LOVE
in an
ENGLISH
GARDEN

ALSO BY VICTORIA CONNELLY

The Rose Girls

The Book Lovers

Rules for a Successful Book Club

The Secret of You

A Summer to Remember

Wish You Were Here

The Runaway Actress

A Weekend with Mr Darcy

The Perfect Hero

Mr Darcy Forever

Molly's Millions

Flights of Angels

Irresistible You

Three Graces

LOVE
in an
ENGLISH
GARDEN

VICTORIA CONNELLY

LAKE UNION
PUBLISHING

Published by Lake Union Publishing, Seattle

www.apub.com

Amazon, the Amazon logo, and Lake Union Publishing are trademarks of Amazon.com, Inc., or its affiliates.

ISBN-13: 9781503942264
ISBN-10: 1503942260

Cover design by @blacksheep-uk.com

Printed in the United States of America

To my dear friend, Judy, who loves the Weald!

Chapter 1

Orley Court sat in the Sussex countryside like a jewel. A sprawling Jacobean manor house built in the early seventeenth-century, it was made from pale-gold Wealden sandstone which held a warmth even on the dullest days when the clouds hung heavy over the Downs.

It was set in a gentle landscape of deep wooded valleys, verdant fields dotted with sheep and horses, and villages full of tile-hung homes, cosy pubs and antique shops full of curios.

When Vanessa Abbott had first driven down from London as a twenty-six-year-old, she'd had no idea that Orley Court was to become her home. Back then, it had been merely another commission for her burgeoning interior decorating business, albeit a very lucrative one. Having Orley on her books would do her no harm at all, she remembered thinking.

Her name had been passed to the owner, Oliver Jacobs, by a mutual friend and she'd made the trip to the Sussex Downs with her pattern books and notepad, totally unprepared for what had followed. The owner might have looked like a handsome hero right out of a nineteenth-century novel, but she'd found his manner gruff and had determined to keep her distance, do the job as quickly as possible and leave. That was, until he'd kissed her in the tapestry room.

Vanessa's life had changed forever with that one kiss, and she'd known that she'd never return to London. Having grown up in the capital, she'd been used to the relentless bustle of the city and it came as a bit of a shock to find herself suddenly living in the middle of the countryside, but she'd soon embraced it. After all, who wouldn't fall in love with Orley Court, with its incredible architecture and its rambling romantic garden filled with wisteria and roses? And she'd managed to bring a bit of the sparkle of London with her, organising legendary parties.

'Come down for the weekend!' she'd cry down the phone to her old friends, who would pack their suitcases and catch her up on all the gossip from town. Oh, yes. There'd been a lot of parties over the years at Orley, but not so many in recent times. Not since her beloved husband Oliver had died.

Looking out of one of the great mullioned windows onto the wintry garden now, Vanessa wondered where all those years had gone. All those wonderful years of living, loving and working. She was lucky. She'd had such a fulfilling life with a job she adored, two daughters she worshipped and the man she loved by her side.

As she thought back to that day thirty years ago when she'd fallen in love with both the man and the house, she couldn't help feeling a little sad. Now, only the house remained and it wasn't in the best of conditions.

Orley Court was a hushed and hallowed place with acres of wooden floors, massive oak beams and enormous fireplaces. It truly was a perfect piece of England, but it was also a very expensive piece and it seemed so big and empty these days with only herself, her mother-in-law Dolly, and Tilda and Jasmine living there. They could no longer afford the luxury of a full-time housekeeper and cook, relying on a local woman from the village to throw a duster around from time to time. Somehow, they got by, but it wasn't easy and it was something that her daughter Tilda was constantly giving her grief about.

She was wittering on about it now – griping about the cost of something or other. Vanessa had tried to zone her out as she watched a wren flitting in and out of the yew hedge which encircled the front lawn, but Tilda was like a very persistent wasp on a summer's day.

'Mother – are you even listening to me?'

Vanessa turned from the window and looked at her daughter, her breath catching in her throat as she realised how much Tilda resembled her thirty years ago.

With her tall, slim build, long vanilla-blonde hair which fell straight down her back like a curtain, blue eyes and pale skin, Tilda had always possessed the power to turn heads, and her looks hadn't done her any harm in her brief career as a singer.

'You're not listening, are you?' Tilda said. 'You've got that vacant look again.'

'Of course I'm listening to you, darling,' Vanessa said. 'I was just thinking about your singing—'

'Well don't,' Tilda snapped.

'You really should think about starting again. It's such a shame all that talent's going to waste.'

'Mum, I don't want to talk about it. I think we should talk about the house.'

Vanessa sighed. 'You're always talking about the house.'

'Well, somebody's got to pay it attention.'

Vanessa frowned. 'What do you mean? I do nothing but pay this house attention.'

'Yes, but a can of paint and a couple of new cushion covers aren't going to solve our problems.'

Vanessa bridled at the insult. Although she'd officially retired as an interior decorator, she still took on small jobs from time to time, and couldn't help sprucing up their home even though she knew in her heart that pasting a sheet of wallpaper over a rotting wall wasn't really the way forward.

'Don't forget that it was my home before it was yours, Tilly.'

'I know,' Tilda said, 'but we just don't have the income to keep it going any longer.'

Vanessa's eyes narrowed. 'What are you saying?'

'I'm saying we need to make a decision.'

'What sort of a decision? Because you know I'll never sell this place.'

'I know that,' Tilda said quickly. 'I'd never suggest that. Only—'

'What?' Vanessa watched as Tilda pulled a strand of hair and twisted it around her finger before speaking. It was a sure sign that something serious was about to be said.

'We could always sell half the house,' she said at last.

The words hung in the air for a few moments before Vanessa responded with a laugh.

'Half the house?' she said. 'What do you mean, half the house?'

Tilda got up from the sofa and started pacing up and down the room. 'I've been thinking about this for some time. We don't want to sell outright, do we?'

'No, of course not.'

'And we wouldn't want lodgers.'

Vanessa shook her head. 'Heavens, no! We tried that before, remember?'

'I remember. He stole the sketch by Holbein, didn't he?'

'It had been in the family for generations. Thank goodness we got it back,' Vanessa said, shuddering at the memory. 'And then there was that strange woman who arrived with a car full of cats.'

Tilda's mouth curved into a smile. 'I liked her.'

Vanessa walked across to the sofa and sat down, patting the space beside her. Tilda joined her.

'Tell me more,' Vanessa said.

'Well, I was thinking that we might be able to sell half the house. You see it all the time on those property programmes,' Tilda explained. 'There'll be this massive old manor house and it'll be split into apartments.'

'But isn't that just like having lots of lodgers?'

'That's why I thought that half the house would work better. That way, you'd only get one family moving in. Orley naturally divides itself from the hallway, doesn't it? It's not quite symmetrical like some of the Elizabethan E-shape houses, but it could definitely work. The north wing even has its own kitchen, and we don't use that part of the house.'

'How can you say that?'

'Because it's true,' she said. 'It's glorified storage.'

Vanessa thought of the rooms that had once been full of house guests. They were now sadly empty, she had to admit.

'But if we sold half the house, that would be like sharing, wouldn't it?'

'Kind of,' Tilda said.

'So Orley would become a semi? Is that what you're saying?'

'Well, a very large, expensive semi.'

Vanessa shook her head. 'It would be sacrilegious.'

'It would be worse to lose it altogether, wouldn't it? At least this way we all get to stay here.'

Vanessa looked at her daughter. 'You're serious about this, aren't you?'

'I think it would definitely take the pressure off us, yes. Our earnings have gone down drastically over the last few years, the bills have gone up and this old place seems to cost us more and more to repair all the time. Remember the bill we got for fixing the oast house roof after the storm?'

'Don't remind me!'

'But that's just it, Mum – you need to be reminded about this sort of thing. You say everything's going to be all right, but how can you be sure of that?'

Vanessa sighed. 'I can't take all this in,' she said. 'You think this is the right thing to do?'

Tilda nodded.

'But how would we do it?'

'Split it down the middle, north–south from the hallway. Roughly. There'd be communal areas like the entrance, and shared access through the garden to certain areas. But you have to admit that the north wing is going to waste.'

'But who'd want to buy the drafty old north wing?'

'Somebody who loves fine architecture with far-reaching views across the Downs? Somebody who wants to own a little bit of English history but can't afford a whole manor house?'

Vanessa shook her head. 'I don't know.'

'Just think about it, Mum.'

Vanessa looked at the earnest face of her daughter and knew in her heart that Tilda was speaking a great deal of sense.

'I need time,' she said.

'We don't have much time,' Tilda told her. 'Have you seen our bank balance?'

Vanessa had. Well, she had a couple of months ago. She hadn't dared to look any more recently than that. It was far too depressing.

'If I agree to this – which I'm not sure I will – I wouldn't know where to begin.'

'You won't have to worry,' Tilda said. 'I'll take care of it – surveyors, estate agents . . . leave it to me.'

Vanessa stared down at the threadbare carpet beneath her feet and then glanced up at the peeling wallpaper to the right of the fireplace, which was hiding goodness only knew what horrors behind it. If they sold, they'd have money in the bank for repairs, for heating and other bills. They wouldn't need to worry anymore. She had to admit that it was a tempting thought.

But to hand over half of Orley to a stranger . . . Wouldn't that be like losing a limb? Vanessa couldn't quite imagine it, even though she could see it made practical sense.

'Okay,' she said at last. 'I'll think about it.'

'That's all I'm asking,' Tilda said.

Tilda closed her bedroom door and breathed a sigh of relief that the moment was over. She'd been keeping an eye on the estate accounts for a while now and knew that her family was in trouble. Her mother must have realised it too, although she'd never said anything. She'd sooner pore over the latest swatches from her favourite designers than examine Orley's accounts. Something had to be done, Tilda knew that, and she also knew it would fall to her to get things moving in the right direction.

But was selling half the house the right direction? It was so drastic, so final.

'So frightening,' she whispered to herself. But not selling was even more frightening because she knew that they couldn't go on living the way they were. The heating bills alone were enough to bankrupt them, especially now that Tilda's own income had dwindled to almost nothing.

Orley was Tilda's special place and she couldn't bear the thought of losing it. It had been her sanctuary when the fickle world of music had turned against her, and it was where she'd come to hide and lick her wounds.

She groaned as she thought about the recent past and cursed the television talent show that had started it all. Tilda had always loved music and had been scribbling lyrics in notebooks for as long as she could remember. When the show had been advertised, she'd leapt at the chance, auditioning with a song she had written herself – which made her stand out from the crowds doing cover versions. Hers had been a catchy little number that won her the show, and a manager from a big record label had picked her up. After that, a head-spinning few months passed as the label groomed her, moulded her, flung a song at her and launched her onto the unsuspecting public, and 'Tilly' had been born.

A UK tour had ensued with guest performances at arenas and stadiums. It was all a blur now. A blur she preferred to try and forget. That meteoric rise to fame had ended as quickly as it had begun: the record label moved on to the newest hottest talent and Tilly was forgotten.

She'd come back to Orley, her bank balance swollen and her ego deflated, and she hadn't written a single lyric since.

She hadn't totally forgotten her music, though, and was teaching singing and piano to both children and adults in the local area. She was a good teacher and she enjoyed her work, but she felt that there was more to her. Her pupils always got a big kick out of recognising her and a lot of them were desperate to have a taste of that same fame. Tilda always brought them back down to earth, however, warning them of the unpredictable nature of the business and how very unforgiving it was.

She looked at the little desk in her bedroom now. It was littered with notebooks, and she flipped through one of them. Filled with half-written songs and random thoughts and feelings, it made Tilda feel both guilty and miserable. She should be writing. Her songs had once been her life and, at twenty-seven, she was much too young to throw her dreams away. But, somehow, inspiration just wasn't finding her anymore and nothing seemed to be helping. She'd tried haunting all the places in which she'd used to hide away with her notebooks, but no amount of hiking in the hills or sitting in the garden produced anything.

Perhaps she was a one-hit wonder, she thought. She had walked out onto the world stage and been applauded and, even though it had only lasted a brief time, she had achieved something. But maybe that was it. She'd had her time in the spotlight and now she had to accept the fact that she was a teacher. Maybe that was one of the reasons why she was taking control of Orley now – because she felt as if she couldn't control her own career.

Well, one thing was certain: she was going to do her very best to save the house and ensure that her family's future there was secure, and if that meant selling half of it to another family then so be it.

Chapter 2

'You're selling my oast house?'

'No, Jassy,' Tilda told her younger sister. 'The oast house is yours.'

'We'd never take that away from you, darling,' Vanessa said.

Jasmine Jacobs didn't look convinced. Her normally rosy complexion had paled alarmingly.

'Finish your breakfast,' Vanessa told her.

'I'm not hungry.'

'Rubbish. You're always hungry.'

Tilda sighed. She hated to see her sister upset. At eighteen, Jasmine was a full nine years younger than Tilda. A surprise arrival, she was still treated as very much the baby of the family, even though she was now a young woman. A complication during her birth had meant that she had been oxygen-starved at a critical moment and, although she looked like a normal adult, she could be incredibly child-like. She'd been home-tutored after it was discovered that she was on the autistic spectrum, and Vanessa had initially taken on the role of teacher before private tutors were hired. Her patience had been endless and the rewards had been great indeed.

'Special,' Vanessa called her daughter, and she was. A little taller than Tilda, Jasmine had inherited her father's height and, although her hair was the same vanilla-blonde as her mother's and sister's, it bounced around her shoulders in enormous curls. But, although she might look like a supermodel, she was anything but feminine in her dress, spending most of her days painting in old jeans and overalls.

The eighteenth-century oast house which stood in the grounds of Orley had once been used as servants' quarters but Oliver Jacobs had had it converted into a studio for Jasmine. She spent most of her time there, sleeping in a room upstairs that had its own en-suite, and only coming into the main house if she was bored or hungry. She loved the place and guarded it fiercely. Only her tutor was allowed inside without a formal invitation.

'Jassy,' Tilda began again, 'do you understand what's happening?'

'You want to sell Orley.'

'Yes, but not all of it. Nothing's going to change for us. We'll still have all the rooms we use every day, and the south garden and walled garden.'

'And the oast house?'

'Of course. But we'll be selling the rest.'

'What does Grandma think about it?' Jassy asked.

Tilda swallowed hard and looked at her mother. 'We haven't told her yet.'

'You're too scared to,' Jassy said, speaking the truth as only she could.

'We're going to tell her today.'

'It's her house too.'

'We know, but it won't be anybody's house if we can't afford to live here.'

Jassy frowned. 'But this is our home.'

'And it will stay our home,' Tilda said. 'Just with the addition of a few more people.'

Jassy stared down into her cereal. She wasn't always good around people. She found talking to strangers very difficult and preferred the company of those she was familiar with. The thought of strangers actually living at Orley was obviously upsetting to her.

'It'll be fun,' Tilda said, not quite believing her own words. 'Think of it as a new chapter in the story of Orley. An adventure!'

'I don't like adventures,' Jassy said.

❧ ⁓ ❧

Dolly Jacobs wasn't known to like adventures either. The wife of Robert Jacobs and mother of Oliver, she'd grown up in a cottage on the outskirts of the nearby village of Elhurst and, as far as Vanessa knew, had never left the county. She'd moved into Orley as an eighteen-year-old bride and now resided in a set of downstairs rooms overlooking the south garden.

The job of telling her that they were selling half the house had fallen to Vanessa who, despite being in her fifties, still felt like a schoolgirl in the presence of Dolly Jacobs.

She's never liked me, her inner voice told her now. *She wanted somebody else for her beloved Oliver. A nice plump country girl who liked horses, instead of some skinny businesswoman from London. She's never forgiven me for capturing Oliver's heart.*

Vanessa shook her head as if trying to dislodge her negative thoughts as she ventured towards Dolly's rooms in the south wing. Dolly was an early riser and had breakfast long before anybody else was up, then spent most of the rest of the day in her living room during the winter.

Reaching her living-room door, Vanessa took a deep breath and tentatively knocked. An immediate sound of barking was heard. It was Reynolds, Dolly's Jack Russell, who also didn't like Vanessa. Named after Dolly's favourite painter, Reynolds was a typical terrier with an instinct to protect and an addiction to ankles. Tilda and Jassy adored him and his half-white, half-chestnut face, but Vanessa sincerely believed that Dolly had trained him to hate her.

'Who is it?' Dolly's voice came from behind the door after Vanessa knocked for the second time.

'It's me. Vanessa.' She opened the door and walked in. It was a beautiful room with an ornate plasterwork ceiling and a large fireplace

11

in which a wood-burning stove had been installed to keep it cosy in the cooler months. There were some very nice pieces of furniture too – pieces that had been hauled in there soon after Oliver's death, as if Dolly didn't quite trust Vanessa with them – as well as a fine eighteenth-century portrait by Sir Joshua Reynolds. Dolly wasn't going to leave *that* anywhere near her daughter-in-law.

'What do you want?' Dolly asked. She was sitting in an armchair by a window which overlooked the garden. In the spring, Dolly had a fine view of the glorious magnolia tree in bloom and, in the summer, she enjoyed the colours of the herbaceous border, which she could see comfortably from her chair.

'I've come to have a little talk,' Vanessa said, fixing a smile onto her face as she took a seat in the chair next to Dolly's. Reynolds, who was sitting by his mistress's feet, growled at her, baring his nasty little teeth.

'Are you okay, Dolly? Your hair looks pretty this morning,' she said. She never knew what to say to the old woman and invariably said the wrong thing.

'Never mind the nonsense,' Dolly snapped. 'Tell me what you've got to say.'

'It's about the house,' Vanessa began hesitantly. 'The girls and I have been talking and we've made a decision.'

'A decision without me?'

'Well, I'm here now to run it by you.'

'And what's this decision?' The old woman narrowed her eyes. She had once been very beautiful, with a lovely round face and thick mahogany-coloured hair, and Oliver, her only child, had adored her. But Vanessa's relationship with Dolly had always been somewhat prickly so she was understandably anxious about talking to her now.

'You know how we've been struggling. Bills and things. Running Orley.'

'I've never known anyone mismanage a house quite like you do,' Dolly said cruelly.

12

'I haven't mismanaged anything, Dolly. You know as well as I do that these big old houses are expensive to keep and, well, we need to be able to ensure its future for Tilda and Jasmine. We need to know that it'll be in sound condition for us to pass it on to them, don't we? Just as when you and Robert handed it to Oliver. And we simply can't do that without a huge injection of cash. Our combined incomes are laughably low and we think it might be in the best interests of everyone if we sold half of the house.' Vanessa paused, waiting for the tirade that would follow, and was quite surprised when Dolly said nothing at all. The old woman simply stared at her.

Vanessa swallowed hard. 'We're thinking of the north wing. The rooms are large and very beautiful. It has its own entrance as well as the main front door. There's a separate garden and I think it would make a really wonderful home for somebody. We hardly ever use that wing and it would raise an enormous amount of money for us.' She stopped, her heart racing and her head thumping.

At last, Dolly spoke. 'You always were trouble,' she told Vanessa. 'I knew the minute you arrived from London with your city ways. I told Oliver, "That one will be the end of Orley!"'

'You did not!' Vanessa said, shocked by the admission. 'Anyway, this is Tilda's idea,' she said, feeling awful for trying to put the blame on her daughter, but perhaps Dolly would feel better about the decision if she knew it had come from a blood relative. 'And I think it's a very good one.'

'This isn't your home,' Dolly said.

'How can you say that? It's been my home for thirty years. I've raised two Jacobs children here and it's their birthright.'

'You're not a Jacobs.'

'And neither are you!' Vanessa said.

Dolly sucked in a lungful of air.

'But my children are Oliver's children,' Vanessa continued, 'and he left the house to them and they've now chosen to sell part of it, so it's our role to support that decision.'

'What about all the portraits and furniture?' Dolly asked.

'Everything will be moved into our half of the house.'

'It's outrageous! If Oliver were alive—'

'But he isn't!' Vanessa cried. 'He's dead and we've got to cope as best as we can, and we'd like your support with this, Dolly. We don't need it, but we'd like it, okay?'

Vanessa stood up, instantly making Reynolds growl. She was shaking. It was probably best if she didn't say anything else at this stage. She'd let Dolly think about things in her own time.

Leaving Dolly's room, Vanessa went upstairs to her bedroom and sat down on the bed. She felt like crying. She missed Oliver so much. It had only been two years since he'd died from cancer, but it seemed like a lifetime ago. An age without his arms around her, without his words of comfort when he knew his mother was getting to her. She tried not to think about how unfair it was that it was Oliver who'd been taken and not Dolly. How much easier life would have been if Dolly had been the one to die.

Vanessa sighed, determined not to be sucked into a vortex of negative emotions. She had work to do and it couldn't wait a minute longer.

***

The estate agent arrived in a very nice Audi and got out of the car with a large clipboard in her hand.

'And you're sure you don't want to sell the whole place?' she asked, a hungry look in her eyes as if she were working out her commission.

'Good heavens, no!' Vanessa cried. 'We have to live somewhere!'

Things got pretty hectic after that, with surveyors, builders, people from building regulations and photographers arriving. A small fence was put up to divide part of the garden. A new door was installed and all of the paintings, furniture and rugs were moved from the rooms which were going to be sold.

Finally, they were presented with a beautiful brochure of the north wing and informed that it was now being advertised.

'That's it then,' Vanessa said to her daughters. 'No going back now.'

'It'll be okay,' Tilda told her. 'It'll all work out.'

'How can you be so sure?' Vanessa said.

'Because things always have a way of working out, don't they?'

'I hope you're right,' Vanessa said, wondering if she dared show the brochure to Dolly. 'I really hope you're right.'

Chapter 3

Laurence Sturridge hadn't been able to face the tyranny of the Tube that Friday night and so he'd walked home, pushing through crowded pavements, crossing busy roads and jogging through darkened parks back to his flat south of the river. He'd needed to clear his head after a stressful week of meetings and mergers he didn't wholeheartedly agree with. His job as a financial consultant used to excite him and he'd enjoyed the pressure but, somewhere along the way, the pleasure had fizzled out and been replaced with resentment. Now, each morning when his alarm clock shook him out of sleep, he would wake with a groan.

'And that is no way to live,' he said to himself as he reached his street at last. It was a quiet road full of large Victorian houses that had been converted into flats, with a couple of modern blocks towards the end. Laurence lived in one of the newer buildings which overlooked the River Thames. He'd been tempted by a ground-floor apartment in one of the Victorian houses because it'd had a garden but, truth be told, he didn't really have time for a garden. And that was another gripe he had with the world. When had life got so busy that he no longer had time to plant some bulbs and grow a few vegetables?

His childhood home had been a cottage on the edge of Elhurst in Sussex, with stunning views across the wooded valleys of the Weald. He'd loved it. From an early age, he'd been allowed to venture out on his bike, exploring the country lanes, paddling in streams and swinging from the great limbs of trees. He'd made dens with friends from the village, climbed hills in the winter and sledged back down them; he'd learned to ride a horse and even had sailing lessons on the south coast. It had been a life led outdoors and he missed that. He hadn't realised how much until the past few days.

When had it all started to go wrong? he wondered, thinking back to when he'd left home for university. He'd immersed himself in his studies, which had led him into the lucrative world of finance. He had no complaints about his salary, that was for sure, but what had it cost him in terms of lifestyle?

Entering the communal door to his block, he crossed the lobby to the lift and took it up to the eighth floor. He hadn't thought about Elhurst for years but, recently, the green and golden landscape of his childhood home had been filling his mind. The cottage at the edge of the village. The village at the head of the valley. The valley in the loveliest county of England.

He smiled as he got his key out, unlocking the door and stepping into the hallway. It was dark, which surprised him.

'Dad?'

Perhaps his father was out, although Laurence doubted that very much. And sure enough, after leaving his briefcase in the hallway and taking off his shoes, he walked through to the living room and spotted his dad sitting in the chair by the window that looked out onto the river. Laurence cocked his head to one side. His father seemed to be asleep.

Leaning forward, Laurence switched the lamp on, flooding the room with light.

'Dad?' he said softly.

Slowly, his dad came to, staring at his son as if trying to remember who he was.

'I'm home. It's the weekend.'

His father nodded. 'Good day?'

'In a manner of speaking. I've had a bit of a crazy idea.'

'Oh?'

'Yes. We should talk. I'll make us a cup of tea.'

He walked into the tiny kitchen. Although well situated, it was a horribly small flat and had been made to seem even smaller since the arrival of his father, but he hadn't had the heart to turn his dad away. Since Laurence's mother had died, his father had been like a lost soul, wandering the earth without a purpose. He seemed to do very little other than sit in the chair by the window, reading a book whose pages never seemed to turn, Laurence had noticed.

Marcus Sturridge had been living with his son for six months now. When his beloved wife Tara had died suddenly in a car crash, he had sold their home in Kent and taken off to South America for a year. There'd been very little communication between father and son during that time and Laurence had been worried sick, imagining a phone call coming any minute from the authorities saying his father had been either kidnapped or thrown in some dive of a prison. To Laurence, it had been as if he'd lost both his parents that year.

But then his father had returned. Hopelessly dishevelled, horribly bearded and somewhat homeless. He'd been sitting in that chair ever since.

Something needed to change, and fast.

'Dad?' Laurence said, coming back with two cups of tea.

Marcus looked up from the book he wasn't reading and took the proffered cup.

'I've been thinking . . .' Laurence sat down opposite his father. 'I've been thinking that a change would do us good. I mean, a total change.'

'Oh, God. You don't want to join a gym again, do you?'

'No, I don't want to join a gym,' Laurence said with an exasperated sigh. 'I want to move.'

'Move where? What's wrong with here?'

'I don't fit here anymore,' Laurence said. 'My life feels like it doesn't belong to me. I get up in the morning and, when I realise that I have to go in to the office, this dead weight lands square on my chest and I'm wishing the hours away!'

'You need a job, son,' Marcus said.

'I know,' he said. 'But I think I can go it alone now. Set up my own business.'

'Isn't that a big risk?'

Laurence took a deep breath. 'I don't like what's happening to the company. It's different from when I joined. Decisions have been made – choices I don't agree with. I'm not happy there anymore. I need to get out, and of course it's a risk, but it's something I feel I need to do. And surely you can't be happy here, Dad? Don't you want to get back to the country?'

'The country?'

'There's the money from the house in Kent, and I could sell this flat in a heartbeat.'

'And do what?'

'*Move*, Dad! Get out of here. Go to the country and start living again. Really living.'

'Where?'

'Sussex.'

'You want to go back to Sussex?'

'Sure. Why not? We were happy there.'

His father didn't look so sure. 'That was a long time ago, Laurie.'

'I know, but it's a time I've been thinking about a lot lately. Look, I've got something to show you.'

He went through to his bedroom and came back with a magazine. It was a big glossy one – the sort which had pages and pages of property advertisements. One of the pages had been dog-eared. He turned to it now.

'I found this on the Tube seat next to me last week. It's like it was fate.'

'Fate that someone had left an old magazine they'd probably sneezed into?'

'Take a look, Dad.'

Marcus shook his head, but took the magazine from his son. 'What am I looking at?'

'The first property on the page.'

Marcus squinted and looked at the photograph, then up at Laurence, then down at the page and then up at Laurence once more.

'It's Orley Court,' Marcus said.

'Yes!'

'Why are you so excited about that?'

'Because it's for sale. Well, part of it. The north wing and a little bit more.'

'And why's that of interest to you?'

'Because I'm going to buy it!'

His father looked at him as if he were quite mad. 'What do you want with an old manor house?'

Laurence laughed. 'It'll be fun! I've got money to invest and property is one of the best investments around, so why not make the most of things and buy something really amazing? I'm always advising people to do that – to put their money not only into sound investments but also into things that will give them joy. Well, it's about time I took my own advice.'

'But what about me?'

'You're coming with me.'

'You expect me to put money into this old ruin?'

'It's not an old ruin. It might need a bit of restoration, but I've got plenty put aside. You can chip in if you want, but it's fine if you don't. The sale from this flat and the money I've got put by will more than cover it.'

He watched as his father looked at the photograph and read through the accompanying text. When Marcus finally glanced up, he wasn't smiling.

'I don't believe in going backwards,' he said.

'What do you mean?'

'I mean, I think it'll be a mistake going back to Sussex.'

'Why?'

'That chapter's closed, son.'

'Yeah? Well I say we reopen it.'

His father got up from the chair, dropping the magazine and stalking out of the room.

'Where are you going?' Laurence asked.

'For a walk.'

'It's dark.'

'I need to get some air.'

Laurence watched as Marcus grabbed his coat, put his boots on and left the flat. It wasn't the response he'd hoped for but, then again, he should have expected it. His father had been running away from things ever since Laurence's mother had died, but he'd have to stop sooner or later, and that might as well be in Sussex.

Going into the kitchen to make himself some dinner, Laurence again thought back to that childhood home in the Ridwell Valley – to the cottage whose windows seemed to be permanently open during the summer months, to his father out mowing the lawn and his mother pegging washing on the line. Was he a fool to think that he could recapture some of that perfection? Was his father right? Should you never try to go back?

But something in Laurence was rebelling. He couldn't remember the last time he'd felt genuine excitement and that was a rather sorry thing to admit, wasn't it? The colour had been slowly seeping out of his life and he was anxious to get some of it back.

He picked up the magazine, looking at the friendly golden facade of Orley Court nestled in the ancient wooded valley in which he'd once played. How he longed to go back there. He'd never wanted anything more in his life, he realised, and he was going to make it happen.

The estate agents had organised an open weekend for Orley Court, arranging viewings back to back. The family were advised to stay away from home, but decided that they wanted to keep an eye on things and spent the two days camped out in the morning room which overlooked the front lawn, so they could see each and every one of the prospective buyers arriving. The room was dual aspect, which meant they could watch anyone wandering through the south garden too.

'Ooooh, I don't like the look of her,' Jassy said as the first viewer arrived.

'Did she just snip off that flower head?' Dolly asked later on that morning. She'd taken position at the window overlooking the south garden, her beady eyes watching every single viewer's every single move. Though she'd made her feelings about the idea of selling very clear, she wasn't going to miss out on spying on any potential new owners.

'Oh, no,' Jassy said sometime after lunch. She was still looking out of the front window. 'A family's just arrived. We don't want young children running around making noise, do we?'

'Or men on their own,' Grandma Dolly said. 'Always suspicious!'

Tilda sighed. 'I'm going out.'

'Where?' her mother asked.

'Just for a walk.'

'I don't think you're meant to mingle.'

'I won't mingle, Mum. I just need to walk about a bit.'

As Tilda left the room, she breathed a sigh of relief. She'd found the atmosphere in the morning room stifling, and yet felt she had to be there because the whole idea of selling had been hers and she would have felt traitorous had she left her family to it.

Pausing on the landing as the estate agent welcomed a couple into the hallway, Tilda turned around and headed for a side door. Although only a portion of the house was for sale, the estate agent had asked permission for the viewers to walk around the south garden so that they could see the property from there and get excited about what they were buying into. This meant that Tilda was very likely to run into some of them at some point, but she was doing her best not to.

Leaving from one of the less frequented doors into the garden, she crossed the gravel path and walked across the south lawn which led to the fields beyond. She could escape there, even if it was just for a few minutes.

The drive down from London was like travelling back in time for Laurence. All the familiar names greeted him. Lamberhurst, Maplehurst, Ticehurst. But they weren't his 'hurst'. He was looking for the turn-off for Elhurst. And there it was. The country road off the main road. He slowed his speed and took in the wide main street that ran through the village. There was the baker's that used to make the most mouth-watering doughnuts, and the newsagent's where he'd once been a paper boy. There was the great stone memorial commemorating the local men who'd given their lives in the First World War, and there was the parish church perched up on the hill, its squat tower topped with a fabulous spire. The village gardens weren't looking their best on this wintery morning but, come summer, they would be frothing with flowers.

Laurence slowed the car further still at a junction turning into a lane that dipped deep into the valley, between the church and a row of pretty cottages. He couldn't resist winding his window down despite the coldness. There was something about the quality of the air here – perhaps due to the proximity to the sea. How he'd missed it. There was nothing like this in London, he thought, not in all the grand parks or along the famous river. Nothing could compare to the sweetness of the Sussex Weald.

'Should be getting close,' he said to himself, remembering the lane from childhood bike rides.

The first thing he spotted were the chimneys rising high above the bare hedges, which were yet to grow their spring plumage. There were at least a dozen stacks in fine red brick, proclaiming that the original owners of the manor had been rich enough to afford a good many fireplaces. Little glimpses of the rest of the building could be seen through the silhouettes of winter trees which crowded the fields. Then, as he rounded a corner, the whole house came into view. Orley Court. It was just as lovely as he remembered, with the beautiful mullioned windows and the warm local stone of the Weald. Could he really afford to live here? It still amazed him that he might just be able to.

Suddenly, he felt a sad twinge of regret that his father hadn't wanted to accompany him.

'You've made your mind up already about this,' Marcus had said. 'You don't need me with you.'

'I'd still like you to come,' Laurence responded, but his father had picked up his book and pretended to read.

Now, following the sign to the parking, he wished he'd been more forceful. Maybe that's what his father needed – to be told what to do.

Laurence shook his head. No, that wasn't the way forward, was it? He'd just have to be patient and hope that his father would come round and see that returning to Sussex was a great idea.

After locking his car, Laurence walked back into the lane and round the great yew hedge which framed the front garden at Orley. There were quite a number of people walking around. He'd been told that it was an open viewing, but he'd secretly hoped that it wouldn't be popular. Maybe these were just nosy parkers who wanted to snoop and who weren't actually interested in making an offer. Still, he couldn't help feeling threatened by their presence. Part of him wanted to swat them away and tell them that this was his future home and they should go and find somewhere else.

He shook his head. He shouldn't get so excited about things. Orley Court was not his yet and might never be, not if there were several good offers for it and the owners got to choose which lucky bidder they accepted. All he could do was hope.

He followed the signpost which read *Viewings this way*, taking a moment to look around. An undulating field with a scattering of white sheep greeted him. It was a peaceful country lane and he remembered cycling down it a number of times as a boy with his friends, off out on a day's adventure. He wondered if he could perhaps buy a bike now or if that would be ridiculous. They say you never forget how to ride one, but he'd certainly forgotten how to make time for one. He grinned as a sudden image of his work colleagues entered his mind. The only bikes they rode were in a gym. They wouldn't dream of riding one in order to get to a real place.

He turned back towards the house. The long yew hedge gave way to a gateway flanked by pale stone pillars, from where Laurence got his first wonderful view of the front of Orley Court. How beautiful it was with its pale gold stone and its inviting arched doorway. He remembered how the front was a riot of wisteria in springtime and smothered with red roses in summer. Today, some scarlet berries were doing their best to colour the stone.

Checking his watch, he saw that he was on time and so walked through the gate and entered the porch. The great wooden door was open and he didn't have to wait long until he was greeted by the estate agent and his tour began.

Of course, the house was everything he'd hoped for and more, and he knew he had to live there. The rooms were numerous, spacious and full of character, and each window framed one of the gardens and the landscape beyond to perfection.

The estate agent was horribly official. There were no cute stories about the house that an owner might impart. None of the quirks were pointed out. It was just: 'And here's the kitchen . . . This is the largest bedroom.' That was all. So, when Laurence spotted a young woman in the grounds after his official tour, he couldn't help but stop her. She looked like someone who actually lived at Orley rather than another prospective buyer, he thought.

'Excuse me,' he said.

'Are you lost?' the woman asked. She was tall and slim with long blonde hair, which was blowing out behind her in the cold wind. She was wearing a waxed jacket and a pink scarf and looked absolutely frozen.

'No, I'm not lost. Are you the owner?'

'The daughter of the owner. Why?'

'I've just been viewing the property,' he explained. 'I'm thinking about buying it.'

'Oh.' Her tone was flat, he couldn't help noticing, as if she didn't approve of him considering buying it. But maybe he was reading too much into things.

'I was wondering if you might tell me a bit about it,' he said hesitantly. 'You know – like what it's like living here.'

She looked completely baffled. 'You have the brochure? I can get you a copy if you don't.'

'I have my brochure,' he said, tapping his bag, 'but that's just the facts, isn't it? What I'd love to know is what it's like living in a seventeenth-century manor. I mean, what is it *really* like? How does it make you feel when you walk around the gardens and look back at the house and know you're living in a little bit of history? It must be incredible! And coming home on a winter's evening and lighting one of the fireplaces, knowing that it's been used to warm people up for almost four hundred years – is that the most amazing thing? Do you feel truly connected to the past?'

The young woman still had a puzzled expression on her face. 'I think you've just answered your own questions,' she said.

Laurence laughed. 'I suppose I have.'

'But, yes, it is a rather special place.' She turned to look at the great house. 'I remember sitting by the fireplace in the drawing room on cold winter evenings, listening to Grandma telling us about the history of Orley. There were so many names and dates from the past. It was hard to believe that these distant strangers had anything to do with us living here now, because it's always just been our home. I guess you take the

26

place you grow up in for granted, but I've always been aware of how beautiful it is and how lucky I am.'

He smiled. 'I'm sure you have.'

They looked at each other for a moment.

'Well, I'd better get—' she began.

'Perhaps you can show me the garden? Tell me something about it that's not in the brochure?' he said with what he hoped was a winning smile.

'Well, I—'

'I'd really appreciate it.'

She seemed to consider this for a moment. 'Okay then.'

'I'm Laurence, by the way. Laurence Sturridge.' He held out his hand to shake.

'Tilda Jacobs.'

'Pleased to meet you,' he said. 'I'd love to see the walled garden.'

'That's not actually part of the sale,' Tilda told him.

'I'd still love to see it. I mean, if that would be okay.'

'I don't think that would be fair on the other viewers.'

Laurence leaned a little closer to her. 'I won't tell if you don't.'

Tilda gave him a quizzical look and he couldn't help noticing how blue her eyes were. Like forget-me-nots.

'I don't suppose it'll do any harm,' she said at last, leading the way.

'I was thinking about the house,' Laurence said as they walked down the brick path. 'It's quite small to be called a court, isn't it?'

'Part of the west wing was lost to fire back in the twenties, so what you see today is only some of the original building.'

'I see. That's a shame.'

'It belonged to some dignitary from Jacobean times and would have been even grander.'

'You see, the estate agent told me nothing about all this.'

'Well, there are a lot of people to show around today.'

'No doubt,' Laurence said. 'When did you decide to sell?'

'It was a recent decision.'

He noticed Tilda's voice was neutral, but he was sure he could see a touch of regret in her expression.

'And you're sure the oast house isn't part of the deal?' Laurence said as they walked by it. 'It's really amazing.'

'Definitely not. It's in constant use by my sister.'

'Really? She lives there?'

'Kind of. She sleeps there and uses it as a studio. She's an artist.'

'I'd love to see some of her work.'

Tilda shook her head. 'It's not for public consumption.'

'Now I want to see it even more.'

Tilda stopped suddenly and Laurence almost crashed into her. 'I agreed to show you the walled garden.'

'Yes.'

'And that's all.'

'Sorry,' he said, running a hand through his hair. He wasn't handling this very well, was he? 'It's just I'm really interested in this place. I grew up in Elhurst.'

Something in her face softened at this admission. 'Did you?'

'I left after university. Moved to London. Never stopped missing it, though. I loved it here.'

'I can't imagine living anywhere else,' she said.

'Nor can I now.' He cleared his throat, suddenly feeling very insecure. 'I really want this to work out.'

Tilda's blue eyes narrowed a fraction. 'And you're hoping that this little chat of ours will mean I put in a good word for you?'

He laughed. 'I wouldn't object. I mean, if you wanted to do that.'

'The final decision won't be mine, I'm afraid,' Tilda said as she opened a paint-cracked wooden gate into the walled garden. 'This is it.'

Laurence looked around at the enormous space with its weathered red-brick walls and neat gravel pathways. There was a scattering of fruit trees in a grassy orchard and some beaten-up obelisks, but the soil was bare bar a few leeks and winter greens.

'It's not looking its best, I'm afraid,' Tilda said.

'I think it's marvellous. But this is what I've come for,' he said, nodding back towards the house, its fine chimneys and tile-hung portion on the north side showing splendidly. From here, you could see just how snugly it sat in the valley, like a teacup in a saucer, he thought.

'I remember this view from one of the fetes you held here in the summer.'

Tilda's eyes widened a fraction. 'You came to those?'

'Never missed one,' he said.

'Wow,' she said. 'I haven't thought about them in years.'

'You don't hold the fetes anymore?'

'No,' she said. 'They kind of fizzled out when—'

'When what?'

She shook her head. 'They just fizzled out.'

'That's a shame,' he said. 'You should start them up again. They were a real highlight of the village year.'

He watched as Tilda shoved her hands in her pockets and looked down at the ground.

'I'd better get back,' she said.

Laurence frowned. Had he said something to upset her or had she just grown bored?

'Well, look, thank you for showing me around,' he said. 'It's really kind of you.'

'You can get to the car park through that gate,' she said, 'you don't have to walk all the way back to the house.'

'Yes, I remember.'

'Give it a good shove. It swells in the winter and we had to shut it so people wouldn't come in through the walled garden, which isn't meant to be part of the viewing.'

He nodded. She knew how to put a person in their place.

'Thanks again,' he said. 'I'll be in touch.'

She nodded and turned to go, her shoulders hunched against the cold.

When Laurence made it back to his car, he let out a loud groan. What had he been thinking? He'd been too pushy by far. He'd seen how awkward she'd felt about showing him around and answering his questions, and yet he'd gone and pressed it anyway. His enthusiasm would probably do him no favours when he put his offer to the estate agent later. His joy at being back at Elhurst had got the better of him and he'd made a fool of himself.

Driving out into the lane towards the village, he glanced wistfully back, taking in the beauty of the building and its setting amidst the gentle fields. It would probably be the last time he saw it and he only had himself to blame.

Tilda had walked straight back to the house after leaving Laurence, dodging an elderly couple who were viewing the gardens and who, in her opinion, would never cope with a winter at Orley.

Her mother greeted her as soon as she entered the morning room. Tilda shed her coat and scarf and made her way towards the radiator. Grandma Dolly was nodding off in a chair by the south window and there was no sign of Jassy, who'd probably locked herself away in the oast house to paint, having got bored of watching the endless stream of prospective buyers.

'You've been gone a while,' her mother said.

'I met one of the viewers in the garden,' Tilda said.

'Yes? What were they like?' Vanessa asked.

Tilda considered what Laurence Sturridge had been like.

'Enthusiastic,' she said at last. It seemed like the perfect word to sum him up. She declined to mention that he was also quite attractive, because that wasn't relevant to the conversation, was it?

'Well, that's good, isn't it?' Vanessa said. 'We'll need someone enthusiastic to take this place on.'

'I suppose,' Tilda said. 'I think he really wants the place. He was asking me all sorts of questions.'

'I hope you didn't go telling him about the awful plumbing and the leaking windows in the north wing,' Vanessa said.

'No, of course I didn't. He wanted to know about odd things like the walled garden and our summer fete.'

'Really? He knew about our fetes?'

Tilda nodded and a melancholic look passed across her mother's face. Her father had loved the summer fetes – they had been his pet project – but they'd come to a halt when he'd become ill.

'He knows the place, then?' her mother continued.

'Yes. He grew up in Elhurst.'

'What's his name?'

'Laurence Sturridge.'

'Never heard of him. So, what's brought him back?'

'He said he missed it.'

Vanessa smiled. 'This place will do that to you.'

Her mother looked out of the window and Tilda followed her gaze to the fields and woods beyond, but she wasn't really looking at the view because she was still thinking about Laurence Sturridge, and the light in his eyes as he'd looked back at the house from the walled garden, and that boyish smile of his. She'd liked his smile. She might not have returned it, but she'd liked it.

Chapter 4

The Jacobs received only two offers for the north wing after the open house weekend. One had been ludicrously low and came with a whole host of requests for work to be carried out before the couple moved in. The other offer was for the full asking price.

'But so many people viewed the place,' Vanessa said.

'They were probably just being nosy,' Tilda said. 'It would have made a nice day out.'

'So, are we going to accept?' Vanessa asked.

'It's for the full asking price,' Tilda pointed out.

'Who's it from?' Grandma Dolly barked from her chair.

'Laurence Sturridge,' Vanessa said. 'He's the man you met in the garden, isn't he?'

Tilda nodded.

'A single man?' Dolly asked. 'I thought we weren't going to accept any single men!'

'He seemed very nice,' Tilda said, 'and he grew up in the village.'

'Suspicious men have to grow up somewhere,' Dolly replied.

'He didn't seem suspicious.'

'How could you tell? He might be some lunatic who'll host those rave things and turn Orley into some hippie festival.'

'That's not the impression he gave me,' Tilda told her grandmother.

Vanessa sighed. 'I don't think we've got the luxury of being picky. You think he seems sane and he's made us an offer.'

'Don't we get to meet him first?' Jassy asked. She'd been ripping up old magazines for some work she'd begun, but was now paying close attention to what was going on.

'The estate agent said he'd like to make an appointment for a second viewing. You can meet him then.'

Jasmine sighed and returned her attention to the magazines. 'I'm not sure I want to,' she said.

Vanessa shook her head. 'Well, I'm going to give her a call and set something up.' She hesitated for a moment as if waiting for somebody to stop her, but nobody did. 'Right. I'll do it now.'

'You okay, Mum?' Tilda said. 'Do you want me to ring her?'

'No, no! I'll do it.' And she left the morning room before she could change her mind and hand the whole horrible business over to her daughter.

Vanessa hadn't slept well over the weekend. She'd kept waking up in the night, fearful that they were doing the wrong thing. What would Oliver think of them selling half the house? Dolly had told her in no uncertain terms that he would be horrified, and Vanessa had been weighed down with guilt ever since.

Last night, she'd tossed around, twisting herself up in the bed sheets and fighting with the blankets until, finally giving up on sleep, she got up, switched on a lamp and pulled a jumper over her nightgown. She'd then left her room and walked to the kitchen, where she made herself a herbal tea. She had finally acquired a taste for it after several years, having given up regular tea when Oliver kicked the sugar habit as part of his dietary recommendations whilst undergoing treatment for cancer. Vanessa had been a five-cups-a-day girl before then – and each one had had a large sugar in it. She felt a lot better for having given it up, she had to admit, but it hadn't saved her husband.

Taking her cup of peppermint tea through to the living room, she'd switched on the large temple jar lamp she loved so much. Orley had a fine collection of antiques. She remembered how her mouth had dropped open when she'd seen the house for the first time: the innumerable paintings, fine tables and chairs, rugs and lamps, chaises longues and longcase clocks, tapestries and chandeliers. It had been overwhelming and she'd had to be very subtle when she'd decorated the rooms, carefully embracing the past whilst bringing the house into the present.

And now she was selling half of it. How could she have agreed to such a thing? She would probably be sent straight down to hell when her time came. Perhaps there was a special corner reserved for such people – people who sacrificed beauty, history and tradition for cold, hard cash.

But it had been much too cold to hang around contemplating such things in the living room in the middle of the night. The middle of the day was bad enough during the winter months, unless you were on top of the radiators or the wood burner. That was one of the problems about living in a big old house. It might look glorious and people might envy you your splendid home, but the reality could be bone-chillingly awful. So she had finished her cup of tea and returned to bed.

Now, Vanessa caught sight of the photograph of Oliver on the mantelpiece above the fireplace in the living room. It was her favourite. She'd sneaked it into her bedroom after he died because she'd needed to have it close to her, but Jassy had complained and so she'd returned it. As she looked at it now, Oliver's handsome face stared back at her with those warm brown eyes of his and that mess of sandy-coloured hair, the curls falling over his brow in just the way that Jassy's did.

'What should I do, Oliver?' she whispered, listening intently to the silence around her as though she might hear the tiniest of voices, the merest hint of help. But she didn't. She was on her own with this.

All the fears of the night before came rushing back to her as her hand hovered over the telephone. Once she made that call, there would be no going back. This was about as final a decision as she could make. Orley would never be the same again, would it?

Taking a deep breath, she picked up the phone.

When the call had come from the estate agent to tell Laurence that his offer had been accepted, he'd thought he'd burst with joy. This changed everything. This was the catalyst for his new life.

And nothing could come close to describing how Laurence had felt when he told his boss he'd be leaving the company. The look on Mr Murgatroyd's face had been priceless.

'Are you sure?' he'd said.

'Absolutely sure,' Laurence had replied as he'd tried to keep his smile from taking on a life of its own.

'But nobody ever leaves here voluntarily.'

Yes, he could easily have frittered away his whole life in that stifling building. It would have been a good life, he knew that – secure, with money coming in and all the luxuries that provided – but it wouldn't be satisfying. He could see that now.

His father, meanwhile, had shaken his head when Laurence had told him.

'You're crazy' he'd said. 'I knew you should have taken one of those gap years after university and got all that madness out of your system back then.'

'This isn't madness, Dad. This is absolute sanity. I've already had an offer on the flat too.'

Flats with a view of the Thames were like gold dust and he had to admit that he'd actually started taking pictures off the walls after the call from the estate agent. He just needed to feel that things were moving forward.

'I'd really love to have you on board with me, Dad,' he said to Marcus one evening when the subject could no longer be avoided. 'You'll come and see Orley with me this weekend, won't you?'

Laurence watched his father's reaction as he slowly put his book down.

'You know my feelings,' Marcus said. 'I have no wish to return to Sussex.'

'But we had such great times there, and I think we can have those times again.'

Marcus shook his head. 'Not without your mother.'

'Dad, Mum's gone, but we're still very much here and, well, I don't know about you but I've got an awful lot of life I want to live and I don't want to do that in London anymore. So are you coming or not?'

The two men stared at one another for an interminably long moment.

'You don't leave me much choice, son.'

'You've got a world full of choices, but you've got to put that bloody book away and get out of that chair.'

Laurence's heart was racing as he spoke. Was he being wickedly cruel to put his dad through this? he wondered. Mind you, his father didn't have to come with him – he could start a new life for himself. But Laurence had the feeling somehow that he wouldn't; that he'd be quite content to spend the rest of his years staring out at the river and occasionally pretending to read.

'I'd like to have you with me, Dad. We rub along okay, don't we?'

His father nodded, but he still hadn't committed himself one way or the other.

'Look,' Laurence said, 'at least come and see the place and then make your mind up, okay?'

His father nodded again and Laurence watched as he got up and left the room.

Well, it was some kind of progress, wasn't it?

The Jacobs women were at the morning room window again. At least, three of them were: Vanessa, Tilda and Grandma Dolly.

'I can't stand waiting,' Vanessa said. 'I suppose it's hard to time a journey from London, though.'

'I'm sure he'll be here soon,' Tilda replied.

'Oh, there's a car now!' Vanessa pointed at the lane as a black BMW pulled up. 'My word, look at that car! Did we ask enough for the north wing?'

'That's really expensive-looking,' Tilda said.

'Huh!' Grandma Dolly said. 'Not very practical for these country roads. First pothole and he'll be done for.'

Vanessa smiled at her mother-in-law's grim prediction.

'Who's that?' Vanessa asked as she watched two men get out of the car.

'There's two of them!' Dolly announced. 'You didn't say there'd be two of them!'

Vanessa turned around to face Tilda. 'Who's that other man?'

'I don't know.'

'You said a single man was buying the north wing,' Grandma Dolly said.

'Maybe it's a friend,' Tilda suggested. 'Lots of people take friends with them to view a property. Anyway, I thought you said a single man would be suspicious.'

'A single man is always suspicious, but that doesn't mean two men is a better option.'

'Let's just wait and see, shall we?' Vanessa said. 'Where's your sister, Tilly? I thought she wanted to meet our new neighbour.'

'Your guess is as good as mine.'

'I specifically asked her to make an effort and be here to greet them.'

'You know she hates that kind of thing.'

'I know, but this Mr Sturridge will be living with us and it's important that we all make him feel welcome.'

'I'm not going to make him feel welcome,' Dolly said. 'I'm going to tell him that he's trespassing.'

'Please don't!' Vanessa was aghast at the sudden image of Dolly chasing poor Mr Sturridge off the premises with her walking stick. 'He's paying a lot of money to live here.'

'Huh! A lot of money indeed. This place is priceless. It should never have been for sale.'

'I'm not getting into all that again,' Vanessa said, tidying her hair with an anxious hand as she crossed the room. *Calm*, she told herself. She needed to be calm.

Tilda followed her out the door. They'd have to bring Mr Sturridge and his companion up to Grandma Dolly if they wanted to meet her.

'He's very nice,' Tilda said as they walked down the stairs, just as the knocker sounded.

'Yes, I'm sure he is.' Vanessa took a deep breath as she reached the door and then opened it.

'Welcome to Orley,' she said, holding her hand out. 'I'm Vanessa Jacobs and this is my daughter Tilda.'

'Laurence Sturridge,' the younger man said, shaking her hand, 'and this is my father, Marcus.'

Vanessa nodded and smiled as she took in the rather stern expression on Marcus's face.

'I met Tilda last time,' Laurence said, nodding towards her. 'She kindly showed me the walled garden.'

'Yes, she mentioned that. Come in. How was your journey?'

'Oh, unbearable,' he said.

'Oh, no!'

'Well, just getting out of London,' he said with a nervous little laugh.

'It's so long ago since I made the journey by car that I've forgotten what a nightmare it can be.'

'You used to work in London?'

'Off and on. I used to live there too, but then I found this place.'

'And saw the light?' Laurence said.

'Fell in love with the owner,' Tilda said. 'My father.'

Laurence smiled. He had a nice, warm smile, Vanessa thought. The same couldn't be said about his father, however, who looked as if he'd rather be any place other than Orley.

'Can I get you a cup of tea before you have a look around? There's somebody you should meet – my mother-in-law, Dolly. She's upstairs.'

The two men followed her and Tilda.

'Isn't it amazing, Dad? Just look at the stairs,' Laurence said.

'This is the original Jacobean staircase,' Vanessa said.

'I love these thick oak posts.'

'Newel posts,' Vanessa told him. 'These are some of the best in the county.'

'Are they yours?' Marcus asked his son.

Laurence laughed at the impertinence of his father's question.

'This will be a communal area,' Vanessa said diplomatically, 'but the staircase still belongs to us.'

Reaching the top of the stairs, they turned left into the south wing and entered the morning room. Dolly was sitting in the armchair overlooking the south garden.

'Dolly? Mr Sturridge and his father are here,' Vanessa announced.

There was a moment's hesitation before Dolly deigned to turn her head.

'So, you're here, are you?' she said.

'A pleasure to meet you, Mrs Jacobs,' Laurence said, moving forward and extending his hand.

'I wish I could say the same to you,' Dolly said, 'but I can't. I'm not going to lie and say I welcome this intrusion because I don't.'

'Dolly, please!' Vanessa said.

Laurence frowned and his hand dropped by his side, unshaken.

'And will you be living here too?' Dolly asked, narrowing her eyes as she gave Marcus Sturridge the death stare.

'No,' Laurence said. 'My dad isn't—'

'Yes,' Marcus contradicted. 'I'll be living here with my son.'

Vanessa noticed the surprised look on Laurence's face, as if his father's admission were news to him.

'Well, I don't know about that,' Dolly said, as if the final decision were hers. 'We believed there was just the one of you.'

'I'm sorry for the confusion,' Laurence said.

'It's all right,' Vanessa assured him. 'There's plenty of room, as you'll see. There won't be any problems.'

Dolly rudely turned back to face the window and Vanessa nervously cleared her throat. 'Tea!' she declared brightly.

'I'll get it, Mum,' Tilda told her, leaving the room.

'I do have another daughter, Jasmine, but she's – well – she's somewhere,' Vanessa explained.

'I'm sure we'll meet her when the time is right,' Laurence said, daring to walk over to the south window. 'What a marvellous garden. Come and see, Dad.'

'I can see it from here,' Marcus stated.

'No wonder you can't take your eyes off it, Mrs Jacobs,' Laurence said, addressing Dolly, who resolutely refused to look at him. 'If I was you, I wouldn't want to share any of this either. I'd see somebody like me as an intruder, I really would.'

Vanessa was watching, her heart in her mouth.

'It must have been a difficult decision to make,' he went on.

'It wasn't my decision,' Dolly said, looking up at him.

'Then it must have been difficult for whoever made it.'

'I wonder what's keeping Tilda . . .' Vanessa said, wishing her daughter would hurry up with the tea things.

'But I can't help but be thankful that your family did make this decision, because it gives me the opportunity to start a brand-new life here,' Laurence went on. 'Totally selfish, I know, but there it is. I'm really excited to be here.'

Dolly made a funny sort of harrumphing sound.

'Please, come and have a seat,' Vanessa gestured to two sofas next to the east window overlooking the front lawn.

'Another wonderful view,' Laurence said as he gazed out of the window.

'And one you'll have from your part of the property.'

'I remember it from the first viewing,' he said. 'Looks right up into the Ridwell Valley. Look, Dad.'

Marcus walked to the window and looked out. He gave a little nod, but didn't say anything.

'Ah, here's Tilda,' Vanessa said, mightily relieved when she saw her daughter returning with a tray on which sat five mugs, a teapot, a jug of milk and a bowl of sugar.

Laurence sprang forward. 'Let me help.'

'It's okay,' Tilda insisted, placing it on the coffee table in between the two sofas before pouring the tea. She took Dolly a mug so she could drink it sat by her own window.

'So,' Vanessa began, encompassing Marcus and Laurence in what she hoped was a friendly smile, 'Tilda tells me you're from Elhurst.'

'That's right,' Laurence said. 'I grew up here. A little cottage on the edge of the village. I used to ride my bike past this house and wonder what it would be like to live here.'

'And now you're going to find out. I hope the reality won't disappoint you.'

'I'm sure it won't.'

Vanessa smiled. Laurence looked so happy to be there and she couldn't help feeling a little of his joy. It reminded her of the day when she had moved into Orley, packing her small car with a few cardboard boxes of possessions and making the drive from London pretty much as Laurence and his father had done today. It had been a strange feeling to know that the big old country manor house was going to be her home, and she'd been filled with a mixture of excitement and trepidation. Tilda and Jasmine had never experienced it, having been born and raised here, but Vanessa had been an outsider, as Dolly had before her.

'What sort of place are you leaving in London?' Vanessa asked.

41

'A flat overlooking the river,' Laurence said. 'I think the river's the only thing I'm going to miss about London.'

'Well, we've got the Ridwell here, as you may remember,' Vanessa said, 'and it often comes a little closer to the house than we'd like.'

Tilda shot her a warning look and Vanessa gasped.

'Not to the north wing, of course!' she quickly added. 'But it often floods the south garden.'

'Not often,' Tilda said. 'Occasionally.'

Laurence nodded, Marcus frowned and Vanessa wished that the wooden floorboards would swallow her up.

'So, it's just the two of you?' she continued, desperate to change the subject.

Laurence cleared his throat. 'Yes. My mother died two years ago.'

'Oh, I'm sorry,' Vanessa said, once again mortified that she'd brought up an unsuitable subject.

'Just me and my dad these days.'

Marcus shifted uneasily on the sofa.

'Well,' Laurence said, finishing his tea, 'perhaps we could—'

'Yes, of course.' Vanessa stood up. 'You'll want to have a good look around. Take your time, and feel free to explore the gardens too.'

'River's not flooded today, then?' Laurence said, a little smile lighting his face.

'No, no! Not for years.'

'I'll show you the way,' Tilda said, and Vanessa watched in relief as her daughter led Laurence and Marcus out of the room.

A horrible silence descended after they'd left, filled with the malevolence of Dolly Jacobs, who was still sat in the chair by the south window.

'You stupid woman!' she said to Vanessa. 'I wouldn't be surprised if they backed out of the sale now. In fact, I hope they do!'

As soon as Tilda had left and they were in the privacy of the north wing, Laurence turned to face his father.

'You're really going to live here, Dad?'

Marcus shrugged. 'Sure.'

'When did you make your mind up?'

They entered a large room, which was cold and echoey, and moved across to the window.

'As soon as you turned off the motorway,' Marcus said.

Laurence nodded. So, the Sussex Weald had worked its magic on him as Laurence had hoped it would.

'I'm right, aren't I? This is a pretty special place.'

Marcus didn't say anything, but Laurence could see that there was gentleness in his father's eyes as he stared out of the window, taking in the full beauty of the Ridwell Valley with its soft green fields and wooded hills. Had his father missed it as much as he had? he wondered.

'Listen,' Laurence said, 'I'll leave you to it, okay? Let you have a look around by yourself. I'll – I'll be around somewhere.'

It was a strange feeling to walk through the big bare rooms without an estate agent, but Laurence welcomed the silence as his thoughts roamed. This was going to be his home. Their home. He was so glad that his father was going to be part of this new life, and Laurence couldn't help thinking that the peaceful setting could only do them good after the stresses of the last couple of years and the noise and strain of life in London.

He could hear his father's footsteps on the wooden floorboards as he moved around. Laurence managed to keep one room ahead of him, giving Marcus the space and time that he would need to accept this place as his new home. He would give anything to know what was going through his father's mind – the questions he might have and the memories that he must be reliving by being back in Sussex – but they would have plenty of time to talk later, he thought. Now was the time for dreaming.

Jasmine had left the door of the oast house open. The sun was still very weak at this time of year, but it was a welcome change from the grim grey days of the last few weeks, and she wanted to try and capture some of that light on canvas. In truth, she was also hiding out from the Sturridge man her mum and sister kept talking about. She didn't want anything to do with him. She had nothing to say to him and wasn't going to be a part of some fake welcoming party when he arrived. Nobody wanted him there, not really, so why pretend?

Jasmine didn't do pretending very well and couldn't understand people who did. It was absurd. If you felt something then you should just come out and say it. Although Jasmine suspected that her grandmother probably wasn't mincing her words that day.

It was as she was washing some brushes, which really should have been washed the night before, that she heard footsteps. Turning around, she saw a man standing in the doorway.

'Oh, sorry,' he said, quickly backing away.

Jasmine could feel a blush heating her face. 'You're him, aren't you?'

'Him?'

'Mr Sturridge. The man who's going to live with us.'

'I'm one of them,' the man said.

Jasmine frowned.

'I think you're thinking of Laurence. My son. He came to view the property before. I'm Laurence's father.'

'Oh.'

There was an awkward silence, but despite having been quite determined not to be a part of the welcoming committee, Jasmine's innate kindness got the better of her and she introduced herself.

'I'm Jasmine, but most people call me Jassy.'

'I'm Marcus. Most people call me grumpy.'

Jasmine found herself smiling, much to her surprise.

'Look, I didn't mean to disturb you,' Marcus said.

'You're not. I haven't begun yet. Actually, I'm not sure I want to.'

'What – what were you doing?' Marcus asked, looking around the oast house from the doorway.

'I was going to paint, but I'm not really in the mood. I'm in one of my funny moods. At least, that's what Tilda calls them. I'm just a bit restless, you know?'

'I know.'

They held each other's gaze for a moment and then Jasmine looked away. She wasn't quite sure why she'd just told this Marcus Sturridge such a thing. She didn't usually tell people how she was feeling.

'Are all these paintings yours?'

'Yes.'

'Can I have a closer look?'

She shrugged. 'I suppose. But don't touch that one!' she cried as the sleeve of his coat almost brushed a canvas as he walked into the room. 'It's still wet.'

She watched as Marcus Sturridge walked around her studio. It was an odd feeling. Tilda and her mother usually got thrown out if they tried to enter and yet here she was inviting this stranger in.

'You didn't come for the first viewing, did you?' she asked him.

'No, I didn't.'

'Why not?'

'I guess I didn't think this was going to happen. I thought Laurence was just – well – messing about.'

'Why would you think that?'

'You ask a lot of questions.'

'I like finding things out,' she said. 'Mum's always telling me that it isn't polite to ask questions, but I can't help it.'

Marcus gave a tiny smile.

'Where did you want to live?' she asked.

He sighed. 'Nowhere really.'

'What do you mean? You have to live somewhere!'

'I didn't care.'

'That's sad,' Jasmine told him. 'You should love where you live.'

'And you love it here?'

She nodded.

'I don't blame you. It's beautiful.'

'You'll be happy here,' she said.

He looked as if he were about to laugh, but something seemed to hold him back. 'I wish . . .'

'What?'

'I wish I could be as confident as you.'

'I'm not confident,' she stated. 'I have a condition. It makes me honest, that's all, which isn't like normal people, is it?'

'I see,' Marcus said. 'Well, honesty is always good, I think.'

'Me too.'

'So many people shy away from it, don't they?'

Jasmine nodded. 'I like you,' she said. 'Which is really odd because I don't normally like strangers and I didn't think I was going to like whoever was going to be living with us.'

Marcus laughed at that. 'And that's about as honest as you can get,' he said.

Laurence was on his second lap of the south garden when he spotted his father.

'Dad!' he called, waving a hand. 'How are you getting on? I thought I'd lost you.'

'I've just had a very nice chat with Jasmine,' he said.

'Since when do you chat, Dad?'

'What do you mean?'

'I mean, we haven't chatted for years!'

'Well, I chatted with Jasmine.'

'I have yet to meet the mysterious Jasmine,' Laurence said. 'What's she like?'

His father looked thoughtful. 'She's like . . .'

'What?'

'No, you'll laugh.'

'Why would I laugh?'

'Because she reminded me of . . .'

'What, Dad?'

Marcus cleared his throat. 'Spring.'

'Pardon?'

'She reminded me of spring. You know – fresh and bright, and full of life, but with a rawness about her.'

Laurence did a double take. 'You're suddenly a poet now you're moving back to the country?'

'I told you that you'd laugh.'

'I'm not laughing,' he said and they walked down a path flanked by flowers. 'So, do you think you'll be happy here?'

His father didn't answer at first, but his long stare took in the fields full of sheep and the distant hills.

'I think the chances are fairly good,' he said.

Chapter 5

What exactly was it that solicitors did that took such an inordinate amount of time? Laurence wondered. When he made his mind up about something, he could be very impatient indeed, expecting the world to move at the pace he had set. Unrealistic, he knew, but he just couldn't help it.

The last few weeks in London were torturous for him, knowing that his beautiful new home and garden awaited him and yet weren't quite his. He did his best to throw himself into his work, tidying up all the loose ends and preparing himself for the life of a self-employed financial consultant. He had made many good friends in the business and already had a list of potential clients, which was heartening because he couldn't help feeling some trepidation.

Finally, with papers signed and money exchanged, Laurence and his father left London on a crisp spring morning. As they entered the Ridwell Valley, they noticed that the river was twice its normal size as the ice waters had melted. It had already broken its banks several times over the long, dark winter months, but now it was receding. Snowdrops, crocuses and violets were emerging in the hedgerows, and the fields looked so very green now their snowy cloak had been finally shaken off.

Laurence kept sneaking little glances at his father as they drove towards Elhurst. Marcus hadn't spoken since they'd left the motorway and didn't even say anything when he saw the two large farm vehicles blocking the main road through the village.

'This could take a while,' Laurence said.

His father sighed.

'Shall we?' Laurence put the car into reverse. It would mean doubling back through the village and taking another lane that linked up with the one that led to Orley, and they both knew what that meant. It meant driving past their old home.

Laurence had avoided seeing it on his first viewing of Orley as he'd wanted the trip to be about the future rather than the past. It was about fourteen years since he'd last seen the place, his mother and father having moved to a property on the Kent coast for a change of scene and a breath of sea air shortly after Laurence had left university.

Turning left out of the village, the road dipped and the valley opened up to them. There were a few small cottages lining the lane that never seemed to change and Laurence slowed the car down as they reached the last one.

Field End Cottage.

It was a sweet little cottage with tiny sash windows that looked out onto the expanse of the Ridwell Valley. Surrounded by a garden with raised beds and an old greenhouse, it wouldn't have looked out of place on a jigsaw puzzle.

'You okay?' Laurence asked.

His father nodded. 'They've got a new front door.'

'Yes, and the old apple tree has gone too.'

'Well, it was looking iffy when we were here.'

'Nothing stays the same forever.'

'We should never have moved,' his father said. 'If we'd stayed, perhaps your mother would still be alive.'

'You can't think like that, Dad.'

'She wouldn't have been out on that road that day.'

'No, but she would have been driving on different roads in different circumstances,' Laurence told him. 'We can't change the past and you'll drive yourself mad if you think that way.'

His father turned away, looking resolutely out of the window as the cottage grew smaller in the rear-view mirror.

It wasn't long before they joined the lane which led to Orley.

'I can't believe we're really doing this,' Laurence said as he caught his first glimpse of the manor house. 'You ready for this, Dad?'

'I guess I'm going to have to be.'

They turned onto the driveway before parking in their own personal space which had access to the north wing. The removal van had arrived and the main entrance hall was full of boxes.

'Mr Sturridge – welcome!' Vanessa said, greeting Laurence as he entered the hallway.

'Please, call me Laurence,' he said. 'Or Laurie. But not Mr Sturridge.'

She nodded and smiled. 'And you must call me Vanessa. I hope your journey was okay,' she said, switching her attention between the two men.

'I think the worst part was getting through Elhurst,' Laurence told her. 'A slight agricultural hold-up.'

'Oh, the roads round here are impossible, aren't they? If anything larger than a Land Rover comes along, it's absolute chaos! Can I get you a cup of tea or something?'

'No thanks,' Laurence said. 'I think we're just going to dive in.'

'Well, you know where we are if you need anything.'

'Thank you,' he said, watching as Vanessa left the hallway, entering a room on the south side.

North and south, he thought. He and his father had journeyed south from London and now they were heading north.

'What a horrible din!' Dolly Jacobs complained when Vanessa entered her rooms.

'It won't last forever,' Vanessa assured her.

'It wouldn't happen at all if I made the decisions round here.'

'Everybody knows how you feel about it,' Vanessa said, trying to keep her cool. 'You've made your thoughts perfectly clear. But it's going ahead – right now – and I think this is the best thing we could possibly do for Orley.'

Dolly heaved herself up from her chair and turned to glare at her. Leaning on her stick, she made her way to the corner of the room and opened the drawer of a beautiful old desk that had once been in Oliver's study, handed down from father to son for countless generations. Vanessa had always been curious as to what Dolly kept in it and knew she was about to find out.

'What is it?' she asked as Dolly crossed the room holding something which she shoved into Vanessa's hand. It was a black-and-white photograph of Orley.

'See this?'

Vanessa looked at the beautiful old image. 'When was it taken?'

'Sometime in the thirties. Just before the war.'

'And you're showing it to me because . . . ?'

'Because I want you to see this place has always been here, unchanged, unsullied. People have come and gone. Fires raged. Wars have been fought. But Orley remains, and it's remained in the same family.'

Vanessa swallowed hard because she knew what was coming.

'This house has been through all those challenges, but never has one of its owners thought to sell it off.'

'Dolly—' Vanessa began as she tried to return the photo.

'Keep it,' she hollered as she turned her back to Vanessa. 'I want you to remember what you've done to this place.'

Vanessa didn't hear Tilda coming into the morning room.

'Mum – what's the matter?'

Vanessa tried to hide her face, but it was too late.

'You've been crying!' Tilda was on her knees by her mother's chair. 'Is it the Sturridges?'

'No, no,' Vanessa said.

'Then what's happened?'

Vanessa took a deep breath. 'I know she's your grandmother, but she can really be a nasty old woman sometimes!'

'Oh, Mum! What's she said now?'

Vanessa shook her head. She was always careful not to talk ill of Dolly in front of her two daughters.

'She gave me this.' She handed the photograph to Tilda, who looked at it, a huge smile spreading across her face.

'It's lovely. I've never seen it before.'

'Neither had I.'

'And this is what's upset you?'

'Dolly launched into this tirade about the history of the house and how nobody ever thought of selling until I came along.'

'Oh, Mum! Did you remind her it was my idea?'

'No, of course not, darling.'

'I'll go and have a word with her—'

'Best to leave it, I think.'

'You sure?'

Vanessa nodded. 'I think I'll just try and avoid Dolly for a while. Say the next ten years?'

'That might actually be a good idea!' Tilda laughed and Vanessa managed to join in.

'When I met your father, I had no idea how huge a part Dolly would play in my life. But the families of these sorts of houses are tightly knit.'

'Do you think you'd have married Dad if you'd known?'

'Of course I would have! I loved your father so, so much. I would have put up with a hundred Dollys to be with him. Anyway, when I first moved here, we were so busy with our own lives and raising you that I really didn't notice her little ways so much. She would poke her nose in from time to time, telling me how I should be dressing you and what I should be feeding you. But all grandparents are like that, I suppose. I think the real trouble started when your grandfather died. Dolly lost the main focus of her life and fastened onto Oliver and me. Then, when she lost her son, I began to feel the full force of her. I think a little bit of Dolly died when we lost your father.'

'She doesn't see how hard you work for us all,' Tilda said.

'It's not just that. She doesn't like me; it's that simple.'

'Of course she likes you. She just doesn't show it.' Tilda gave her a weak smile.

'She's very good at showing her disapproval,' Vanessa pointed out.

'That's the way some people are.' Tilda looked at her watch. 'Look, I've got to scoot. Got a lesson in Robertsbridge.'

'Old Mr Bromley?'

Tilda nodded.

'How's it going?'

'He's tone deaf and hates taking instruction from a young woman.'

'Why does he keep at it then?'

'I think he likes the company,' Tilda said.

Vanessa smiled. 'Have fun.'

'And don't worry about Grandma, Mum. She hates change. Remember when you wanted to plant a new herbaceous border and she even complained about that?'

Vanessa laughed. 'I've never known somebody able to find fault in absolutely everything. It's quite a skill, isn't it? And one I'm very glad you didn't inherit.'

Laurence would never forget the feeling of freedom on waking up on his first morning at Orley. He didn't have to rush to catch the Tube and make it into the office for an eight-thirty meeting. He could have a leisurely breakfast and venture out into the garden, take a footpath across the fields and up into the hills. He could just be.

He couldn't remember the last time he'd done that – let a day unfold. Of course, that way of living wasn't sustainable and he'd have to get his business off the ground but, for the time being, he'd allow himself a little holiday.

Walking around the north wing that morning, Laurence couldn't help smiling. He truly felt as if he'd found a place he could live forever, but he soon began to realise that he wasn't accustomed to having quite so many large rooms. His London flat had been modest in size. Here at Orley, his father had taken just a living room and an en-suite bedroom for his own personal use, and most of his boxes had been unpacked already. Laurence still had a few to go. But he'd never been much for hoarding and he was rather regretting that trait now because all the rooms looked half empty.

Heading towards his father's rooms at the end of the north wing, Laurence thought about what he was going to do next. He'd given each of the rooms the once-over and realised that he'd have to get a bit of work done on a few of them, but he didn't want to get bogged down with something so serious so soon. He wanted to think of fun things like coffee tables and sofas, maybe even a new bed.

'Dad?' he called, knocking on the door of his father's living room.

'Come in.'

'How are you getting on?' Laurence asked as he walked in. 'Wow! You look really at home already.'

'There wasn't a lot to do. Just a few books and CDs. I got rid of most of my things before I moved in with you.'

Laurence nodded. Like him, his father wasn't much of a hoarder.

'But you don't need much at my stage in life,' Marcus added.

'Dad, you're not exactly ancient. I think you've still got a few good years yet.'

'Maybe, but I'm quite happy to sit with a book or the newspaper. I don't need things anymore.'

'You know, I was thinking that we could give our new garden a makeover together.'

'Were you?' Marcus made it sound as if the idea were preposterous.

'It would be fun,' Laurence said. 'Remember how beautiful the garden was at Field End? You used to spend hours out there.'

'The garden here's north-facing.'

'Yes, but we could still do a bit of landscaping and planting, couldn't we?'

'I don't know.'

Laurence sighed. It was going to take more than a house move to forge a closer relationship with his father, wasn't it?

'Listen, I'm going to go out – have a look around and maybe buy some furniture or something. You want to come?'

His father shook his head.

'Want me to look out for any pieces for you?'

'No, thanks.'

'Dad, you can't live in a room that's half bare.'

'Why not?'

'It looks sad.'

'I think it looks restful.'

Laurence shrugged. 'Okay,' he said. 'I'll see you later.' He paused at the door and looked back at his father, who'd picked up a book and seated himself in a chair positioned by the window. It was the same book and the same chair as in London, Laurence observed, but at least it was a different window and view now.

It was as Laurence was walking downstairs that he heard it. Somebody somewhere was playing the piano. At first, it was a few hesitant notes, but then a stream of beautiful music floated through the hallway, stopping abruptly as he stuck his head around the door of the living room in the south wing.

'Sorry!' he said quickly as he saw Tilda sitting at the piano. 'I didn't mean – I know this is your part of the house, but I had to see who was playing.'

'I should have shut the door,' she said. 'I didn't mean to disturb anybody.'

'You didn't. I was just being nosy. Sorry,' he said. She stood up and shut the lid of the piano. 'Please don't let me disturb you.'

'I was done.'

'It was lovely.'

'No, it wasn't.'

He frowned. 'It was. What was it?'

'What do you mean?'

'The music – I don't know much about music. Was it Chopin or something?'

She smiled. 'No. It wasn't Chopin. It was just a little something. Nothing, really.'

He saw the way she anxiously knotted her fingers together and looked at everything in the room but him, and then it clicked.

'You wrote it?'

She shrugged. 'It's not finished. It's not even started, really.'

'Well, you should finish it. It really was lovely.'

She gave the faintest of smiles. 'How are you settling in?'

'I'm having problems.'

'You are?'

'Nothing fits,' he said.

'What do you mean?'

'Come and see. I mean, if you wouldn't mind. I could use someone's advice.'

'Okay,' she said, and he led the way out of the living room to the north wing.

'Oh dear,' Tilda said a moment later.

'See what I mean? I haven't got enough stuff, and the stuff I do have is exactly wrong,' he said, scratching his head in despair. 'All these modern pieces looked great in my flat in London, but they're not right here.'

'What are you going to do?'

'I'm going to have to go shopping. Got any ideas where? It would be nice to get a few antiques. Not too pricey, though. I've kind of spent a lot of money recently.' He grinned at her.

'Well, there's the big antiques centre just outside Elhurst,' Tilda said. 'It's a bit more rough and ready than the shop on the main street, which mostly sells overpriced pieces of mahogany.'

'Rough and ready would do me nicely,' he said. 'I think I'm too clumsy to justify any purchases in mahogany.' He cleared his throat. 'Would you like to come with me? I could do with your opinion. I've no idea what I'm looking at when it comes to this sort of thing. I asked my dad if he wanted to come shopping and he – er – well, he declined.' He paused, feeling a little awkward. 'We're going through a slightly tricky time at the moment.'

She looked startled. 'So I'm your second choice, am I?'

'No, no! I didn't mean it like that.' He raised his hands in the air as if in panic. 'You're absolutely my first choice. After all, you're the daughter of an interior designer and you've been brought up surrounded by beautiful antiques. That makes you a tad more experienced than me and my dad.'

Tilda looked at her watch. 'I suppose I could come with you. But I've got an appointment this afternoon so we can't be too long.'

'Okay,' he said, clapping his hands together. 'Let's get going.'

They left the house together, walking round to where Laurence's car was parked.

'I've not met your sister yet,' he said.

'She's a bit shy,' Tilda said. 'I expect she's in the oast house.'

'My dad met her there on our last viewing.'

'Yes, she mentioned him. I think she likes him.'

'He said they had a chat,' Laurence said. 'I envy your sister that. I haven't been able to chat to my dad for years.'

'What do you mean?'

He took a deep breath as they both got into the car. 'Dad's still struggling with my mum's death.'

'I'm sorry.'

'I'm hoping this move might shake him out of himself.'

'You think it will?'

'I'm not sure. We used to live here, you see, and I'm wondering now if coming back was such a good idea. We drove by our old house on the way here yesterday. Field End Cottage.'

'I know it,' Tilda said. 'It's a sweet place.'

'We were all really happy there.' He started the engine and pulled out of the driveway onto the lane. 'I guess I'm trying to find some of that happiness again by coming back.'

'It's a good idea.'

'You think so?' he asked. It would be good to get her opinion, he thought, because he didn't have anyone else to talk to about this stuff.

She nodded. 'This is definitely my happy place.'

He turned and smiled at her and then he unwound his window. 'Well, it definitely has the best air in the world, doesn't it?'

'The best what?' Tilda asked.

'Air – the best air!'

She frowned. 'I've never really thought about it.'

'Says a true local who's known nothing else in her life.'

She turned and stared at him. 'That's some assumption to make. You think that I've only ever lived at Orley and that I've never experienced anything else?'

'Did I say that?'

'Not in so many words.' She shook her head. 'I've been away, you know. I've seen places.'

'I'm sure you have!' he said, glancing at her quickly. 'You know, there's something familiar about you.'

Tilda turned her head slightly away from him, as if pretending to watch the passing landscape.

'We haven't met before, have we? I'd have remembered.'

'No, we've not met. I've just got one of those faces, I guess.'

'You haven't told me what you do. For a living, I mean.'

'I teach music.'

'The piano?'

'And singing.'

'You sing too?'

'A little.'

They drove up the hill out of the valley, passing the church and turning onto the main street of Elhurst. As it was Saturday morning, it was busy with shoppers walking with children and dogs, and people riding bicycles and horses.

'It's up here, right?' Laurence asked, passing the war memorial.

'Yes. There's parking at the back.'

The antiques centre was housed in an impressive converted mill and had three floors to explore.

'Where shall we begin?' Laurence asked as they entered the building.

'The ground floor tends to have the largest pieces of furniture,' Tilda told him.

'Okay. Are you looking for anything?'

'No,' she said. 'We'd be more likely to sell things to the buyers here than to purchase them.'

'You've got some pieces to sell at Orley?'

'Don't get your hopes up. I think Grandma Dolly would kill us if we tried to sell anything else.'

They looked around, spotting a wonderfully large refectory table that wouldn't look out of place in a monastery, several huge wardrobes which were probably all portals to Narnia, as well as beds, mirrors, chairs, clocks, sofas and paintings – more than Laurence could ever have dreamed of.

'I think I'll have to do some maths,' he confessed after they'd walked around a second time. 'I'm definitely going to have that bed with the carved headboard.'

'You're going to have guests?'

Laurence looked thoughtful. 'Probably not, but it's nice to be prepared and I've certainly got the room for it.' He grinned. 'You know, I spent all those years in London and yet I can't think of a single person I want to keep in touch with. Is that bad? I don't imagine I'll invite anyone down here to visit.'

'You should be careful about that.'

'What do you mean?'

'I mean, it's easy to isolate yourself somewhere like Orley. It's a bit of a bubble. We're very cut off from the outside world. Mum came down from London, and she had such a huge circle of friends and there were always lots of parties and things, so it kept the place alive but, since Dad died, we haven't really seen anyone much.'

'I'm sorry to hear about your father.'

Tilda nodded. 'Orley isn't the same without him. He *was* Orley.'

'All this must be a huge upheaval for your family.'

'It is. These old houses might not seem to change over the decades, but they do. People come and go and leave their marks, their memories.'

'Hey, that's rather beautiful. You should write that down. It might make a good song.'

She smiled. 'You might be right. Anyway, what else is on your shopping list?'

'Ah, yes. So, we're going for the bed, one of those wardrobes, the second-largest table that we saw and the chairs around it, the bookcase with the glass front and the side table with the cabriole legs. Do you think they'll cut me a good deal?'

'I sure hope so, otherwise it might be you selling part of Orley!'

He grinned.

Then, as they were making their way towards the desk at the front of the store, something rather strange happened. A woman who looked to be in her early thirties was walking towards them with two girls who looked about eleven and nine. 'Hey – it's Tilly!' the older one suddenly shouted. 'Mummy, it's Tilly!' And she grabbed her mother's arm and pulled her towards Tilda.

Laurence looked on in amusement. He assumed that they were either friends of Tilda's or perhaps two of her pupils. That was, until they asked her for her autograph.

'I hope you don't mind,' the mother said. 'They love your song.'

'It's no bother,' Tilda said as she dutifully signed a notepad the mother got out of her handbag.

'This is so kind of you. You know, they both know all the words, and all the moves too!'

'We do!' the older girl said.

'Really?' Tilda said. 'I'm impressed.' She handed the notepad to the younger girl.

'Oh wow!' she said. 'Thank you!'

'You're welcome.'

'So, when's the next song out?' the mother asked.

Laurence watched as Tilda's face paled.

'I'm not sure,' she said.

'Well, we'll be the first to buy it! Say goodbye, girls.'

'Goodbye, Tilly!' they chorused.

'Bye!' Tilda said, waving to them as they disappeared out of the door.

Laurence cocked his head to one side. 'What on earth was all that about?'

'I – er – it was nothing.'

'Nothing! They asked for your autograph.'

She shrugged. 'I sang a song once.'

'A song that seems to have made you famous.'

'Maybe just a little bit. To locals.'

'I think you're being very modest,' Laurence said. 'What was it called, this song of yours?'

Tilda sighed. '"Summer Girl".'

Laurence's mouth dropped open. 'That was you? You were Tilly?'

Tilda nodded.

'Blimey. I remember that song. They used to play it on the radio all the time. It was really annoying!'

Tilda stared at him in horror. 'Thanks a lot!'

'No – I mean, the song wasn't annoying. I meant the constant playing of it.'

'It was on a lot,' Tilda admitted.

'So that's where I know you from. You were on the TV and in the newspaper all the time.'

'For a little while.'

'Well, this is really—'

'I think you should buy this furniture, don't you?' Tilda said abruptly.

Laurence managed to get a bit of a discount and free delivery on the items he wanted to purchase and felt very excited about seeing them in situ in his rooms, but it didn't distract him from the incident with Tilda. As they left the antiques centre, he zoned in on her again.

'Do you mind me asking how it all happened?'

'How what happened? How you came to buy half the antiques centre?'

'No!' he said with a laugh. 'How the whole Tilly business happened.'

They got in the car and Tilda took a deep breath. 'Do you really want to know?'

'Yeah! I really do. I'm a boring financial consultant. I don't often get to meet famous people.'

'I'm hardly famous.'

'No? You've just been on the TV, radio and in newspapers, and cause little girls to have heart attacks in public places.'

Tilda shook her head, but he could see that she was doing her best to suppress a smile.

'Tell me, Tilda. Or should I call you Tilly?'

'No, please don't. Only my family is allowed to get away with that and they were doing it long before the madness began.'

'So how *did* it all begin?' he asked, starting the engine and driving through Elhurst.

'Well, I entered a talent contest and then got signed up to a record label, but I only had the one hit. It did pretty well, though. It was summer, so the timing was right and I got involved in a nationwide tour, but that was it. It was a corny, cheesy song. I had the lyrics pushed into my mouth. But it made a lot of money. It helped us out at Orley with some pretty big bills.'

'And you're not singing and performing now?' he asked, taking a right turn into the valley.

'I was kind of pushed aside. Another artist from another talent show came along and became the next big thing.'

'That's brutal.'

'That's the business.'

'But you've still got your talent – your music. You still write, don't you?'

She didn't answer and gave a funny little shrug.

'Because what I heard coming from that piano was really beautiful. You can't bury talent like that.'

'But can't you see that nobody's going to take my music seriously now? I'll always be "Silly Tilly" of that summer song.'

'Then reinvent yourself. Artists do it all the time. Pick a new name, a new identity. Find a new sound.'

'I don't have a new sound, unless silence is a sound.'

'I'm afraid "The Sound of Silence" has already been a big hit.'

'Very funny,' she said.

'Seriously, write your music, Tilda. It's beautiful, and people will always want that in their lives. You don't have to hit great heights again like you did. Music isn't all about money, is it?'

'Says the investment accountant or whatever it is you do!'

'No, I mean—'

'It's totally about the money. I have to earn a living and these days I do that by teaching music. I've no right to think I can be a musician anymore.'

They'd reached Orley and, as soon as Laurence had parked the car, Tilda jumped out.

'Hey!' he called after her. She stopped and turned back to face him. 'Thanks for today.'

She nodded, but she didn't say anything.

Chapter 6

Tilda wasn't in a good mood as she packed her bag and got her things together for her afternoon's teaching. Who did this Laurence Sturridge think he was, telling her what she should be doing with her music? Just when she'd started to think of herself as a teacher, he'd come in and done his best to throw her off course again. Well, she wasn't going to allow that to happen. Nothing and nobody was going to persuade her that she could do anything more than teach. Teaching was safe, it was reliable and, if she could get enough pupils, it could become a really viable career. The same could not be said for becoming a full-time singer-songwriter. There were too many variables, too much luck involved. The industry was frighteningly fickle and she wanted nothing more to do with it. At least, that's what she told herself.

The truth was, Tilda knew that there was more to her than teaching. However wonderful it was to guide a pupil towards a love and appreciation of music, it was nothing when compared to composing your own pieces, and she missed that, oh how she missed that. She was an artist, pure and simple. She needed to write, to play, to sing. But what was the point, really, if she was never going to find an audience? She truly believed what she had told Laurence – that the music industry would never consider her as a serious artist after her incarnation as Tilly. She was as good as dead and so she had tucked her dream away, burying it under layers of remorse, and regret that she had ever entered that stupid competition.

Oh, she was so mad that Laurence had managed to get her all stirred up about things again. He might have a cute smile, but she was going to have to avoid him in the future if she was going to keep sane. As it was, her mother and sister were always telling her she should be singing rather than teaching. The last thing she needed was another voice chiming in. Was she the only one who could see the truth of the matter?

She shook her head. She wasn't going to think about it anymore. She had promised herself that, one night in a lonely hotel room in the middle of her tour. The tour on which she had been replaced.

Her manager had been less than tactful about it, telling her to go back to her hotel and ride things out. 'Don't take it personally,' he'd told her, but how could she not? Just a few months before, she'd been told countless times that she was the most personable girl on the planet and that everybody loved her. So, where had all that love gone? Had it simply transferred to the next young act? Had she been forgotten so quickly? They had built her up and then hadn't even stuck around to watch her fall.

Tilda still carried some of that hollow feeling around inside her. It was like a kind of disease, but she was doing her best to make sure that she never caught it again.

Grabbing her bag, she left the house and drove into Elhurst for her Saturday appointment with old Major Finnegan. He lived in a large Georgian house opposite the church and Tilda parked outside, glancing up at the eight enormous sash windows that looked out onto the main street and wondering if the major was looking out of one of them, awaiting her arrival.

Sure enough, as soon as she was out of the car, the front door opened and the tall, portly figure of Major Finnegan greeted her.

'Ah, there you are,' he said, ushering her in. 'I expect you'll want to try and teach me something, eh?'

'That's the general idea, Major,' Tilda said.

'Well, come on through, come on through.'

He led the way into the sitting room. It was a beautifully light space with two windows which took in the panorama of the church and the Ridwell Valley beyond. The room itself housed an old sofa with a threadbare cover and a scattering of old cushions and even older cats, whom the major would chase out before they began their lesson as if he were afraid he might upset his pets with the racket he made on the keyboard.

The major was a widower and a large portrait of his very large wife dominated the room, glowering down at the piano. It was quite off-putting really, but Tilda did her best to ignore it.

'Cup of tea?'

'No, thank you,' Tilda said. It was one of the major's delaying tactics, she had found. A cup of tea, a plate of scones, a quick tour of the garden to see what was growing, a rifle through the newspaper to read her the latest book reviews – the major was a great one for putting off his actual lesson. 'I think we should get straight to it, don't you?'

'Hmm, I suppose we should,' he said, cracking his knuckles, which made Tilda wince.

'Now, Major—'

'I do wish you'd call me Herbie.'

Tilda nodded silently. She couldn't even call him by his full Christian name of Herbert, let alone Herbie. It just wasn't right. Even though she was the teacher in this scenario, she always felt like the schoolchild.

'Let's see how you've been getting on with that Bach piece I left you with, shall we?'

The major grumbled something into his beard which Tilda couldn't quite make out, but she seriously suspected that it had something to do with him not having played a single note since her visit the previous Saturday.

When she got home, she felt absolutely drained. Some of her pupils did that to her, she found. She seemed to pour more into their lessons than they did. Honestly, she wondered why some of them took up such a pastime as the piano. Her younger pupils were often pushed into it by ambitious parents, but what on earth was the major doing, torturing himself every week when he didn't have to? Music should come from the soul, she thought. It shouldn't be forced, or thrust upon a person who had no interest and no natural aptitude.

Tilda sighed. She mustn't allow herself to become so despondent. She knew that not all of her pupils would be astonishingly talented protégés who would light up her world with their talent and enthusiasm. No, the reality was that it was her job to push a few reluctant children through their grades in order to appease their parents. That was the lot of the piano teacher and she had better get used to it.

As soon as Marcus had seen Laurence's car take off down the driveway, he'd put his book down and got out of his chair. He walked around his rooms for a bit, looking out of the windows at the new view. It wasn't London, that was for sure. But, then again, London had never really been his home. If he was perfectly honest with himself, which he rarely was these days, he hadn't felt at home since Tara had died and he'd sold their house in Kent and gone travelling, putting as many miles between himself and the memory of the tragedy as he could.

In all his years, Marcus had never felt so unsettled as he did right now, and that was saying something for a man who'd joined the navy as soon as he'd left school and had sailed the seven seas. But this was different. This was the kind of unsettled feeling that came from deep within, squatting in one's insides and seemingly unable to respond to anything – even a year-long trip to the other side of the world and two house moves. Maybe he'd feel better if he took a walk, he thought, putting on his coat and boots.

He saw her as he was walking down the stairs. Vanessa. The well-meaning woman he really didn't want to see at that particular moment. He sensed that there was something needy about her; he had absolutely nothing to give her and so he deliberately avoided eye contact and hoped that she was going about her own business and would ignore him.

'Oh, Mr Sturridge!' she cried as she spotted him. Marcus took a deep breath and looked up.

'How are you settling in?' she asked. He nodded and continued walking towards the door.

'Anything I can get you?' He shook his head. He was at the door now. He was very nearly outside.

'Okay then. I'll see you later.'

He hoped not.

Once outside, he took a deep breath of spring air. He didn't mean to be rude, he really didn't, but it was easier sometimes. Politeness often encouraged intimacy and that was the last thing he wanted. Swapping pleasantries led to personal intrusions so it was best not to begin.

He wasn't really sure where he was heading. If he'd been earnest about a walk, he should have gone straight out into the lane and across the fields, but he found himself walking around the garden and soon realised that he was at the oast house. There was something about the round building that had captured his imagination, he realised, remembering his conversation with young Jasmine on his last visit. Was she in there now? he wondered. He didn't want to disturb her and, to be fair, he shouldn't even have been walking by the oast house as it was very much a part of Orley that belonged to the Jacobs family. But, as he walked past, the door opened and an old cat streaked out.

'Stay out of here, Skinny, or you'll get paint on your nose like last time!' Jasmine called after the frightened feline. She looked up and caught his eye.

'Hello,' he said.

'Oh, it's you!' She pushed a large blonde curl out of her eyes and adjusted her hairband, which was a swirl of wild colours. 'You coming in?'

'Well, I—'

She disappeared inside and Marcus tentatively followed, watching as Jasmine returned to a large canvas she was obviously working on.

He cleared his throat. 'How are you?'

'I had a cold last week and my nose swelled up and turned red, but I'm fine now.'

He smiled. Her honesty was so refreshing. 'Can I see what you're working on?'

'Sure,' she said with a shrug and he took a step towards her, looking at the brilliantly bright colours on the canvas but unable to make out exactly what it was. 'It's called *Spring*. Not very original, but I'm not feeling very original today. Today is an ordinary day and I never paint well when I feel ordinary.'

He took in the warm pinks and yellows that seemed to dance before his eyes. 'I like it.'

'It's a mess, but I'll get something from it. I usually do.' She put her hands on her hips and frowned, and Marcus suddenly felt uncomfortable being there.

'I – er – I know this is your family's part of the property. I shouldn't really have trespassed.'

'I'm glad you did.'

'You are?'

'Yes. You can help me move this bench,' she said. 'I can't shift it on my own and it's driving me nuts.' She nodded towards a long bench on the far side of the room. Like everything else in the building, it was covered in paint.

'Where do you want it?' Marcus asked as he grabbed one end and Jasmine grabbed the other.

'To the right of the door.'

They moved it together, being careful not to scrape it along the beautiful wooden floorboards, which were also covered in paint splats.

'That's better,' Jasmine said. 'I can use that space over there for my new easel. The light's better.'

Marcus nodded, but he didn't really understand these things. He'd always envied artists and their ability to see the miracle of something as simple as light and to create something from absolutely nothing – to fill a blank canvas with colour and expression.

Looking around the oast house now, he took in marvellous sketches and paintings, abstracts and landscapes, portraits and still lifes.

'You're frowning again,' Jasmine said.

'Am I?'

She nodded. 'You frown a lot, don't you?'

'Well, I don't know.'

'You do. I'm telling you that you do. Your forehead goes all wrinkly and you look serious and sad. Why are you sad?'

'I'm not.'

'You know what I do when I'm sad?'

'No.'

'I paint. Well, I paint when I'm happy too. And mad. But it's particularly good to paint when I'm sad. That's what you should do.'

'What do you mean?'

'Paint it out.'

'I don't under—'

'Paint out all your feelings. Let them go. Put them down on paper or canvas.'

'But what would I paint?'

'Doesn't matter.'

Marcus felt completely baffled by this young woman. 'I can't.'

'Sure you can,' she told him, and she looked around the room before grabbing a brush. 'This one will do. I've got a nice bit of hardboard here. It's been primed and it's ready to go. Paint on it. Go on!'

'I don't know how.'

'Don't think. Just do it!'

Marcus gave a funny kind of laugh. It was the first time in a long while that anything approaching a laugh had sounded from him and, before he could talk himself out of the situation, he took the proffered paintbrush.

Vanessa had tried not to take Marcus's abruptness personally as he'd left the house, but she couldn't stop it from bothering her. He was obviously a man who was carrying around a great deal of hurt and she so desperately wanted to reach out to him. Her late husband had often told her that this was a great fault in her because she always wanted to help those in need and one simply couldn't. It was an impossible task to want to make the whole world smile. Still, Vanessa couldn't help wanting to try.

But it wasn't going to happen this morning, she thought as she put her coat on and left the house, walking to the little shed where she kept her bicycle. The misty, silvery mornings of winter were slowly being replaced by the gently golden ones of spring and it felt really good to be outside.

The road from Orley to the village of Elhurst was a narrow and winding one full of potholes, but Vanessa loved it. Flanked by gently undulating fields, it was a joy to ride down even on a rather ancient bicycle with the wicker basket shaking. Oliver had hated his wife riding the old thing.

'Take the car!' he used to shout, terrified for his wife's safety with the speed of the traffic. But there really wasn't ever much traffic on this road other than the dog walkers or horse riders, and Vanessa couldn't imagine life without her bicycle. It was a little freedom which she loved.

Arriving in the village, she dismounted and leaned her bike up against the wall of the shop. She was just about to enter when a tall man opened the door and came out. She didn't recognise him. He looked to be in his mid to late forties and was wearing a checked shirt unbuttoned at the neck, a dark gilet and a pair of steel-capped boots. His hair was the colour of a redwood tree and his face had a healthy bronze glow about it that told of a life spent in the great outdoors.

Vanessa stood to one side to let him pass and it was then that Barbara, the owner of the shop, appeared in the window, sticking up an A4 poster with some Blu-tack. The man gave her the thumbs up and looked at Vanessa.

'Hello,' he said. 'Need a gardener?'

She laughed at his opening line. 'I need one, but I can't afford one.'

'Jonathan,' he said, holding out a big strong hand. 'Jonathan Dacre.'

'Vanessa.'

He nodded. 'You live up at Orley Court.'

'Yes,' she said. 'Have we met?'

'Not officially, but I've visited your gardens a few times on open days. They're wonderful.'

'They're overgrown,' she said. 'We used to have a full-time gardener but we – we don't anymore.'

'I see.'

'It's a lot of work. We get by with a part-timer who mows the lawn and trims the yew hedges, but it isn't the same. I feel so guilty that the place just doesn't look its best these days. I'm sorry I can't offer you work. Good luck, though.'

'Thanks,' he said.

Vanessa opened the shop door and was just about to enter when the man spoke again.

'Listen,' he said, 'maybe we could be of some use to each other.'

'Oh?'

'I've got a group I work with twice a week. Our current project's just coming to an end and we need something new to tackle.'

'They're horticultural students?'

'Er, not exactly.'

Vanessa frowned.

'They're' – he stopped as if gauging her likely response – 'young offenders.'

'Oh, right,' Vanessa said.

'I need to find a project for them. There are a lot of gardens around here, but most of them are too small or the owners – well – they wouldn't exactly welcome us. They're hard-working youngsters who just need a bit of guidance and some inspiration.' He paused and Vanessa realised that he was waiting for her response.

'Right,' she said again.

'I'm sorry,' Jonathan said, 'it's a lot to ask.'

'No, no – I admire what you're doing, I really do. If everybody ignored these problems and didn't help then where would the world be?'

'Exactly,' he said.

'It's just that – well – Orley is a delicate place.' She grimaced. 'Delicate's not the right word. It's—'

'A house stuffed full of valuables?' Jonathan said.

'Yes!' Vanessa gave an embarrassed laugh.

'I totally understand your reservations, but I would hold myself personally responsible for my team. I work with an ex-policeman and we monitor the group at all times, and I'm insured for any damage done. Not that there's ever any damage,' he quickly added. 'And, of course, we'd be based in the garden, so nowhere near the house.'

'Gosh,' Vanessa said, 'this is all so unexpected. I only came out for a book of stamps.'

He grinned. 'It's a lot to spring on you. Why don't you have a think about it? I've got a card.' He reached into the pocket of his gilet and brought out a small business card with a muddy fingerprint across the back. 'Sorry. Occupational hazard.'

'Thank you,' she said, taking it from him.

He nodded. 'I'll – er – leave you to your stamps. It was nice meeting you.'

'You too,' Vanessa said, watching as he walked towards a beaten-up old van.

'Mr Dacre!' She wasn't sure what caused her to shout the way she did, but she had the strangest sensation that she shouldn't let this man walk out of her life – that there was something about this meeting that was meant to be.

'Why don't you come out to Orley?' she said, shutting the shop door and crossing the pavement towards him.

'Really?'

'Have a look around. See what you think?'

'Okay,' he said. 'If you're sure.'

'I am. I'll give you a call.'

'Great.' He gave her a wonderfully warm smile.

She watched him drive away and then wheeled her bicycle onto the road and began the ride back home.

It wasn't until she caught the first golden glimpse of Orley that she realised she'd forgotten to buy her stamps.

Chapter 7

Laurence was so cross with himself. He'd upset Tilda, hadn't he? He hadn't meant to; he'd only meant to encourage her because it was strikingly obvious to him that she was an incredibly talented young woman. But he'd obviously hit a nerve and brought back nothing but bad memories for her. Whatever had happened must have been pretty traumatising for her to write off all thoughts of giving the business another go, and how he wished there was something he could do about it.

After making a quick call to a new client, Laurence left his rooms and went to see how his father was getting on, but there was no reply when he knocked on the door.

'Dad?' he called as he went into the living room. The chair was empty and his father's book was lying on the windowsill. He called again and checked the bedroom, but Marcus wasn't there. For a moment, Laurence looked at the sparsely furnished room and wished that his dad had come antique shopping with him. There was just a bed and a wardrobe and a little nightstand, which Laurence walked towards now. Sitting on top of it was a guidebook to South America and a small round photo frame. Laurence swallowed hard as he took in the smiling face of his mother, Tara. It was a pre-Laurence photograph and he had no idea where or exactly when it had been taken, but he knew that it had travelled all around the world with his father like some kind of talisman, crossing seas and oceans with him.

After his father had taken up a position with the Ministry of Defence in Whitehall, he'd worked long hours away from home, but it was a definite improvement on his deployments while part of the Royal Navy and he'd been home for weekends. Laurence remembered with affection the time his parents had spent in the garden together. Tara had always been begging Marcus to take early retirement, but he'd loved his job too much. Was that something he regretted now, Laurence wondered, that he hadn't spent more time with his wife?

He'd retired shortly before her death, but it had been too late then. It was a bleak and desperate year after she died. Marcus had been paralysed with grief and Laurence took some time off work to be with him, moving into the house in Kent and helping to sort things out. His father hadn't said a word – not about anything important anyway – and Laurence had the feeling that he was holding something back. But what?

'What happened, Mum?' he asked the photograph, wishing that, somehow, she could tell him. At that moment, he sincerely believed he had as much chance hearing it from his mother as he did from his father.

Laurence retraced his steps, grabbed his coat and headed outside. The sun had come out and it was possible that his father had taken a walk. Or maybe he was pottering around the garden somewhere. He did hope so. One of the reasons Laurence had wanted his dad to move to Orley with him was because of the beautiful gardens. He hoped that Marcus would show an interest in them and that they would work alongside each other like they'd used to do.

It was as Laurence was walking through the north garden that he heard a car coming up the driveway and he soon saw that it was Tilda.

'Hello,' he said as she got out of the car.

Tilda turned around; her long hair was loose and blowing back from her face in the light breeze and the sight almost took his breath away. She really was a beautiful young woman.

'Did you want something?'

A beautiful young woman who was always on the defensive, he thought.

'I've been looking for my dad. I don't suppose you've seen him, have you?'

'No. I've been out.'

'Of course,' Laurence said. 'I guess it's going to be harder keeping tabs on him here than in our old flat.'

'Do you need to keep tabs on him?'

Laurence was surprised by the question. 'Well, I don't suppose . . .' He looked around as if trying to spot him. 'I guess I like to know where he is.'

'I'll let you know if I see him.'

'Thanks.' He watched as she retrieved her bag from the car. 'Listen, I wanted to apologise for before.'

'Oh?'

'You were nothing but kind to me – coming shopping and helping me choose pieces for my rooms. It was really nice of you.'

'That's okay.'

'But then I went and upset you.'

'You didn't upset me.'

'No?'

'I . . .' she paused. 'I overreacted.'

'It's been eating me up,' he said.

'Don't let it worry you,' she told him. 'It's just that I don't like talking about that part of my past now. Ancient history.'

'Right,' Laurence said. But it obviously wasn't ancient history because he could see the pain etched across her face and the echo of it in her eyes at the mere mention of the subject. Her ancient history was still very much a part of her present, wasn't it?

'I was thinking about doing some gardening,' he blurted.

'Really?' She gave him a look as if to say, *why are you telling me this?*

'But our north garden isn't great for growing things, is it?'

'What do you want to grow?'

He shrugged. 'Thought I might try my hand at cabbages.'

'Cabbages?'

'Amongst other things,' he said, remembering how proud his father used to be at growing produce for the dining table. 'I envy you that walled garden. I don't suppose you'd want to sell me that, would you?'

Tilda looked at him aghast. 'No!' she cried.

'Or a portion of it, perhaps? What about half? I could probably run to ten thousand pounds.'

Tilda's eyes were nearly out on stalks. 'Ten thousand—' she stopped. 'No,' she said, shaking her head. 'It's not for sale. You can't just wave your London money around and expect us to want to sell.'

'Okay,' he said, holding his hands up, acknowledging defeat. 'But let me know if you change your mind.'

'I think we've sold you every last bit of Orley that you're going to get,' she said, locking her car and making her way to the front of the house. Laurence fell into step beside her.

'Just as well, really. I haven't got my business running properly yet. I'd better stop furniture shopping and wondering whether to grow cabbages and start thinking about getting some clients. Know anyone who needs a financial consultant?'

Tilda gave a little smile. 'You could advertise in the shop window in Elhurst.'

'Oh, really?'

'I'm totally serious. Everyone knows that all the best businesses advertise there. It's how I started my piano teaching.'

Laurence smiled back. 'I'll get a postcard written at once.'

'See you later,' she said as they walked into the house and she disappeared into the living room in the south wing.

Once again, Laurence wondered if he'd been too pushy with Tilda, but he hadn't been able to help himself. The idea for the walled garden had just occurred to him. It would be such a fabulous project for him and his father to tackle together. But perhaps they could make something of their more modest and challenging north garden.

What Tilda had said had made him reel inside too. He did just think that he could wave his London money around and get what he wanted. He'd been wrong to do that and he'd been wrong to think that money could automatically buy him and his father a little bit of their past back. It couldn't, could it? And buying the north wing wasn't necessarily going to make his father suddenly open up to him, was it?

When Laurence got back to the north wing, he noticed his father's boots in the hall.

'Dad?' he called, walking into his father's living room. 'Where've you been?'

'Out.'

'Out where?'

'Just around the garden.'

'Really? I was out there myself just now and didn't see you.'

'Did you want something?'

'Yes. I'd – I'd really like to talk to you sometime.'

Marcus frowned. 'What about?'

Laurence took a deep breath, dreading saying the words and yet knowing that he had to. 'You know what about.'

'There's nothing to talk about.'

'Dad, there's everything to talk about. You've never told me what happened that night. Not fully. Where was Mum going? Why was she on that road at that time? All I've got is the police report and it's not good enough. I've waited for you to tell me, given you space and time. I've been patient until I can't take it anymore. I need to know, Dad! You owe me.'

His father glared at him. 'I owe you nothing!' he said. 'What happened that night had nothing to do with you. You know all you need to know. Now, just leave it at that.'

There was a thread of menace in his father's tone and Laurence felt himself die a little inside. Why wouldn't his father open up and talk to him? What the hell had happened that night?

'There's something I should tell you,' Tilda said. She was in the living room in the south wing with her mother, who was sewing up a cushion that Reynolds had done his best to destroy in one of those mad terrier moments Vanessa couldn't abide and which she felt sure Dolly actually encouraged in the little dog.

'What is it?' her mother asked.

'It's something Laurence said. I thought he was joking at first, but I think he's quite serious.'

'He's not unhappy here, is he?'

'No, of course not! He's only just got here!'

'Oh, thank goodness,' Vanessa said. 'I thought you were going to say that he hates the north wing and wants to sell it.'

'He doesn't want to sell. He wants to buy.'

'What does he want to buy?'

Tilda looked at her mother as if gauging if she could take the shock. 'The walled garden.'

Vanessa's face drained of all colour. 'Well, he can't have it.'

'Or a part of it. He offered us ten thousand pounds.'

'Who offered us ten thousand pounds?' Grandma Dolly asked as she walked into the room.

'Laurence,' Tilda said. 'He wants to buy the walled garden.'

'Ten thousand pounds?' Vanessa cried as if just registering the amount properly.

'Apparently, he wants to grow cabbages.'

'That's some very expensive cabbages,' Grandma Dolly said. 'Can't he just go to the supermarket like everyone else?'

'I know it sounds like a lot of money,' Tilda admitted, 'but it isn't really.'

'Isn't it?' Vanessa said.

'It's our walled garden, Mum. Our beautiful, private garden where we wander around at dawn in our nightgowns.'

'Oh, yes. I like to sunbathe topless there too.'

'Oh, Mum!'

'What? It's the best place for it. Those walls really hold the heat and it's a lovely private spot.'

'Well, it wouldn't be if Mr Laurence Sturridge bought half of it,' Tilda said. 'I don't want you sunbathing topless there when the Sturridge men turn up with their forks and spades. Honestly, he's got some nerve. Just because he's got big pockets and is handsome, he thinks he can get away with anything!'

'You think he's handsome?' Vanessa asked, jumping on her daughter's words.

'No!' she said quickly. 'Well, a little bit. But we're still not accepting his offer.'

There was a moment's pause and then Vanessa cleared her throat and spoke.

'Anyway, we can't sell it.'

'I wasn't going to suggest that we did,' Tilda said.

'Good. Because I have plans for the walled garden.'

'What plans?' Dolly and Tilda asked in unison.

'Plans that don't concern either of you at this stage.'

'Anything that happens at Orley concerns me,' Dolly said. 'And, after the north wing fiasco, I want to be told everything in advance of any decisions being made.'

'Yes, well we don't always get what we want in life, do we?' Vanessa said and, with that, she left the room.

Marcus really hated himself sometimes. He hated the way he was around his son. This was the one person on the planet he should be closest to, especially after the loss of Tara, and yet he felt such a chasm between them – one that he feared he could never cross and that it was all his fault. He could see that Laurence was doing his very best in moving them to Sussex, but that didn't mean Marcus was just going to suddenly divulge everything to him. At least in London, Laurence had spent each weekday away from the flat with his work. Here, however, he had yet to get himself up and running. He'd got a few clients on his list and would no doubt be commuting to London on occasion, but more often than not he would be working from home, which meant he would no doubt be poking his nose into Marcus's business.

Suddenly noticing that he had paint on his wrist, he walked through to his en-suite to wash it off. His morning with Jassy had been so much fun – he couldn't remember the last time he'd experienced anything like it. She'd been wonderfully bossy, barking orders at him like an admiral – and he'd loved it. He wasn't quite sure if what he'd produced could be classed as art, but he'd enjoyed himself nevertheless. When was the last time he'd done anything remotely creative? It had been a truly freeing experience and certainly one he'd like to repeat if Jassy was accommodating.

He smiled as he thought about her. There'd been a time in his life when he'd longed to have a daughter. Tara had wanted a girl too, to make their family complete, but a series of miscarriages had left her raw and unwilling to try again. Watching Jassy had made Marcus think about what it might have been like to have a daughter. A sister for Laurie. Marcus would have liked that.

Yes, he'd felt really good after his painting session with Jassy. Then Laurence had showed up and dispelled the mood. He had a knack for doing that even when he wasn't so direct as he had been today. Sometimes, his son only had to walk into the room for Marcus to experience that awful feeling of dread and guilt because he knew he couldn't give him what he wanted.

So why hadn't he used Laurence's move to go their separate ways? He must surely feel that there was something to salvage in their relationship – that they could reach out to each other. The trouble was, Marcus didn't know how to begin.

Chapter 8

Vanessa was hovering by the window. She'd made the phone call the night before and was surprised at how fast her invitation had been accepted. Now, she began to feel anxious. Was she doing the right thing? What if this was a huge mistake?

'I wish you'd sit down. You're giving me indigestion,' Dolly said with a weary sigh from the breakfast table. 'Are you expecting somebody?' The old woman got up and moved towards the window with alarming speed, just as a van was pulling up in the lane. 'Who's that? He's not going to park that disgusting old van there, is he?'

Vanessa had to bite her lip to stop herself from laughing at the sight of Jonathan Dacre's mud-splattered vehicle.

'That's for me,' she said.

'I might have known it would be something to do with you.'

Vanessa chose not to rise to her mother-in-law's comment, but left the room with alacrity. As she made her way to the front door to greet Jonathan, she realised that she was feeling excited at seeing him again. He'd made quite an impression on her the day they'd met at the shop and she was eager to find out more about his gardening project.

She'd just reached the hallway when he rang the bell.

'How are you?' he asked her as she opened the door.

'I'm very well.'

'Good.' He smiled at her and she noticed the way his hazel eyes seemed to dance with merriment. She liked that.

'Can I get you a tea or coffee?' she asked.

'No thank you. Just had a tea.'

'That's good because Dolly's hanging around and would no doubt scare you off if you came in.'

Jonathan's eyebrows rose a fraction. 'Your mother-in-law, right?'

'Right. And she's not to be crossed,' Vanessa said.

'To the garden then?'

'Definitely.'

Vanessa led the way around the side of the house, passing the oast house where Jasmine had already been for hours. The door was closed but the sound of loud rock music could be heard, which meant she was probably working on a very large and energetic abstract.

'So, this is the walled garden,' she said a moment later.

Jonathan nodded. 'I remember it from my last visit. It's such a great space.' He stood with his hands in his trouser pockets. He was wearing his steel-capped boots, but he didn't have a jacket on. Was he one of those people who didn't feel the cold? Or perhaps his job meant he was on the go all the time and so kept naturally warm.

'I'm afraid we haven't kept it in the best order,' Vanessa explained unnecessarily. 'We do what we can, but there are only so many hours in the day and growing vegetables comes a long way down on our list of priorities.'

'But it should be right at the top,' Jonathan said. 'I feel very strongly about that. The food we eat is the most important thing in our lives, isn't it? It's something that we do every day – we can't live without it – and we have an obligation to ourselves to know where it comes from. That's what I think anyway, and you've got the perfect place here to grow good organic food.'

'I've never thought of it like that,' Vanessa admitted.

'Not enough people do, I'm afraid. That's why I like working with young people, and encouraging them to really think about where food comes from and teaching them how to get involved with growing it.'

Vanessa nodded. 'That sounds really rewarding.'

'It is. It can be frustrating too. Some of the young ones just don't want to get their hands dirty, and the thought of pulling something out of the ground and eating it is totally alien to them.'

'I have friends from London like that. I'll try to give them fresh home-grown produce and they look at me as if I'm quite mad. I don't think they've ever seen a vegetable that doesn't come washed, trimmed and pre-packed in a tray from a posh supermarket.'

Jonathan laughed. 'Society's grown so far away from the basics of life.' He shook his head sadly.

'So, tell me more about your – what do you call them?' Vanessa asked as they walked down the gravel path between the overgrown raised beds.

'Team,' he said. 'We're a team. They're mostly kids with alcohol or drug-abuse problems and – well – the crimes that go with addiction. Usually petty thefts, things like that. Nothing big time, you understand, although a few of them have been in and out of prison.'

'Right,' Vanessa said, acknowledging the fact that this was a world so far removed from her own that she couldn't even begin to understand it.

'Introducing them to gardening and the concept of making something from scratch, of getting your hands into the earth and growing something you can then eat – it's really liberating. Most of these kids have never even been in a garden before.'

'Really?'

'Truly.'

'I can't imagine,' Vanessa said. 'To grow up without a garden.' For a moment, she thought back to her own childhood which, although it'd been in London, had always encompassed a garden even if it was the tiniest of spaces. It would be unthinkable to live without a garden now, not after so many years at Orley.

'I always have to stop and remind myself that everything I take for granted is new to them,' Jonathan said.

'And what are they like?'

'The team? They're great kids. They've simply lost their way because they've never been given any guidance before, or maybe they've taken a couple of wrong turns and made some bad decisions. They're damaged, but they can be repaired – they just need time, love and a little bit of guidance, and a garden can give all that. There's something incredibly good and honest about gardening and manual labour. Being outside in all weathers and watching things grow – things that you've planted and nurtured. That gives people an enormous sense of self-worth. I've seen it over and over again. Even if you only grow a bit of salad in a window box, you know that those leaves on your plate at lunch wouldn't exist without you.'

Vanessa smiled. She liked listening to him. He was so passionate about what he did and about sharing that love with others and making their lives all the richer.

'And how many of you will there be?' she asked.

'There'll be four to seven of the kids at any one time, and Rod too. He's the ex-policeman and keeps a beady eye on everyone. I've known him for years. He doesn't say a lot, but he's a really decent guy and he knows how to keep the kids in line.'

Vanessa felt a little easier having heard this. 'I look forward to meeting everyone,' she said.

'So, you're really on board with this?'

'You sound surprised!'

'I am. I get a lot of rejections,' he explained. 'People see me coming now and draw their curtains or pretend they're out. So many people turn their backs and close their minds. They think these problems are city problems, but these kids are from our own neighbourhood and we have to take responsibility for them.'

Vanessa bit her lip. This was a serious business, she realised. She hoped she hadn't taken on something that she couldn't handle – that

Orley couldn't handle. But Jonathan would be there and she felt quite certain that, with him leading the way, nothing could go wrong.

They continued walking around the garden together.

'So, you've got a little orchard too,' he said, nodding towards the fruit trees.

'Yes, some lovely old varieties of apples, pears and plums.'

'They need a good pruning.'

'No doubt.'

'Is that something you'd trust my group with?'

'Absolutely,' she said. 'You'd be doing us a favour.'

'And general maintenance too – like repairing fences and some of these raised beds? We have a little money put aside for materials and we have bits and bobs donated by folk.'

'Whatever you think needs doing. I'll be guided by you,' she told him. 'It'll be a relief to have a bit of help around here. As I said, my daughters and I have done our best over the years, but there are never enough hours in the day.'

'You still work?'

'Part-time. I'm an interior designer. I don't do as much as I used to. I cut my hours back when my husband fell ill. I became his carer.'

'I was sorry to hear he died,' Jonathan said. 'He was a good man.'

'The best,' she said, looking away for a moment as her eyes misted with tears. It could still get to her – a mention of Oliver from a stranger. 'Then there's the house to take care of,' she continued. 'That's a full-time job in itself.'

'I bet it is,' he said, glancing back at Orley Court before bending down and picking up a handful of earth, letting it crumble through his fingers. 'Good stuff.' He brushed his hands down the front of his trousers as he stood back up.

'We have several compost heaps and bays around the grounds. You're welcome to use those. And we've got a tool shed, although I should warn you that a lot of the tools are old. Some should be in a museum really.'

'That's okay,' he said. 'I've got tools. I've accumulated a grand collection over the years and it's all I seem to get bought for Christmas and birthdays.'

Vanessa smiled. 'So, when do you want to start?'

'As soon as possible. Spring's upon us and we need to do a lot of preparation work before we can start planting. Can I give you a call once I've spoken to Rod and organised the team?'

'Of course,' she said. 'You've got my number?'

He nodded. 'I can't tell you how grateful I am for this opportunity.'

'You don't have to thank me.'

'I absolutely do,' he insisted. 'You've no idea what this means to me and the group. It's a huge weight off my mind having somewhere to work like this and it will be so great to finally get all the plants into the ground. I've been growing seeds in my own greenhouse and cold frames and I'm rapidly running out of space.'

'It will be wonderful to see this garden being put to good use again. I've felt so bad about it being neglected over the last few years.'

They walked over to the small orchard at the far side of the walled garden and Vanessa watched as Jonathan reached out and touched the bark of one of the old, gnarled apple trees.

'That's an Egremont Russet,' Vanessa said.

'One of my favourites.'

'Mine too! Oliver used to refuse to eat them though – said they were far too sharp.'

'I like that about them. Better than the insipid watery varieties you get in the supermarkets.'

'Exactly.' She smiled.

'Well, I've probably taken up enough of your time for one day,' he said, and she suddenly realised that she didn't want him to go. She liked being out in the garden, talking about apples and compost.

'You'll let me know when you want to start?'

'I will.'

They walked back through the garden, passing the oast house once again to the blast of rock music, and she accompanied him down the path in front of the house and out of the gate into the lane. It had been a cloudy morning but the sunshine now peeped out and shone on Jonathan's hair, turning it a wonderful auburn.

'Okay then,' she said, suddenly feeling awkward.

'I'll call you.'

She watched as he got into the van, turning the key in the ignition once, twice before it fired. He shook his head in despair and wound down the window.

'Seen better days,' he confessed.

'Like me!' Vanessa winced. Why on *earth* had she said that?

He smiled at her and raised a hand in farewell, and she watched as he drove round the corner and back towards Elhurst. Vanessa turned and immediately saw Dolly standing by the morning room window. She'd probably been stood there the whole time, raining curses down upon Jonathan's old van.

You're going to have to tell her, a little voice said as she walked back to the house. As much as Vanessa would have liked to hide away in a private corner of Orley she knew Dolly would find difficult to get to with her slow gait and arthritic knee, she thought it would be just as well to get things over and done with. She returned to the morning room and hadn't even got through the door before Dolly pounced on her.

'So, are you going to tell me who he is or am I going to be the last to know about that too?'

'His name is Jonathan Dacre and he's a gardener. He's going to be working in the walled garden.'

'We can't afford—'

'We're not paying him.'

Dolly glowered at her. 'I don't understand.'

'He's working with a group of young people. They need somewhere to – to train,' she said, giving just as much information as she thought would satisfy the old woman.

'You mean these young people don't know what they're doing? That they'll be wielding tools around the property that they don't know how to use and doing all sorts of damage?'

'Jonathan will be supervising them. Rod too.'

Dolly frowned. 'Who's Rod?'

'I haven't met him yet. He's an ex-policeman.' Vanessa bit her lip. She'd said too much.

'An ex-policeman?'

'I've got a call to make,' Vanessa said, making to leave the room.

'You're not telling me everything, are you?'

That's right, Vanessa thought to herself. *That's absolutely right.*

Laurence had taken Tilda's advice and placed a postcard in the window of the village shop, and he had been pleasantly surprised by the response. So far, he'd received half a dozen phone calls and had met with three of the callers, who had already signed up to become new clients of his. He felt rather pleased with that result. He might not be on the best of terms with his father at the moment, but it seemed his new business was moving in the right direction.

He was also in the process of setting up his office – the space where he would work from home and meet with the occasional client. It was funny being his own boss after so many years of working for a large company. He would have to be very disciplined, he realised, setting up his own workdays and not being tempted to slack off when the sun was shining and the garden looked glorious. It would be all too easy to put down the paperwork and venture out into the countryside, forgetting his obligations and frittering his days away.

The furniture he had bought at the antique centre in Elhurst had arrived and his father had helped him to place it around the rooms. Marcus hadn't said much. He'd nodded a few times when Laurence had asked him if he liked the pieces, but he hadn't hung around when he'd been offered a cup of tea.

Laurence shook his head as he thought about it now. What did his father do all day? he wondered. Did he really read? He had seen Marcus leaving the house a number of times and been tempted to follow him to find out exactly where he was going and what he was doing, but that would be a bit freaky, wouldn't it?

Perhaps his father was bored down here in Sussex. That was Laurence's main concern – that he'd cut him off from civilisation. Mind you, he hadn't ever gone out when he'd been living with Laurence in London, despite being a stone's throw away from some of the world's most fabulous theatres, museums and restaurants.

Maybe Laurence could involve his father in his business, he thought. He'd have to go about it slyly, though. Asking directly wouldn't work. It would be better if he approached the subject obliquely, maybe suggesting that he needed help and wasn't sure where to turn.

Tara Sturridge had been an accountant and Laurence had inherited his mother's fascination with numbers. He remembered watching her for hours as she pored over columns of figures, balancing books for her clients.

'Figures calm my mind,' she'd told him. 'In an ever-moving world, numbers settle me.'

His mother had been the sweetest woman. She'd had a head for business, but a heart that reached out and touched all who knew her. No wonder his father felt the loss of her so keenly.

Returning to Sussex had made Laurence think about Tara more. He could hardly believe it was two years since she'd died. Just two years. It was hard to comprehend that he'd never see her again, never hear that warm voice on the end of the phone, never sit at the kitchen table whilst she buzzed around making tea. When a person died, they took away so many little everyday things that could never be replaced, and Laurence felt intense guilt at not having spent more time with her. During his years in London, he'd been so wrapped up in his work that he'd turned down many an invitation to visit his parents in Kent.

'Not this weekend, Mum, sorry,' he'd say lamely.

What he'd give now to have one of those weekends. He'd have been in his car and on the motorway within ten minutes. But time only moved forward and his mother was gone. The only thing he could do to make himself feel better would be to forge a real connection to his father. The fact that Marcus had moved to Sussex with him was a really good indication that he too wanted to repair their relationship.

Unless he just had nowhere else to go. Laurence couldn't help but wonder this, considering that his father had yet to make an attempt to hold any sort of conversation with him.

'Give it time,' Laurence told himself.

He was just looking around his study when he realised that he'd left an important file in his car. Leaving the north wing, he walked into the entrance hall just as Tilda was coming through the front door with another young woman.

'Hello,' he said with a smile.

'Hello,' she said back. 'Laurence, this is my sister, Jasmine. I don't think you've met yet, have you? Jassy, this is Laurence.'

Laurence looked at the girl who was a little taller than Tilda and who had gloriously curly hair. Other than that, she was strikingly similar to her sister, with her pale heart-shaped face and bright-blue eyes.

'Pleased to meet you,' Laurence said, stepping forward to shake Jasmine's hand. She looked startled by his action and glanced at Tilda as if for direction.

'This is Marcus's son,' Tilda explained.

'I know who he is,' Jasmine said, and she walked across the hallway and disappeared into a room, closing the door behind her.

Laurence frowned. 'Was it something I said? Or didn't say?'

'No,' Tilda said. 'She's – she's just like that. Please don't think anything of it. She gets a little anxious around strangers, that's all.'

'I hear that she's befriended my father.'

'Yes,' Tilda said. 'She mentioned him to us. Jassy doesn't make friends easily. Your father must be a pretty special man.'

'Oh, well, yes,' Laurence said, feeling temporarily stunned.

'Listen – I've got to make a call. I'll see you later.' She left him, going into the same room that Jasmine had disappeared into.

Laurence left the house and walked towards his car. He was pleased that his father had found somebody to talk to, but he couldn't help feeling a little jealous of Jasmine's ability to reach his father when he was unable to do so himself.

Chapter 9

It was with a mixture of anticipation and trepidation that Vanessa woke up on the morning when Jonathan and his team were due to arrive. What exactly did one wear to greet such a bunch? she wondered. She wasn't actually going to be working alongside them and so didn't need to wear gardening clothes, but she didn't want to come across all lady of the manor either.

She opened her wardrobe. There to the right were the suits and shirts that had belonged to Oliver. Tilda had helped her sort out a few things to take to a local charity shop about a year after he had died. Vanessa hadn't been able to think about giving anything away until then and had hung on to a few of his favourite things, like the simple checked shirt in the softest of cottons which had been a favourite of his and the suit with the threadbare elbows. Parting with those would be like parting with Oliver all over again and she stroked the sleeve of the checked shirt now, remembering how handsome he'd looked in it. A real country gentleman.

She closed the wardrobe door. She wasn't going to find anything in there and so opened a drawer and took out a pair of jeans and a jumper. That would do. Neat but not too posh.

By the time she got washed and dressed and had breakfast, it was ten o'clock. Vanessa had been surprised that Jonathan hadn't wanted to start earlier in the day, but he told her that his young team weren't early risers and that he'd failed miserably to enforce earlier starts on them in the past. So, they started at ten and finished at six, with a half-hour lunch break and two tea breaks.

She was looking out of the east window in the morning room when Jonathan's van pulled up in the lane beside the yew hedge, followed by a minibus. Vanessa watched as Jonathan got out and was soon joined by another man. She assumed this was Rod, the ex-policeman – he looked shorter than she'd expected but had a wiry strength about him. They were quickly joined by four young people and Vanessa gasped at her first sight of them. They were a scruffy-looking bunch, there was no way around it and, if Dolly saw them, she'd have something to say for sure.

Grabbing her waxed jacket and quickly making her way downstairs, Vanessa opened the front door and was there to greet them as they walked up the path towards her. Jonathan was a little way ahead of them and gave her a nod.

'Good morning,' she said, glad she'd popped her coat on as there was a keen breeze that counteracted the effects of the spring sunshine.

'You look worried,' he told her.

'I'm not worried.'

'No? Because you look worried,' he said with a grin. 'Come on, I'll introduce you. They don't bite. Well, Rod does if he hasn't had his morning coffee.'

'Let's go round to the garden first, shall we?' Vanessa said, aware that Dolly could appear at a window or a door at any moment.

'Sure.'

Vanessa led the way, only slightly alarmed by the rough-looking group following in her wake with an assortment of dangerous tools.

Once in the walled garden, she turned to face Jonathan.

'Okay, let me introduce you,' he said. 'First of all, this is Rod. Rod, this is Mrs Jacobs.'

Rod held out a hand towards her. He looked to be in his mid-fifties, and his eyes were tiny slits in his face as if he were permanently squinting, but there was something about him that Vanessa liked immediately.

'Pleased to meet you,' he said.

'Call me Vanessa.'

He nodded. 'Nice place you have here. Very nice.'

'Thank you.'

He nodded again, and took a step back as if to signal he was done talking and was ready to work.

'Everyone – listen up!' Jonathan said to the others, who were having a little conversation of their own by this stage. 'This is our host, Vanessa Jacobs. She's kindly said we can use her walled garden and I think you'll agree that it's the nicest site we've ever been given permission to work in.'

The group of four eyed her warily but didn't say anything.

'This is Nat,' Jonathan said, indicating a young lad of no more than twenty to his right. He was tall and skinny and wearing ripped jeans and an old T-shirt under a leather jacket.

Vanessa nodded him a hello.

'And Austin,' Jonathan continued, nodding towards a lad who looked a little older than Nat. 'Everyone calls him Oz.'

'Hello, Oz,' Vanessa said.

He grunted a response at her and looked down at his trainers, which were absolutely filthy even before he'd begun work.

'And this is Michael. He's known as Fingers. I'm not sure why.'

There was some surreptitious laughter from the group.

'We probably don't want to know why,' Jonathan added. 'And this is Jenna. Our one and only girl.'

Vanessa looked at the young woman. She was thin and pale and had long hair that had obviously been dyed blonde at some stage, but which had long since grown out, leaving great black roots on display. The thing that struck Vanessa was how much Jenna reminded her of Tilda. Perhaps it was the fineness of her hair or her sharp cheekbones, but how very different her background must be, Vanessa thought, swallowing hard and trying to imagine the sort of life that this girl must have had.

'Hello, Jenna,' Vanessa said with a smile.

Jenna didn't smile back; she nodded and then she whispered something to Jonathan.

'She wants to know if there's a toilet,' he said.

'Oh, yes,' Vanessa said. 'If you go towards the oast house, there's a building just after it with a toilet and sink. You're welcome to use that. There's also a worktop and socket too, so you can plug in a kettle.'

Jenna made to leave, but Jonathan stopped her.

'We'll all go together,' he told her and the rest of the group. 'Make sure you all know where it is and that you don't go poking around anywhere else. Don't forget that this is somebody's home.'

Vanessa led the way out of the walled garden.

'Oz, put that fag out,' Jonathan said.

'But we're outside,' Oz said.

'You know the rules – no smoking on site.'

'But it gives me energy.'

'That's rubbish and you know it,' Jonathan said.

The lad muttered something unsavoury under his breath, and Vanessa caught Jonathan's eye and he shook his head as if in despair.

'We try and promote all things healthy whilst they're here with us,' he whispered to Vanessa. 'Good wholesome food, no alcohol or cigarettes – that kind of thing. You should have heard the stink when I first told them that cola was banned too.'

Vanessa smiled. 'I can understand that. I'm partial to a can myself.'

'You're joking? It's disgusting stuff.' He shook his head again.

'I'm going to side with your team on this one!' she teased.

'Is this, like, really your house?' Jenna interrupted.

'It is,' Vanessa said. 'It's my husband's family's home. It's belonged to the Jacobs family for generations.'

'It's huge,' Jenna cried. 'Do you ever get lost in it?'

'I did when I first moved here,' Vanessa said. 'But you quickly learn.'

The girl's eyes widened as if she'd never seen anything like it in her life.

'And what's that building?' Jenna asked, noticing the oast house.

'It's an oast house.'

The girl looked none the wiser.

'You must have seen them around the countryside, Jenna?' Jonathan said.

She shrugged. 'No.'

'They were used for drying hops during the brewing process,' Vanessa said.

'Making beer,' Jonathan elaborated.

'Oh, cool,' Jenna said.

'Not many of them are used for that purpose anymore. Most are private homes and ours is used by my daughter as an artist's studio,' Vanessa said, stopping outside an old brick and tile-hung building. 'Well, this is it.' She opened the door and flipped a switch, showing them the small sink and toilet. Jenna went in and, when she came out, Jonathan spoke to the rest of the team.

'If you lads need the loo, go now, okay? We don't want you sloping off behind a tree like you did at Mrs Pilcher's. It isn't any wonder she didn't invite us back.'

Nat quickly disappeared inside.

'Do you have everything you need?' Vanessa asked once they'd returned to the walled garden.

'I think so, thank you,' Jonathan said.

'So, what are your plans for today?'

'I thought we'd have a good warm-up by removing some of these perennial weeds and digging over the raised beds.'

'Sounds great. Well, I guess I'll leave you to it.'

Jonathan nodded and gave her that smile of his which seemed to reach inside her and banish the blues away. It felt like a long time since a man had smiled at her like that and she had to admit that she rather liked it.

Vanessa returned to the house and made herself a cup of tea and then settled to work in the south wing's smallest room, which functioned as her office. Although 'office' was too grand a word for a space that was really just a glorified dumping ground for rolls of material, stacks of paint pots and an assortment of old pieces of furniture she'd picked up over the years, intent on breathing new life into them. But this was Vanessa's own place in a house which she was constantly being reminded wasn't her own. It was one room in which Dolly would not interrupt her and Vanessa felt safely cocooned, surrounding herself with her beautiful fabrics, mood boards and notebooks.

She'd recently started working with a newly married couple who'd moved into one of the big Georgian houses in Elhurst. It was a stunning property, but it was a tad dated with its swirling patterned carpets and wallpaper from a particularly gaudy period in the 1970s. The couple, Geoffrey and Elouise, wanted a total makeover and had the sort of eye-watering budget that made Vanessa pant with envy. So, it was all fabrics from Zoffany and paint from Farrow and Ball.

But, as much as Vanessa adored the little worlds she was creating for each of their rooms, she just couldn't seem to settle down to anything knowing that Jonathan and his team were in the garden. How were things going out there? she wondered, tapping the end of her pencil against her chin. She was desperate to know and so put her sketches down and returned outside. It was much too nice a day to stay cooped up anyway. It had been a particularly long winter and, now that the days were getting longer and the borders were colouring up with tulips and irises, it would be a crime to stay indoors.

'Well, that's my excuse anyway,' she said to herself as she made her way to the walled garden. She soon saw that the team were at the far end and hadn't noticed her, so she got a chance to study them. Rod and Oz were tackling a large area choked up with nettles. They were both wearing heavy-duty gloves and were really putting their backs into it. Jonathan and the rest of the team were all wielding forks and spades as they cleared an area surrounding one of the raised beds. It was weed city there and, once again, Vanessa felt a surge of guilt that things had become so very overgrown.

'Can I help with anything?' she asked as she approached them. Jonathan turned around.

'I didn't expect to see you again.'

She shrugged, suddenly feeling awkward at being there. Perhaps they didn't want her interfering.

'I thought you could use another pair of hands.'

Jonathan leaned on his fork. 'We can always use another pair of hands. You really want to help?'

'I have done this before, you know.'

'I believe you,' he said.

Jenna had turned around and was watching the pair of them.

'Hey, get back to work, you,' Jonathan told her. She grinned at him, but did as she was told.

'So, where do I start?'

Jonathan eyed her warily as she took off her jacket. 'Is that cashmere?' he asked, nodding to her jumper.

'Oh, it's very old,' she told him. 'I was going to wear a sweatshirt I had, but Mrs Carstairs came round collecting for the homeless last week and I gave it to her.'

Jonathan shook his head. 'Come with me.'

'Where are we going?'

She followed him out of the walled garden and around the side of the house. Arriving at his van, he opened the back door and pulled out a large red-and-black checked shirt.

'Here, try this on.'

She took it from him and put it on over her cashmere jumper. It was fleece-lined and wonderfully cosy.

'Fit okay?'

'It's a bit big.'

'You can roll the sleeves up.'

'I really don't need to wear it. I'm perfectly fine in my own jumper.'

'It's much too good a one to risk damaging. Come on.'

He led the way back to the walled garden and she followed. He then handed her his fork and nodded down at the earth.

'I think you can see what needs doing.'

'Oh yes,' she said. 'Everything.'

'Basically.'

So she got digging. At first, she had to admit to it all feeling rather alien. She was far more used to wielding a pencil than a garden fork these days. It had been many years since she had dug over these beds and her body had forgotten what it was like but, as the morning progressed, she got into her stride and made a real contribution.

'You're doing well,' Jonathan told her when break time approached.

'Don't sound so surprised,' she replied.

'Join us for a cup of tea?'

She nodded and the group made their way to the little outbuilding. Rod immediately took charge and plugged in a kettle that he'd brought with him, and Jonathan put out a selection of old chipped mugs and teaspoons.

'The travelling tea caddy,' he said, pointing to the plastic box Rod had brought in from the minibus. 'Seen all sorts of action, hasn't it, team?'

'Make sure you've all washed your hands,' Rod shouted above the kettle. 'Especially you, Oz. I know where your hands have been this morning.'

'God, you're like a drill sergeant,' Oz said.

'You could do with one of those, my lad,' Rod told him.

Oz shook his head and Vanessa did her best to suppress a giggle at the exchange.

'Hope you've still got my mug,' Jenna said.

'It's right there,' Jonathan told her, picking up the mug with the teddy bear on the front. Jenna took it from him as if afraid somebody else might grab it. 'Very protective of her mug is our Jenna.'

'I don't want to be drinking out of any of your mugs,' she said. 'I don't know where you've all been.'

'Yeah, well we don't know where you've been,' Oz argued.

'I can guess,' Nat said, and Jenna elbowed him in the ribs.

'Ouch!' he cried.

Vanessa smiled as she studied the group. She couldn't help but wonder what their backgrounds were and what had happened to them all. She looked at Jonathan, hoping she could find out. He looked up from making the tea and caught her eye.

'Have you got a minute?' she asked.

'Sure.' He motioned to a sky-blue mug.

'Black, no sugar,' she said.

He sploshed some milk into his own mug and took them outside, handing hers over.

Once Vanessa was quite sure that the group couldn't hear them, she began.

'I'd love to know more about everyone,' she said.

'What do you want to know?'

Vanessa shrugged. 'What can you tell me?'

Jonathan sighed. 'They're a mixed bunch and we haven't got everyone here today of course. Let me see. Michael there, he's the youngest of six children and has been in and out of foster homes all his life. He once told me that his biological father was a drunk and used to beat him.'

'Oh, God!'

'Yep. Imagine growing up like that. With Nat, it was his mother who was the problem. She was in and out of prison and he had a succession of carers. Aunts, uncles . . . One time, he and his siblings were left to fend for themselves for two months. Nat was the eldest and he was only thirteen.'

'How awful,' Vanessa said.

'Oz was expelled from his first school when he was nine. He's pretty much been in trouble ever since, but I'm sure there's a heart of gold in there somewhere. We've just got to dig a bit to find it. And then there's Andy and Ryan, who aren't here today. They just fell in with the wrong crowd. Andy's got such promise, though. He's really smart and a good worker when he puts his mind to it.'

'And Jenna?'

'Broken home. Her mum died young and her dad never really cared about her. She's been living with friends since leaving school.'

'That's sad. To have no real family. I can't imagine what that's like.'

Jonathan gave her a look she didn't quite understand.

'What?'

'Don't get attached, Vanessa.'

'I'm not!'

'I saw the way you kept glancing at her in the garden.'

She felt her face flame in embarrassment. 'I didn't mean to stare, but she looks a little like my daughter, Tilda, and I couldn't help thinking . . .'

'There but for the grace of God?'

'Yes. There's so much luck involved in life, isn't there? Where we're born and who we're born to.'

'Who our parents get involved with and the friends we meet along the way.'

Vanessa nodded.

'And the decisions we make,' he added and, for a moment, Vanessa thought that she saw a dark shadow pass across his face as if he were remembering something. 'Jenna's pretty mixed up,' he continued a moment later. 'Her moods can be up and down, but she's special. I've got great hopes for her.' He cocked his head to one side. 'Where's that music coming from?'

'What?' Vanessa said. 'Oh! It's Jassy in the oast house. She's my younger daughter and she must be painting a still life because she's listening to Corelli. She likes to listen to Baroque music when working on still lifes.'

'Really?'

'And hard rock when she's painting abstract, and absolute silence when painting portraits.'

Jonathan grinned. 'Do you think our team would work harder if we played some heavy metal?'

'They might, but you'll have me complaining if you do.'

'And we don't want to upset our lovely host,' he said.

She smiled at him but, before she could ask him any more questions, he had returned to supervise the washing of the mugs.

'Right,' he said, addressing the team, 'use the loo if you need it and then straight back to the walled garden. Rod will be waiting for you, so no loitering.'

Vanessa smiled. She loved his bossiness, which was probably just what these kids needed – rules and boundaries. He clearly adored them and she couldn't help wondering what had led him into this work. Perhaps there was more to this than just passing on his love of gardening. Maybe there was something in Jonathan's own past that made him reach out to connect with these young people.

Vanessa left them at lunchtime, giving them a bit of privacy to do their own thing, but rejoined them in the afternoon.

'You know, I've really enjoyed today,' she said when it was finally time to down tools.

'Good,' Jonathan said. 'It's done you good too, judging by your complexion.'

Vanessa's hands flew to her face. 'Really?'

'You were pale as snow this morning, but you've got roses in your cheeks now.'

'And dirt under your nice nails,' Jenna pointed out.

Vanessa laughed and then realised that she was still wearing Jonathan's shirt. 'Thank you for this,' she said as she began to unbutton it.

'Keep it.'

'I couldn't.'

'It's a bribe really,' he said. 'It'll force you into coming to help us again.'

'I don't need to be bribed to help you. I've had a really great day.' She watched as Rod and Nat cleaned the tools with an old rag.

'Jonathan goes nuts if we leave dirt on anything,' Oz told her.

'Tools are expensive,' Jonathan said. 'It's taken me a long time to put this collection together and I don't want it rusting away through neglect. Make sure you put that stuff on the compost heap before you leave.' He nodded towards a pile of weeds which had been pulled from one of the raised beds.

'You've got them all really well-trained,' Vanessa said.

'Only taken eighteen months,' he said with a grin.

They spent another ten minutes tidying around the garden and making sure everything was safe and neatly put away for next time.

'I'm knackered,' Nat complained as they returned to the minibus.

'Good,' Jonathan said. 'Means you've done a proper day's work and won't have the energy to get up to any mischief tonight.'

'I wouldn't be too sure,' Oz said. 'He's seeing somebody.'

'Are you?' Jonathan asked, and Nat gave a sheepish look.

'Might be.'

'Good for you,' Jonathan said and then turned to Vanessa. 'Thank you for today.'

'Thank you. I can't believe how much land you've cleared.'

'We'll finish off next time and then we can start enriching the beds and planting.'

'I'll see you in a couple of days then.'

'You bet.' He gave her a funny little salute before leaving via the gate in the yew hedge with his team.

Vanessa returned to the house and wasn't a bit surprised to see Dolly in the hallway ready to pounce on her.

'Where've you been all day?'

'Out in the garden,' Vanessa said.

'What's going on out there? That horrible van and minibus have been parked in the lane all day, blocking the road.'

'They're not blocking the road,' Vanessa said.

'You're up to something. You're always up to something.'

'I'm not up to anything, Dolly.'

'You've got dirt on your face.'

'I've also got roses in my cheeks,' Vanessa said, undeterred.

'There's dirt in your hair too.'

And you've got poison in your heart, Vanessa thought, but she didn't say anything because she wasn't going to allow Dolly to spoil what had been a wonderful day.

Chapter 10

It was a new experience for Laurence to wake up in the middle of the night and experience total darkness and hear absolutely nothing. His flat in London had been in a relatively quiet street and yet was never completely silent. There was always traffic and the sound of people coming and going, and street lighting that meant he could safely wander around in the early hours without needing to turn the lights on. But, here at Orley, the middle of the night was a strange place indeed, and one of the first things Laurence had made sure he bought was a bedside lamp so that he didn't stumble across the sloping floorboards of his bedroom or crash into walls he was not yet familiar with.

Getting up now, he wondered when his disjointed sleep had begun and pinpointed it back to the time just after his mother had died. The unreality, the suddenness, the brutal ugliness of it all had disturbed him greatly. He'd had nightmares too when he had actually managed to fall asleep, nightmares which had caused him to wake up sweating. He didn't have those anymore, but his sleeping patterns hadn't been quite the same since.

Putting on a pair of jogging bottoms and an old jumper, he opened his bedroom door, praying that the appalling squeak wouldn't wake his father. He'd have to get that fixed as soon as he could, although he liked the way the old house seemed to talk to him in a succession of squeaky doors and floorboards. He'd heard that old houses breathed and moved, but he hadn't really paid that any attention until he'd experienced it for himself. Field End Cottage had had a few rattly windows and sloping floors, but it had been nothing compared to Orley.

Doing his best not to step on any vocal floorboards, Laurence decided that he might listen to a chapter or two of one of the audiobooks he had on the go. That might not help him sleep, but it was, at least, a good way to pass the time.

It was as he was crossing the landing that he thought he heard something, and he opened the door overlooking the entrance hall. *Music.* He could hear music. Somebody was playing the piano and he had a very good idea who it might be.

Running a hand through his hair, he slipped on a pair of trainers and made his way downstairs, listening to the music coming from the south wing. There was a touch of melancholy about it, he thought, as well as intense sweetness. It was the kind of music one could listen to for hours and always find something new, something wonderful to remark upon.

He approached the room where the music was coming from. It was much louder now and he stopped and listened to it for a moment before he entered. Sure enough, there was Tilda sitting at the piano. She was wearing a big baggy jumper just as he was – a prerequisite for mooching around a big old manor house in the middle of the night. Her hair was slightly dishevelled, as if she'd managed to get into bed at least but perhaps hadn't slept well there.

'Hello,' he whispered, trying to come into her line of vision and hoping he didn't frighten the living daylights out of her.

'Oh!' she cried, catching sight of him.

'Sorry!' he said, coming into the room. 'I didn't mean to frighten you.'

'What are you doing up?'

'Couldn't sleep. Then I heard you playing.'

'You can hear me in the north wing?' she asked, her face a picture of mortification.

'Just faintly.'

'I'm so sorry. I didn't mean to disturb anyone.'

'You didn't,' he said. 'I was awake anyway. I'm a light sleeper. I used to get up all the time in London and sit and listen to audiobooks in the dark.'

'Yeah? Which books?'

'Thrillers mostly. A bit of crime.'

'I don't think those kinds of books will ever help you sleep!'

'Maybe not, but they kept me amused in the wee small hours.' He watched as she gently closed the piano lid. It was a very expensive-looking grand and a thing of great beauty, though it was obviously much loved rather than a piece that had been inherited and used to place photo frames on.

'What was that you were playing just then? Was it something you wrote?' Laurence asked her.

She nodded. 'A long time ago.'

'It was lovely.'

Tilda gave a little smile. 'When Dad was ill, he'd find it hard to sleep some nights and he would ask me to play for him.'

'What, he'd wake you up?'

'No, I pretty much couldn't sleep either. We'd sit up for hours together, talking and playing the piano.'

Laurence took a step towards her and nodded to a sofa before sitting down. Tilda turned around on the piano seat to face him.

'I was just thinking about my mum,' he said. 'I found it hard to sleep after she died. I haven't really been right since.'

Tilda frowned. 'But wasn't that two years ago?'

'Yep.'

'That's a long time to not be able to sleep properly.'

'Tell me about it!' He sighed. 'There's been a lot of upheaval since then too. It's not been an easy time for me or my dad.'

Tilda gave him a sympathetic look. 'How did she die? I mean, if you don't mind me asking.'

'I don't mind. It was a car crash in Kent. A little country road. It had been raining. Dangerous conditions, the police told us, and maybe she lost concentration or control of the car. We don't really know,' he said. 'She died instantly.'

'Oh, no,' Tilda said. 'That's so sad.'

Laurence sighed. 'Dad didn't deal with it well. *Isn't* dealing with it well.'

'I'm sorry. Is that why you moved here? A fresh start?'

'I suppose it is,' he said. 'I thought it would do us both good. We were happy here in Sussex. It was a good life.'

'And is he happy to be back?'

Laurence shrugged. 'To be honest, I don't know what makes him happy these days.'

'Have you asked him?'

'Whenever I ask my dad a direct question, he shuts down on me completely. It's really frustrating. I've tried to talk to him so many times, but he'll just leave the room or clam up.' Laurence paused. 'I think we've always had trouble communicating. I've been thinking about that a lot lately. We've never really chatted together. Not like I used to with my mum. Dad would ask how my day went and what the football score was – that kind of thing – but we never really talked about anything meaningful. And I really wish we could. I want to know how he's feeling and what's going on in that head of his.'

'Well, these things take time.'

'It's been two years and he spent one of those years travelling around South America.'

'Really?'

'Yep! I had no idea where he was. The occasional postcard would arrive, but he'd always moved on by then. There was no way of getting in touch with him.'

'He obviously needed to escape. When my dad died, my sister escaped into her art and my mum into her work, and Grandma into silence. That was scary. She didn't talk to anybody. We just couldn't reach her. It was awful. We didn't know what to do.'

'Nobody prepares you for this kind of thing, do they?' Laurence said.

Tilda knitted her fingers together in her lap. 'We all knew Daddy was going to die, but it didn't make it any easier. I think it just makes you sadder for a longer time.'

'But at least you got to say goodbye.'

Tilda nodded.

'You could talk about all the things that really mattered too,' he said.

Suddenly, there were tears in Tilda's eyes.

Laurence was beside her in an instant, kneeling down in front of the piano seat. 'Sorry! I didn't mean to upset you. I should have been more mindful.'

'It's okay. I'm okay.'

'It's just that I don't often get to talk about all this, and I guess it's still very much going round my head.'

'It's fine,' she said, mopping her eyes with a tissue from the sleeve of her jumper. 'It's good to talk.'

'Are you sure?'

She nodded and Laurence slowly stood back up and walked across to the window, drawing the curtains and staring out into the moonlit garden.

'The middle of the night is a strange place,' he said, 'but it can be a great friend. I did a lot of thinking in that year after my mum died. I'd never really had time to think before. But I guess I needed to talk as well.' He turned around, smiling suddenly. 'Want to go for a walk?'

'What?'

'In the garden. Right now. Do you want to come with me?'

'No, not really. It'll be freezing!'

'It'll be fun. Come on. Don't forget I'm new here. This is all still an adventure.'

'I thought you wanted to talk,' Tilda said, obviously confused.

'I do. But let's talk and walk.'

'You're crazy!'

'Come on!' he said again, taking her hand as he walked past her.

They crossed the hallway together, through the eerie shadows, to the front door.

'You'll need a coat,' Tilda said, grabbing two from a hook by the door and putting one on. 'Here – this is a spare.'

'Your father's?'

'No. I think it belonged to the gardener we used to have. It's got a huge rip up the back so it'll be a bit draughty, but it's better than nothing.'

She stuffed her feet into a pair of wellington boots, and they opened the front door and Laurence immediately turned right.

'We can't go round that way,' Tilda whispered. 'Grandma's rooms are on the south side and we'll set Reynolds off if we walk past them.'

'Shall we go to the walled garden then?'

'I suppose,' she said, sounding reluctant and probably thinking that he was absolutely mad.

They tiptoed down the garden path, only speaking again when they were away from the house.

'Wow – just look at those stars,' Laurence said, craning his neck back and taking in the enormous expanse of the heavens. 'I've forgotten what a night sky is meant to look like. Isn't it fantastic?'

'I guess.'

'Says somebody used to seeing millions of stars every single night.'

'Only a madman would come out here every single night.'

'I used to try and see the stars from my flat in London. I had the tiniest of balconies outside my bedroom, but there was so much light pollution that you couldn't see a thing or, if you thought you had, it turned out to be an aeroplane.'

'Is this what you came out for – to see the stars?'

He turned to look at her. 'I just wanted to come out because I could. It's been a long time since I had a garden to roam about in at night.'

'Well, it's freezing.'

'You want to go back in?'

She paused before answering and then shook her head. 'No, I'll brave it a bit longer, but can we start walking so I can keep warm?'

They continued towards the walled garden and Laurence glanced back at the great bulk of the house and the comical conical shape of the oast house's silhouette against the night sky. The outline of the hills looked ominously dark against the star-studded heavens. He couldn't remember the last time he'd walked in the countryside at night. It must have been when they'd lived at Field End Cottage. He had often sneaked out into the garden on a summer's evening, climbing up the beech tree and sitting on one of its smooth grey boughs and just staring into the sky until he felt quite dizzy. How long ago that seemed now. The young boy who had climbed trees and jumped over brooks, whose childhood had seemed to stretch to infinity during those long summer holidays – the boy who had been the centre of his parents' world. Where had he gone? And the family too, and that perfect little life? It was all gone, it had stopped existing; it had morphed into something quite different: the boy was now a man, the father was a recluse and the mother was dead.

Laurence took a deep breath of the cold night air.

'You've gone very quiet,' Tilda said as they entered the walled garden.

'Just thinking.'

She turned to look up at him and the moon shone full on her pale face. What a lovely face she had, he thought. So full of warmth and kindness, but sadness too. Just as he was nursing a bruised heart, so was she. That was something else he'd learned from his mother's death: so many people were carrying great hurts and you never really knew what somebody was suffering. Not until it happened to you. Until recently, Laurence had always been the kind of man to work at full speed and pay very little attention to the emotional needs of those around him. He just hadn't been aware of them. But he was now.

'Tilda?'

'Yes?'

'Did your mum talk about your father's death?'

They were walking in the orchard now, the silvery moon making beautiful twisted shadows on the grass.

'She did nothing but talk,' Tilda said. 'Dad wasn't just her husband, he was her best friend. We were all so close and there were never any secrets. We all knew what was happening and Mum was amazing when he died. She's always been good like that – talking about emotions. The only thing she's never been good at is talking about money. She tends to bury her head a bit when it comes to financial difficulties. It was my idea to sell the north wing. She'd never have thought of doing that.'

'Then I have you to thank?'

'I suppose.'

'Were things always difficult for your family here? I mean financially?'

'Well, it's not cheap running a place like Orley.'

'I can imagine.'

'The utility bills are horrendous and you don't even want to imagine the repair bills just to keep everything intact. So it's always been a struggle, but it became more difficult after Dad died. He took care of all the books and managed the land.'

'It must have been hard on your mum.'

'It was. Financially as well as emotionally. For a while, we had some money coming in from my singing, but Dad got ill around the time I retired from that life and Mum refused to use the money anyway. I paid for a few things on the sly like new guttering, repointing a wall and a chimney repair, but I knew we needed to do something to raise significant funds.'

They were quiet for a moment, standing under the apple trees together, letting their thoughts drift. Laurence could hardly believe what Tilda had just told him. What a great burden she'd been carrying – the very future of Orley Court. And no wonder she found it impossible to contemplate going back into the music industry. She no doubt associated the whole bad experience of being in the spotlight with the awful time of her father's illness. Was that why she was hiding herself away at Orley? He couldn't really blame her.

He looked out beyond the walls of the garden to the hills and the sky again. His father might have travelled the world with the navy and spent months hiking through the Peruvian rainforest, but Laurence was pretty sure that there weren't many views that could rival this one – a glorious English landscape.

'Hey,' he suddenly said as he remembered something. 'What was your mum doing out in the garden with those people yesterday?'

'What people?'

'There was a whole group of young people. I think they were working here in the walled garden.'

'Really?'

'You didn't see them?'

She shook her head. 'I was out teaching most of the day. I teach at a couple of local schools one day a week,' she explained. 'So, what was going on?'

'Well, I think they were gardening.'

Tilda frowned. 'We can't afford a team of gardeners.'

'Work experience students?'

'I don't know,' Tilda said. 'Mum said she had plans for the walled garden. I'll have to find out what's she's up to.' She stomped her feet in her wellies. 'Are you done with the stargazing yet because my feet have turned to ice!'

He laughed. 'Let's get back inside.'

They left the walled garden, stumbling a little as the moon went behind a bank of cloud.

'I didn't bring a torch,' Tilda hissed. 'Did you?'

'I don't think I even own a torch,' Laurence said.

'Well, you'd better get one fast if you're going to live here for any length of time. We get our share of power cuts, you know.'

'Ouch!'

'What was that?' she asked.

'I walked into something hard.'

'One of the galvanised planters. It'll be safer if we walk on the grass.'

'Where is the grass?' Laurence felt Tilda's hand reach for his; she guided him away from the path and he felt the soft wetness of the grass beneath his trainers. 'You've done this before, haven't you?'

'What – dragged clueless Londoners around our garden in the middle of the night?'

He laughed. 'Just get me back in one piece. I think there was a pond around here, wasn't there?'

'It's more of a puddle.'

'I still don't want to end up in it.'

A second later, the garden was flooded with moonlight once again as the clouds dispersed across the heavens. Laurence felt relief fill him but, as Tilda dropped his hand, he wished that the moon had been elusive for a little longer.

'Nearly there,' she said, leading the way back onto the path and reaching the front door at last.

'Listen,' he said, 'I've really enjoyed talking to you tonight.'

She looked up at him, her eyes wide as she smiled. 'Me too. I've enjoyed talking to you.'

'We'll have to do it again sometime.'

'Although maybe not in the middle of a freezing-cold night.' She opened the door and they went inside. Tilda took off her boots and Laurence returned the ripped coat to its peg.

'Tilda?'

'Yes?'

Laurence paused, hoping he was doing the right thing. 'I know it's not my place. I know we've just met, but I have to say this.'

'Say what?'

'You have a real talent. You've been out into the world and proved it. You can't turn your back on it.'

'But I already have,' she said, her voice sounding darker.

'I don't believe that,' he said. 'You're much too young to bury yourself out here in the countryside. The world needs people like you. Young, vibrant, talented people.'

'No it doesn't. It gobbles them up and spits them out.'

'Well, if it does, you've got to learn to spit back.'

She grimaced. 'What are you talking about?'

'You mustn't give up on your dreams, Tilda. Not ever.'

She shook her head as if dismissing him. 'And what are your dreams, Laurence?'

'Mine?' he said, shocked by her question.

'Yes – yours. You accuse me of burying myself in the countryside. Well, isn't that exactly what you're doing?'

'No,' he insisted. 'It isn't. I didn't come here to bury myself. I came here to find myself.'

'Oh, really? You think that leaving London for some obscure little hamlet in the middle of nowhere is going to help you find yourself?'

'Yes, I really do,' he said. 'Anyway, I wasn't talking about myself. I was talking about you.'

'Yes, well, I don't want to talk about me, okay?'

'What would your father have wanted, Tilda? He surely wouldn't have wanted you to give up on your great talent?'

For a moment, Tilda looked completely stunned and her mouth dropped open but no words came out.

'I'm sorry,' Laurence quickly said, realising he'd overstepped the mark.

'How dare you talk about my father! You have no right to do that.'

'I know I don't. I'm just trying to help here.'

'Well, you can help by keeping your nose out of things. Just because you live here now, it doesn't give you the right to interfere in our lives.'

Laurence watched in dismay as she stormed across the hallway and ran up the stairs. He let out a long slow sigh. How on earth did he keep messing things up with Tilda?

Chapter 11

'You're not standing right,' Jasmine said. 'You're all hunched. You'll make yourself ache before you've even got any colour on the canvas.'

Marcus flinched as he felt Jassy's hands on his shoulders.

'You've got to loosen up. Do some stretches. Roll your shoulders. Wiggle your wrists.'

'Wiggle my wrists?'

She nodded. 'Wiggle your wrists. Go on!'

'Has anybody ever told you that you're really bossy?'

'Uh-huh,' she said, 'and I'm really bad-tempered if people don't do as I tell them.'

Marcus snorted. 'I've never met anyone like you before.'

'I'm one of a kind. Mum's always saying that. Dad used to say it too.'

'I can believe it,' Marcus said.

Jassy gave a little shrug and then returned to her own canvas.

'Actually, you're a bit like my dad,' she suddenly said.

'Am I?'

'A bit. Not just because you're a man and you're a lot older than me. You – you let me say things to you and you don't get cross or upset. Mum and Tilda – they always try to calm me down, but Dad never did. Dad listened to everything I said, even if I shouted or got a bit hyper. I miss that. I miss him.'

Marcus looked at her as she painted, taking in the earnest expression on her face. He liked this girl. He liked her a lot.

'Grandma lets me get good and mad too,' she said. 'She knows I sometimes need to get things outside of me, and she never interrupts when I'm like that. But she's been different recently. We used to talk loads, but she's gone all quiet. I think she misses Dad. I tried to persuade her to take up painting, but she said painting was my thing.'

Jassy was painting a still life of a group of old glass bottles that had been found in a corner of the garden one year when they'd cleared away a dead shrub. They were beautiful things. Some were tall and some short, some a very clear green and others an opaque white. Marcus was doing his best to paint them too, only he was struggling. Perhaps his eyesight was going, he thought. Or perhaps he just wasn't very good at this art business. He'd done a bit of sketching during his time in the navy, picking up a pencil and pad whenever he had a spare moment, but he'd never painted before.

It was funny. He hadn't planned on painting with Jassy that morning, but he'd woken early and had been walking in the gardens when he'd heard music drifting over from the oast house. It was classical music. Something with strings. Vivaldi, perhaps, he wasn't sure.

When he'd knocked lightly on the door, Jassy's bright voice called him inside and she'd immediately thrust an apron at him.

'Wear this,' she'd said. And that was it.

One thing was certain about painting: it made you focus on the thing you were doing – the image before you. It made you concentrate and that meant the mind was full and unable to dwell on anything else, and that was good. That was exactly what Marcus needed and what he'd been lacking in recent months. When he'd gone travelling, he'd found a certain element of escape, but travel necessitated long times in airports and tedious journeys by plane, train and bus, and that meant that the mind would drift. His certainly had and it had filled with images he'd rather not have entertained. So was that why his feet kept finding their way to the oast house? Had Jassy helped him to find oblivion at last?

He turned to look at her now. Her hair was piled on top of her head, its curls wildly exploding and giving her the look of the Medusa – there was a paintbrush in there somewhere too, and another between her teeth. He wanted to laugh, but thought he'd better not.

'Concentrate!' she said, growling at him through the paintbrush.

'I am,' he protested. 'My brain's going to explode if I concentrate anymore.' He shook his head. He just couldn't get the shape of these bottles right, and what made matters even worse was that Jassy had placed a mirror behind them which meant that they had to paint not one but two groups of the blooming things.

'I thought painting was meant to be relaxing,' he said.

'That,' Jassy said, removing the paintbrush from her mouth, 'is a common misconception. It is never relaxing – not if you're doing it right. You should be focused, and that's always hard.'

Marcus nodded. 'Focused,' he repeated as if that might help him.

He was just managing to capture what he thought was the essence of one particular bottle when a cat ran into the oast house.

'Hey, kitty!' Marcus said.

'That's Skinny,' Jassy said. 'Don't encourage her. She doesn't live here.'

'But she's always hanging around. I keep seeing her in the garden.'

'I know.'

'She doesn't belong to you?'

'Nope,' Jassy said.

'You don't want to keep her?'

Jassy shook her head and Marcus turned back to the black cat, who looked horribly thin.

'She needs feeding up.' He turned to Jassy, whose eyes were narrowed in concentration. 'Don't you think?'

'Probably,' she said.

'I might take her in with me.' He put his brush down.

'What, now?'

He bent down, putting a hand out for the cat to sniff. She seemed friendly enough, and her eyes were a beautiful green just like one of the bottles he'd failed to capture.

'I could paint you,' he told the cat as he scooped her up in his arms. 'One day. If I improve.'

'Where are you going?' Jassy asked.

'I'm going to find Skinny some food. I'll be back later.'

'Don't let your brushes dry out!'

'I won't, teacher,' he said, smiling as he left the oast house with the cat in his arms.

The spring sunshine was pleasantly warm on his back as he walked to the house.

'I think I've got a tin of tuna in the cupboard,' he said. 'How would you like that?' The cat purred as he stroked her soft fur. 'We'll get you nice and plump in no time.'

'Dad! There you are.'

'Laurie?'

'Who's that?'

'Skinny.'

'Skinny?'

'She's coming in.'

'You're taking her into the house?' Laurence asked in surprise.

'Sure. Why not?'

Laurence frowned. 'I never had you down as a cat person.'

'There's a lot you don't know about your father,' Marcus said. 'I used to have a cat growing up. Albert.'

'Albert?'

'Albert the cat. A big fat ginger tom.'

'I didn't know.'

Marcus kept walking and, a moment later, entered the house followed by Laurence. The two men walked to the north wing and Marcus put the cat down once they reached their shared kitchen. It was a modest-sized room, large enough to have a small table in the middle, but a little dated. It could really do with a makeover, but there were some nice features like the old range and the butler sink.

As soon as they were in the room, the cat sprang up onto the kitchen table.

'Oh, Dad!'

'Off there, Skinny,' Marcus said, quickly picking the cat up and putting her onto the floor. 'Now, where's that tuna?'

'You're not thinking of adopting him, are you?'

'*Her*, and I don't see why not. It'll be nice to have a companion around the place.'

'Just in case you hadn't noticed, I live in the next room,' Laurence said, and there was something in his tone of voice that caught Marcus's attention.

'What's that supposed to mean?'

'It means that you can talk to me if you need a companion.'

'I know that, son.'

'Do you?'

Finding the tin of tuna, Marcus put it down and turned to face Laurence.

'What's got into you?'

'What do you mean? Nothing's got into me,' Laurence said.

'You've got that strange tone.'

'No I haven't.'

'You sound narked.'

Marcus heard his son sigh. 'Dad, I wanted to ask you something.'

'I've told you, I'm not going to talk about your mother—'

'No, not that,' Laurence interrupted. 'It's about my business.'

Marcus opened the tin of tuna and tipped the contents onto a white saucer before placing it on the floor in front of Skinny.

'There you go, little one.'

'Dad!'

'What is it?'

'I'm trying to talk to you.'

'Go on.'

'I've got quite a lot of work on at the moment.'

'So, what's new?'

'What's new is that I'm my own boss now, or had you forgotten?'

Marcus turned to face his son. 'How could I forget that? It's why we moved here, isn't it?'

'Partly,' Laurence said. 'Anyway, it's a lot of work and I've been thinking of hiring an assistant. Just part-time.'

'Good idea.'

'Any thoughts? I mean, can you think of anyone who might be interested?'

Marcus thought for a moment. Who did he know with a head for business who might be able to help his son?

'Wait a minute,' he said. 'Is this your ham-fisted way of asking me to work for you?'

Laurence frowned. 'Of course not! Although, now you come to mention it, that's not a bad idea.'

Marcus shook his head. 'Not interested.' He searched the kitchen cupboards until he found a suitable bowl, which he filled with water and placed on the floor for the cat.

'I could pay you,' Laurence added.

'I don't need your money.'

'I know, but wouldn't it be great to have something to do?'

Marcus frowned. Had he heard his son right? 'I've got plenty to do,' he said.

'What? What have you got to do, Dad?'

'You want me to keep a diary so I can show you how my hours are filled?'

'No, of course not!'

'I don't need this, Laurie. I don't need you buzzing around me all the time.'

'I'm not buzzing. I'm—'

'I admire what you're doing, setting up your own business from scratch, but that's your dream. That's what you want to do. You don't need to include me in it. I can take care of myself.'

'I know you can, Dad.'

'Just let me be, will you?' And he left the room with Skinny the cat – having finished her tuna meal – trotting behind him.

Laurence was pretty shaken after the confrontation in the kitchen. He had to accept some of the blame himself as he hadn't handled things in the best way imaginable, but Marcus wasn't the easiest man to deal with and Laurence found himself becoming increasingly frustrated by this. All he wanted to do was reach out to his father – he had thought that encouraging him to become part of the business was a really great way forward, but maybe he'd been wrong.

He bent down to pick up the now-empty saucer and placed it in the sink to wash. When had things last been good between him and his father? Laurence wondered. *Really* good, and not just tolerable? When had they last had a real conversation that wasn't just about what was in the newspapers or what was on the television – about something that really mattered? Laurence genuinely couldn't remember, but it was probably a long time ago, certainly before his mother had died and probably on one of his rare weekend trips down to Kent. Then again, his mother would have been there, presiding over everything and lightening every moment with her warmth and humour.

Laurence was beginning to wonder if he'd ever really had a normal relationship with his father. Maybe he hadn't. What did he really know about his dad? He certainly hadn't known that he'd once had a pet cat.

And where on earth had that new cat come from? The scrawny thing was getting more attention than he was.

It was ridiculous, Laurence thought. He was even jealous of a cat now.

Tilda had woken up in a bad mood. She'd gone to sleep in a bad mood too, tossing and turning in anger at what Laurence had said to her. What right did he have to come wading into her life like that? Mind you, she couldn't help feeling that she'd encouraged him by going out into the garden at midnight and taking his hand on the way back to the house. Perhaps she'd given him the wrong idea. Perhaps she'd created a feeling of intimacy and he'd felt he could say anything to her. Well, he couldn't.

It was just as well that Tilda didn't have any pupils until later in the day, because she was feeling too grouchy to teach. Her mother was sitting at the table in the kitchen, flipping through a lifestyle magazine, when Tilda entered.

'Look at these horrible chairs,' she said as Tilda approached. 'Can you imagine anyone wanting to have them in their home?'

Tilda looked at the lurid green plastic chairs. 'Not everyone likes Chippendale, Mum.'

'Imagine these at Orley. No, don't! The mere thought gives me indigestion—'

'Mum,' Tilda interrupted.

'Yes, dear?'

'Laurence said there were some people out in the walled garden yesterday.'

'That's right.'

Tilda waited for her mother to elaborate. 'And?'

'What?'

'What were they doing?'

'Gardening, darling.'

'But we can't afford one gardener, let alone several.'

'I know.'

Tilda shook her head in exasperation. 'Are you going to tell me what's going on?'

Her mother smiled at her. 'It's a special group who will be working here from now on under the guidance of Jonathan Dacre. I met him in the village.'

'And what do you know about him?'

'Jonathan?'

'Yes. Have you done a background check on him? Got references or something?'

Her mother laughed lightly. 'He's a gardener with years of experience. He was putting an advert up in the village shop.'

'Anyone can put an advert up in the shop.'

'And he's working with Rod – an ex-policeman.'

Tilda frowned. 'An ex-policeman?'

Vanessa chewed her lip. 'Look, your grandma doesn't know this yet—'

'Know what?'

'About the group. The team, Jonathan calls them. They're—'

'What? What are they, Mum?'

'They're young offenders.'

'Oh, Mum! Are you sure it's safe having them here?'

'Of course it is. They're amazing people, Tilda. They deserve a second chance.'

'I'm sure they do. But here at Orley?'

'Darling, if everybody had that attitude – and a fair few people do – then these people would never get an opportunity to change. Jonathan told me that they've been turned down countless times and I can understand why, I really can, but think of the difference you can make by giving these people a chance.'

'Mum, that's really admirable, but I can't help being a bit worried.'

'You don't need to worry. Jonathan's a really great guy. Rod too. And you should see the work they're doing. We're lucky to have them.'

'Well, if you're sure.'

'I am,' her mother said. 'I really am. You should come and meet them. There's a girl – Jenna. I'd like you to meet her.'

'Okay,' Tilda said.

'Good. Now,' Vanessa said, getting up, 'I suppose I'd better let Jassy know what's going on too. Is she in the oast house?'

'I guess.'

'I can't remember the last time I had a conversation with that girl. She's always preoccupied with one of those paintings of hers.'

'She's getting good. Have you seen the latest abstracts?'

'No, I haven't,' Vanessa said. 'I'll take a walk and see if I can catch her. I suppose Mr Sturridge is out there, is he?'

'Laurence's dad?'

'Yes.'

'He does seem to be spending a lot of time with Jassy.'

'I know,' Vanessa said. 'I can't say I've warmed to him yet, and I have tried to make conversation with him. He's a little tricky, don't you think?'

Tilda's ears pricked at her mum's use of the word 'tricky'. Wasn't that how Laurence had described his current relationship with his father? Tilda couldn't help wondering if she'd perhaps been a little harsh with him the night before. He'd only been trying to help her after all, and if he was having his own troubles, it had been doubly kind of him to want to reach out to her with advice.

Yes, she thought, she'd been unkind as well as ungrateful to Laurence, hadn't she?

Vanessa pulled on a cardigan before leaving the house. The sun might be shining, but the spring air was still cool. She walked towards the oast house, smiling at the cheerful yellow and red tulips. It was the time when one could dream of glorious things for the gardening year ahead, when seeds could be planted and new borders created. Vanessa was already planning a new lavender path in the south garden and was hoping to buy some more climbing roses for the south face of the house and some more bush roses. Roses were always so glorious to have in the house and were much too extravagant a thing to buy from a florist.

That was another of the great luxuries of having an old house and beautiful country garden, she thought: there was always something to cut for a vase and she got infinite pleasure from browsing the borders for colourful blooms to place around the house. She adored matching the right flowers with the right vase; there was a glorious collection of vases at Orley, from blue and white Chinese pieces and handmade studio pottery to the most delicate English porcelain and the finest crystal.

Vanessa made sure that the borders had plenty of flowers to cut each year. There were majestic giants like lilies and gladioli, and blowsy beauties like roses and peonies, as well as the more delicate glories of sweet peas and pinks. There was always something, even in the depths of winter when vibrant berries in reds and oranges could be matched with evergreens to bring a bit of cheer to a bare windowsill.

The garden had been a special sort of sanctuary for her when Oliver had been ill and, in the moments he'd been sleeping, Vanessa had strolled down the pathways, taking comfort from the flowers and the trees. And she'd always bring something back with her to place on Oliver's bedside table.

Yes, the garden was a special place and Vanessa felt happy that she was able to share it with Jonathan and his team. She wasn't going to let the ever-cautious Tilda sow seeds of doubt in her mind. It was much too lovely a thing to keep to oneself. That had been one of the reasons for hosting the summer fete – to allow the locals to enjoy the garden when it was at its very best. But that had only been for one day a year.

Vanessa pondered this for a moment on her way to the oast house. East Sussex and the bordering county of Kent were well known for their gardens, from Vita Sackville-West's Sissinghurst to Christopher Lloyd's Great Dixter, from Nymans to Standen. Visitors to the region were spoilt with what was on offer. Could Orley really compete with such gems if they decided to open it to the public? Vanessa smiled. Of course it could, because it had one advantage that none of the other properties had: it was Orley.

She took a deep breath as she looked out across the south garden and the view to the hills beyond. This valley was a special place and Orley had one of the best vantage points. Perhaps they should share that. Maybe she should talk to Jonathan about it.

She had once suggested opening the gardens at weekends to Oliver and he'd been interested in the idea initially, but had backed down completely when Dolly had made her thoughts known.

'You want to invite the public in every weekend?' Dolly had barked.

'Only between April and October,' Vanessa had said.

How disappointed she'd been when Oliver hadn't supported her scheme. There'd been several other occasions over the years when she and Dolly had played tug of war with Oliver's loyalty, but Oliver wasn't around now, Vanessa thought, and she certainly didn't have to ask Dolly's permission before making decisions. If Vanessa wanted to open the gardens to the public or start the summer fetes again then she jolly well would.

Reaching the oast house, she heard the uplifting notes of a Vivaldi mandolin concerto.

'Still life,' she said to herself, knocking on the door before entering.

'Mr Sturridge!' she said in surprise as she came face-to-face with Marcus.

He cleared his throat. 'Mrs Jacobs.'

'What are you doing out here?'

'Isn't that obvious, Mum?' Jassy said. 'He's painting. He's not very good yet. He's still learning about perspective.'

Marcus chuckled. 'Your daughter is very honest.'

'I know,' Vanessa said, taking in the fact that Marcus Sturridge was standing behind an easel and wearing one of her daughter's paint-splattered aprons.

'Did you want something, Mum?'

Vanessa had walked into the room so that she could get a look at what Marcus Sturridge was painting.

'Did I what, darling?'

'Did you want something? Only, we're rather busy as you can see.'

'Oh, right. Of course.' Mr Sturridge was indeed painting, and it wasn't a bad effort either. 'The garden.'

'What about it?' Jassy asked.

'We have someone working in the walled garden now. Jonathan Dacre and his friend Rod. They work with a group of young people and they're coming twice a week.'

'That's nice,' Jassy said.

Vanessa cleared her throat. 'They're young offenders.'

Jassy frowned and Marcus did a double take.

'What does that mean?' Jassy asked.

'It means they've been in trouble.'

'What sort of trouble?'

'Drink, drugs, crime.'

Jassy seemed to consider this for a moment. 'And does gardening make them feel better like painting makes me feel better?'

Vanessa smiled. 'I think it does,' she said. 'I hope it does.'

'That's good.' Jassy returned to her painting. Vanessa caught Marcus's eye and he did something he hadn't done before: he smiled at her.

Chapter 12

The primroses and cowslips were a distant memory, and the daffodils which had smiled upon the garden for so brief a time were over just as the first roses were beginning to open. They seemed to be getting earlier each year, Vanessa thought, remembering how she'd seen the first pink buds of the Old Blush China roses begin to unfurl in March. Now that it was the end of May, they had been joined by several other beauties which lit up the south garden with wondrous colour.

The stately irises had put on a marvellous display too this year, with their vivid purple and ghostly white flowers and the rich chocolate blooms that her husband had been particularly fond of. The fruit trees in the walled garden were smothered in delicate blossom, giving the appearance of low-floating white clouds when viewed from a distance and, everywhere, the tiny blue flowers of forget-me-nots threaded their way around the garden in a floral river.

The countryside had been a joyous sight too: the woods glowing with bluebells, the scent filling the air with heady perfume. Vanessa could never get enough of them, walking through each day and drinking in their beauty.

Jonathan and his team had made excellent progress in the walled garden. Each of the raised beds was planted with a fine array of vegetables and Vanessa smiled as she recalled the day – just a few weeks ago – when he'd arrived with his trays of plants which took up the entire back of his van.

'Somebody's been busy,' she'd said.

'That would be me.'

'What have we got here?'

'All sorts of things,' he said. 'Beans, peas, cabbages and kale, salad crops, squashes and carrots. A little a bit of everything really.'

And now they were all in the ground, planted with care by the team. Walking around the walled garden today, she marvelled at how everything was so neat.

Vanessa had joined them on and off over the last few weeks, helping where she could, but her daughters had yet to meet everybody. Vanessa had to admit that she was rather upset by that. Still, this was her project, and her daughters had their own lives to lead and she had to respect that. Just because Tilda and Jasmine were still living under her roof, it didn't mean that they had to be involved in everything that Vanessa did or every decision she made. Still, it would have been nice if they'd shown some interest, other than Tilda's initial warnings about Jonathan and how they didn't really know anything about the man.

Vanessa had managed to forget her daughter's caution until an incident in the post office just the week before. She'd been standing behind two elderly women who were waiting to collect their pensions. They hadn't turned round to see her behind them and had been gossiping quite happily.

'I can't believe she did that,' the first woman had said and Vanessa instantly wondered who they were talking about and what this woman had done.

'Mind you, she's a Londoner. She's used to that sort of thing, isn't she?' The other woman declared and Vanessa had tried to guess the identity of this particular Londoner. Perhaps it was Elouise, Geoffrey's wife, whose house she was giving a makeover.

'But criminals, for pity's sake!' the first woman said, and then Vanessa had known that they were talking about her.

'They call them young offenders,' the second woman corrected, 'but a criminal is a criminal.'

'Serve the family right if Orley Court gets burgled.'

'It would that. But what if they come into the village? I bet she hasn't thought about that. As long as she's getting free labour, she's not thinking about anybody else.'

At first, Vanessa was too dumbfounded to react, but then she found her nerve and her voice.

'I really think you should keep your opinions to yourself,' she said, and the two women turned around looking suitably shocked.

'We didn't know you were standing there, Mrs Jacobs,' the first woman said. Vanessa recognised her as Mrs Lancaster who did the flowers at the local church, but she didn't recognise the second woman.

'Oh, and it would have made a difference if you had, would it?' she countered.

'Of course,' Mrs Lancaster said. 'We wouldn't dream of talking about you—'

'Just think,' Vanessa interrupted, 'if one of those criminals was your son or daughter or grandchild. Wouldn't you want them to be given a second chance? Don't you think they'd deserve one? We can't just write these young people off, you know. They're our future! And to think that you're Christians! Where's your compassion?'

She'd left the shop, desperately blinking back tears that had been threatening to spill, and yet, at the same time, a tiny niggle of doubt assailed her because, just the day before, Dolly had said she'd lost a little jewellery box in which she kept a gold necklace Oliver had given her. But that couldn't have anything to do with Jonathan's team, could it? None of them would have sneaked into the house and stolen anything, would they? She'd quickly dismissed the idea.

Now, watching Jonathan and his team in the garden, her heart filled with love and pride. She was getting to know a little bit more about each of them as the weeks went by and had now met Ryan and Andy too. They were all hard-working, but had a tendency to get distracted. Jonathan and Rod had a full-time job on their hands keeping them all on task, especially with Andy who seemed to be a bit of a joker and liked nothing more than to recount stories which were highly amusing, but highly aggravating to Rod, who would slap him down with a reprimand and tell him to put his energy into the earth.

Vanessa was doing a bit of light weeding with a hoe when Jonathan approached her.

'You okay?' he asked.

'I'm fine,' she said, smiling quickly.

'You looked thoughtful. Something on your mind?'

He was very attentive like that. He seemed to be able to read her so well; she knew that there was no point in hiding anything from him and so she took a deep breath.

'It was something I heard. In the village,' she said.

'What? What did you hear?'

'It was about the kids. Two women were talking and they weren't happy about them being here.'

Jonathan frowned. 'And you let that upset you?'

She took a deep breath. 'I guess I did. I mean, I have.'

'Don't,' he told her. 'You've got to shut all that noise out. Keep your head down and just get on with the work. Accept that your vision of the world doesn't always line up with everybody else's.'

She gave a little laugh. 'You've got such a healthy attitude.'

'It's taken a while to cultivate.'

'Cultivate!' she said with a smile. 'Do you always use gardening terminology?'

'What can I say? I dig it!'

'Very funny,' she said. 'Listen. I was wondering – I was thinking . . .'

'What?'

'Well, we don't really know much about each other.'

'Is that bothering you?'

'No,' she said, perhaps a little too quickly to be totally convincing. 'It's just—'

'You'd rather know who it is you've got hanging around your walled garden?'

She couldn't help but smile at that. 'You must think I'm being silly.'

'Not at all,' he said. 'Tell you what. Why don't you come round to mine this evening? I'll make us dinner.'

'Oh, I didn't mean for you to—'

'It's the least I can do. You can come and see my garden. That's a pretty fair exchange for sharing yours with us, isn't it?'

Vanessa looked at his smiling face and she had to admit that she liked the idea of seeing his place. As an interior designer, she was appallingly nosy.

'Okay,' she said.

'I'm at Beeches. It's one of the cottages on the Brightling Road. Last one on the right, the same side as the church. Seven o'clock okay? That will give us some time in the garden before the sun sets.'

'I'd like that,' she said, acknowledging how everything with Jonathan revolved around gardens.

Beeches was a tiny cottage on the edge of Elhurst. It was an end terrace with a small patch of front garden that led to a neat wooden door painted red. Vanessa, who had brought a bottle of wine and was now regretting it, wondering if it would give out the wrong signal, knocked on the door, pulling her light jacket around her. The dress she'd chosen to wear was a little too low-cut, she'd decided as she checked her reflection in the car mirror. But there wasn't much she could do about that now.

She took a deep breath. She suddenly felt nervous, which was silly really as they were just two adults having dinner together and talking about gardening. That was all. She needn't get all anxious, because it wasn't a date. Yet, she couldn't help thinking that this was the first time she'd shared the company of a man since her husband's death, and what would Oliver make of that?

She shook her head. It was silly even to ask such a question. If Oliver were still alive, she would never be having dinner with Jonathan. But he was dead and, although she felt his presence still close to her whenever she walked in the garden and moved around his favourite rooms of the house, she knew he probably wasn't looking down on her and guiding her every move. She was on her own now and she had to make her own decisions.

In all the novels she'd read and the films she'd watched over the years, characters would always say that the departed spouse would have wanted the partner left behind to be happy. It was a comfort to hear those words and Vanessa had heard her fair share of such platitudes from her own friends, who had tried to persuade her to see other men, to date again, but she hadn't had the heart for it. The happiness she'd known with Oliver could never be replicated so she wasn't even going to attempt to find something similar, but there was something about Jonathan that she liked. He was easy to talk to. He was easy on the eye, she couldn't help acknowledging that too, but she most certainly wasn't thinking about him in terms of romance. They were simply two mature adults who had something in common: a passion for gardening.

So why had she panicked in front of her wardrobe just an hour before? Because she wasn't used to spending time with a single man?

Suddenly, something occurred to her. What if Jonathan wasn't single? After all, he'd never discussed his private life with her. Maybe he was married and Vanessa was about to join him and his wife for supper. She looked down at her outfit. She'd chosen a simple but elegant dress in a light linen. It wasn't new or anything special but, then again, nothing in her wardrobe was new these days. She couldn't remember the last time she'd bought a dress. It would seem like such an extravagance even though they now had money in the bank from the sale of the north wing. But why would Vanessa need a new dress? She never went anywhere. She had a few good suits she wore when working with clients and they all still had years of life in them. But she'd wanted to wear a dress tonight – not to be noticed or admired, but simply to feel feminine again.

She knocked on the door and it wasn't long before Jonathan answered it.

'Have you been here long?' he asked in a panic. 'I was out in the garden.'

'No, not long,' she assured him.

'Come in.'

He was wearing a navy shirt and clean jeans and his dark red hair looked slightly less tousled than usual. She'd never seen him in anything other than his work clothes and had to admit that he scrubbed up very well indeed.

'This is beautiful,' Vanessa said as she entered Beeches.

'It belonged to my grandmother. She left it to me, knowing how much I loved the garden. Come and see it.'

'Is it just us?' she asked.

'For dinner? Yes. Why?'

'Just wondering,' Vanessa said.

'Is this a woman's roundabout way of asking if I'm married?'

Vanessa smiled. 'Well, I wasn't sure.'

'I'm not married,' he said. 'It's just me here.'

'Okay, good,' she said. 'I mean – that's good if you're happy and if you . . .' She shook her head in embarrassment. 'You know what I mean.'

He grinned at her. 'I wish I did!'

'I'm sorry. Let's start again, shall we?' She gave a nervous little laugh and they walked down a short hallway, entering the kitchen. 'I brought some wine,' she said, handing the bottle to him.

'Oh.'

'You don't drink?' She noted that his expression was suddenly serious.

'I don't. No.'

'Silly of me. I should have checked.'

'No, no – it was kind of you.'

'I'll just leave it here,' she said, popping it on one of the kitchen counters.

Jonathan looked flustered for a moment as his eyes followed her movement, but then he cleared his throat.

'The garden,' he said, opening the back door from the kitchen.

'Oh my,' Vanessa said as she saw it for the first time.

'It's quite something, isn't it?'

The garden was much larger than one would have imagined being attached to such a modest-sized cottage. It sloped away from the house and was bordered by a fine hawthorn hedge, which was delightfully frothy with its white blossom. Two large beech trees stood sentinel-like at the bottom of the garden – the trees Vanessa imagined had given their name to the house – but it was the view beyond the hedge that took her breath away.

'I've never seen the valley from this point before,' she said, taking in the sweep of wooded hills with the Downs in the distance.

'It's pretty spectacular, isn't it?'

'It's wonderful.'

'We didn't have much of a garden growing up and I used to love coming here. Grandma let me use her little trowel and fork to dig around. I think that's when I got hooked on gardening. She'd buy me packets of seeds to plant and then would give me all the credit when they grew, even though I wasn't around to take care of them. I learned about the changing seasons and the rhythm of nature. She helped me see things – really see them.' His voice was gentle and full of fond remembrance.

'That's really lovely,' Vanessa said, feeling as if she'd glimpsed a little bit of this man's soul.

'She was a special lady.'

'I'm sorry I didn't know her.'

Jonathan nodded. 'You would have liked her. She liked you, you know, even though she never really met you. She loved your garden.'

'She came to Orley?'

'Every year. She used to talk about your summer fete. I think it was the highlight of her year.'

'Really?' Vanessa said in surprise. 'I wish I'd known.'

'She used to talk about you too.'

'Did she?' Vanessa asked in surprise.

'She talked about "the lovely lady of the manor".'

'Oh, you're making this up!'

'I'm not!' Jonathan protested. 'She used to tell me what you'd been wearing. What you'd said at the opening speech and . . .' He paused.

'What?'

'She especially liked your hats.'

'Really?'

'She did. In fact, she once bought one at the village jumble sale. She was thrilled to find it. Apparently, there'd been quite a scrum to get it, but Grandma was victorious.'

Vanessa laughed. 'She sounds like quite a character.'

'She was.' A sad look crossed his face.

'You miss her, don't you?'

'Every day,' he said. 'No exaggeration. Every time I'm in the garden, I'll see something that I'd love to share with her or think of a little job to do that reminds me of her.'

'When did she die?'

'Twelve years ago.'

'Are your parents still living?'

'They retired to Portugal. They were hoping I wouldn't want this cottage so they could sell it.'

'But your grandma left it to you,' Vanessa said.

'My dad still thought he had a right to sell it and do what he wanted with the money, but I made sure he didn't get a chance.'

'Good for you.'

'Whenever he visited, he'd be eyeing things up that he could sell in the future. He once even asked if he could take Grandma's dressing table. I think it's some kind of antique. Anyway, he'd clocked it.'

'And did she give it to him?'

'No way,' Jonathan said, a gleam in his hazel eyes. 'My dad is the kind of man who always knows the price of something but never its true value. He never loved this place and Grandma knew that. He would pace around the garden as if measuring it out. I think he would have sold it to a developer.'

'No. Surely not?'

Jonathan shrugged. 'I'm not giving him a chance to find out.'

'It's so beautiful,' she said, taking in the neat raised beds full of produce and the flowering shrubs and perennials in the borders, all set against the fantastic backdrop of the Weald.

'Can I get you a drink?' he asked.

'Thank you.'

She followed him back into the kitchen.

'I have some elderflower cordial,' he said. 'Unless you'd like me to open the wine?'

'Oh, no. Elderflower cordial sounds lovely!'

He poured them both a glass.

'I've just got to check on dinner.'

'Can I . . .' She motioned to the garden and he nodded.

Taking her glass with her, Vanessa returned outside, walking down the herringbone path which led to a small greenhouse stuffed with plants. Everything was so neat and tidy. Vanessa believed that you could tell a lot about a person from their garden – almost as much as you could from their house – and she looked around now, clocking the fruit trees, flowers and vegetables. There was a birdbath too, and several nest boxes in secretive places.

Vanessa took in the old metal obelisks that were supporting plants in the borders. They'd seen better days, but there was a wonderful rustic charm about them, as with the heaps of terracotta pots in all shapes and sizes which stood alongside the greenhouse. They were chipped and mossy, but utterly beautiful. She also noticed the homemade willow supports for the beans and peas and the recycled galvanised tubs that were now planted with herbs, and she smiled at the elegant columbines which nodded happily along the path, their pale flowers almost luminous in the fading light.

The garden was at least three times the size of next door's and Vanessa guessed that Jonathan's grandmother had been able to purchase land from the neighbouring farmer at some stage. She'd certainly made the very best of it and Jonathan was obviously in love with it as much as his grandmother had been.

Walking around it now, Vanessa couldn't help thinking how wonderful it must be to have a manageable garden – a garden that didn't need an army of people to take care of its acres of lawn, massive hedges and elaborate borders. But she adored Orley and got so much pleasure from walking in the grounds, and she truly couldn't imagine life without it even though it was jolly hard work and caused her endless worry.

'Dinner's nearly ready,' Jonathan said, joining her.

'This is such a lovely garden,' she told him.

'I'm glad you like it. It's very special to me.'

'Do you get a lot of bird life?'

'There are two blue tit families in the nest boxes and a blackbird's nesting in the hedge over there.'

'It's a magical time of year.'

He nodded. 'I like coming out here in the evenings and listening to the nightingales in the valley.'

Vanessa smiled. Nightingales had been one of Oliver's favourite things too. She remembered a time when he'd taken her for a walk into the valley. The sky had been darkening and a cool breeze had made her shiver; she'd been on the verge of asking to return home when she'd heard that extraordinary sound for the first time: the song of the nightingale – a quizzical, complex song full of magic and mystery and so unlike anything she'd ever heard before. She'd stood transfixed, forgetting the cold of the night air with Oliver standing close behind her, his hands resting on her shoulders. They'd been there for an age as the sky changed from navy to black and the stars came out to shine upon the valley. Then they'd walked home, holding hands, without speaking, knowing that they had shared a little miracle.

'Vanessa?'

She turned to Jonathan, almost shocked to see him there.

'Sorry!' she said.

'You were miles away.'

'Just remembering something.'

'About Oliver?'

'Silly of me.' She quickly blinked away the tears that had mischievously arisen.

'Not at all,' he said kindly. 'It's not been that long, has it?'

'No, I suppose not,' she said, thinking how incredible it was that moments like that could still creep up on her and catch her unawares.

'And you were together a long time. You can't just forget a person who's been a part of your life for so long. It wouldn't be right or normal.'

Vanessa nodded, not trusting herself to speak.

'Listen,' he said, laying a hand lightly on her arm, 'I'll just switch the oven off. Take your time and come in when you're ready, okay?'

It was sweet of him to give her a moment. She needed that and she took a few deep breaths of the evening air to centre herself. Would it ever go away, this terrible grief she carried around with her? It had eased somewhat over the months, but it still weighed her down, making her ache with longing for the man she'd loved so much. Jonathan was right: you can't forget somebody you'd loved for so long just because they're no longer there. All of the feelings you had don't die with the person who has departed; they go on.

She took a moment longer, listening to a startled cry from a blackbird who obviously wanted the garden to itself at this time of night. She took the hint and walked back into Jonathan's cottage, entering the kitchen where a wonderful smell greeted her.

The small table had been set with a white damask tablecloth that Vanessa guessed to have been another hand-me-down from Jonathan's grandmother.

'Take a seat,' he said as he placed two white plates, which had been warming in the oven, on the table.

He'd made a vegetable lasagne and served it with a fresh baguette and a bowl of crisp salad leaves.

'From the greenhouse,' he said.

'It all looks delicious,' she told him.

'Let me top up your drink.'

'Thank you.'

They ate in silence for a moment before Jonathan spoke.

'So, what did you want to talk about?' he asked.

Vanessa looked up from her plate. 'You make it sound so official.'

'I just wondered if you had anything particular on your mind.'

'No, not at all,' she said, and she really didn't, although she couldn't help being curious about this man and had indeed wondered about his past, especially since Tilda had pointed out that they knew absolutely nothing about him. 'I just thought it would be nice to get to know each other a little better.'

'Okay,' he said. 'You start.'

She grinned. 'I was hoping you'd start. After all, you have the advantage. You know all about Orley and have an impressive record of each and every hat I've ever worn to the fetes.'

He laughed. 'True enough. Okay then. Where to begin?' He picked up the breadboard and offered her another slice of baguette which she took, spreading it with gloriously golden butter. 'I was born in Sussex, grew up in Sussex and will no doubt die in Sussex.'

'And that's it?' she asked.

'There's been some other stuff along the way,' he said with a wry grin.

'Then tell me about it. Have you brothers and sisters?'

'Nope. Just me.'

'And you were close to your grandma. What was she called?'

'Elsie.'

'Elsie Dacre?'

He nodded.

'That name rings a bell. Was she on any committees?'

'She was secretary for the WI for more years than I care to remember.'

'Of course! I remember her now.'

'You knew her?'

Vanessa cast her mind back. 'I once gave a talk to the WI. About the garden at Orley.'

'Yes. I remember her telling me about it.'

'I don't remember any of the details, but Elsie came up to me afterwards and said she had a terrible confession to make. I couldn't for the life of me think what it might be, but she told me that she'd taken some columbine seeds from Orley to sow in her own garden. She said she loved our garden and that she was trying to capture a little piece of it in her own.'

'And the descendants of those seeds live on today. Did you see the columbines?'

'I did. I was actually admiring them. How funny! I think there are probably little pieces of the garden at Orley scattered right across the village.'

'You're probably right.'

'I can't believe that was your grandmother. I'm so glad I met her.'

'She was a big fan of yours. She loved her local lady of the manor.'

Vanessa shook her head. The idea of having a fan was way outside her comfort zone, and as for the title 'lady of the manor', that had never sat easily either. Yes, she opened the annual fete and, yes, she was happy to give the occasional talk to a local group, but that was it. She was a private person who just happened to live in a rather extraordinary house.

'So,' she said, eager to move the subject away from her, 'have you any family of your own?'

'Er, no,' he said.

'No lady in your life?'

Jonathan took a mouthful of elderflower cordial before answering. 'I'm pretty much married to my work.'

Vanessa watched his face closely as he gave his evasive answer. 'So nobody special?'

'Not at the moment,' he said. 'Next question?'

She took a breath. So, that was the end of that particular subject, she thought. 'Have you always been a gardener?'

'Pretty much. Although it was tough at first to make a full-time living from it. I was working for a small company for a while before breaking out on my own, but it's pretty good now. I like being my own boss. It suits me.'

'And how did you become involved with your team?'

There was a pause before he answered, and he gave a little shrug. 'I believe in giving back. I knew Rod and he told me a bit about what he was doing and I got on board with it.'

'I think it's really wonderful – what you're both doing. It must feel good to make a difference.'

'I hope I do.'

'Of course you do,' she said. 'Have you seen the looks on the faces of those kids when they finish for the day? They're practically glowing and that's not just from all the fresh air. I think they have a real sense of pride in what they're doing with you.'

'You think?'

'You must know that.'

He looked thoughtful for a moment. 'It's hard to tell sometimes. You think you're making headway with a youngster, that you're really getting through to them. You show them that life can be good, different – that they can make wholesome choices.' He stopped. 'It doesn't always work out, you know. We can't save everybody.'

A sudden chill seemed to descend and a feeling of sadness encompassed her. Perhaps it had been a mistake to come here, she thought. She had no business prying into this man's private life, picking at him with her questions when he clearly wasn't happy answering them.

'I'm sorry,' she said, scraping her chair back and standing up. 'I should—'

'Vanessa – no, wait.'

'I shouldn't have come.'

'Please sit down. I'm sorry.' He got up himself and reached a hand out towards her, touching her shoulder and encouraging her to stay.

Vanessa sat back down. 'I didn't mean to upset you,' she told him.

'You didn't. It's just, well, I don't normally talk about this stuff.' He sat down again. 'Well, that's gone and ruined a perfectly nice evening, hasn't it?'

She gave him a sympathetic look. 'No, it hasn't.'

'You see why I stick to plants now? I don't do company well.'

'Yes you do,' she said. 'The way you talk to those kids is pretty amazing. You have something special with them. And we've been getting along all right, haven't we? Until I started probing you, that is. I'm sorry about that. Shall we just erase the last ten minutes and start again? I'd really like to do that if I haven't put you off talking to me forever.'

'It would take more than that to put me off you,' he said, and there was something in his tone that put her at her ease, knowing that he valued her friendship.

They finished their meal and then Jonathan led her into the tiny living room at the front of the cottage.

'Make yourself at home,' he said. 'Can I get you a cup of tea or coffee?'

'A tea would be lovely,' she said.

'Coming right up.' He left the room and Vanessa's eyes began to dart around as they had done in the garden. His shelves were crammed with books and Vanessa was delighted to see that many of them were books about gardening – everything from encyclopaedias and journals, to guides on how to plant or prune and manuals about landscaping.

After perusing the shelves for a couple of moments, her designer's eye noted the old-fashioned wallpaper of the room, which was a sweet floral pattern from, she guessed, the 1980s. It was actually very similar to a modern one she'd seen recently which had been incredibly expensive.

But this one was lovelier because there was a mellowness to it that only age could bring.

The curtains, which weren't yet drawn against the night sky, were Sanderson, she thought, a classic country style that suited a property of this period. The colours were faded and she guessed there wasn't a lot in the cottage that was Jonathan's choice. It was very much a hand-me-down home, but he seemed completely at ease there and she guessed that his real home was the garden anyway.

Turning around, she saw a beautiful if battered-looking notebook sitting on a side table. It was bulging slightly because it was filled with newspaper clippings and loose pieces of paper. Curious, Vanessa opened it and saw that it was a journal. Was it Jonathan's? She'd never seen his handwriting before, but guessed that it must be. He had nice writing. It was slightly forward-sloping with big loops. He wrote in blue ink. She liked blue ink. There was something tremendously beautiful about blue ink in a world of black typeface and she couldn't resist reading a few lines.

July 21st – the garden is parched and the soil cracking. No rain for weeks now and the water butts are long empty.

So, it was a gardening journal, she thought as she read on.

R not good today. I stopped work early and came home.

Who was R? Rod perhaps?

A teaspoon clattered onto the floor in the kitchen, causing Vanessa to jump and close the journal before being discovered.

It was then that something caught her eye: a framed engraving hanging on the wall behind a standard lamp. She walked towards it. At first, it appeared to be of a man striding across a field, a hilly landscape threaded through with a river far below him but, on closer inspection, Vanessa saw that the arm she had thought was merely swinging was, in fact, sowing seeds and that he was carrying a large container strapped around his neck.

'You like it?' Jonathan asked, coming into the room with a tray on which sat two fat pottery mugs of tea, a sugar bowl and a milk jug.

'I do. Who's it by?'

'It's a Clare Leighton print from the nineteen thirties. It's called "Sowing". From her book – *The Farmer's Year*.'

'It's wonderful. There's a real sense of his movement, isn't there? He's so graceful. It's like a kind of dance over the land.'

Jonathan nodded. 'I like the clouds. They're so alive.'

'And the church amongst the huddle of houses in the valley. It's really lovely. We don't have many engravings at Orley. I wish we did. They're special, aren't they?'

Vanessa's eyes drifted away from the picture and looked at the bookshelves again, and that's when she saw a small photo frame in silver and black. It was a portrait of a young woman, a very beautiful young woman with short fair hair and a pretty smile. She turned to Jonathan, who seemed to have clocked her looking at it and turned away. Vanessa's mouth opened but she didn't say anything, remembering the awkward scene in the kitchen. It wasn't her place to probe into this man's life and so she tactfully returned her gaze to the books before her.

They talked for a while about their favourite gardening titles and she watched as Jonathan pulled down volume after volume, opening up pages to share his favourite photographs and reading out passages that were special to him. She noticed that many of the pages were dog-eared. She did that too, which used to annoy Oliver intensely even if it was a brand-new novel and not one of the ancient tomes which belonged in the library at Orley. She knew better than to manhandle those. But Jonathan had no such qualms when it came to making a book his own and she saw that some passages were underlined and that he used empty seed packets in lieu of bookmarks.

'Anyway,' he said at last, returning one of the books back to the shelf, 'you were going to tell me about yourself.'

'Was I?'

He nodded.

'Well, I'm the hat-wearing lady of the manor,' she said with a smile.

He gave her a quizzical look. 'There's more to you than that.'

'I'm not so sure.'

'What makes you say that?'

Her hands surrounded her mug of tea in a tight embrace, finding a comfort in the warmth. 'Everything changes, doesn't it?'

'All the time.'

'I find that hard.' Their eyes met and she saw him swallow. 'But one gets on.'

'And you have two wonderful daughters,' he prompted.

'Yes,' she said. 'I'm sorry you haven't met them yet.'

He shrugged. 'That's okay.'

'I'd like you to, and I'd like them to meet you.'

'Then I'm sure we will,' he said.

She looked anxiously around the room as if trying to fasten onto something they could talk about without doing too much damage.

'I'm sorry,' she said at last. 'This hasn't been very successful, has it?'

'What do you mean?'

'I mean, this was meant to be about getting to know each other and I'm afraid that I upset you with my questions and I haven't been able to answer yours.'

'It's been a complete disaster, hasn't it?'

She was about to nod, but saw that he was smiling, and there was a definite twinkle in his bright hazel eyes which made her smile too.

'Listen,' he said, 'you've been through a hard time losing Oliver and it takes a while to bounce back from such things. Don't put so much pressure on yourself. You're a good person, doing wonderful things for your community.'

'I am?'

'Of course you are.' He gave a little laugh. 'Have you any idea of the difference you're making to me and the team just by letting us dig a bit of earth?'

'But you're helping me.'

'Then that's what I'd call a success. Just as this evening has been.'

She gave a wry grin. 'How can you say that?'

'How can you not?' he asked. 'You've seen my garden. We've established that you knew my grandmother, you've looked at my treasured gardening books and I sincerely hope you enjoyed my cooking.'

'Oh, I did!' she said quickly.

'There you go then. That's not too bad as evenings go, is it?'

'No, I don't suppose it is.'

They chatted a little while longer, keeping comfortably to subjects like books, music and the latest gossip from Elhurst, and the atmosphere between them was definitely more relaxed. Finally, Vanessa checked her watch and stood up.

'It's been a lovely evening,' she said, 'but it's time I was getting back.'

'Dolly keeping tabs on you, is she?'

'I wouldn't be surprised. She doesn't miss much.' Jonathan escorted her to the front door. 'Thank you for dinner.'

'You're welcome. I'm really glad we did this.'

'Me too.' She opened the door.

'Wait just one moment,' he said, disappearing into the kitchen.

Vanessa was about to ask him what he was doing when he returned a moment later with the bottle of wine.

'Here. It's wasted on me, I'm afraid.'

'You sure you don't want it? For guests?'

'I never keep alcohol in the house.' He handed her the bottle.

'Okay,' she said. 'If you're sure.' She turned to leave and he followed her out, standing on the pavement as she got into her car.

'See you soon,' he called, and she waved before starting the engine.

It was with mixed feelings that she left Beeches that night. She'd sincerely enjoyed Jonathan's company but, as she drove back through the village and turned into the valley towards Orley, she couldn't quite work out who had been holding back the most that evening: herself or him.

Chapter 13

'You were out. All night!'

Vanessa jumped as her mother-in-law crept into the kitchen. Turning around to face Dolly, she noted the red face glaring back at her as if the old woman had been hoarding all the resentment of the night before, ready to unleash now.

'You're exaggerating. I was home well before eleven. Not that it's any of your business,' Vanessa said, turning her back on Dolly as she cleared away the breakfast things.

'It jolly well is my business whilst you're living under my roof.'

Vanessa didn't rise to the bait. They'd had this argument so many times in the past and she didn't have the energy for it this morning. Besides, she was in a good mood. The more she thought about her evening with Jonathan, the more she realised how much she liked him. He was a good man. A kind man. And how often did you find one of those? Okay, so their conversation had hit a few walls, but perhaps they'd been going too fast too soon.

Too fast too soon. Honestly, it was as if she were dating again, which she certainly was not. She must stop putting such notions in her head. They were friends – friends who still knew relatively little about each other, but who were content with things the way they were.

'Where were you anyway?' Dolly asked.

'Are you still here?'

'Of course I'm still here. Where else would I be?' She made a derisive noise.

Vanessa could think of all sorts of amusing responses to that particular question, but held her tongue.

'Well,' Dolly said at last, 'I can't be standing here all day. Hermione's on her way.'

'Don't let me keep you,' Vanessa said, deciding to steer clear of Dolly's old crony. Hermione Warbouys was one of Dolly's oldest friends and would come to Orley every week or so. Vanessa wasn't really sure what they talked about, but she had a feeling that she got more than a few mentions judging by the evil looks she received from Hermione whenever they happened to cross paths. One thing Vanessa took comfort in was the fact that Oliver hadn't been able to stand Hermione.

'The Witch of Ridwell', he'd called her, because she used to terrify him as a child and things hadn't got much better when he'd grown up. Now, she was terrifying Vanessa.

Perhaps it would be better if she took her cup of tea into the garden, she thought, moving quickly in order to get away from Dolly and avoid Hermione, but she didn't move fast enough because she ran right into Hermione as she opened the front door.

'Oh, it's you,' Hermione said. Like Dolly, she was in her late eighties.

'Good morning, Hermione,' Vanessa said politely. She had always been polite to this woman even though she'd never received a civil word from her. 'What a lovely morning. I'm just on my way out.'

'With a cup of tea?'

'Yes.'

The old woman tutted. 'And what does Dolly have to say about you taking the family china out of the house?'

'She can say what she likes.' Vanessa gave a little smile and walked down the path to the sound of Hermione harrumphing. She would no doubt enjoy her morning with Dolly all the more now that Vanessa had given her something to grumble about.

The May morning was still and perfect. The sky was a heavenly blue with a few wispy clouds playing over the distant Downs, and the air was warm enough for rolled-up sleeves. The wisteria on the south-east corner of the house was at its peak right now, its rich purple flowers vibrant against the golden stone. Wisteria had always been a favourite with Oliver. He used to lean out of the mullioned windows and scoop the drooping flowers in his large hands and inhale their scent. Vanessa smiled as she remembered, and then went out into the walled garden.

She liked coming here in between visits from Jonathan and his team, walking around to see their progress. Now, she sat on an old metal bench which was slowly rusting away into the ground. It was the type of bench that was kinder on the eye than it was on the bottom and Vanessa wished she'd brought a cushion with her. What would Hermione have said about that? she wondered with a rebellious grin.

She cast her eyes over the garden, taking in the glory of the raised beds, which would still have been a tangle of weeds had she not met Jonathan.

'Jonathan.' She spoke the name softly, thinking of the night before. She still couldn't help feeling embarrassed when she thought about it. Instead of easy conversation, they'd done an uneasy dance around each other. And yet there had been moments when she'd felt a certain warmth between them, like when they were in the garden as the light was beginning to fade and the air was cooling. Perhaps they should never talk in any place other than a garden. Maybe that was their natural setting.

She was just finishing her tea when she saw a young man entering the garden. He was wearing ripped jeans and sunglasses, which seemed a very odd look first thing in the morning in a country garden.

'Can I help you?' Vanessa asked, instantly on her feet and on her guard. Maybe he was one of Jonathan's lot, although he looked too expensive, she thought, noticing his designer jacket.

'You live here?' he asked.

'Yes.'

'I can't get in.'

'Why do you want to get in?' she asked, wondering if he was a new breed of burglar who asked for the key first.

'I'm here to see Tilly.'

Vanessa was immediately on alert. Nobody but her family or her music fans called her Tilly. Was this young man somebody from the press hoping to get a story?

'Nobody's answering the door,' he said and Vanessa thanked her lucky stars that Dolly hadn't answered. Heaven only knew what would have become of the young man if she had.

'Who are you?'

'Morton.'

'Morton?'

'Morton Singer.'

She wasn't sure if that was a name or a job description. It was hard to tell. 'And you know Tilly?'

He slowly took off his glasses and gave her a long slow smile. 'You could say that.'

'Oh,' Vanessa said, wishing she hadn't asked.

'I'm a producer,' he said.

'Oh!' Vanessa said, mightily relieved.

Morton Singer put his glasses back on and then motioned towards the house. 'Shall we find Tilly?'

His confident manner almost had her marching straight to the house in search of her daughter, but she checked herself in time. 'Is she expecting you?'

'Probably not. She's been ignoring all my texts and emails.'

'Then it's likely she doesn't want to see you,' Vanessa said.

Morton Singer scraped a toe into the gravel path and dug his hands deep into the pockets of his expensive-looking jacket.

'It could be in her best interests to see me,' he said, staring down at the gravel.

Vanessa examined him. She wasn't at all sure about what she saw before her and certainly wasn't going to take his word on things.

'How did you get here?'

'I drove down this morning. From Knightsbridge,' he added, as if that might make all the difference in the world to his reception.

'Where's your car?'

'Beside a really big hedge.'

So he'd parked in the lane, which probably meant that Dolly had clocked him.

'Follow me,' she said, leading the way back to the house but not inviting him in. 'Wait here.' She went inside, closing the front door on him.

She stood in the hallway a moment, seeing if she could hear the sound of the piano being played. Sure enough, Tilda was at the keyboard in the drawing room.

'Darling?' Vanessa said as she entered. 'Do you know somebody called Morton Singer?'

Tilda stopped playing and looked up, her expression one of shock. 'Why do you ask?'

'Because he's here.'

She stood up. 'Where?'

'In the porch. He says he wants to see you. He said it's in your best interests to see him.'

'Oh, did he?'

'That's what he said. So, you do know him?'

'We met a few times. He's a producer.'

'Yes – he said. Look, I can get rid of him if you don't want to see him.'

Tilda shook her head. 'It's okay, Mum. I'll see him.'

'Well, if you're sure.' Vanessa watched as her daughter's hands flew to her hair, tidying up what didn't really need to be tidied. 'I'll be in here if you need me, okay?'

Laurence had just come off the phone as he opened the window in the room he was using as his office in the north-east corner of the house. It was a glorious morning and, although he'd set up a couple of meetings with clients, he couldn't help feeling that he'd wasted his time being inside. He gazed across the front lawn and out into the fields and wondered if he could slope off for the day. He could take his mobile with him and then he could kid himself that he was working instead of just walking.

As he debated the ethics of this with himself, he noticed a strange young man walking up and down the path at the front of the house. He was wearing ripped jeans, dark glasses and had the sort of hair that managed to look untidy and affected at the same time. Laurence watched him for a moment, wondering who he was – he couldn't even begin to imagine. But it didn't take long before he found out who the man was visiting.

'What are you doing here, Morton?' Tilda said. Laurence couldn't see her, but he recognised her voice instantly.

'Nice to see you too,' the young man said.

There was a pause.

'You never answered my messages,' Morton complained. 'Where'd you go?'

'I've not been anywhere.'

'You're telling me. You vanished off the face of the earth. What the hell happened?'

'What do you mean, what happened? You know the business. You know what it's like.'

'Yep,' he said. 'It's pretty brutal out there.'

'And it's not much of a compliment if you've only just noticed I've not been around for a while.'

'I noticed as soon as you were gone.'

'Liar!'

'I did!' he protested. 'It was after the Manchester gig, wasn't it? You got pulled—'

'Don't say it. Don't come here and say that sort of thing.'

There was a moment's silence.

'Listen,' Morton said at last, 'I'm sorry I've not been down sooner. I've been busy – that's all – but you've been very much on my mind.'

'Oh, really? Well, I'm retired from that business now.'

'You're joking, right?'

'Why would I joke?'

'Because somebody with your talent doesn't just shut themselves away like this. You've got to get back out there.'

'God, you sound like Laurence.'

Laurence flinched at the mention of his name and then grinned. So, Tilda *had* been listening to him, then.

'Who's Laurence?'

'Nobody.'

Laurence frowned, but tried not to take it personally.

'Look, I want to work with you, Tilly,' Morton said.

'Please don't call me that.'

'What should I call you?'

'History?'

'Ha ha. Listen, I've got my own studio now,' he went on, 'and I've got a great team and I'm ready to do something new and exciting and the first person I thought of was you.'

'Then you'd better think of a second person.'

'Tilly!'

'Don't call—'

'Sorry,' he said quickly. 'Is it Matilda?'

'Just Tilda.'

'Can I have a cup of coffee, Tilda?'

'I suppose,' she said.

Laurence watched as they disappeared. They were coming into the house and he couldn't hear them anymore, so he left his office and walked out onto the landing just as Tilda and Morton were crossing the entrance hall.

'Everyone still talks about you,' Morton was saying. 'You haven't been forgotten, you know.'

'I really don't care,' she said.

'Yeah, you sound like you don't care.'

Laurence was just about to lean over the railing as much as he dared when his father suddenly appeared on the landing.

'What are you doing?' his dad asked him.

'Shush! I'm trying to listen.'

'To what?'

'To Tilda and some guy called Morton.'

'And should you be doing that?'

'I am doing that.'

His father sidled up to him and peered over the stair railing.

'Dad! They'll see you.'

'They're not looking up,' he said. 'What is that guy wearing?'

'Haven't you seen ripped jeans before?'

'Not ripped like that. It's obscene!'

Laurence couldn't help smiling. 'He's some friend of Tilda's from the music industry. It sounds like he wants to work with her again.'

'And does she want to work with him?'

'I don't think so. She sounded mad that he was here.'

'You going to wade in?'

'No!' Laurence said in outrage.

'Then what's the point of listening in if you're not going to do something?'

Laurence pondered this. 'I want to know what she's going to do.'

There was a pause. 'Because you care about her?' his father asked at last.

Laurence flashed a look at him. 'Sure. I care about her.'

Marcus nodded and Laurence realised that it was the first personal question his dad had asked him in a long time.

'She's a nice girl,' his father added.

'I know, and she's got this fierce talent, but she's too afraid to use it again.'

'Fear can often stop us from reaching our full potential,' his father said. Laurence looked at him again. His face was solemn and Laurence wondered if he was going to elaborate, but he became distracted when Skinny the cat made her way onto the landing.

'Hey, she's not looking so skinny now,' Laurence observed.

'I'm taking good care of her.'

'So I see.'

'We'll have to rename her.'

'I kind of like Skinny,' Laurence said.

'I was thinking of Silky. Her coat's really improved since I started feeding her properly.'

'I prefer Skinny. It's got character.'

His father smiled. Actually smiled. It took a moment for Laurence to take this in but, before he could do or say anything, his father had bent to pick the cat up and was on his way. A missed opportunity, he thought. He might have been able to have an actual conversation with his dad, but Marcus was heading back to his room now and the moment was lost.

Laurence returned to his office but he couldn't settle down to any work. He kept wondering what was happening downstairs with Tilda and, when he heard a car start up in the lane and realised that Tilda's visitor must have left, he just couldn't help himself.

Leaving his office, he walked back out onto the landing before heading downstairs.

'Tilda?' he called.

'Yes?' She appeared in the doorway of the living room.

'Who was that?' Laurence asked as he came into the room.

She frowned at him. 'Why do you ask?'

'I heard him talking about your music.'

'Were you earwigging?' Her forehead wrinkled in displeasure.

'Er, kind of. Sorry.'

'God! I can't get any privacy in this place!'

'I couldn't help overhearing.'

'Yes you could – you could have gone to another part of the house. It's big enough.'

'I'm sorry. I guess I was listening because I was worried about you.'

She stared at him as if trying to work him out. 'Why would you be worried about me?'

He shrugged and suddenly realised that he didn't know what to say. *Be honest*, he told himself. *It's the only thing that works.*

'Because I care about you.'

'You don't even know me,' she said, sounding alarmed as she turned and walked towards the window.

Undeterred, Laurence followed, watching as Tilda started picking up old magazines and leaflets and stuffing them into a magazine rack by the coffee table.

'It's funny,' he said, 'because I feel that I do know you.'

'Oh, really? Well, that's creepy.'

He grimaced. Perhaps he'd been a little too honest, he thought. 'Sorry,' he said, 'I really didn't mean to sound creepy.'

Tilda stopped torturing the magazine rack and looked up at him. Her usually pale face was flushed.

'I know,' she said. 'You're a good man and I'm just in a foul mood.' She grimaced down at the carpet and then looked back up. 'Sorry.'

'No need to apologise.'

'I'm mad at Morton – not you.'

'Why are you mad at him?'

'Because he's trying to drag me back into the music business.'

'And that's such a bad thing?'

Her mouth parted slightly. 'Yes,' she said, her voice barely above a whisper.

Laurence nodded. 'And you told him that?'

'I think I made it abundantly clear how I feel about it.'

'Then you can relax. He's definitely gone. I saw his car speeding back towards Elhurst.'

'But Morton's the kind of person who doesn't take no for an answer. He's bound to be back sooner or later.'

'Then tell him again.'

'I thought you wanted me to go back into the industry too?' she said.

'I didn't say that.'

'Yes you did.'

'I said I didn't think you should turn your back on your talent.'

'Isn't that the same thing?'

He shrugged. 'I don't know. Do you need the music industry in order to write and produce your own music? I thought you just needed a YouTube channel these days.'

'I wouldn't ever go back,' she said. 'Not after what happened in Manchester.'

'What happened there?'

She looked down at her nails and took a deep breath. 'I only play for myself these days.'

Laurence nodded. She wasn't going to fill in the gap about Manchester then.

'Listen,' he said, 'I'd better get back to work.'

She looked up. 'Thanks,' she said.

'What for?'

'For listening. You're a good listener.'

'I thought you hated me for earwigging?' he said with a teasing grin.

'Yeah, well, maybe you can do slightly less of it in the future.'

'You got it,' he said, giving her a little nod before leaving the room.

As soon as Laurence was back in his office, he just couldn't help himself. He had to know what had happened in Manchester and so he Googled.

Tilly. Summer Song. Manchester.

The first thing that came up was a link to her performing on stage. It was a sweet, lively performance with Tilda leaping around the stage in a yellow dress, her blonde hair flying around her face and the crowd cheering. What was so bad about that? He scrolled through the comments and there was the usual stuff – the compliments, the coarseness, and the stuff written by totally insane people who shouldn't be left alone with a keyboard and Internet connection. He shook his head, hoping she hadn't read all this because it was enough to make the strongest person bury their heads.

But there was one comment that halted him.

Check out this link! Tilly really knows how to sing.

Laurence followed the link to another video. It seemed to follow on from Tilly's performance of 'Summer Song'. She was talking to the crowd and he turned the volume up to listen to her.

'*Thank you so much! It's been a real pleasure to perform "Summer Song" for you here today, but there's another song I'd like to sing for you now. Would you like to hear it?*'

The crowd cheered and Laurence watched as the musicians behind her shrugged shoulders and exchanged baffled looks. One of the guitarists walked towards Tilly and whispered something in her ear but she simply shook her head and waved a hand at him. This, Laurence thought, definitely wasn't part of the routine.

'*The song is called "Forgive Me"*,' Tilly told the crowd.

And then she began to sing without any musical accompaniment. Her voice was pure and beautiful and the song was moving and melancholy – nothing like the pop piece she had just performed. At first, the crowd kept cheering, but then it went quiet. Were they listening to her, rapt by the beauty of the song and her voice? Laurence could feel himself going tense as he waited to find out what happened.

And then the booing started. It was just vague background noise at first, barely audible, but then it grew with the speed and malevolence that only a crowd can manufacture. But Tilly kept on singing, her angelic voice rising above the appalling noise below her – and then the video ended.

'What?' Laurence cried at the screen. What had happened next? He needed to know.

Then he saw a link to another video. This one looked as if it had been taken on a mobile phone and was a bit shaky, but it followed on pretty much from where the other had ended. Tilly was still singing and the crowd was still booing. The guitarist who had approached her before now laid a hand on her shoulder. Some people emerged from backstage and Laurence watched as one of them took the microphone from Tilly. She tried to grab it back but another man came between them and then took hold of Tilly's arm and led her off the stage. The video ended.

Laurence sat back in his chair and let out a huge sigh.

'My God,' he said. What had she been thinking? But maybe just having that live audience in front of her had persuaded her to take a chance. It was a brave and foolish thing to have done and Laurence admired her tremendously, but he could see how it might have put her off ever performing again. That crowd had been swelling with love and adoration one minute and then boiling over with hatred the next. And why? Because a young woman had dared to shake off her manacles and sing a song that came from her heart. They hadn't wanted that.

That's not what they'd come for and they hadn't given her a chance, and neither had the team backstage. Laurence could only imagine what it must have felt like to have been up on that stage, giving the very essence of your being only to be humiliated and then dragged off.

He shook his head. Now he was beginning to understand the extent of the problem.

When Laurence had found her in the living room just after Morton Singer left, Tilda had quickly hidden something from him. Now, she removed it from underneath the book on the coffee table. It was a CD. Silver-bright and dangerous. She looked at it for a moment, as if it was a foreign object and she was trying to make out what she should do with it.

'Just listen to it,' Morton had said, handing it to her before he left. She had made no promises, but her curiosity was getting the better of her and so she slid it into the music centre in the corner of the room, making sure it was at a volume that could only be heard by her as she perched on a nearby chair.

She didn't recognise the piece at first, but then it all came back to her. It must have been from the recording he'd done of her in the hotel just before the Manchester gig. They'd been fooling around and he'd been recording her on his phone. She hadn't thought anything of it at the time but, from those brief lines of hers, he'd made a song.

She listened to it twice through. It wasn't 'Summer Song', that was for sure. This was a much purer sound – a simple song full of emotion. This was the real Tilda. And she couldn't stop the tears from falling because as much as she protested that she didn't want to be a part of the music industry anymore, and as much as she said that she wasn't going to write and perform any more songs, she knew in her heart that it was what she wanted to do more than anything in the world.

Chapter 14

The acid-green flowers of the euphorbias were looking absolutely perfect, Vanessa thought as she walked through the garden. Placed next to the blowsy blooms of the pearly-pink peonies, they seemed almost incandescent. Love-in-a-mist was rippling through the borders, and clematis was throwing out its flowers, smothering the arches in the south garden.

Oliver had once told Vanessa never to overlook the importance of verticals in the garden and so Orley was filled with towering spires of mystical-blue delphiniums, lemon-yellow hollyhocks, white lupins and magenta larkspurs, which caught the eye and provided interest at a level that many gardeners disregarded.

Vanessa had learned so much from Oliver over the years and, although her main interest would always be interior design, she had come to share his passion for the garden, which was why she was so thrilled that Jonathan and his team were helping to restore it.

Walking into the walled garden now, she caught Jonathan's eye and he waved her over.

'Hey, what do you think of these supports for the beans and peas?'

'You made these?' she asked, looking at the impressive structures that the team were placing in one of the raised beds.

'I merely supervised,' he told her.

'They're beautiful. I love them.'

'Remember all the pruning we did? Never throw anything away. All these supports have come from around the garden.'

'They're great,' she said. 'They've got a real Beatrix Potter feel to them.'

'Yes, well as long as Benjamin Bunny doesn't pay us a visit! We're about to direct-sow some French and runner beans. I think we've had the last of the frosts, but I like to wait until the end of May to be absolutely sure.'

Vanessa watched as Ryan and Oz worked on the bean and pea structure, making one long support system whilst Andy and Jenna placed wigwam-like constructions in each corner of the raised bed. It truly was a work of art – both functional and beautiful, and didn't that make for the perfect garden?

'We've got some flower seeds and herbs to plant amongst the vegetables. Things like chives and marigolds, which not only look great but are fantastic companion plants and help deter pests,' Jonathan told her. 'Jenna? Tell Vanessa why we're planting the chives.'

The girl looked up from the wigwam she was trying to make straight. 'In with the carrots,' she said.

'Not where. Why?' Jonathan said.

'You testing me?'

'Yep!'

Jenna rolled her eyes. 'It helps improve the flavour and keeps away carrot flies.'

'That's right.'

She gave a smug smile and got back to work.

'I knew that too!' Andy chimed in.

'I'd hope so,' Jonathan said.

'Test me next time.'

'I will,' Jonathan promised, a touch of pride colouring his voice.

'That's really impressive,' Vanessa said.

'It's not just about manual labour here, you know,' Jonathan boasted. 'We do try and teach them something too. Something they can take away and hopefully use in gardens of their own one day.'

'Gardens of our own?' Andy cried. 'We've got a stairwell we share with five other flats. No chance of growing anything anywhere.'

'Have you got a nice sunny windowsill somewhere?' Jonathan asked.

Andy looked unsure. 'I suppose. Maybe. I'd have to check.'

'Try a few herbs in a pot.'

'I could try growing some pot.'

'Basil would be better for you,' Jonathan said and Vanessa couldn't help but smile.

'Hey, I've got a good joke about pot,' Andy began.

'Unless it's about a pot used for growing things in, we're not interested,' Rod warned.

Andy rolled his eyes and got on with his work.

'Listen,' Vanessa said once everyone was concentrating on the garden again, 'I hope you won't mind, but I thought it was time that my daughters met you. I feel so rude that I've not introduced them yet.'

'That's okay,' Jonathan said, wiping his hands down the front of his corduroy trousers. 'I'm sure they're busy young women.'

'That's no excuse not to say hello.'

'So, you want to do this now?'

She nodded. 'If we could.'

'Where do we go?' He glanced towards the house and Vanessa thought she could see apprehension in his eyes.

'I'll bring them out here,' she told him. 'I'd like them to meet everyone.'

'Okay.'

'Right,' she said, 'I'll do that now.' She bit her lip, suddenly feeling anxious.

'You okay?'

'Yes. I'll be back in a minute.'

He nodded. 'I'm looking forward to it.'

Vanessa gave a weak smile. She'd been wanting to do this for weeks but, now that the moment was finally upon her, she couldn't help feeling intensely nervous, which was silly really because she was just introducing some of the dearest people in her life to one another. Why should that make her nervy?

She walked back to the house, barely noticing the swallows wheeling and screaming above her.

'Tilda?' she called as she entered the house. 'Jassy?'

'We're in here, Mum!' Jassy called back, and Vanessa entered the living room.

'Ready?' she said.

'Let's get this done,' Jassy said.

'Well, you might sound more enthusiastic about it,' Vanessa tutted, annoyed by her daughter's tone.

'I just mean I want to get back to my work.'

'I'm not going to keep you long, don't worry. Are you ready, Tilda?'

Tilda nodded. 'Shall we go?'

Vanessa led the way back out into the garden.

'So, Mum – with you introducing us like this, does that mean you like this guy?' Jassy asked, peering at her with those intense blue eyes of hers.

'What?' Vanessa could feel her face heating up under the scrutiny of her daughter. 'Jonathan is a part of life at Orley now and I think you should meet him.'

'You do like him!'

'Well, of course I like him. He's a good and kind man.'

'And handsome?'

'What's that got to do with anything?' She saw Jasmine cast a glance at Tilda and Vanessa wondered what was going through their minds. She was about to introduce her daughters to a man. A man who wasn't their father. But he was a gardener, a friend. Did Jassy and Tilda think that she was in a relationship with him?

'Listen,' she said. 'Jonathan Dacre is a friend. A good friend. Nothing more. He's working here with his team and he's doing us a very great favour in the process. The walled garden hasn't looked this good since your father was able to take care of it.' She paused, the mention of Oliver shaking her a little.

'It's all right, Mum. We didn't mean anything,' Tilda said.

'You said to me that they had dinner together,' Jassy said to Tilda.

'We did have dinner together. I told you – we're friends. That's what friends do.' She looked from one to the other. 'Look, girls, if you feel uneasy about this—'

Tilda reached a hand out and touched her mother's arm. 'We don't,' she said with a smile. 'We want you to be happy, Mum, and if Jonathan is a friend, that's fine. And if he's more than a fr—'

'But he isn't.'

'But that's fine too,' Tilda said.

'Well, that's very kind of you to say, Tilda, but it's not something you need to think about.' Vanessa moved on, picking up her pace.

They reached the walled garden a few moments later and everyone looked up as they entered.

'There are so many of them,' Jassy said.

'It's a good turnout today,' Vanessa said. 'Come on. Let me introduce you.'

'Which is Jonathan?' Jassy asked. 'That one with spiky hair and a nose ring?'

Tilda elbowed her sister in the ribs just as Jonathan approached.

'Hello,' he said, stretching to shake both Tilda's and Jassy's hands.

'Girls – this is Jonathan. Jonathan – this is Tilda and Jassy,' she said, indicating each in turn.

'You've been working really hard out here,' Tilda observed. 'It looks great.'

'We do what we can,' Jonathan said.

'I should come and paint you all,' Jassy declared.

'Please do!'

'But I don't like painting outside. Too many flies.'

Jonathan laughed. 'I agree!'

The girls then met Rod and the rest of the team. The boys seemed particularly keen to meet Tilda and Jassy and it wasn't long before the inevitable happened. It began with Andy whispering something to Jenna, pushing her to say something.

'He wants to know if you're Tilly,' Jenna said quietly.

'I used to be,' Tilda said.

'What's that mean?' Andy asked, finding the courage to speak to her at last.

'It means that I'm a piano teacher these days.'

'No, really?' Andy said.

Tilda nodded. 'Yes, really.'

'Can I have your autograph?'

'And me,' Oz added, coming forward. 'I'm Oz and I'd still take you out for a drink even if you're just a piano teacher these days.'

'Right!' Jonathan shouted, clapping his hands together. 'I think it's time we got back to work.'

The team groaned.

'Things were just getting friendly,' Oz moaned.

'Yeah, and that's why it's time you grabbed that hoe and got to work in the raised bed,' Rod said. 'Go on now, lad!'

'Spoilsport!' Oz said, winking at Tilda, who gave him a smile, Vanessa couldn't help but notice. Now that was something she had naively overlooked: she was introducing her two daughters to a group of young offenders. But wouldn't it be awfully hypocritical of her to prevent her daughters from seeing who they liked when she'd so recently reprimanded the ladies in the post office for judging these young people without even knowing them? Still, the thought of her Tilda running around with a young man like Oz – as funny and endearing as he might be – was enough to bring her out in hives, she had to admit.

'Thanks, everyone,' she said, raising an arm to guide her daughters away.

'I might come and paint you after all,' Jassy said.

'Please do,' Jonathan said.

Was it her imagination or was Oz now eyeing up Jassy? Vanessa wondered.

'I think you'd better stick to painting in the oast house,' she whispered to Jassy.

'Why?' Jassy said loud enough to turn the heads of the team.

'Too many flies,' Vanessa said. 'Way too many flies out here.'

Jassy looked up and down the garden as if trying to spot them.

They'd just left the walled garden when Jonathan caught up with them.

'Hey!' he said. 'Are you forgetting something?'

Vanessa turned to look at him. 'I – er – am I?'

'Wasn't I going to meet somebody else? Dolly, isn't it?'

'You're introducing him to Grandma?' Tilda asked.

'Oh my God!' Jassy exclaimed. 'Good luck with that!'

Vanessa sighed. 'Run along, you two,' she said as if talking to two young kids rather than grown-up daughters.

'I'll see you later, Mum,' Tilda said. 'It was good to meet you, Jonathan.'

'You too,' he said.

'Jassy – haven't you got somewhere you need to be?'

Jassy shrugged. 'Not in a hurry.'

'Oh, I thought you were. Haven't you got something you should be painting?'

She frowned and then, finally, it seemed to click. 'Oh, right!' And she leaned forward to whisper something into her mother's ear before leaving.

'What was that about?' Jonathan asked.

'Nothing,' Vanessa said.

'So, you want to introduce me to Dolly?'

'Let's do it another day, shall we?'

'Why?' he asked. 'I'm all buoyed up after meeting your girls – who are wonderful, by the way.'

'Thank you.'

'So why stop there? I want to meet everyone.' He grinned and then narrowed his eyes. 'Vanessa?'

'I just feel . . .'

'What?' he asked softly.

'Jonathan!' Jenna's voice cried out from the direction of the walled garden. 'Nat's cut himself. There's blood everywhere!'

'Oh, crikey! Look – wait here, I'll be right back.'

Vanessa watched as Jonathan ran towards the walled garden and decided to make the most of the opportunity to flee, finding a favourite spot in the south garden and sitting on the bench which overlooked one of the herbaceous borders. It was a secluded spot where one could see but not be seen and it had been a favourite place of Oliver's. After a long day's work, the two of them would often walk out into the soft summer evenings and sit there side by side, listening to the last of the birdsong as the garden slowly sank into darkness.

Sitting there now, her fingers plaiting themselves together, Vanessa could feel the presence of her husband. He was always so close to her when she was in the garden and, if she looked out across the lawn, she could almost imagine him walking towards her, his long stride eating up the grass until he was by her side.

'All right if I sit here and hold your hand?' he'd ask her.

'I think that would be all right,' she'd reply.

Thirty years of hand-holding, she suddenly thought, and how it pained her that there would be no more. She looked down at her hands. She still wore her wedding ring. Her engagement ring, which was a large emerald-cut diamond, lived in a jewellery box in her bedroom. She didn't wear it when she was in the garden for fear of losing it. But she'd never be without her wedding ring. In fact, it hadn't left her finger since Oliver had placed it there on their wedding day, sliding the slim gold band on with such love in his eyes that it made her gasp just to remember it.

She twisted the ring on her finger now and wished with all her heart that she could bring him back. That perhaps there'd been some sort of mistake and she'd merely imagined the last couple of years, and that she'd walk across the lawn back to the house and would hear his voice calling to her.

'There you are! Where've you been all this time?'

'In the garden,' she'd explain.

And he'd laugh. 'I thought I'd lost you!'

'I thought I'd lost *you*!'

'Silly girl,' he'd chide, and they'd laugh.

Oh, how she wanted to be able to laugh.

'There you are!' a voice startled her out of her reverie. But it wasn't Oliver's longed-for voice – it was Jonathan's. 'I couldn't find you.'

She looked up at him, blinking back the tears which had risen as she'd thought of her husband.

'Everything okay?' Jonathan asked.

She nodded. 'Nat okay?'

'Yeah. He had a little accident with a pair of secateurs, but we've got him all plastered up. May I?' He motioned to the bench and Vanessa nodded, feeling the weight of the seat change as he sat down. She'd never sat there with another man before and she couldn't help feeling that she was somehow betraying Oliver's memory.

'You – er – seem anxious about something,' Jonathan said.

'I'm fine.'

'Really?'

She nodded.

'Okay,' Jonathan said, leaning back on the bench, his long legs stretched out in front of him. 'I'll just sit here until you tell me what's wrong.'

Vanessa blinked in surprise. He sounded serious. 'What makes you think—'

'Don't lie to me, Vanessa. I know you better than you think.'

For a moment, she was too bewildered to speak.

'Go on,' he said, 'try the truth.'

She looked down at the gravel path, noticing a weed that she was itching to pick, but she resisted and looked back up at Jonathan, who remained steadfastly on the bench beside her, going nowhere.

'Tilda and Jasmine,' she began hesitantly.

'Yes?'

'They think we're – er – seeing each other.' Her fingers knotted in her lap.

'I see,' Jonathan said calmly. 'Is that all?'

'What do you mean, *is that all*? Isn't that enough?'

'No. I thought something really significant was bothering you.'

'This isn't significant to you?'

He sat up straight and leaned towards her. 'I didn't mean it to come out like that. I meant' – he ran a hand up and down his left leg – 'I meant that this is natural, you know?'

'No, I don't know.'

'We've been spending a lot of time together. We like each other, don't we? It's only natural that your daughters are going to start thinking—'

'I don't want them to start thinking that.'

'What?'

'I'm not ready for that. For *this*!' she cried.

'Listen—'

'No – *you* listen! Oliver is here. He's right here in this garden. On this bench!'

Jonathan blanched and looked uneasy at this confession.

'You're getting all worked up over nothing,' he told her.

'How can you say that? This isn't nothing!' She stood up, needing to get as far away from Jonathan as possible.

'I think we should talk about this.'

'There's nothing to talk about,' she said, and turned her back on him before marching across the lawn towards the house.

'Vanessa!' he called after her, but she didn't look back and nor did she stop until she reached the sanctuary of her bedroom, where she sat on the edge of the bed and closed her eyes against her hot tears.

Chapter 15

Tilda stood in the doorway of the oast house wondering if her sister was going to invite her in. 'We might have a problem,' she said at last.

Jasmine looked up from the sink where she was washing her hands with a bar of green soap. Tilda had once made the mistake of using it only to be shouted down.

'Don't touch that!' Jassy had cried. 'It's expensive stuff and only meant for artists.'

Tilda wondered if it was discriminatory that painters had their own bars of soap but pianists didn't.

'Did you hear me?' Tilda said.

'What's the problem? Is it Grandma? Is Reynolds chasing Skinny the cat? I told Marcus he shouldn't encourage her.'

'No, it's not Grandma; it's Mum.'

Jassy dried her hands on an old checked towel by the side of the sink and turned to face her.

'Is it about that man?'

'If you mean Jonathan, yes, I think it's Jonathan-related.'

'Is she mad at me for teasing her?' Jassy's expression was suddenly that of a six-year-old, and Tilda didn't have the heart to admonish her even though that had been her original intention.

'I don't think she's mad,' Tilda said. 'I think she's more sad than anything.' She walked further into the room and, after checking that the paint splats were dried, perched on a stool.

'Why's she sad?'

'Because I think she's having feelings for this Jonathan and it's making her sad because she feels disloyal to Dad.'

'Really?'

Tilda shrugged. 'I'm just guessing, Jassy. I don't know for sure, but she's certainly been in an odd mood.'

'Should we say something?'

'You saw how she reacted when we did. I think she's denying her feelings. I really think she likes Jonathan.'

'I like him.'

'Yes. He seems like a good man, doesn't he?'

'I like his red hair. I want to paint him.'

Tilda smiled. It always came down to art with Jassy, and her wanting to paint somebody was probably the highest compliment you could hope for.

'You should,' Tilda said.

'Would it make Mum happy?'

'It might.'

'I'll put it on my list.'

Tilda nodded, knowing that her sister lived by her lists. She had daily ones, weekly ones, annual ones and lifetime ones, and Tilda watched as Jassy took a pencil out of her apron pocket and scribbled this newest addition to one of the lists she kept in the oast house.

'Well,' Tilda said, jumping down from the stool, 'I thought I'd let you know.'

'Thanks,' Jassy said. 'Hey – you've been sad too.'

'Have I?'

'Uh-huh,' Jassy said as she retied her scrunched-up ponytail and grabbed a couple of brushes from a nearby jar. 'Are you in love with Jonathan too?'

'Very funny!' Tilda said. 'Of course not.'

'Someone else?'

'What on earth makes you say that?'

Jassy shrugged. 'You've been mooning about, looking miserable.'

'Rubbish!'

'You so have!'

Tilda frowned, knowing that she wouldn't be able to escape Jassy's scrutiny unless she fed her something.

'It's my music – that's all,' she said.

'Yeah?'

'Yeah. I've just got some stuff going on. Nothing to worry about.'

'Okay,' Jassy said, seeming to take her at her word.

Tilda hovered by the door for a moment, wondering if Jassy would press her for more, but she didn't. She'd picked up her brushes and was leaning over her CD player. A blast of rock music filled the building a second later. An abstract painting was on its way, Tilda thought with a grin, and she made a hasty retreat.

Vanessa held up the swatch of material and waited for Elouise's response.

'What do you think? Too dark?'

Elouise grabbed a pair of diamanté-encrusted glasses from a nearby table and examined the swatch.

'No, I like it. It's prettier than the other one.'

'It's also more expensive than the other one,' Vanessa confessed, trying to calculate how much it would cost to cover the sofa with the fabric.

Elouise waved a hand in the air. 'Don't worry.'

Vanessa smiled and made a note in her book. Elouise wasn't constrained by budget, that was for sure. The beautiful Georgian house she'd recently moved into in Elhurst was being lavished with the very best in interior design, from luxurious fabrics to bespoke furnishings.

'Vanessa?' Elouise said. 'I've heard some rumours about young offenders working at Orley. Is it true?'

Vanessa swallowed hard. She liked Elouise and was loving working on her house, but if she was about to give her an ultimatum then Vanessa would be forced to leave.

'Yes. It is true.' She held her client's gaze, wondering which way this would fall.

Elouise slowly nodded. 'Good for you,' she said.

'You approve?'

'Well, of course I do! I used to work on a community project in East London. Making gardens, planting trees, creating wildlife corridors.'

'Really?'

'Don't tell Geoffrey,' she said in a hushed tone. 'He'd have a fit. He's a terrible snob and thinks I was working on some posh charity committee.'

Vanessa couldn't repress a smile and she was still smiling as she parked outside the village shop. People never failed to amaze you, she thought, getting out of the car. She'd been bracing herself for a reprimand from her client but, instead, she'd got a wonderful insight into another side of her.

Crossing the pavement, Vanessa caught sight of Jonathan's card in the window, his beautiful blue handwriting making her heart skip a beat. She was still feeling pretty shaken after their fight. Well, 'fight' was too strong a word perhaps, especially since it had all been one-sided. She'd probably gone and blown their friendship after that outburst.

Quickly buying a loaf of bread and some eggs, Vanessa left the shop and drove the short distance to the other side of Elhurst, pulling up alongside Beeches, Jonathan's home.

A moment later, she tentatively knocked on the red front door and waited before knocking again, but nobody answered. Of course, she should have guessed he'd be out during the day. His van wasn't there and it was most likely that he was working somewhere, but oh how she wished he was at home because she felt as if she was carrying around a great weight in her heart. She wanted to do nothing more than talk to him, without screaming or blaming him for something that wasn't his fault.

Walking back to her car, she determined to call him later. With any luck she'd be able to smooth things over, because losing Jonathan's friendship was the very last thing she wanted.

Laurence was taking a mid-morning break from his work and decided to stretch his legs in the garden. What a great joy it was to be able to down tools and walk outside into the midst of so much beauty, he thought. May he never take it for granted. He didn't think he would, after his years spent in an office where lunch breaks were inevitably spent at his desk and mid-morning breaks were unheard of. Even if he had been able to take a proper break, there'd been nowhere to go. Well, nowhere he could inhale the sweet aroma of a hundred different flowers and soak in the richness of the landscape.

He was just heading back to the house when he saw Jassy.

'Where's your dad?' she asked him without any preliminary niceties. 'He's not with you?'

She shook her head. 'I thought we were going to be sketching in the garden today, but he hasn't shown up.'

'Oh. Well, he's bound to turn up sooner or later.'

Jassy stepped into line alongside him. 'I'm sorry about your mum,' she said.

'Pardon?'

'Tara,' Jassy said. 'That's a pretty name.'

Laurence stopped and turned to face her. 'Dad's been talking to you about her?' he said, unable to hide his shock.

'Not much. Just said she'd died and that he often thought of her. Especially at this time of year.'

'Really?'

'She liked to walk in the garden and collect flowers for the house.'

Laurence swallowed hard at that particular memory of his mother. She had loved to fill endless jam jars with anything from marigolds to cow parsley. There was nothing too ordinary or too common. Anything that had a bloom was a thing of beauty in her eyes.

They reached the front door together and, without so much as a goodbye, Jassy disappeared up the stairs, leaving Laurence dumbfounded in the hallway. He stood, feeling utterly lost as he tried to imagine the scene between his father and this girl. It was so unfair, he thought. Why had his father trusted a stranger with his deepest-felt emotions when he wouldn't breathe a single word to his own son?

Laurence returned to his office, but he felt much too agitated to work. Still, he sorted out a few spreadsheets and rang a client, but abandoned his desk as soon as he saw his father's car in the lane. He'd recently bought himself a little runaround. There hadn't been the need for a car in London, but Laurence was pleased that his father could enjoy some independence now.

He waited a few moments until he heard Marcus entering the north wing and went to meet him in the kitchen, where he found him boiling the kettle.

'Where've you been?' Laurence asked.

'I took Skinny to the vets to give her the once-over. Why?'

'Jassy's been looking for you.'

'Oh, right. I forgot. I've got an appointment, haven't I? She's a very demanding teacher.'

'Dad?'

'What?'

'I spoke to Jassy. You've been talking about Mum. To a stranger.'

Marcus frowned. 'Jassy isn't a stranger.'

'You know what I mean.'

'No, I don't. What do you mean, Laurence? What's eating you up about this?'

'You have to ask? You really have to ask that?' He cast his eyes up to the sky in desperation. 'You're talking to Jassy about my mother, but you won't talk to me.'

His father held his hand up between them. 'I don't need this.'

'No? Well, you're getting it,' Laurence said.

'Jassy and I talk. Why have you got a problem with that? You were always telling me to get out and make friends when we were in London and now I'm doing it and you're chastising me.'

'I'm not chastising you and you're twisting this around.'

'Let's not do this,' Marcus said. 'I really don't want to do this with you.'

'You can't keep running away from this. You've got to face it.'

His father gave him a look like no other look he'd seen before. It was a desperate, haunted sort of expression that seemed to beg Laurence not to press him on this matter.

'There's nothing to face,' Marcus said slowly. 'There's nothing to face and there's nothing to say.'

'You're lying to me. You're hiding something, I just know you are.'

Marcus simply shook his head and walked out of the kitchen without having made his cup of tea.

Vanessa's hand hovered over her mobile. All she had to do was press a button, but she was so nervous that she could barely even pick the phone up for shaking.

You've got to do this, she told herself. *You've got to put things right otherwise you'll be miserable.*

She reached for the phone.

'Jonathan?' she said a moment later. 'It's Vanessa.'

'How are you?' he asked her kindly.

'I'm good. Thank you. How are you?'

'Fine.'

There was a pause.

'Vanessa? Was there something—'

'I'm sorry,' she blurted. 'I wanted to say sorry for the other day. In the garden. The whole bench thing.'

'You don't need to—'

'Yes I do. I was really rude and I'm so sorry. You've been nothing but kind to me. I guess I was just feeling a little bit raw after what the girls said.'

'It's okay.'

She took a deep breath. Her eyes were closed and she wished that there was an easy way to get through this, but it seemed like there wasn't.

'I'm still a mess,' she said quietly. 'I'm still working things out, you know?'

'I know,' he said, his voice gentle as it always was. 'There's no need to explain it to me.'

'But I want to. I want you to understand.'

'I do.'

She took a moment, nodding even though he couldn't see her. 'We're still friends then?' she asked.

'Of course we're still friends, silly!'

She laughed, relief flooding her. 'That's good.'

'Listen,' he said, 'I was thinking of taking a walk this evening. Just into the valley. Maybe along the river.'

'Sounds nice.'

'Would you like to come with me?'

A thousand thoughts somersaulted through her mind at the implications of such an invitation. It would be so easy for her to read something into it and to start getting anxious all over again about what Oliver would make of it. But Oliver wasn't there and she was, and this wonderfully kind, sweet man was asking her to go on a walk with him.

'I mean, don't worry if you'd rather not.'

'No, I'd love to.'

'Really?'

'Yes.'

'Okay. Good. Well, shall I call in at yours? Say seven thirty? We can drive into the valley and take a path from further along the river.'

'Y – yes,' she said again and then paused.

'Vanessa? You still there? You still breathing?'

She gave a little laugh. 'I'm breathing.'

'Deep breaths,' he said. 'Deep breaths and little steps.'

It was just what she needed to hear.

The day passed unimaginably slowly after that. Vanessa had placed the latest orders after her visit to Elouise and had sorted out a pile of fabrics, which had accumulated on the top of a dear little Hepplewhite chair that seemed almost startled to see daylight again.

She tidied some drawers where a pretty assortment of tangled ribbons and homeless buttons lived, and idly flipped through the pages of her notebook where she jotted down ideas for colour schemes but, with every minute that passed, she thought about Jonathan and the agonising moments that separated her from seeing him again. She told herself it was just nerves – that she'd be more settled as soon as they'd said hello and had sorted out the awkwardness between them once and for all – but she knew it was more than that. She was starting to have feelings for him.

She couldn't stomach a big meal before he was due to arrive and so had a couple of slices of toast with some WI jam that had crystallised rather beautifully in its jar. She then did her best to settle in the living room, looking through an old magazine whilst Tilda sat in the chair opposite her reading a book.

'Are you expecting someone?' Tilda asked after a moment, putting her book down and giving her mum her full attention.

'Why do you ask?'

'Because you're all fidgety.'

'Rubbish!' Vanessa said, glancing at the clock on the mantelpiece. 'Is it Jonathan?'

'We're just going for a walk,' she blurted.

'You don't need to explain,' Tilda said. 'I was just wondering.'

'We're friends and we're going for a walk.'

'Good.'

They were silent for a moment and then the little clock chimed the half hour and, precisely ten seconds after that, their front doorbell rang. Vanessa sprang up out of her chair, tossing the magazine onto it and fleeing out of the room.

'Have a nice time!' Tilda shouted after her.

'Bye, darling!'

Reaching the front door and grabbing her jacket, Vanessa paused to compose herself. She was aware that her heart was racing, which was ridiculous. Maybe it was just the rush to get outside. But she knew that it wasn't. She wanted to see Jonathan again and, opening the door, couldn't help smiling.

'Hi,' he said, giving her one of those warm smiles which instantly made the world a better place. 'How are you?'

'I'm good. You?'

'Yep. Pretty good. I hope I'm not late.'

'Not at all,' Vanessa said.

'I lost my watch today and kind of feel a bit odd without it. I removed it whilst clearing out a client's pond and then their terrier grabbed hold of it and promptly dropped it right in the water.'

'It wasn't waterproof?'

'Apparently not.'

'Oh dear!'

'That watch has seen a lot of gardening action. I'm going to miss it. Do you wear a watch?'

Vanessa pulled her sleeve back to reveal a slim gold watch.

'Wow,' he said. 'That's a beauty.'

'Nineteen thirties,' she said. 'A wedding gift from my parents. I used to be afraid to wear it but, as one gets older, one realises that it's important to live in the moment and enjoy things.'

'Absolutely,' he said. 'Like this evening. It's too perfect to stay indoors.'

'I agree.'

They walked out of the east gate into the lane where Jonathan had parked his van and he went round to the passenger door, which he held open for Vanessa before running round to his side.

'Excuse the mess,' he said, removing a plant pot from the footwell. 'The van's a glorified potting shed, I'm afraid.'

Vanessa smiled. She liked it. It smelled of the earth and all things green.

He started the engine and they drove the short distance along the valley, where they parked by the side of the road and got out opposite a tile-hung cottage.

'I love that place,' Vanessa said. 'It's like one of those divine Helen Allingham paintings – you know, the Victorian watercolourist?'

Jonathan nodded and they took a moment to admire the cottage garden with its blue delphiniums and foxgloves, its pink peonies and heaps of lavender. Great swathes of climbing plants smothered the front and threatened to take over the thatched roof, and a forest of hollyhocks made it hard to see any of the downstairs windows.

'The house looks as if it's going to be swallowed up by the garden at any minute,' Jonathan said. 'Do you know who lives there?'

'Mr Taylor. He's a widower. He spends all his time in the garden.'

'I can tell.'

'He used to bring us plants to sell at our summer fete. They were glorious and would sell out as soon as I announced the fete open.' She smiled. 'You know, I'd forgotten all about that until just now.'

'The fete was special to a lot of people,' Jonathan told her. 'I really think you should start it up again.'

Vanessa took a deep breath. 'It's something that's crossed my mind too.'

They glanced at each other and then took one last look at the garden before crossing the road towards the footpath. The sun had blazed a rich pink trail across the sky and the air was still warm. All the same, Vanessa was aware of how quickly it cooled down in the evenings and put her jacket on. She was wearing a pair of old blue jeans and a white blouse covered in tiny sprigged flowers, over which she wore a pale pink jumper. It was a cosy, feminine look which she'd made her own over the years.

Looking at Jonathan, she noted the light waxed jacket that was full of rips and tears and the corduroy trousers that looked old but were neat, just like his big walking boots.

They took a narrow path which sloped steeply into the valley. Vanessa was perfectly capable of managing by herself, but she accepted Jonathan's hand when he stretched it towards her. It was warm and strong and surrounded her own small cool hand, making her feel wonderfully safe as he led the way.

'I often come into the valley on summer evenings. It's a good way to cool off after a hot day's work,' he said as they entered a wood.

'I love walking through the woods just as it's getting dark,' she said.

'I hope you don't do it on your own.'

'Of course I do!'

He turned and looked at her, eyebrows raised.

'I've lived here for thirty years, Jonathan.'

'What's that got to do with anything?'

'I'm not scared of going for a walk in the countryside.'

'You should get a dog or something,' he told her. 'A big one. Something that would defend you.'

'Oh, rubbish!'

'I'm serious. I don't like to think of you wandering around on your own.'

He was being silly, of course, but she couldn't help liking his protective streak.

The floor of the wood was carpet-soft, with last year's leaves and needles making a wonderful cushion for their feet. It hushed their steps too, so that they could drink in the peace of it all.

Suddenly, they'd left the trees behind them and the valley opened out with the river running through the middle of it. They stood side by side as they gazed upon the serene scene. There was something very special about the countryside at dusk; it seemed to be breathing out, relaxing into itself after a long day, Vanessa thought, smiling at her fancifulness.

She cast a sideways glance at Jonathan. His face was relaxed as if he too was breathing out for the first time that day.

'We're very lucky to have all this on our doorstep,' she said in a hushed, reverent tone, noticing that they were still holding hands.

'I tried to bring the team out here one evening after work,' he said.

'What did they make of it?'

'We didn't even get this far, I'm afraid. Nat hit his head on a branch in the wood and Oz said he was getting bitten by mozzies. Jenna wasn't impressed either. She kept asking what did the countryside have to do with her.'

'Oh dear. You'll have to try again.'

'They've grown up in a totally different world and this one seems so alien to them.'

'That's really sad.'

'Isn't it? I mean, I can't imagine a life without woods and hills and fields. I'd be lost. Still, they seem to be adapting to life in a garden so that's something. Good progress.'

They stood for a moment longer and then they heard it: the song of the nightingale, filling the air with its melody. Suddenly, Vanessa was back in time, standing with Oliver, listening to that same song. Hot tears pricked at her eyes and it was all she could do to blink them away. *Don't go there*, she told herself, because she could so easily go there and make tonight about her and Oliver again. But she was with Jonathan. He was the one who'd invited her to join him and she wanted to be here with him, and so she had to make tonight about her and Jonathan.

There were so many things that would remind her of Oliver, she knew that, and it was only right – he'd been her beloved husband and best friend for thirty years – but she had to start making new memories if she truly wanted to live her life.

'Isn't that incredible?' Jonathan said. 'It was waiting for us.'

She smiled, willing herself not to cry. 'Yes,' she said.

'You okay?' he asked, seeming to sense that something was wrong.

She blinked quickly before looking at him, giving him the biggest, brightest smile she could muster.

'Yes.'

'Good.'

They crossed a field where sheep were grazing. The river was softly silvering the landscape, wending its way past an oast house whose roof and cowl looked like a witch's hat against the darkening sky. A ghostly barn owl flew low over the long grasses of a neighbouring meadow, its wings sleek and silent, and still Jonathan held her hand. She didn't want the moment to end, but she was all too aware that night was approaching.

'We'd better head back to the car,' Jonathan said. Did she detect a certain reluctance in his voice?

They'd taken a circuitous route which brought them out a little further up the lane from Mr Taylor's cottage.

'I wish it was lighter just a little longer,' Vanessa said.

'The longest day of the year will be here soon.'

'I know. I love that. I hate winter, when the darkness forces you inside.'

They got back into the van and drove the short distance back to Orley, where yellow lights spilled onto the garden from the mullioned windows.

'Can I show you something?' she asked as he cut the engine.

'Of course.'

They got out of the van and entered the east gate through the yew hedge, and Vanessa led the way through to the south garden. Their feet crunched softly on the gravel pathway but, thankfully, Dolly's curtains were drawn and Reynolds the terrier must have been asleep because they managed to miss being barked at.

'What did you want to show me?' Jonathan asked.

'Everything!'

He laughed, and all of a sudden the garden was flooded with moonlight, causing Vanessa to gasp.

'I didn't know there was a full moon tonight.'

'It's been hiding behind the clouds.'

'Well, there you are,' Vanessa said, giving a little 'ta-da' gesture with her right hand. 'Everything!'

'And I thought the garden at Beeches was pretty spectacular at night.'

'But it is,' Vanessa assured him.

'Yes, but this is something else.'

They stood next to each other in silence, drinking in the splendour.

'White flowers are magical at night, aren't they?' Jonathan said. 'It's like they've captured the essence of the moon in their petals and are shining it back at the heavens.'

Vanessa looked up at him, his hair bright in the moonlight and his eyes dark and intense. He took a step towards her and Vanessa knew exactly what he was going to do. He was going to kiss her.

She didn't move, didn't say anything and, when his hands reached out to cup her face, she knew that she truly wanted to be kissed by this man right here, right now in the moonlit garden, with the glow of the white flowers all around them like wondrous candles. And oh, how right it felt.

'Was that okay?' he whispered a moment later.

A little laugh escaped her. 'That was very okay.'

'Because I wasn't sure how you'd respond. I thought you might . . .'

'What?'

'Slap me.'

'I'd never slap you!'

He gave a shrug. 'I know you've been through a difficult time and that you're still going through it, but I couldn't help myself. I wanted to show you how I feel about you.' He reached out and stroked her cheek with his garden-roughened hands.

'I'm glad you did,' she said.

'Yeah?'

'Yes.'

All of a sudden, it began to rain. At first it was a sweet and gentle summer rain that made them laugh, but it soon turned heavier.

'Here!' Jonathan said, reaching into one of the pockets of his jacket and pulling out a squashed hat before placing it on Vanessa's head.

'What about you?'

'I'm fine.'

'Let's run for the south porch!' she said, and she took his hand and they tore across the lawn, huddling together against the wooden door and its tiny covered arch. There wasn't much room, but Vanessa didn't mind the fact that Jonathan's body was close to hers and neither did she mind when he turned to face her, bending down to claim her mouth in another kiss. Only he crashed into the peak of the cap.

Vanessa laughed and quickly removed the hat, lifting her face so that he could kiss her without injury.

192

'Wow!' he said a moment later. 'I didn't expect this tonight.'

'Neither did I,' she said. 'It must be the moonlight.'

He shook his head. 'It's not the moonlight; it's you. I've been wanting to kiss you for a long time.'

'You have?'

'Oh, yes.'

'Tell me.'

He took a deep breath and caressed her face. 'It probably goes back to when I was coming out of the shop in Elhurst and I saw this strikingly beautiful woman.'

'No!' she said incredulously.

'Fine, don't believe me,' he said, grinning at her.

'Really?'

'Truly,' he said, 'but I didn't think grabbing hold of a stranger and kissing her in the middle of the village would be the best of ideas.'

'Good call.'

The rain continued to fall, softly quenching the summer lawn and showering the plants.

'Jonathan?'

'Yes?'

'Let's start the fete again.'

He leaned back a little so that he could see her face properly. 'You really want to?'

'More than anything!'

'Well, that's great!'

She laid a hand on his chest. 'But I'll need your help. I can't do it on my own.'

'I'll help. Rod and the team will too.'

'Really?'

'Vanessa – this will be brilliant. It'll give the team something real to aim for – we can sell some of our produce from the garden. There'll be loads to choose from over the coming months. You've seen what we've been growing.'

'Yes! And I can cut fresh flowers to sell. We can even get Mr Taylor to bring some of his plants too.'

They smiled at each other as if they were sharing a great secret. Vanessa couldn't remember feeling this happy in years.

'I'd better get going,' he said at last. 'Not that I want to.'

'I don't want you to,' she said.

'Maybe we could move into the porch here together. I think it could be a very cosy home.'

She laughed and they kissed again.

'I'll see you tomorrow, okay?'

'Yes,' she said, resting her head against his chest for a moment. He kissed her brow and she watched as he walked down the path and out into the east garden. She listened to his van as it drove away and only then did she open the door and go inside. Closing it behind her, she stood with her back against the ancient wood, reliving the moment in the moonlit garden over and over again. It had been crazy – crazy and wonderful – and she felt giddy at the realisation that she could still fall in love.

Chapter 16

Tilda opened her laptop in the living room and grimaced at her inbox. *Morton Singer . . . Morton Singer . . .* Bloomin' Morton Singer. Her inbox was full of messages from him, as was her mobile. He was trying to wear her down, wasn't he? And he probably knew that her curiosity would get the better of her and that she'd have to listen to each and every attachment he'd sent her.

She clicked on the first message.

Check this out, Tilda. It's a hit for sure! M.

She looked at the attachment, her eyes wary. Perhaps there was a virus attached. Perhaps that's the excuse she could give him for not opening any of them, but the cursor was hovering over it, nevertheless, and she clicked on the file. For a moment, nothing seemed to happen and then, suddenly, box after box came up on her screen. There *was* a virus attached!

'Oh, God!' Tilda cried. 'Shut it down! Shut it down!'

She pressed key after key, trying to stop the boxes from opening, and was just about to switch her laptop off altogether when she heard a light tapping at the door.

'Everything okay?' Laurence asked, his head popping round.

'No it isn't,' Tilda admitted. 'It's my laptop. It's going into meltdown.'

'May I?'

'Please.'

Laurence joined her on the sofa and took the laptop from her. She watched as his fingers danced over the keys, restoring order on the screen and calm in her.

'There you go,' he said a moment later.

'Oh, thanks! I thought I'd killed it.'

'No. Not quite.'

'I hate computers,' she said. 'Well, when they're not working.'

'I'm kind of reliant on mine now for my business. It's become the centre of my world.'

'That would drive me crazy,' she confessed.

'So how do you write your songs and music?'

'With good old-fashioned pencil and paper.'

'Really?'

'Yes. There's something about the connection between the brain, the heart and hand that works best for me. I did once try composing on my laptop, but it was a complete disaster. There wasn't that special connection.' She smiled, but then her smile turned into a frown as she realised that Laurence was staring at her. 'What?'

'Nothing,' Laurence said. 'I just love hearing how artists work. It's a different world from mine. I really admire you. You and your sister – you're both so talented.'

'Oh, I don't know. We just do what's in our hearts and hope for the best.'

'So, are you going to open those?' he asked, nodding towards the emails.

Tilda looked at the screen. 'I haven't made my mind up yet.'

'No? Because I'd have had them all opened by now.'

Tilda continued to stare at her inbox as if it were her mortal enemy.

'Just open the first one,' Laurence said, whispering in her ear like a little devil sitting on her shoulder.

Her hand hovered over the keyboard and, a couple of clicks later, a blast of music filled the room.

'Oh, God!' she exclaimed, a look of horror on her face.

'Is that you?' Laurence asked as Tilda struggled to find how to close the file.

'I suppose,' she said.

'You suppose?'

'I've never heard it before. Morton—'

'The guy who visited you?'

'Yes. He keeps sending me these downloads. He's been manipulating songs of mine.'

'I like it.'

'Do you?'

'It's great! Can you turn it up?' Laurence asked.

'I really don't want to do that.'

'Why not?' The music suddenly ended. 'What did you stop it for?'

She swallowed hard. 'I've had enough.'

'Play another.'

'I don't think so.'

'Go on! This is more fun than I've had in ages and, if you don't play another, I'll be forced to return to my boring old desk and get on with some boring old work.'

She looked at him and the silly, sad expression he was pulling, and something in her felt just a tad sorry for him.

'Okay,' she said, 'one more.' Laurence nodded eagerly and Tilda opened another track.

'What's this one?'

She read the email. 'Morton says it's an artist he's working with.'

'Play it.'

Tilda opened the file.

'The music's pretty decent, but her voice is nothing compared to yours.'

She smiled, stopping the music. 'Thanks.'

'One more?' Laurence asked.

'Laurence—'

'Go on – humour me!'

She opened the next file.

'There – that lovely voice of yours again.'

'It's another track of mine he's been messing with.'

'It's good. It's really good.'

'You think so?'

'Of course I do! You must be able to hear how good that sounds?'

'Well, I suppose,' she said.

'It's full of life and energy and fun! But it has a real heart to it too. Listen to that part again.'

'Which part?'

'Just before the chorus-thing.'

'Chorus-thing?'

'I don't know how to talk about music other than, "Oh, I like that" or "Oh, that's terrible!"'

She rewound about twenty seconds.

'There – that bit. That's lovely, isn't it?'

Tilda's head cocked to one side. She had to admit that it was.

They listened to all the tracks Morton had sent her, replaying some over and over again and, before they knew it, a whole hour had passed by.

'I didn't mean to open any of those,' she said, closing the lid of the laptop and leaning back on the sofa.

'Come on,' he said, 'you must admit that was fun!'

'Well, I—'

'There's no denying it – you glow when you talk about music.'

She frowned.

'You do. You really do.'

'Maybe,' she said, 'but none of this is going anywhere.'

'What do you mean?'

'Morton wants to work with me. He wants to produce my music.'

'But that's great,' Laurence said. 'Isn't that what you want?'

'No, it isn't.'

'Tilda – you love writing music, you love singing, you've proved yourself in the past, and now you've got a hungry young producer begging you to work with him. What's holding you back?'

She looked at Laurence, his face serious as he tried to understand what was going on in her head. Should she give him a glimpse?

'I know what happened to you,' Laurence said when she didn't answer him.

'What do you know?'

'I know about Manchester. I know what you did on stage.'

'How do you know?'

'I saw it on the Internet.'

'Of course you did.'

'I'm sorry,' he said. 'I had to find out.'

'Blimey, Laurence. You're the nosiest person I've ever met.'

'It's the worst thing about me – I have to know what's going on with people.'

'Don't joke about this.'

'I'm not joking. I'm just trying to understand. And I do – I really do. What happened to you was horrible. I can't even begin to imagine what it must have been like to have been on that stage with that huge crowd—'

'Don't!'

'Sorry,' he said.

'I'm never going to put myself in that situation again.'

'But there must be another way.'

'There is – teaching!'

'No, I mean to go on singing and getting your music out there – without going up on stage. What about all those online channels like YouTube? Have you thought about doing anything like that?'

'It's still the public arena, Laurence. Have you seen some of the comments people leave online?'

'I have and it can be pretty vitriolic, but there's always something about a job that's going to be disagreeable.'

She gave a hollow laugh. 'It's all right for you to say that; you don't get publically attacked in your job. You hide behind a computer.'

'But you can too – surely? There must be a way of doing what you love without the need to perform in public.'

'I'm sure there is, but—'

'So it's got to be worth a go. What does Morton say?'

'I haven't read all his messages properly yet.'

'Then you should,' Laurence said. 'Promise me you will.'

She frowned. 'Why are you so determined to make me do this?'

He grinned at her and she remembered why she was letting him get away with talking to her like this – because he was very cute.

'You've got a great gift, Tilda. I wish I'd been born with one. If I had, perhaps I'd be doing something more exciting than sitting at a computer all day.'

'But you like what you do, don't you?'

'Sure I do, but I'm not going to inspire applause or adulation,' he said.

'Those things are highly overrated,' she told him. 'Believe me.'

'Maybe, but it pains me to see that you're hurting because you can't do the thing you love most in the world.'

'How do you know I love it the most?'

He shrugged. 'I can tell. When I watched you perform at that concert, you were so alive! I couldn't take my eyes off you. You lit up the whole stadium. You can't fake that.'

Tilda felt stunned by his words. Nobody had ever talked to her like this before. She'd had a lot of flattery from her manager, and some pretty scary adoration from fans, but that hadn't seemed as real as this. Here, sitting on the sofa next to her, was an ordinary man who seemed to be able to see right into the centre of her being.

'Speak to Morton. See what he's got to say,' he told her. 'Go on! Don't live to regret this, Tilda. Promise me you'll ring him.'

Tilda felt faint at the merest prospect of getting in touch with Morton and starting things up again, but there was a tiny thread of excitement in her too and she found herself nodding.

'I'll get in touch with Morton,' she told Laurence, noticing that he was still smiling at her and realising, perhaps for the first time, that she liked him smiling at her very much.

Vanessa had lain awake most of the night, staring up at the ceiling as the summer rain drummed on her bedroom window. She still hadn't been able to believe what had happened in the garden and so got up to stare out of the window, the moon still brilliantly bright. Had that really happened, she wondered, touching her lips. Standing there by the window in the middle of the night, it all seemed so dreamlike, but the revelation that he'd wanted to kiss her for a long time made it very real.

And just how long had she been attracted to him, she asked herself now as she put her pencil down and pushed the pattern books to one side. She'd managed to put in a good hour's work at her desk before Jonathan and his team were due, but she rose now and left her office and went straight out into the garden.

Jonathan had texted her as soon as he'd got in the night before.

Miss you, he'd written, and she'd messaged back: *Miss you too.*

She felt as giddy as a schoolgirl falling in love for the first time, which was silly really because she'd been a married woman for so long, but perhaps she'd thought she'd never get to feel like that again after Oliver's death. She'd never expected to meet somebody else. When Oliver died, Vanessa had believed that the happiest years of her life were over. She still had her daughters and their futures to look forward to, but her own time for love and happiness had passed.

Until Jonathan.

There was just one little thought niggling at the back of her mind. He still hadn't opened up about his past. His reaction to the bottle of wine she had brought to his home told her that he was clearly hiding something. Had he a history of addiction? Or was he teetotal for another reason? She really wanted to know but it was obvious that he wasn't going to bring the subject up, and was it that important anyway? Vanessa was anxious about his past more from a trust point of view – that he trusted her enough to tell her about it – rather than simply knowing what had happened to him.

She picked up her pace as she neared the walled garden. She could hear the team before she saw them and, entering through the south gate, she saw them all setting up for the day ahead.

'Hey!' Jonathan called as soon as he saw her, putting down the box he was carrying and walking towards her.

'Hi,' she said, flashing him a smile. He was wearing a sky-blue cotton shirt with the sleeves rolled up, revealing tanned arms that she couldn't help imagining around her. His red hair was bright in the morning sunshine and his smile made her feel as if she were floating.

'You're just in time. I was telling the team about our idea for the summer fete,' he said.

'What do they all think?' Vanessa asked.

'Well, Andy wasn't really sure what a fete was, but when I said we'd be selling some of our produce, he was on board immediately. Of course, any money made will be going straight back into the project.'

'You made that clear to him?' Vanessa said.

'Absolutely. And Oz said that he'll only come if he can throw a wet sponge at the local vicar.'

'What?' Vanessa asked with a laugh.

'Apparently, he's got some grudge against the poor man.'

'Well, we have been known to have wet sponge–throwing in the past, but I think poor Reverend Allsopp wouldn't be up to it these days.'

'Fair enough. I'll tell Oz that he's coming anyway.' He leaned in towards her and whispered, 'There's something I want to tell you too.'

'Yes?' She waited, barely able to breathe.

'Jonathan?' Andy shouted from the other side of the walled garden. 'What are we meant to do with this?'

Jonathan rolled his eyes and turned around. 'I'll be with you in a minute,' he told Andy.

'What is it anyway?' Andy called back.

'It's a cloche. Put it down before you damage it. No, don't put it on your head! It's not a traffic cone!' He sighed and turned back to Vanessa.

'What did you want to tell me?'

'What's a cloche?' Andy called.

Jonathan sighed. 'I think I'd better talk to you later.'

So Vanessa had to wait in agony as she worked in the walled garden with the team. She and Jonathan kept swapping little smiles, savouring the secret of their shared kisses in the porch but, each time they tried to get close to have a private word, someone would interrupt them. It was as if the team knew that something was going on between them. Maybe they did, Vanessa thought. Maybe they'd known long before she had.

It was as she was helping Jenna repot some tomatoes in the greenhouse that it became clear.

'He likes you,' Jenna said with a sniff.

'Who?'

'Jonathan of course!'

'How do you know that?'

'He's always looking at you and he's always talking about you when you're not here.'

'Is he?'

Jenna nodded. 'Do you like him too? I think you do, but Oz says he thinks it's that unreq—' She stopped. 'I don't know the word he used.'

'Unrequited?'

'That's it! What's that mean?'

'It means a love that isn't returned,' Vanessa explained.

'That's the one. Oz said you're posh and that you'd never look at someone like Jonathan.'

Vanessa took a moment to take this in. 'Is that what he said?'

'I don't believe him, though.'

'You shouldn't.'

'So you do like him? I mean, like – you know – romantically?'

Vanessa paused with a tomato plant in her hand. What should she say? She hadn't even told her own daughters yet, although they suspected something was going on, and it would be fun to share something with Jenna in this quiet, female time in the greenhouse with the two of them crouching over pots and growbags.

'I like him,' she said at last.

'I knew it!' Jenna said, punching the air.

'Just keep it between us for now, all right?'

The girl nodded. 'Our secret,' she said with a wink.

'So, is there anyone special in your life?' Vanessa asked.

Jenna looked unsure for a moment. 'Kind of.'

'Kind of?'

'It's kind of on and off. More off than on really.'

'And do you love him?'

Jenna shrugged. 'I suppose, but he never sticks around for long. He flits about. I think he's seeing somebody else.'

Vanessa frowned. 'Why do you put up with that – a pretty girl like you?'

'Me? Pretty?' She laughed.

'Of course.'

'You must be confusing me with someone else.'

'I'm looking at a young, attractive woman,' Vanessa said, 'who could do anything she wanted in life and have any man she set her heart on.'

Jenna's eyes widened at this revelation and Vanessa thought that the girl was about to cry, but then she gave one of her little shrugs.

'Nah!' she said. 'I'm just me, aren't I?'

'Vanessa?'

Vanessa and Jenna looked up to find Jonathan standing at the greenhouse door. 'You got a minute? I need a hand with something.'

'Sure,' Vanessa said, standing up. Jenna gave her a wink, which Vanessa hoped Jonathan didn't see.

She left the greenhouse, following him into the orchard.

'So,' she said a minute later, 'what needs doing here?'

'This,' Jonathan said, taking her face in his hands and kissing her.

'Jonathan!' she cried. 'The team – they'll see!'

'They're busy.'

'Are you sure?'

'Nobody suspects a thing anyway.'

'Except Jenna.'

'What?'

'She knows.'

'You didn't tell Jenna, did you?'

'No, of course not! She guessed.'

'How?'

'Oh, I don't know – because she's got eyes and her head.'

'But we haven't said anything or—'

'It's all in the eyes apparently.'

Jonathan scratched his chin. 'Good grief. They're more observant than I give them credit for.'

'We've got to be more careful.'

'But the secret's out now.'

'Well, we don't need to make an announcement or anything.'

'You wouldn't want to do that?' Jonathan asked, head cocked to one side in a teasing manner. 'Because I was thinking of painting a banner on the side of my van which says I've been kissing the lady of the manor!'

'Stop calling me that!' She play-punched him and he laughed. 'Seriously, I'd like to keep this thing quiet.'

'That's okay,' he said.

'You're all right with that?'

'I'm fine with that. As long as it's got nothing to do with the fact that I'm a lowly gardener.'

'Jonathan – don't even joke about something like that.'

'Sorry,' he said. 'I really don't care if we have to keep it a secret from the whole world forever. Just as long as I get to be with you.'

'You know how to say all the right things, don't you?'

He smiled and picked up her hands and squeezed them. 'I hope so, because I want to make you happy.'

'You do,' she said, and they shared another kiss and then Vanessa remembered something. 'Jenna was telling me a bit about her boyfriend.'

'Carl? He's bad news.'

'Really?'

'I tried to get him involved in our gardening team, but it was a waste of time.'

'What does he do?'

'As little as possible. I think he's a dealer. He's involved in some sort of criminal activity anyway.' Jonathan sighed. 'He's violent too.'

'Has he ever hurt Jenna?' Vanessa asked in concern.

'If he has, she'd deny it.'

'What can we do?'

Jonathan reached out and stroked her cheek. 'We give Jenna as much encouragement as we can to make better choices. It's up to her whether she listens to us or not.'

Vanessa nodded, determined to play her part in helping this young woman.

'Hey!' she suddenly said. 'What was it you wanted to tell me?'

'Pardon?'

'You said you wanted to tell me something. You know – before Andy interrupted you.'

'Oh, right!' Jonathan said with a light laugh, but then his face became more serious and he held her gaze. 'I couldn't stop thinking about you last night.'

'No?'

'You kept me wide awake.'

'I didn't sleep much either.'

He nodded. 'We've got a bad case of this, haven't we?'

'Very bad indeed,' she said. 'Now, let's get back to work before we're missed and everyone works out exactly what we've been doing!'

Since Laurence had persuaded her to open the files, Tilda had lost count of the number of times she'd listened to the tracks Morton had sent her. She felt as if she were getting to know this funny, passionate person all over again and she realised that she'd missed her friend since walking out on the music business. She missed their banter and their fooling around. It had been such an easy relationship between them but it had come at a time that was far from easy for Tilda, and her friendship with Morton had been one of the sacrifices she'd made when she turned her back on her career and came home to brood. And she missed him. She could admit that now, after reading his emails and texts and listening to the tracks he'd put together, and she instinctively knew how much fun it would be to work with him. Certainly more fun than teaching the reluctant children of pushy parents how to play the piano or sing, that was for sure.

But getting in touch with Morton, responding to his messages, would start a whole chain of events she wouldn't altogether be in charge of and that thought terrified her. Could she really allow herself to go through all that again – potentially put herself in a position which could so easily bring hurt and humiliation? Was her love of her music worth gambling on that again?

She reached for her phone, calling Morton's mobile and hoping it would go to voicemail, but he answered it almost immediately.

'Tilda?' he said.

'Hi,' she said.

'You okay?'

'Yes. Well, no. Not really. I'm – I'm not really sure.'

'Oh. Sounds complicated.'

'It is.' She shook her head. She was messing this up already and she hadn't even started.

'Can I help you uncomplicate things?' Morton asked after a moment. 'Tilda? You still there?'

'I'm still here,' she said and she took a deep breath. It was, perhaps, the deepest breath she'd ever taken in her entire life. Her mouth was dry and her hand shaking, but when she spoke, it was with a clear and determined voice.

'Morton?'

'I'm still here.'

'I think I'd like to work with you.'

Chapter 17

It was after lunchtime when Vanessa joined the team in the garden again. She left them to it for lunch, feeling that her presence might be intrusive even though Jonathan had assured her that it wouldn't be. She figured they'd want to talk openly and freely without the 'lady of the manor' around. So she'd gone into the house, checked the messages on her answerphone, rung a client and fixed herself a sandwich. And that's when Dolly had entered the kitchen.

Vanessa took a few deep breaths now as she walked into the walled garden.

'Hey!' Jonathan said in greeting. Then he frowned. 'You okay?' He peered closer at her. 'You're not, are you?'

'I'm fine. Give me a fork for those nettles over there. I need to dig the living daylights out of something.'

'Okay,' he said. 'Let's dig. But let's talk first.'

Vanessa shook her head. 'I don't want to talk about it.'

'Whenever somebody says that, it usually means that they really should talk about it.'

'Yes? Well I don't want to.'

'Why not?'

'Because it's private. It's a family thing.'

'Screw that,' he said. 'Tell me!'

'Why? Why should I tell you?'

He shrugged. 'Because I'm here and I'm a pretty good listener.'

'Believe me, you do not want to hear my gripes about my mother-in-law.'

'Ah, the dreaded mother-in-law.'

'What do you know about her?'

'Only what I've heard in the village. She's pretty well known around these parts, isn't she? I haven't had the pleasure of meeting her myself.'

'Count yourself lucky then.'

Jonathan grinned. 'Is she really that bad?'

'She's worse. She's worse than anything you can imagine. You don't believe me, do you?'

'I admit I'd like to see the evidence first.'

'Fine,' she said. 'Come and meet her if you insist.'

'Really?'

'Well, you've met Tilda and Jassy and you said you wanted to meet Dolly too.'

'Okay,' Jonathan said. 'Rod? You hold the fort for a bit?'

'Sure thing,' Rod said.

Jonathan waved a hand. 'I'm good to go.'

'Fine,' Vanessa said and she stomped out of the walled garden.

'Hang on a minute,' Jonathan called after her, running to catch up. 'What exactly did she say to make you so mad?'

'She said I shouldn't be stooping so low as to work in the garden with a bunch of criminals,' she told him, briefly remembering her fear that Dolly's missing necklace might very well have something to do with Jonathan's team and that Dolly might be right about them after all.

'And what did you say?'

'I said something very rude.'

'Good for you!'

'It was horrible,' Vanessa said. 'But then all my encounters with Dolly seem to be horrible. I can never do anything right.'

They'd reached the house now and Vanessa could feel that her face was flaming with heat which had nothing to do with the summer sunshine. She looked up at Jonathan, who was running a hand through his dark-red hair.

'You're nervous?' she asked.

'Er, maybe just a little,' he said. 'Should I take my boots off?'

Vanessa looked down at the steel-capped boots. 'No. Keep them on. You need all the protection you can get. You sure you want to go through with this?'

He nodded. 'You've got me curious now. I want to see this bully.'

'You might regret it when she verbally attacks you and kicks you out.'

Jonathan grinned. 'She won't do that, will she? I'm a charmer.'

'Maybe you should have brought a hoe in with you to defend yourself.'

'Oh, come on, Vanessa. She can't be that bad.'

'Just don't say I didn't warn you.'

They made their way to Dolly's rooms on the ground floor.

'When my husband died, Dolly shut herself away in here for weeks,' Vanessa explained. 'She didn't talk to anyone – not even her granddaughters, and she adores them.'

'It must be hard to lose a child. An only child especially,' Jonathan said.

'Yes. She took it badly. I don't think she'll ever get over it.'

'She doesn't talk to you about it?'

'No, never. Which isn't really surprising. We've never had the kind of relationship where we just talk to each other.'

'And her granddaughters – does she talk to them?'

'Not about anything important.'

'That's really sad. We all need somebody to talk to.'

She glanced at him. His face was etched with concern and she realised that she'd never once thought about Dolly's feelings in that way before. Vanessa had been so consumed with her own pain and that of her daughters after losing Oliver – and then on the defensive against Dolly all the time – that she hadn't really thought about the old woman's feelings. But was it really as simple as Dolly just needing somebody to talk to? Vanessa found that hard to believe as she tentatively knocked on the door of Dolly's living room.

When there was no answer she knocked again, only louder this time.

'Dolly? There's somebody who'd like to meet you.'

'Who?' Dolly barked. Just that one harshly spoken word and Vanessa's hackles were up. She couldn't help it. Dolly had always been able to rile her so easily. Jonathan seemed to sense it too and rested a hand on the small of her back.

'Relax,' he whispered, and she took a moment to calm herself before opening the door.

As soon as they were in the room, Reynolds the terrier leapt off the chair he'd been sitting on and made a beeline for the intruders. He looked all set to have a naughty nip at Vanessa's ankles when he caught sight of Jonathan and stopped to sniff his boots.

'Hello, little fellow,' Jonathan said, bending down to pat him. 'What a sweetheart.'

'Who are you?' Dolly cried.

'Mrs Jacobs?' Jonathan began, undeterred by her gruff manner as he made his way straight to Dolly's chair. 'I'm Jonathan Dacre.' He held his hand towards her and she was so startled that she automatically reached out to reciprocate, her eyes wide in her pale face. 'It's a real pleasure to meet you.'

'Is it?' Her eyes narrowed as she took him in. 'You own that old van, don't you?'

'I do.'

'It's horrible.'

'Dolly!' Vanessa admonished.

'I'm only telling the truth,' Dolly said.

'It is, indeed, a horrible old van, but it's all I can afford to run and it gets me from A to B.'

'I don't like it parked out there.'

'Oh,' Jonathan said. 'Well, perhaps I can park it somewhere else so you don't have to look at it.'

Dolly harrumphed, which was her way of showing that she was somewhat appeased.

'You have a very fine view here,' Jonathan said, looking out of the large window onto the south garden.

'I do, and I don't like being disturbed when I'm looking at it.'

'I can understand why. You know, this is a really special place you have here, Dolly. May I call you Dolly?'

'Well, I—'

'It's such a pretty name. Why aren't there more Dollys these days?'

'It was my father's choice. He always had impeccable taste.'

'He certainly did. I can't think of a lovelier name.'

Vanessa blinked as she saw the beginnings of a smile in the corners of Dolly's mouth. No, she thought, she must surely be mistaken. Dolly didn't smile. Well, not since the days before Oliver became ill. That was the last time that Vanessa had seen Dolly happy.

'You know what we're doing out in the walled garden, don't you?' Jonathan asked her.

'Vandalising the place, no doubt.'

'Not at all,' he said, managing to remain impervious to her insults. 'Vanessa's told you about the amazing team we've got working here?'

'Yes, she ha—'

'They're young people full of energy and enthusiasm and I can't thank you enough for the opportunity you've given them. The walled garden is such a great environment. I've never seen the team so excited to be anywhere. The chance to work in your orchard and greenhouse and to use the raised beds – it's been really great.'

'But they're crimin—'

'They're young people who might have made a few bad choices,' he interrupted again, 'but let me ask you this, Dolly. Haven't we all made a few bad choices in our lives?'

'Well, I can't say I have—'

'And haven't we all needed a helping hand to get us back on track? That's what me and Rod are trying to do, but it's people like you who make the real difference by giving us the time and space we need in order to turn our dreams into reality. Without people like you, our society would be all the poorer, and that's why I wanted to come in here and personally thank you – for allowing us to share your extraordinary home. It's an honour and a privilege – a real privilege to be here.'

He finally stopped to draw breath and Vanessa stared at him in wonder. What on earth had just happened there? He'd given her no warning that he was going to launch into a full speech and flatten Dolly into submission. She almost felt sorry for her poor mother-in-law because she hadn't stood a chance. He had completely bulldozed her with his enthusiasm.

Dolly sat in her chair looking completely stunned. 'Well,' she said. 'Well indeed.'

Jonathan took a step closer to her and crouched down so that he was at her eye level.

'Dolly,' he said, and Vanessa couldn't help wondering if he was going to start up again, 'would you do me the very great honour of walking to the walled garden with me? I'll show you around, tell you what we've been doing, and the team would love to thank you, they really would.'

Dolly's mouth fell open and, instead of the angry tirade that Vanessa would surely have got, she squeaked a little 'yes'.

Jonathan stood up and held out his arm for her to take and the two of them left the room, Reynolds trotting behind them. Vanessa stood completely dumbfounded. She couldn't ever remember Dolly being at a loss for words – she always had far too much to say for herself, in Vanessa's opinion.

'You coming?' Jonathan said, looking over his shoulder at her.

'Don't worry about her,' Dolly said with a little laugh.

A laugh, Vanessa thought. The old woman could actually laugh.

They left the house together, Vanessa following Jonathan and Dolly. Dolly's progress to the walled garden was slow, but Jonathan was endlessly patient with her, placing her hand in the crook of his arm and guiding her along the path.

'I've been in a lot of gardens, Dolly, but I have to say that there is something very special about Orley.'

'Well, of course there is,' she said. 'It's the best in the county. In the *country*. Only we're not as flashy as some.'

'Nothing worse than a flashy garden.'

'Exactly,' Dolly said. 'We're very understated here. Everything's in good taste. You won't find any model railways or nasty theme-park rides.'

'That's very reassuring.'

They reached the walled garden and Jonathan cleared his throat.

'Everybody? Can I have your attention for a minute? I'd like to introduce you to a very special lady.' He waited until everyone had put their tools down and come forward, wiping their hands on the fronts of their trousers. 'This is Dolly Jacobs, Vanessa's mother-in-law, and I think we'd all like to thank her for letting us use her stunning walled garden.'

Everybody applauded politely and Vanessa watched as Dolly gave a tiny smile, clearly loving being the centre of attention.

Jonathan led her around the garden, introducing her to Rod and the team and showing her the work they'd been doing. Rod was particularly attentive, telling her what all the plants were and pushing Andy back when he got too close.

'She doesn't want you near her with those mucky hands of yours,' Rod told him.

Victoria Connelly

Dolly seemed to take a real interest in it all, rather like a visiting dignitary who'd been briefed on what questions to ask.

Vanessa watched on in amazement as Jonathan's charm seemed to win Dolly over completely. She couldn't believe that Dolly would respond to such obvious flattery, but it seemed that she was as susceptible as anybody else.

Finally, they escorted her back to the house. Vanessa made them all a cup of tea and freshened Reynolds's water bowl. The little dog was mightily thirsty after tearing around the walled garden and being petted by everyone.

Dolly sat back down in her chair and Vanessa saw that her mother-in-law had real colour in her cheeks, which made her look rather attractive.

'What do you think of the work being done, Dolly?' she asked her.

Dolly looked up from her chair. 'Where's Jonathan?'

'I'm right here, Dolly,' he said, walking forward, teacup in hand.

'Thank you for showing me what you're doing.'

Vanessa blinked in surprise. First a smile, then a laugh and now a thank you. This was a truly momentous day.

'It's us who should thank you,' Jonathan said. 'I hope today has helped to put your mind at rest. I hope you're happy with what we're doing.'

'I am, Jonathan,' she said, sipping her tea and treating him to one of her rare smiles again. Reynolds, who was now sitting by her feet, looked up at his mistress, head cocked to one side in response to this strange phenomenon.

'Well, we'd better get back to work,' Jonathan said as he finished his tea.

'I'll see you later, Dolly,' Vanessa said.

'Jonathan?' Dolly called as they were leaving the room.

'Yes, Dolly?'

'You can park your van in the lane. I don't really mind.'

Jonathan grinned. 'Thank you,' he said. A moment later, when they'd left the house, he turned to Vanessa. 'So, how do you think that went?'

Vanessa put her hands on her hips and shook her head. 'Amazingly well. I can't believe how you—'

'How I what?'

'Tamed her!'

He laughed. 'I wouldn't go that far.'

'I jolly well would!'

'Let's just say I've met one or two like her in my time,' he said. 'You just need to flatter them into submission.'

'But she likes you. She really likes you!'

Jonathan didn't look too convinced. 'I think she'd like any man who paid her a bit of attention.'

'You do?'

'I really do. You said her husband died?'

'Yes, years ago.'

'And her son. Oliver.'

Vanessa nodded. 'It's not been an easy time.'

'I think she needs some male company.'

'Are you applying for the job?' Vanessa teased.

'Ah, no,' he said, taking a step towards her. 'I'm already taken, aren't I?'

'Absolutely. She's not having you!'

He leaned forward and kissed her forehead. What he'd said made Vanessa think. Perhaps he was right about Dolly. Perhaps the thing that had been lacking in Dolly's life was male companionship – and this was what had been making her miserable.

Dolly had been a very beautiful woman and much admired, Vanessa had heard. She had probably never wanted for male attention, but then her husband had died and Vanessa took her son's attention away from her. At least, that's how Dolly had viewed it. She was one of those women who needed to be adored by a man and, no matter how much attention her beloved granddaughters gave her, it just wasn't the same thing at all.

'Laurence, are you in there?'

Laurence almost leapt out of his office chair when he heard the voice. 'Tilda?' He got up, crossed the room and opened his study door.

'I didn't mean to disturb you. I can come back later if—'

'No, no – come on in. You're not disturbing me.' The truth was, he was glad of a break from the appalling financial muddles one of his clients had got himself into.

'There's nobody around I can talk to,' she went on.

'Oh, so I'm the last resort, am I?' he teased.

She grinned. 'Sorry. That didn't come out right.'

'Come on in. It's a bit messy, I'm afraid. I've been trying to find some documents that have got misplaced in the move.'

She looked around the room, her eyes darting anxiously. 'I hope it's okay, me coming to your wing like this.'

'Why wouldn't it be okay?' he asked.

'Well, this is your home now,' she said, shoving her hands into the large pockets of her blue dress. She looked horribly nervous and he was mindful to put her at ease.

'You're always welcome here, Tilda. It's still taking me a while to get used to spending the working day on my own. I kind of miss the interruptions of an open-plan office.'

'So I *am* interrupting you?' She looked embarrassed. 'Oh, I'm so sorry. I really didn't mean to. I should have thought—'

'No, no! I meant I need an excuse to take a break. I tend to just push through when I'm on my own and then feel totally burned out at the end of the day.'

'I don't want to bother you.'

'You're not bothering me. Honestly. Now, can I get you a tea or coffee or something?'

'No thanks.'

'Do you want to sit down?'

She shook her head and walked to the window overlooking the front lawn and the great yew hedge.

'Morton wants me to visit the studio.'

'Are you going to?'

'It's in London.'

'Well, it's not very likely to be down the road in Robertsbridge, is it?'

'I don't like London.'

He watched her for a moment. Her shoulders looked stiff and tense and he was tempted to walk over to her and give them a good massage, but that would most definitely be overstepping the mark, wouldn't it?

'What if I go with you?' he suddenly said.

'What?' She turned around to face him.

'I've got some errands to run. I can meet up with a couple of clients, visit a pal. It will save you getting the train and facing the hideousness of the Underground.'

'You'd seriously drive me into London?'

'Sure. Why not?'

'Is this to make sure that I actually go to the studio?'

He grinned. 'Partly.'

'Why's that so important to you?'

'I've told you why, Tilda: because I really think you should do this.' He paused. 'And you want to, don't you? Otherwise you wouldn't be in here discussing it with me.'

'It's so complicated.'

'Only if you make it complicated.'

'No, it really is complicated,' she said.

'Then just take it one step at a time. Go to London. Talk to Morton. Maybe even make some music. You don't have to sign anything or make any big decisions. He's a friend, isn't he?'

Tilda nodded.

'So go and see your friend and just talk.'

She gave a weak smile. 'You should be an agony uncle or something.'

'Why?'

'You're really good with advice.'

He smiled, although part of him was dying inside at her use of the word 'uncle'. Is that how she saw him?

'But what if I . . .' She paused.

'What?'

'What if it all goes wrong? What if I get sucked into it all again and—'

'You can't think like that. You've got to go into this positively. You can't worry about all the ifs, buts and maybes. If everybody did that all the time, nobody would ever leave home or do anything, and think how dull the world would be then.'

She looked out of the window again.

'Let me take you to London, Tilda. Then, if it all goes wrong—'

She turned back to face him.

'Which I'm sure it won't!' he quickly added, his hands up in the air. 'Well, you can blame me.'

She took a deep breath. 'Okay then,' she said. 'I'll come to London with you. I'll see Morton and hear what he has to say.'

'Great.'

'And then I'll blame you, right?'

'Absolutely.'

It was always best to act quickly when momentous decisions were made, Laurence had found, and so he persuaded Tilda to go up to London the very next day, leaving after breakfast.

Laurence went in search of his father to let him know where he was going. When he couldn't find him in his rooms, he went out to the oast house.

A blast of rock music greeted him as he opened the door after knocking several times and not being heard. What did rock mean? he wondered, harkening back to something his father had mentioned. Abstract painting, was it?

'Laurie?' his father said, obviously surprised to see him there.

'You're at it bright and early,' Laurence said.

'Lots to do,' his father said.

'Hello, Jasmine.'

'There's a whole world to paint,' Jasmine explained. 'Isn't there, Marcus?'

'There certainly is.'

Laurence looked from one to the other, but their eyes remained firmly on the canvases in front of them.

'Right, I'm off, Dad.'

'Okay.'

'Can I get you anything whilst I'm in town?'

'I don't think so.'

'Sure?' Laurence said.

'There's nothing I want from London.'

He watched a moment longer as his father stood behind his easel looking every inch the artist.

'Okay then,' he said, half expecting his father to look up but he didn't.

'Bye, Laurie,' Jassy said. 'Shut the door on your way out, please.'

Well, that put him in his place, he thought, closing the door as he left.

Laurence and Tilda left Orley just after nine in the morning. A summer mist was lingering in the valley, its magical skeins enveloping the sheep and promising a hot day ahead. If it hadn't been for Tilda, Laurence would have been more than happy to stay at home, opening his office window and letting the summer air and all its scents pour into the room. But there was no place he'd rather be than with Tilda.

He had to admit it – he was becoming extremely fond of her. Not just because she was incredibly pretty with her English-rose looks and her astonishing talent that left him breathless – there was a sweetness about her that drew him in, and a vulnerability that made him want to protect her.

He knew he was taking a risk pushing her in her career, but he could also see that she was burning to pursue it herself and perhaps this Morton guy was a good option. As a friend of Tilda's, he'd be less likely to betray her trust, wouldn't he?

'You okay?' he asked her as they left the rural villages of the Weald behind and headed towards the motorway.

She nodded.

'You're just normally pale, quiet and pensive?'

'Yep.'

'Well, it's a long drive if you're not talking.'

'You want to talk?'

He shrugged. 'Sure.'

'What about?'

'Your plans for today.'

'My plans for today. Let me see. To get through it and make it back home without having a nervous breakdown and without having sold my soul?'

'Good plan.'

'Yeah, I think it is.'

'Always have a plan,' Laurence said.

She turned to face him. 'You plan things, don't you? I mean, you strike me as the sort.'

'The sort?'

'You're a numbers guy. You're logical, organised.'

'Is that right?'

'Isn't it?'

He shrugged. 'I suppose so.'

'I wish I was more like that,' she said.

'Why would you wish that?' he asked. 'You shouldn't ever want to be something you're not. Take it from me. I once had this crazy notion of being a footballer. I joined a team whilst I was at university and promptly broke my arm in a fall. I'll never forget the pain and humiliation. Put me firmly in my place. I had a lot of time to think with my arm all bandaged up. I should never have been out on the pitch – it wasn't the right place for me.'

'But didn't you enjoy it whilst you were there?'

Laurence cast his mind back. 'Not really because it didn't feel right. I think I was just rebelling a bit and trying to impress people.'

There was a pause.

'So don't ever try and be somebody you're not, Tilda. You'll break your arm if you do.'

'I'll make a note of that,' she said. 'But what if it's somebody else who's trying to change you?'

'What do you mean? Like the music industry?'

She nodded. 'I was just thinking about the time I got a makeover. They dyed my hair blonde.'

Laurence did a double take. 'What do you mean? You are blonde!'

'Apparently, I wasn't blonde enough. They wanted me blonder.'

'Blonder than what?'

She laughed. 'The sun? I don't know.'

'That's crazy.'

'They also asked if I'd ever consider having a nose job.'

'You're kidding, right?'

'I wish I was. It's pretty standard, I've heard.'

'But there's nothing wrong with your nose.'

Her hand automatically flew to her face as if to check and Laurence couldn't help wondering how many times she'd felt anxious about her appearance. The music industry certainly sounded as if it could breed insecurity.

'They also wanted me to wear contact lenses to make my eyes even bluer and fake eyelashes that were so ridiculous, I could hardly see out of them.'

'And what did you say?'

'I said I wouldn't be able to sing to an audience I couldn't see.'

Laurence laughed. 'Did you?'

She nodded. 'And I told them what I wanted to wear too, which they didn't listen to, but at least I won the battle of the eyelashes.'

Laurence cast a look at her now. She was wearing blue jeans and a pretty white lacy blouse. Her hair was loose and natural and he couldn't imagine why anybody in their right mind would want to change her, but that was show business for you, he supposed.

'It wasn't the physical changes that bothered me, though. It was the changes they wanted to make to my sound. They'd taken me on the strength of one of my own songs, so that's what I thought they liked about me, but they didn't want that. They chucked it away.'

'Makes you wonder why they sign artists up if they just want to change them.'

'I think they always have to feel in control. They find the raw talent and mould it into something that they hope will sell. They don't listen to what the actual artist has to say.'

'But that's not going to happen again, right?' Laurence asked.

'Right. Morton knows how I feel about it all. I don't think he's going to mess with me.'

'So I'll recognise you when I pick you up later today? You won't have dyed your hair or had a nose job?'

She laughed. 'No way!'

'Good,' he said, 'because you're perfect just the way you are.'

She looked at him, her eyes bright in that beautiful face of hers, and then she turned away and took her phone out of her handbag and started doing a little dance with her thumbs. It was what Laurence thought of as the 'I don't want to talk to you' thumb dance. She probably wasn't doing anything really; it was her way of sending him a very clear message: *You've overstepped the mark and I think it best we don't talk anymore.*

They didn't speak for the rest of the journey and Laurence was quite relieved when they finally reached their destination.

'Is this it?' Laurence said, peering up at a large building which looked like a warehouse.

Tilda checked the address again. 'I think so.'

'Want me to come in with you?'

'No,' she said hastily. 'Thank you.'

He nodded. 'Good luck.'

'I don't need luck – just a good business head.'

Laurence smiled at that. He was tempted to join her to keep an eye on the proceedings, but he didn't want to totally freak her out. Anyway, he really did have a few errands to run whilst he was in the city.

'Call me when you're ready to leave, or sooner if you need me – if Morton upsets you.'

She sighed. 'I won't let him upset me, Laurence.'

'Here's my number, okay?' He handed her one of his new business cards, which she put in her handbag. 'I'll see you later.'

'It'll probably be late,' she warned.

'I don't mind. Whenever you're ready.'

She flashed him a brief, anxious smile and he watched as she got out of the car and crossed the pavement, pausing outside the large metal door before pressing the buzzer and disappearing inside.

Laurence did his best to fill his day without worrying too much about Tilda. He met with two of his clients, stocked up on some stationery from a favourite store of his, bought a tin of biscuits from Fortnum & Mason for his dad and had a walk by the river. Every half an hour, he'd check his phone to make sure he hadn't missed a call, but she didn't get in touch until after six.

'Hey!' she said. 'You still in town?'

'Of course!'

'Haven't got bored and left without me?'

'No, of course not. You ready to go?'

'As soon as you can get me. We're just going to grab a coffee from round the corner, but I'll be back at the studio in ten minutes, okay?'

'I'll see you there. Probably take me half an hour to get to you.'

'Perfect! Just buzz on the door.'

But Laurence didn't need to buzz because she was waiting for him outside the studio when he arrived. She didn't spot him at first and he watched her as she stood on the pavement, her hair blowing around her face as she did the thumb dance on her phone. Then he sounded the horn, quickly and lightly, and she looked up, beaming him a smile and waving.

'How did it go?' he asked as she got into the car.

'Good.'

'That all?'

'Isn't that enough?'

'It's a good start.'

She chewed her lip.

'You've got to give me more than "good",' he told her.

'What do you want to hear?'

'That you've just cut a new single and have a brand-new album planned.'

'Ha ha!'

'So?'

She took a deep breath. 'He wants to record with me.'

'Well, of course he does. He'd be a fool not to want that.' He looked at her, trying to gauge how she felt about it. 'And what did you say?'

'That I'd think about it.'

'Okay.' He pulled out into the road and set the satnav for home.

'Today was just about listening to what he had to say and looking around the studio.'

'Sure,' he said, not wanting to pressurise her. 'That's good.'

'Yeah.' She stared out of the window at the smart terraces of West London.

They'd just hit the motorway when Tilda started to hum something. Laurence listened for a few moments, scared that if he interrupted her, she'd clam up.

'Is that a new song?' he asked as soon as she stopped.

'What?'

'That tune you were humming.'

'I wasn't humming.'

'You most certainly were.'

'Was I?' She looked genuinely surprised and then her forehead crinkled and she nodded. 'I suppose I was.'

'What's it called? I mean, does it have a name?'

'"Blue-sky Girl".'

'Good title.'

'Yeah?'

'It's really nice, you know? Happy, summery.'

'Don't talk to me about summery songs.'

'Sorry,' he said, remembering that her big hit single that had caused her so many problems had been called 'Summer Song'.

'This is a new one.'

'One you wrote?'

'Co-wrote.'

'With Morton?'

'Uh-huh.'

'Just now – in London?'

She laughed. 'Don't look so surprised.'

'You really wrote a whole song today?'

'Well, it probably needs a bit of tidying up, but it's mostly there.'

'Wow! All I did was meet a couple of clients and buy some stationery. I thought you said you were just talking things through today.'

'Well, we were, but then – you know . . .'

'I'm afraid I don't.'

'I think it was after the third cup of coffee.'

'Ah, so that's the trick! I obviously don't drink enough coffee to be creative.'

'Coffee does help.'

'So, what's that like – to have words and emotions pouring out of you like that?'

She didn't answer for a moment. 'I don't know how to explain it. It's always been a part of me. It's just something I do, like breathing.'

'You breathe out songs?'

'Something like that.'

'I breathe out spreadsheets.'

She laughed again. He loved making her laugh.

'Sing it to me,' he said.

'No way!'

'Oh, go on. I'd love to hear it.'

It took a further three miles of unrelenting persuasion before Tilda sang 'Blue-sky Girl' for Laurence.

'You really wrote that today? Sing it again, will you?'

'Oh, Laurence!'

He started humming.

'What are you doing?' she asked. 'You've got it all wrong.'

'And I'll continue to get it wrong if you don't sing it again. Go on!'

She rolled her eyes. 'Just once, okay?'

By the time they reached Elhurst, they'd sung the song together at least half a dozen times and Laurence was word perfect. They were both laughing and singing in equal measure as they pulled into Orley Court.

'I think you've got a hit on your hands there,' he told her.

She fell silent for a moment. 'I don't want to think about that. I just want to enjoy this song for what it is. I don't want to share it yet.'

'You shared it with me.'

'Yes, but you're different.'

'Am I?'

'You're my friend.'

'I see,' he said. So, she saw him as an agony uncle and a friend, he thought with a little sigh.

'My very good friend,' she added, seeming to sense his disappointment.

They got out of the car and walked to the house through the garden. It was just beginning to get dark and a few swallows were screeching overhead, eating insects on the wing.

'Thank you for today,' she said as they entered the porch together, stopping before she opened the door. 'I'm so glad I went.' And then she did something that surprised him so much he nearly fell over backwards: she went up on tiptoes and kissed his cheek.

'Oh!' he said.

She laughed. 'You look so funny.'

'Do I?'

'And cute.'

'Oh, really?'

'You're sweet, Laurence.'

He smiled and looked into the sky-blue eyes of this blue-sky girl. Her face looked so soft and rosy and inviting. Was she inviting him to kiss her? There was only one way to find out and so he slowly lowered his face to hers and brushed her lips with his. She didn't pull away.

'Tilda?'

'Hmm?'

'Was that all right? I mean, was it okay I just did that?'

'Yes,' she whispered before turning away from him to open the front door.

He swallowed hard, trying to gather his thoughts as they entered the hallway together and she turned back towards him.

'Today's been nice,' she said.

'Nice?' He couldn't disguise his disappointment at her choice of words.

'Interesting,' she said, a tiny smile tickling the corners of her lips. 'Laurence – Laurie—'

'I like that.'

'I've got a lot to think about just now and my head's spinning with it all.'

'I know.'

'Goodnight, then.'

He watched her turn to go. Part of him was frustrated at losing her so soon after they'd shared the most intimate of moments, but he didn't want to put any more pressure on her, so he stood there in the cool silence of the hallway while he tried to calm down, and then he walked into the north wing alone.

Chapter 18

When Tilda awoke the next morning, she had five texts from Morton but none from Laurence, which left her with a strangely deflated feeling. But, then again, they did live in the same building so maybe he was hoping they'd see each other and that they didn't need to text. What could you say in a text anyway? She sometimes hated the impersonal, impossible succinctness of a text. She'd once gone out with someone who'd texted her the weirdest messages. He'd seemed to have his own language or perhaps he was just bad at spelling, she thought. Anyway, she'd wanted to shout at him, 'Just ring me up, okay?' People didn't talk anymore. Perhaps that was why she liked Laurence so much – because he talked to her. He listened too, which had also endeared him to her. He truly seemed to be interested in her and to care, and that was quite addictive.

And the kiss? She smiled as she thought about the cosy, warm feeling of being so close to Laurence in the porch, with the swallows screaming across the inky sky and the evening air cooling their faces.

She really did like him, but wouldn't a relationship complicate things? What if whatever this was between them didn't work out? They were neighbours now and, no matter how attracted she was to him, there could be years of awkward moments ahead of them if they got it wrong. Tilda sighed, chastising herself for being so negative when nothing but good things were happening to her.

She got out of bed and showered, leaving her hair to dry naturally and enjoying the sensation of the warm air on it when she opened her bedroom window and leaned outside. It was going to be a beautiful day. It was a pity she had to teach at the local comprehensive because she would have liked to sit in the garden with her paper and pencil, the way she'd used to before the pop world had claimed her. After her day with Morton and her singing marathon with Laurence, she was finally feeling inspired to write again.

Leaving her room, she made her way to the morning room, standing in the doorway for a moment, looking at the ornate plasterwork ceiling, the mullioned windows and the fine oak-panelled walls as if seeing them for the first time. It was probably the loveliest room in the whole of England and she felt so privileged to have breakfast there each morning. But would that all change if she launched another music career? Would she have to spend part of her week in London, if not move there altogether like last time? What sacrifices would she have to make?

She remembered the sharp agony of missing home when she was on the road promoting 'Summer Song'. How she'd longed to return to Orley, to sneak away from her impersonal hotels in the middle of the night and run back home to the Weald. And yet she couldn't deny how much she'd enjoyed her time in the studio with Morton yesterday. It had felt right somehow, and natural. She'd loved it all – the mad scampering out to get coffee and the buzz of writing with someone. But it could so easily lead her to living in a way that she didn't like.

'What are you doing?' Jassy called over from the breakfast table.

'Yes, darling – you do look funny standing in the door like that,' her mother said, bringing her out of her reverie. 'Come in and have some breakfast. Jassy was just telling me about her latest project. She's painting something new every day for a month. Isn't that exciting?'

'Is Marcus joining in too?' Tilda asked as she walked towards them.

'He is, but he's very slow so I'm not sure he'll keep up.'

'Don't be so hard on him,' Vanessa said.

'You've got to be hard if you're a teacher, haven't you, Tilly?'

'Well, tough rather than hard,' Tilda corrected. 'And don't forget to be encouraging too.'

'Of course I'm encouraging!' Jassy said. 'Just yesterday, I told him that he wasn't making nearly as many mistakes as when he began.'

Tilda and her mother exchanged an amused glance.

'So, how was London?' Vanessa asked.

Tilda had only said a brief goodnight to her mother and sister after getting back with Laurence, claiming tiredness. Now, however, she would face the questions head on.

'It was good. We wrote a song.'

'Really? That's wonderful, darling!'

'What's it called?' Jassy asked.

'"Blue-sky Girl".'

'Oh, lovely!' her mother said.

'Are you going to release it?' Jassy wanted to know.

'I'm not sure,' Tilda said, pouring herself a glass of fruit juice and taking a sip. 'There's a lot to think about.'

'And no need to rush,' her mother told her. 'You take your time.'

Tilda nodded.

'Did Laurie go with you?' Jassy asked.

'Not into the studio. He had his own things to do.' Tilda cleared her throat as she chose a cereal from the middle of the table.

'So, you got on okay?' her mother asked.

'Of course.' Tilda could feel the weight of her mother's gaze upon her. 'What?'

'Are you telling us everything, Tilda Jacobs?'

'What do you mean?'

'You're blushing,' Jassy said, following their mother's lead and staring at Tilda remorselessly.

'I'm not blushing. It's just a warm day.'

'You like Laurie, don't you? And he likes you. I can see that,' Jassy said.

233

Victoria Connelly

'We're friends, okay?'

'Nothing more than that?' Vanessa asked.

'Mum!'

'I mean, he's a handsome man. Sweet too. And goodness only knows *they* don't come along very often. It would be only natural if you became . . .' She paused. 'Friends.'

Tilda sighed, knowing that she wasn't going to get a moment's peace until she told them.

'Oh, all right then,' she said, forgetting all about her breakfast. 'We kissed!'

'You kissed Laurie?' Her mother looked surprised by her admission.

'Well, it was more like he kissed me.'

'Where did he kiss you?' Jassy asked.

'On the mouth,' Tilda said, knowing that's not what her sister had meant at all.

'No, *where*?'

'In the porch.'

Vanessa gasped.

'What?' Tilda asked.

'That's where I kissed Jonathan. Well, the south porch.'

Jassy frowned. 'Is the mistletoe still up there from Christmas?'

Vanessa laughed.

'Since when have you been kissing Jonathan, Mum?'

'Since we went out on that evening walk.' She gave a little smile and Tilda had to admit that it was wonderful to see her mother look so happy again.

'Wait a minute,' Jassy said. 'If you marry Laurie, does that mean we'll get the north wing back or will he get the whole house?'

'Jassy! Nobody's talking about getting married! It was just a kiss.'

'It's never just a kiss,' Jassy countered. 'I've watched films and it never ends in just a kiss.'

'Who's been kissing?' Dolly asked as she sneaked into the room, causing all three of them to jump.

'Everybody!' Jassy cried.

'Traitor!' Tilda hissed under her breath.

'Is there something I should know?' Dolly asked as she approached the table.

'Probably not,' Vanessa said.

'I wouldn't ask if I were you,' Jassy said, noisily scraping her chair back and standing up. 'Right, I'm off to paint before I catch this kissing thing.'

Tilda couldn't help grinning. She'd get her revenge one day when her little sister fell in love.

Laurence had woken as the first light brightened the sky. Instantly, his mind flooded with Tilda and the lyrics from 'Blue-sky Girl' returned to him, making him smile. And the kiss. That sweet, gentle kiss. In all his years, he'd never wanted to kiss anyone as much as he had Tilda, but he'd been anxious about it too, not wanting to cross any boundaries. They were neighbours now and that might make things tricky.

He wondered if she was worrying as much as he was. Probably not. She was most likely writing more wonderful songs.

Laurence suddenly baulked. What if Tilda wrote a song about him? Isn't that what songwriters did? They used all their experience of relationships as material for their music. Her follow up to 'Blue-sky Girl' could very well feature Laurence. He felt cold just thinking about the possibility.

Get a grip, he told himself. *It was just a kiss. She isn't likely to immortalise that in a song.*

235

But it had been a very special kiss – to him at least – and, if he could write songs, he'd have written twenty since the night before, he was sure of it.

'But I'm a financial adviser,' he said as he walked through to the kitchen for a cup of tea. For a moment, he thought about what Tilda had said about coffee. Maybe he should buy a big sack of the stuff.

'Who am I trying to kid?' he said to himself. He wasn't an artist and he had to accept that. He'd never be able to write a song to express how he felt, but perhaps it was time that he did express how he felt about Tilda.

He'd thought about texting her last night, but that would have been just weird, wouldn't it? What would he have said, anyway: *Made it home okay?* He already knew that. But he wanted her to know that he cared about her.

Taking his cup of tea through to his study, he switched his computer on. After his meetings in London, he had a whole heap of work to get through and so, for the time being, he put his blue-sky girl out of his mind and settled down at his desk.

It wasn't until late afternoon when his phone beeped with a text. It was from Tilda.

In south garden. Want to join me? T

He was out of his study before he could press 'Send' on his reply to her.

She hadn't told him exactly where she was in the south garden. There were a number of secluded benches, but Laurence instinctively knew that she would be sitting on the one overlooking the pond and, sure enough, as he approached he saw her there. She was wearing a wide-brimmed summer hat and a simple white dress, and on her lap was a notebook and pencil. She looked so peaceful and he was reluctant to disturb her, but she had summoned him and he very much wanted to talk to her.

'Hello,' he said.

She looked up. 'Hi. Come sit.'

Laurence didn't need to be asked twice.

'Been writing?' he asked.

'Yes. I have.'

'That's good.'

'Been . . .' She paused. 'Spreadsheeting?'

He laughed. 'Something like that.'

'I spent the day in school,' she told him. 'I take one after-school class and a few individual pupils during the day. It's a nice job. I don't have to travel far, the work is rewarding and the pay isn't bad.' She shrugged. 'But it still doesn't fulfil me. It's annoying, sometimes, to admit to this hunger I have for something more.'

'You shouldn't be annoyed by it; you should embrace it.'

'I knew you'd say that.' She flashed him a smile.

'And did you need to hear it?'

'I think I did.'

He watched her closely, waiting for her to go on but she didn't. 'You know what you're going to do, don't you?'

She looked at him and he felt as if he were holding his breath both for himself and for her.

'Yes,' she said at last.

'And?' he dared to ask.

'I'm going to give things a go with Morton.' She chewed her lip and her brow furrowed. 'I can't not do this.'

'Tilda, I'm so pleased.' He reached out and squeezed her hand. 'And excited!'

'I'm so excited, I can hardly breathe!' she confessed. 'But I'm not doing this for the fame or a position in the charts.'

'I know you're not,' he assured her.

'It's purely about the music this time. It's about having a vision and sticking to it. Morton understands that better than anyone. He's on board with this. He's not going to use me or turn me into something I'm not just to take advantage of the public and make a quick buck.'

Laurence nodded. 'Don't forget to breathe!'

She looked puzzled. 'How did you know I was holding my breath?'

'I think you do that a lot – when you're all excited and stressed at the same time.'

She pursed her lips. 'You're right. I do.'

'Take a few good, deep breaths.'

She laughed. 'I'm going to have to employ you as my manager.'

'I'd readily agree,' he said, knowing she was joking, but kind of hoping that she wasn't.

'I used to get like this before a performance. It's like an adrenaline overload where everything's speeded up as if somebody's hit the fast-forward button on your life.'

'Yeah, that's just how I get whenever I open a new spreadsheet.'

Tilda play-punched his arm and he laughed. 'Silly!'

'Sorry. Couldn't resist,' he said. 'There's not a lot in my line of work that gives you an adrenaline rush. That's probably why I'm so fascinated with yours.'

'Yes, but don't forget that adrenaline might drive a decent performance, but it makes you feel really bad!'

They sat quietly for a moment, watching as a pair of swallows dipped low over the pond.

'What's it like?' Laurence asked at last.

'What's what like?'

'Standing in the middle of the stage with a crowd before you.'

Tilda took a deep breath, as if imagining herself in that very position again. 'Wonderful. Terrifying. It's like nothing else in the world. You see all these faces staring back at you, and you know they're waiting for you to perform and entertain them. You have the power to make them love you or hate you and, before you begin, you don't know which way that's going to go. But, when the music starts, you get buoyed along and there's no stopping you, even if the crowd's booing, there's this need – in me at least – to get to the end of that song.'

Laurence must have been staring at her because she frowned at him. 'What?'

He shook his head. 'That must be amazing.'

'It is. But you've seen what the flipside of that can be. It can go from being the best experience in the world to the worst at breakneck speed.'

'So, when do you think you'll begin recording with Morton?'

'I'm not sure. Soon.'

'That's really great.' He took her hand again.

'Laurie?' she said gently.

'Yes?'

She cleared her throat, suddenly looking very unsure of herself. 'You're one of the sweetest people I've ever met.'

He smiled at that confession, but he couldn't help feeling apprehensive too, as if he sensed what was coming next.

'What is it, Tilda?' he asked when she looked down at the ground. 'Tell me. I can take it.'

'I know, but I don't want to . . .' She paused and pulled a strand of hair, twisting it around her finger.

'What?'

'I don't want to have to tell you this, but I need space. For the present.'

'Okay.'

She held his gaze. 'You know what I'm saying?'

'I think so.'

'I mean I can't get involved. Romantically.'

'And you think that's what's happening here?'

'Isn't it?'

'Well, I was hoping so,' he said. 'I wasn't sure how you felt about it all, but I really like you, Tilda. You're talented and fascinating and beautiful.'

'And completely overwhelmed by what's happening at the moment.' She took a deep breath. 'I like you. I really do, but it's not a good time. I need to keep a clear head. I need to be focused. Do you understand?'

'Of course I do,' he told her. 'And I wouldn't want to do anything to stop you reaching your full potential. I really wouldn't. But I'd love to be part of it.'

'How?'

'Perhaps I can just be a good friend? You know, listen to you when you need to talk, and talk to you if you need any advice.'

'You're too good to be true.'

'I assure you I'm not. I'll still want to be kissing you at every available opportunity.'

'Laurie!'

'Sorry. I promise not to kiss you again unless you explicitly ask me to.'

She gave a tiny smile. 'You don't mind then?'

'Of course I mind. I'm only human! I want to get to know you. I think we could be really good together.'

'Do you?'

'Don't you?'

She looked out across the garden and then turned back to him. 'Can I answer that another time?'

He sighed. 'You certainly know how to keep a fellow on tenterhooks.'

'I'm sorry. I—'

'Don't apologise. You don't need to.' He let go of her hand and stood up from the bench. 'Just know I'm here for you, Tilda.'

She nodded and he turned away, walking back through the garden towards the house and trying desperately to believe that she hadn't completely given him the brush-off.

It was later that day when Jonathan's van pulled up in the lane. Vanessa wasn't expecting to see him again that week because the team weren't due until Tuesday, but sometimes he popped round between jobs.

'I just couldn't wait,' he explained when she met him at the front door, leaning towards her and kissing her.

She invited him in, but he turned around and looked up at the sky. 'Come outside.' So she did.

They walked around to the walled garden. It seemed funny being there on their own without the team, but she loved having some peaceful, private time with Jonathan without any interruptions from the likes of Andy and Oz.

'How are things with Dolly?' he asked as they sat on an old wooden bench that overlooked the raised beds.

'Interesting,' Vanessa said. 'She's still gruff with me, but she doesn't seem so confrontational. I think she's hoping I'll bring you to see her again. She's always dropping you into the conversation.'

'Is she?'

'You made quite an impression on her.'

Jonathan smiled. 'I guess I just have a way with the ladies.'

Vanessa took in the smug smile on his face. 'Fine,' she said, with just a hint of humour, 'go flirt with Dolly!'

'I'd rather flirt with you,' he said, taking her hand and giving her the kind of look that heated her up from the inside out. She'd almost forgotten what it was like to feel that kind of adoration. It seemed like such a long time since Oliver had been able to give her attention like that. But she wasn't going to dwell on Oliver today. Not when she was holding hands with a handsome man.

'I love this time of year,' Jonathan said. 'All fear of frost is over and the plants are really going for it. The borders are filling out, the trees have hit perfection and fruit is forming in the orchards.'

'And there's so much to do in the garden!'

'Ah, but you must never forget to take time to sit down and just enjoy it all,' he said.

She nodded. 'I like to come out first thing in the morning when the grass is cool and dewy. I try not to fiddle and fidget with my trowel or run inside for my secateurs. It's just a time for looking, for taking it all in.'

They sat for a while longer, listening to the birdsong and the breeze in the trees, and Vanessa couldn't help feeling intensely grateful for that moment. Life was such a rush and tumble sometimes that it was important to be able to recognise the special moments when one was given them, even if it was just something as simple as sitting on a bench overlooking a garden. But, being with Jonathan, she couldn't be content with just that and she turned to look at him.

'Can I ask you something?'

'Sure,' he said.

Vanessa paused, hoping she wasn't about to go and spoil things. 'I was thinking – you know all about Oliver, but I don't know anything about your past relationships.'

'Well, I wouldn't say I know everything about Oliver. Just that you were married to him for a good long while.'

'So you know that I've been off the market for most of my adult life . . .'

'And?' He frowned at her. 'Where's this going?'

'I'd like to know more about you and your relationships.' There was an awful pause, during which Jonathan looked out across the garden and then up to the sky. 'You don't mind me asking, do you?'

'No, of course not,' he said. 'There's just not that much to tell you.'

'Tell me anyway.' Was it her imagination or did he look decidedly uncomfortable? He was shifting his feet about, scraping the soles of his big boots on the path.

'What can I say?' he said at last. 'I've been involved with a few women in my time but, for one reason or another, it's just never worked out.'

'Why not?'

'Different reasons,' he said evasively.

She left it a moment, hoping that he would elaborate. Finally, he cleared his throat.

'There was Cate. We were together about three years, but she moved away.'

'You didn't want to go with her?'

'We were kind of drifting apart by that stage and I'm ashamed to say that I used my home here as an excuse not to leave.'

'You loved your garden more than her?'

'I think I did,' he said. 'Is that terrible?'

'I don't think so. Gardens can often last much longer than relationships.'

'Mine's outseen quite a few,' he admitted and Vanessa smiled.

'Anyone else special?'

'There was Julia. I thought we'd be together longer than we were. She was a teacher. A bit bossy if I'm honest and she loved to timetable everything. Drove me nuts! She used to sit in the front room marking books and then she'd tell me that she would be finished in exactly forty-five minutes so I should have a shower and shave and she'd meet me in bed.'

'Really?'

'Really!'

Vanessa laughed. 'How funny!'

'I don't envy the poor sod who's ended up with her.'

They watched as a robin landed on the corner of the raised bed, observing them with his sideways glance.

'Rachelle,' Jonathan suddenly said.

'Who's that?' Vanessa asked.

'My last girlfriend.'

'That's a pretty name. Is she the girl in the photo?' Vanessa asked, thinking of the woman who'd looked to be in her late thirties.

'What photo?'

'On the bookcase in your living room.'

His eyebrows raised. 'Oh, so you saw that?'

'I'm a woman. It's my job to notice these things.' She smiled. 'Sorry. I didn't mean to be nosy, but I noticed her pretty face.'

He nodded and a sad expression passed over his face like a cloud hiding the sun. 'She certainly was pretty.'

'So, what happened?'

Again, he shuffled his boots together and stared out over the garden. 'It ended.'

Vanessa waited, wondering if he'd say any more, but he didn't.

'So there was Cate, Julia and Rachelle,' she said quietly.

'And a few – you know – others.'

'Okay.'

'And now Vanessa,' he said, stroking her hand with his work-roughened ones.

She leaned her head on his shoulder and breathed deeply. As much as she wanted to ask him more, she didn't want to push him away with her questions. She had the feeling that he wasn't telling her everything, but did that really matter?

Right then, sitting on the garden bench together, she didn't think that it did.

Chapter 19

There comes a moment in a summer garden when, after the long cold days of winter and interminably wet days of spring, everything just seems to speed up, when it reaches absolute perfection and the gardener wants to shout, 'Stop! Slow down! Let me enjoy this moment.'

So June rushed into July at Orley. Vanessa had lifted the tulip and hyacinth bulbs, Jonathan and his team had been sowing spring cabbages and pruning the wisteria on the south-east corner of the house, and Tilda had been back and forth to London writing, singing and recording. Marcus was still taking lessons with Jassy in the oast house and Dolly was showing an interest in the work being done in the walled garden and had occasionally been seen out there, although Reynolds had taken a dislike to Andy and had attacked his ankles on more than one occasion.

Everything and everyone seemed to have found a place and a rhythm. Except Laurence. He'd found a routine, he supposed, but he didn't feel settled.

Gazing outside at the blue summer sky, he couldn't help but feel isolated. *Alone in paradise*, he thought. When he'd known he and his father would be moving to Orley together, he'd sincerely believed that it would be a new start for them. Well, it was of course. He'd got his business up and running and his father had found an outlet in his painting and friendship with Jasmine and Skinny the cat. But Laurence felt that he and his father were no nearer to becoming closer. Laurence's dreams of starting a garden together had gone nowhere, they hadn't taken any long, ambling walks in the countryside and mealtimes were rushed affairs with his father anxious to flit back to the oast house. They hadn't really talked about anything but the most mundane of subjects even though Laurence had pushed and pushed.

He was just about to make a call to one of his clients to arrange a meeting when he heard a light knock on his study door.

'Laurence?' a voice came.

'Vanessa?' He got up from his chair and opened the door, shocked by the pale face which greeted him.

'You okay?'

'Yes. I'm okay,' she said, 'but I'm worried about Tilda.'

'What's wrong?'

'It's that song of hers – the new one. It's online and—'

'And what?'

'It seems to have got a lot of attention.'

'Okay,' he said. 'And that's not good?'

'Well, it is. There are lots of really great comments, but there are some stinkers too and I think Tilda's focusing on those in that way she has in the past. I'm afraid she's going into meltdown like she did after she came home from that tour.'

'Where's this website?' He motioned to his desk and Vanessa sat on his chair, quickly going online.

'This is the latest site for indie artists,' she told him. 'It's all the rage, apparently. It's been in the press a lot and there's a lot of really good material on here.'

Laurence watched as Vanessa found the page created by her daughter, and Morton too, no doubt.

Blue-sky Girl.

Vanessa played a bit of the track and then scrolled down to the comments before getting up from the chair.

'You'd better read them,' she said ominously.

Laurence sat down and read the comments and then cursed. Some were pure vitriol, as if the people writing them had nothing but bile in their brains.

Isn't this Tilly? someone had written. *She should stick to what she's good at – singing her silly teen girl songs.*

That was one of the tamer comments. Some were full of profanities, insults and obscenities. It was truly horrible.

'Oh, God!' Laurence said. 'Has Tilda read all these?'

'I think she's making a study of them.'

He shook his head. 'That's not healthy.'

'It's like the press she got as Tilly. She became obsessed with it and seemed to internalise all the negative comments.'

Laurence was out of his chair and up onto his feet in an instant.

'I'll go and talk to her.'

'I hope it's okay to come to you with this. You two are close, aren't you?'

'Well, I'm not sure about that to be absolutely honest.'

'Oh dear!'

'But I'll help if I can.'

'Will you?'

'Of course I will. Where is she?'

'In the living room with that laptop of hers.'

Laurence nodded and then placed a reassuring hand on Vanessa's shoulder. 'It'll be okay.'

Sure enough, Tilda was sitting pale-faced at her laptop when Laurence found her.

'Hey,' he said as he walked in and sat on the sofa beside her.

'Did Mum tell you?' Tilda asked, looking at him.

'She's worried about you.'

'I'm okay.'

'You don't look okay.'

She closed her laptop and folded her hands over it as if trapping all the bad things inside.

'I shouldn't have listened to Morton.'

'Why?'

'Because he encouraged me to do this.'

'And you didn't want to do it yourself?'

She bit her lower lip as if knowing Laurence had caught her out. 'I guess I did.'

'I think you did the right thing.'

'How can you say that? Have you seen the comments?'

'I had a quick look.'

'And they're terrible!'

'Sure. Some of them are. Bound to be. You put your work on a public forum, Tilda. A public forum which idiots can access anytime, day or night, whether they've got a brain in their heads or a belly full of beer.'

'It's fine for you to say that. They're not saying those things about you,' Tilda said.

'And they're not really saying them about you either.'

'What do you mean?'

'They're trolls, searching the Internet for places to leave their malicious mark. It doesn't matter who you are or what you've put out into the world, they're going to hate it.'

She shook her head. 'They've made comments about music. The lyrics. The way I sing.'

'You're seriously going to take notice of these imbeciles who have nothing better to do than pour poison on somebody's art because they're not talented enough to create their own?'

He took hold of the laptop and opened it, quickly finding what he wanted.

'Who is this' – he squinted, reading the name of the person who'd left a particularly nasty comment – 'this PJBottoms anyway? The name probably sums them up – a lazy good-for-nothing couch potato. Probably three stone overweight without a creative bone in their body!'

Tilda gave a little laugh.

'You know you can sing and this is a great song, Tilda! These people – these naysayers – would leave a nasty comment on anything good and pure out there. It says a lot more about them than it does you. They're hiding behind a computer and a moniker whereas you've had the courage to put your soul out there. You've dared to step out onto the world stage whereas they're sitting at home in their pyjamas. Anyway, there are plenty of great comments too. You have read those, haven't you?'

She nodded. 'I'm afraid it's the nasty ones that stick in the mind.'

'Well, you've got to focus on the good ones. Here – read this one: "This is such a pretty song. I hope she's got an album coming out soon." And this: "Her voice is so pure. I love it!"'

'Yeah, that's really nice.'

'And there are others – loads of others – just like that. Read those, Tilda. Write them down. Copy them into a document and print them out. And forget the PJBottoms of the world. They're not worth the space in that incredible imagination of yours.'

She smiled. 'You say all the right things, don't you?'

'Do I?'

She nodded and, for a moment, he thought about reaching out to hold her hand, but that was when he heard the front door open.

'She's in the living room,' Vanessa was telling somebody and, before he knew what was happening, Morton Singer had entered.

'Morton?' Tilda said, obviously as surprised as Laurence was.

'I had to come,' he said, crossing the room. Tilda stood up and was instantly in his embrace.

'Are you okay?' Morton asked her, stroking her hair in a gesture that, to Laurence, looked way too intimate for a work colleague.

'I got myself all upset, but Laurence has been really kind.'

Morton cast a glance in his direction and he stood up.

'Oh,' Tilda said, 'you've not met, have you?'

'No,' Morton said, flicking his too-long hair out of his eyes. He was wearing a leather jacket and a ripped T-shirt, which Laurence suspected had been ripped at the time of manufacture. Ridiculous. 'Morton Singer.' He extended a hand sporting a silver skull ring. Laurence shook it with his own ring-free hand.

'Laurence Sturridge.' He saw Tilda glance from him to Morton and back again and, as much as he didn't want to back down and leave the room, he realised that Morton wasn't likely to, having just come from London, and so he did the decent thing.

'I'll leave you guys to it,' he said.

'Yes,' Morton said, throwing a scowl his way.

'Oh, you don't need to go, Laurie,' Tilda said. 'Stay with us.'

'No, no,' he said, knowing his place. 'I'll – er – I'll see you later, Tilda.' He gave her a brief smile and then left the room.

Vanessa had borrowed Jenna from the team and the two of them were staking flowers in the herbaceous border in the south garden. She'd really noticed a change in the girl of late. She'd arrived as a shy, gawky young woman who had to get somebody to ask where the toilet was on her behalf, but now she was taking the initiative, suggesting jobs for both herself and the others and always asking questions. It was quite remarkable. Only the other day, she'd asked if she could stay behind because she wanted to finish a task she'd started and couldn't bear to leave it dangling until the next week. Jonathan had been surprised but delighted, coming back to pick her up later so he could take her home.

Vanessa had worked with her into the evening and the two of them had chatted amiably. Vanessa smiled as she remembered how she'd sneaked into the house to secure the last two slices of a ginger cake that Dolly had bought from a WI function. She'd deal with the wrath of Dolly later, she'd thought. There'd been nobody more deserving of that cake than Jenna.

There had been a time when her daughters had joined her in the garden, working alongside her and Oliver to create something beautiful together, but then Tilda had found her music and Jasmine her art, and every hour of their free time was given to their own passions. She'd expect no less really, but she had to admit that it was nice to have a new companion in Jenna.

Jenna was the first person Vanessa had thought of to help her in the south garden. She liked working there and she was hoping Jenna would enjoy it too. Staking flowers was a peaceful job which Vanessa always enjoyed, especially when the sun was on your back as it was today. Jenna, however, didn't look as happy as usual. Her face contorted in concentration as she seemed to struggle with the brown string.

'Are you all right?' Vanessa asked her.

'I'm fine,' Jenna said through gritted teeth.

'Do you need a hand with that?'

'I'm okay.'

Vanessa watched her, noticing that the girl's hands were shaking.

'How about we get a cup of tea?'

Jenna looked up and Vanessa saw that there were tears swimming in her eyes.

'Come on – come with me.' Vanessa placed her hand on her shoulder.

A few minutes later and the two of them were in the kitchen of the main house. Jenna's eyes had flittered around the rooms as she'd walked through them, but she'd been uncharacteristically quiet.

'Chocolate biscuit?' Vanessa asked as the kettle boiled.

Jenna nodded. She was never one to turn down a chocolate biscuit, Vanessa noted, handing her the tin.

'Help yourself and have a seat.'

Jenna took two biscuits and went to sit at the kitchen table. It was a room that wasn't used much for eating in, which was a shame because it was very pretty with its quarry-tiled floor and view over the garden and the gentle hills to the west of Orley. The family usually ate in the morning room in the mornings and evenings and then grabbed lunch on the go, rarely seeing each other in the middle of the day.

Vanessa made the tea and sat down opposite Jenna, waiting for her to say something because she didn't want to push her. If Jenna was anything like her daughters then the gentlest of prods would make her clam up for good.

'He's seeing somebody,' Jenna said after she'd finished her second biscuit.

'Your boyfriend?' Vanessa said, trying desperately to remember his name.

'Carl,' she said.

'Did he tell you he's seeing someone?'

'He don't need to. I know.'

'How?'

'Because he never sees me anymore, that's how. He just turns up at three in the morning, stinking of beer and needing a place to crash. He's probably been kicked out of hers by then and knows his mum will kill him if he goes home.'

'He still lives with his parents?'

'His mum and sister. They're soft on him. Let him get away with murder, but his mum can't stand him drinking.'

'So you let him stay at yours?'

'I made him sleep on the sofa last night. I told him I didn't want him near me.'

'Good for you.'

'He went before I got up, but he left his jacket behind.' She paused and took a sip of tea and Vanessa felt that there was more to come.

'I checked his pockets,' Jenna continued. 'I don't know why. I suppose I was looking for something. Clues. I don't know.' She looked up and Vanessa saw the haunted look on her face. 'There were some photos in his pocket. You know those little passport ones? It was of him with some girl I've never seen. They were messing about. Kissing and stuff. It was probably the same place he took me to get our photos done.'

'Oh, no.'

She nodded. 'I tore them up. I tore them up and stamped on them before putting them in the bin with some old spaghetti.'

'Oh, Jenna!' Vanessa could feel the waves of pain coming off her.

'I love him. I can't help it. I know he's no good for me, but I love him all the same.' She started to cry.

Vanessa got up from her chair and was by her side in an instant. She wrapped her arms around the girl, noticing her bony shoulders. Was there any pain sharper than unrequited love? Vanessa didn't think so. Not when you were young and hadn't yet experienced the pain of losing a loved one.

She continued to hold Jenna as the girl cried, letting her free all the pain she'd been bottling up inside for goodness only knew how long.

'How are you feeling?' Vanessa asked at last, handing her a tissue to mop up her face.

Jenna gave a little nod and a big sniff. 'Can I wash my face?'

Vanessa pointed to a door which led into a cloakroom and Jenna disappeared, coming out a moment later after she'd calmed her face down a little.

'Why don't I drop you home?' Vanessa offered, not knowing where exactly Jenna lived.

'No,' she said. 'I want to get out into the garden.'

'You sure?'

'Yes. It calms me.'

Vanessa smiled. 'Me too. You know, when my husband was ill, the garden was my sanctuary. I don't know what I would have done without it. It kept me sane during a really rough time. It always has. Even if life is good and you've got no real worries, gardening still helps. It makes you see the bigger picture – the changing seasons, the fact that life goes on.'

'I'd like to have my own one day,' Jenna said.

'I'm sure you will.'

'Will you come and visit it?'

'I'd love to.'

'Thanks,' Jenna said.

'What for?'

'For listening to me. I don't have many people I can talk to.'

Vanessa tried not to look saddened by this admission. 'Well, you can talk to me whenever you need to, okay?'

They exchanged smiles and then left the kitchen and went back into the garden.

It wasn't until the end of the day that Vanessa managed to catch Jonathan and fill him in on what had happened to Jenna.

Jonathan let out a long slow sigh. 'I wish she'd make the break and tell him where to go. He's no good for her.'

'But she's in love with him,' Vanessa said.

'What is that about? How can she love someone who treats her so badly?'

'That's just it – you can't reason when it comes to love. You can't just switch it off when it suits you.'

'But it's making her so unhappy. I hate seeing her like this.'

'Me too.'

'Did she talk to you?'

'Yes. But mostly she just cried.'

'And she's okay now?'

'I think so.'

Jonathan ran a hand through his hair. He looked stressed. 'Look, I'd better get them home. It's been a long day. Did you get on okay with her? I mean, other than the breakdown?'

'Of course I did. She's a great girl. She gives a lot.'

'I know,' Jonathan said. 'Too much sometimes. I did warn you not to get involved, didn't I?'

'You did,' Vanessa said, 'and I didn't listen.'

Jonathan shook his head. 'I knew you wouldn't. You'll pay the price, you know.'

'Very likely.'

He leaned in and kissed her cheek. 'I'll call you later.'

'Hey, I know you're rushing off now but have you thought any more about your plans for you and the team at the fete?' Vanessa asked.

'Why don't you come over tonight and we can talk about it?'

'I'd like that.'

'Good.' He gave her a wink that made her feel like a woman half her age, and she watched as he walked to his van and left for the day.

Everything was changing, wasn't it? That's what went through Jasmine's mind as she saw her mum waving Jonathan off. She'd just come out of the oast house where she'd been working all day with Marcus. They'd run out of teabags and she was making a quick dash to the house when she spotted them. She stopped and watched, unobserved, as Jonathan leaned forward to kiss her mum. That was hard to take in even though it was Jonathan and she liked him. But he wasn't her father, was he? It would be easier when Tilda explained it all to her. Jassy always understood things better with Tilda around to explain.

And so she stood there on the path, trying to process her feelings. When a huge bumblebee landed on a nearby rose, she gladly turned her attention away and watched it and, by the time the bee had moved on, so too had Jonathan and her mother and she was able to sneak into the house for the teabags.

It occurred to her that Jonathan might actually want to move in with her mother. What would that be like? she wondered. They already had two men in the house and it hadn't been half as bad as she'd been expecting. In fact, she quite liked it. She enjoyed Marcus's company and Laurie was sweet too. She could tell he liked Tilda and the revelation that they had kissed hadn't come as a surprise to her.

Men, she thought. They had a way of changing things. She was quite sure that their little unit of women had been happy enough in the last couple of years. Of course the loss of her father had been felt severely by all of them, but they had slowly adapted. Dolly, Vanessa, Tilda and Jasmine. Four Jacobs women living perfectly happily together, although her mother and grandmother still had a few issues to work out.

Walking into the kitchen, Jassy forgot the incident with Jonathan and her mother as she got on with the wonderfully mundane task of gathering teabags into a plastic bag.

Marcus didn't appear to hear her when she walked back into the oast house. At any rate, he didn't take any notice of her. He stood with his back to the door, a large canvas in front of him. He was getting brave. She was always encouraging him to work big. 'Dream big, work big' – that was her motto. Well, Marcus seemed to be running with it.

'I've got the tea,' she told him, stuffing the teabags into a tin of a royal couple Jassy could no longer recognise through all the paint splatters. 'Do you want a cup?'

'Please.'

She boiled the kettle and washed two of the mugs by the sink.

'You're all hunched again,' she shouted across the room when she turned to look at him. 'Don't do that thing with your neck. You're storing up trouble.'

Jassy did a few quick stretches of her own after popping the teabags in the mugs and pouring in the water. It was important to stretch. One could get into some peculiar postures whilst painting. She knew all about that. She'd once gone to a yoga class with Tilda but had had to leave after falling onto the floor in a fit of giggles at the funny poses, which hadn't gone down well with the po-faced yogi. She'd also tried meditation in order to learn how to relax more. The problem was, she kept falling asleep. Perhaps she'd been a little bit too relaxed, she thought, taking out the teabags. She hadn't liked that class anyway. It was all lycra and chakras.

Jassy and Marcus were both serious tea drinkers, preferring it black with no sugar. To Jassy's mind, anything else was an abomination. Although she did enjoy the occasional ginger nut to sweeten the moment a little.

She placed her mug on the stool by her easel and walked over to where Marcus was working, watching him for a moment before speaking.

'Who is she?' Jassy asked him at last, her head cocked to one side as she studied a rather beautiful face.

Marcus stopped painting and stared hard at the canvas.

'Is it your wife?'

He glared at her, took his mug of tea and turned back to the canvas.

Jassy shrugged her shoulders. 'Suit yourself.'

She went back to her own easel. Sometimes, artists needed space rather than questions. That was something she told her family anyway. They always wanted to know what she was doing and would constantly ask to see her drawings and paintings. But she didn't ask them what they'd been doing all day.

'Tara.'

'Pardon?' Jassy said as Marcus turned around.

'Tara. My wife.'

'Oh, right.'

'I – er – didn't mean to paint her. I don't know how this happened.'

'You're unlocking yourself,' she told him.

'What?'

'You're freeing up the real you at last. I knew that would happen. You started off painting the things you could see in front of you: still lifes, flowers, bottles, that sort of thing. Then we went out into the garden. And now you're painting things from within. It's a natural progression.'

Marcus didn't look convinced by this. His face looked dark and stern.

'It's a good painting,' Jassy told him. 'I mean, I don't know if it's a good likeness of your wife or—'

'It's a good likeness.'

'Then finish it. Show it to Laurie.'

'Laurie will never see this, okay?' Marcus's voice was curt and final.

Jassy nodded. 'Okay,' she said. 'We can keep it in here, can't we? Our little secret.'

It was only the second time that Vanessa had visited Beeches, but it was already beginning to feel like a second home to her. She loved the modest size of the property. After the sprawling grace of Orley Court, Beeches was a breath of fresh air with its two small rooms on the ground floor.

Jonathan opened the door as soon as she knocked, ushering her in after the sweetest of kisses.

'You okay?' she asked him. 'You look tired.'

'Just anxious.'

'About Jenna?'

He nodded. 'Yep.'

'I've been thinking about her too.'

'She's a tough little cookie, but she looked like all the fight had gone out of her when I dropped her off tonight.'

'She was probably tired too. I worked her pretty hard in the herbaceous border, you know.'

Jonathan smiled at that. 'Come on through to the kitchen. I've got some spaghetti on the go. Is that okay?'

'Lovely!'

'I've just picked some basil from the greenhouse. Come and smell it.'

Vanessa grinned, loving his enthusiasm for all things green.

A moment later and she was sniffing the basil. It was indeed delicious and still felt warm from having absorbed all of the heat from the day's sun.

'I didn't bring any wine with me,' Vanessa said, remembering his abrupt rejection of the bottle she'd brought last time.

'How about an iced apple juice? Straight from an orchard in the Weald.'

'Sounds perfect.' She watched as he poured the drinks and then he opened the back door out into the garden, which was a tapestry of colour with lupins, larkspur, cornflowers and roses. The tomatoes in his tiny greenhouse had almost reached the roof and the vegetable beds were brimming over with produce.

'So, have you talked any more to the team about the fete idea?' Vanessa asked as they sat down together on a sun-warmed bench.

He took a sip of his drink before answering. 'I ran some ideas by them earlier today.'

'And?' Vanessa asked, eager to hear what they'd made of it.

'Yeah, I think they went for it on the whole.'

'You think?'

'Well, it's hard to tell sometimes. They can be a little unreceptive to change. You know, anything outside their comfort zone.'

'So, what did they say?'

'Well, Andy asked if it was a fete worse than death.'

Vanessa groaned.

'Yeah. You can always rely on Andy for the wisecracks. Nat wanted to know if they got to keep the money made from sales and Oz wanted to know if they got paid to man the stalls.'

Vanessa laughed. 'Good businessmen.'

'I told them that payment came in the form of satisfaction for a job well done, and that we could probably run to tea and cake. I think they were beginning to get excited by the idea of showing their produce to the public. I told them there's nothing quite like selling something that you've grown yourself and knowing that a stranger is going to eat it for their tea. I could see them taking it all in. I think they're actually really looking forward to it.'

'And Jenna?'

'I don't think she said anything. She was pretty quiet and then she went to join you in the south garden.'

'She didn't mention the fete to me. I think she was thinking of that no good man of hers.'

Jonathan put his glass down on the bench beside him and took Vanessa's left hand in both of his.

'Finding someone good isn't easy,' he said.

'I know.'

'That's why I feel so lucky to have found you. Thank goodness I was putting that advert up in the shop that day. We might never have met otherwise.'

'We might have.'

'You think?'

'Elhurst is a pretty small place.'

'But we haven't run into each other before.'

'I think we might have eventually met. Maybe one day, I'd have been cycling down the lane and you'd have been speeding along in that van of yours. You'd have driven right through a huge puddle, splashing me all over.'

'What?' Jonathan cried.

Vanessa giggled. 'You'd have stopped, of course.'

'I should hope so!'

'And we'd have got talking.' She gave a little shrug and Jonathan shook his head.

'I don't think it would have happened like that.'

'No?'

'I think we might have met somewhere in the valley. One evening, just as it was beginning to cool. You'd have forgotten to wear a coat.'

'Oh, really?'

He nodded seriously. 'And I, naturally, would have taken mine off and placed it around your shoulders, stealing a quick kiss from you as I did.'

'Oh! And I would have slapped you!'

'No you wouldn't have.'

She laughed at his certainty.

'Anyway,' he continued, 'we did meet.'

'Yes,' she said, closing her eyes as he kissed her.

They ate at the table in the kitchen, the back door open so that they could enjoy the evening birdsong. It was a much more relaxed affair than the first dinner they'd shared. She cringed whenever she thought of that. Thank goodness they'd managed to get through to the other side of all that awkwardness.

Now, they could happily amble from topic to topic. Most of their conversation was garden-related, she had to admit, but everything seemed joyful and easy between them.

After dinner, Jonathan got up to make them a cup of tea and Vanessa walked through to the living room where she was greeted by the overwhelming scent of sweet peas. She spotted the little vase full of pink, white and lilac blooms and went to inhale them before casting her eyes around the room. There was something particular she was looking for. It had been on the bookcase, hadn't it? Only it wasn't there now and, looking around for a second time, she couldn't see it anywhere.

Jonathan must have moved the photograph of Rachelle.

Chapter 20

At first, Vanessa thought she was dreaming but, after a few moments, she realised that her mobile really was ringing. She switched on her bedside lamp and looked at the clock. It was after four in the morning. Who on earth could be calling her at that time?

She picked up the phone and instantly recognised the number.

'Vanessa?'

'Jonathan – what's wrong?'

'Can you come over?'

'Are you okay?'

'Just come, will you?' And he hung up.

Vanessa sat up in bed feeling stunned. What on earth was the matter?

Whipping the covers back, she swung her legs out of bed and quickly got dressed before running downstairs. She shoved her feet into the first pair of shoes she found and grabbed her bag and car keys.

The summer sky was slowly beginning to lighten as she ran to her car. Her heart was racing as she tried to imagine what was going on with Jonathan. Why hadn't he given her some hint? Was he unable to talk on the phone? All sorts of crazy thoughts went through her mind as she drove the short distance to Beeches.

He was there at the door when she pulled up. He looked terrible. His face was pale and drawn and his beautiful red hair was a mess.

'Jonathan?' she cried as she got out of the car and ran the short distance towards him. 'What is it?'

He guided her into the house, his arm around her shoulder.

'Tell me!'

'Sit down.'

'You're worrying me,' she said as she sat down in the living room. She noticed he was still standing. 'Tell me what's going on.'

'It's Jenna. She's in hospital.'

'Oh, no! What happened?'

'She tried to OD.'

'Oh, Jonathan. Is she okay?'

'She's stable now. They've got things under control.'

'Who found her?'

'A friend she was meant to meet up with. The friend found a bottle of pills and called an ambulance.'

Vanessa got up from the chair as tears began to fill her eyes.

'I knew something wasn't right with her. I should have stayed when I dropped her home.'

She reached up to caress his face. 'You can't be with them all the time. You have to let them live their own lives.'

'Even if that means them tossing those lives away?'

'She's going to be all right, Jonathan.' She placed her hands on his. He was shaking. 'Let's sit down, shall we?'

She guided him to the sofa and they sat next to each other. She ran a hand through his hair and studied his face. She'd never seen him like this before and was thankful that he'd called her because she would have hated knowing that he'd gone through something like this alone.

'Are you okay?' she whispered after they'd been sitting there in silence for a good few minutes.

He nodded, but he looked miles away.

'Jonathan?'

He turned to look at her. 'She's going to be okay,' he said.

'Yes,' Vanessa told him. 'You've done all you can.'

He shook his head. 'I should have read the signs. If anyone should have read them, it was me.'

'What do you mean?' she asked. 'Jonathan? Has this happened to you before?'

Between Vanessa asking the question and Jonathan answering it, there seemed to be the most agonising void of time. Then he sighed and turned to look at her, the pain in his eyes almost too much for Vanessa to bear.

'Rachelle,' he said simply.

'The woman in the photo?'

He nodded. 'I couldn't help her, Vanessa. I couldn't help her!' A tear rolled down his cheek and he turned his head away.

'Shush,' she said, putting her arms around him.

'I loved her, but I couldn't save her.'

Vanessa continued to hold him, now understanding that this was why he worked so hard for his team – because he'd lost someone he cared about deeply.

'I noticed you'd moved her picture,' she said gently.

'I didn't want you to get upset by it,' he said, a little more composed now as he wiped a hand across his face.

'I wouldn't get upset by it,' she told him. 'You have a right to a past just as I have.'

'But I don't want to live in it anymore.' He gave a great sigh. 'I want to tell you something, Vanessa. Something that might change your opinion of me.'

She looked at him, wondering what he could mean by that. 'You know you can tell me anything,' she said, 'and I won't judge you.'

He shook his head. 'Don't make any promises you can't keep.'

'Jonathan—'

'No, listen to me first.' His eyes locked with hers and they were cool and earnest. 'It was a week after Rachelle overdosed. I wasn't coping with losing her. Her parents blamed me and it got pretty ugly at one point.' He ran a hand over his face and then continued.

'I got horribly drunk one night and got in the car. It was a stupid thing to do, but I wasn't thinking straight. I just had to get out of the house. It felt so empty without her. I'm not sure where I drove, but I hit the main road and went a fair few miles before turning off, God knows where, and that's when I crashed.'

'Oh, Jonathan! Were you hurt?'

'I should have been. I hit a tree by the side of the road and wrote off the car.'

'But you were okay?'

He nodded. 'The point is, I could have killed somebody.'

'But you didn't.'

'I was totally out of control. It makes me shudder when I think about it.'

'You were going through a rough time,' she told him.

'But I shouldn't have gone out in that state. I put others in danger. It was a bad decision.' He paused and let out a great sigh. 'You see, I know what it's like to lose control and I can see how people make bad decisions. It can happen to anyone.'

'God, Jonathan. I can't imagine what you must have gone through, losing Rachelle like that, but you've turned yourself around and you're helping others to do the same.'

'But I wasn't there for Jenna when she needed me.'

Vanessa's heart ached for him. 'You can't possibly be there for all of them all the time. It's like being a parent. You do your best – your very best – but you have to give them space, and hope that you've guided them and encouraged them and given them the tools they need to make good choices. That's all you can do. But you do more than that too, you know? You show them that there are amazing things in the world. You show them beautiful things which enrich their lives. You do so much good, Jonathan.'

He looked up at her. His eyes were rimmed red.

'This is why I didn't want you getting involved with her, Vanessa. I know how much it hurts.'

'But you can't go around not getting involved with people on the off-chance that they might hurt you. Life doesn't work like that. Not for me, anyway,' she told him softly. 'And Jenna's going to be okay.'

'I know,' he said at last.

'And you are too.'

He lifted her hand to his lips and kissed it and they sat in silence for a few minutes before Vanessa got up.

'Shall I make us some tea?'

Jonathan nodded and made to get up.

'I'll do it,' she said quickly, but he followed her through to the kitchen and got mugs from the cupboard.

A few minutes later, they sat at the table together.

'You okay?' she asked.

He nodded. 'I'm sorry I—'

'Don't apologise,' she said. 'You know, I've been thinking.'

He looked at her inquisitively.

'There's something we could do.'

'What do you mean?'

'I mean for Jenna. To really help her.'

'Go on,' he said.

'Well, you know we need more help in the garden?'

'Yeah,' he said slowly.

'I've been thinking, if we open it to the public, even if it's just for weekends and public holidays, we'll have money coming in. We could afford to pay her and you. She could be your assistant. Your trainee. I've seen what a great worker she is and she loves learning from you.'

'You'd really want to do that? I mean, have me and Jenna working for you?'

'Of course I would. I'd love to have you there as Orley's gardener,' she said, reaching across the table and holding his hand. 'I mean, if you want the job.'

'You sure you could afford that? I hate to be so base and to talk about money and everything.'

'No, no. It's okay. I don't want there to be any awkwardness between us. But I could definitely afford two part-timers. We've got money from selling the north wing and I really think we could make a go of it if we opened to the public. Maybe we could even sell plants and cut flowers. What do you think?'

Jonathan didn't need long to think about it. 'It's a great idea. It'll keep me close to you too.'

'You can fit me into your timetable, then?'

'Are you kidding? There's nothing I'd rather do than spend time with you at Orley.'

'You know, I sometimes think you only like me for my garden,' she teased.

He smiled. 'So you've found me out!'

She got up from the table and took his face in her hands and kissed him. 'I'm happy to share my garden with you. And my life.'

His expression softened at her declaration. 'What on earth did I do to deserve you?'

She stroked her fingers through his hair. 'Just being you was all it took.'

By the time Vanessa got home, it was after seven in the morning. It didn't seem right to go back to bed even though she felt exhausted. She knew she wouldn't be able to sleep anyway. She had too much going on in her mind what with Jenna in hospital, Jonathan's confession and her idea to hire them both to help in the garden.

She went upstairs to take a shower and change into fresh clothes and, by the time she came downstairs, Dolly and her daughters were in the morning room.

'You're up late, Mum,' Jassy said.

Vanessa smiled. 'You wouldn't say that if you knew the truth.'

'What truth?'

'I've been up for hours. I spent most of the night at Jonathan's.'

'Disgraceful,' Dolly said through a mouthful of cornflakes.

Tilda spluttered on her orange juice. 'Mum!'

'It's not what you think,' Vanessa said quickly and calmly. 'I'm afraid there was a crisis in the night.'

'What crisis?'

'Jenna overdosed.' The news was greeted by gasps. 'She's okay! She's in hospital. They got her there in time.'

'Are you going to see her?' Tilda asked.

'Jonathan thinks it's best if I wait till she's home. He's going to visit her today and let us know what's going on.'

'What happened?' Tilda asked.

'We think it was something to do with her boyfriend, Carl. She's been unhappy for a while.'

'I always knew those kids were no good,' Dolly said. 'It's obvious one of them would get into some sort of trouble sooner or later.'

'Dolly, how can you say such a thing?' Vanessa said, staring at her mother-in-law in undisguised horror.

'Because that's who they are. Don't be so naive, Vanessa. You can't hope to change them by getting them to hoe some weeds and plant a few cabbages.'

'But you've spent time with them. I thought you cared about them.'

'Yes, but I haven't made the mistake of getting close to them like you have.'

'No, you never like getting close to anyone, do you?'

Dolly chose to ignore this remark. 'They're the kind of people who hurt others and you'd do well to remember that.'

'I don't need this right now, okay?'

'You've always been one to bury your head in the sand. That's your trouble.'

'And you've always been one to point out all my faults!' Vanessa countered. 'But no more, Dolly. I've really had enough. You have no right to criticise me in my own home.'

'Oh, your home is it?'

'Please don't start that again.'

'I'm not starting anything, I'm merely—'

'STOP!'

The voice startled the fighting women into instant silence as they stared at Jassy, who was now up on her feet.

'Why are you so mean, Grandma?' Jassy said. 'You're always so mean, especially to Mum, which isn't fair. She does her best and she's doing a bloody good job too, but you just pick and pick at her and it's not right!'

Dolly looked totally stunned by her granddaughter's sudden outburst.

'Jasmine, I—'

'I can't understand why you're never happy. I know Dad died and we all miss him so much it actually hurts here sometimes,' she said, squeezing her abdomen in an alarming fashion, 'but we try and keep going. We're there for each other. Or at least we should be. Sometimes, Grandma, it seems like you don't want to be a part of this family.'

'What?' Dolly said.

'You pick on Mum all the time. She's sad too, you know. If you cared, you'd know that. You'd talk to her rather than shout at her. It's the same with Jonathan's team. If you were nice to them – if you gave them a chance and just talked to them – you'd realise they were really good people.'

Vanessa could feel her eyes filling with tears at her daughter's rather marvellous defence of her. Tilda was looking on in amazement, her mouth open but no words coming out.

There was silence for a moment as none of them spoke for fear of Jassy starting up again. Vanessa hadn't seen her daughter quite so impassioned since she was a young child and less capable of controlling her emotions. It had taken years of patient teaching to get Jassy to understand that emotional outbursts weren't the norm, but Vanessa wasn't going to correct her daughter today because she felt that she had done exactly the right thing and, although a part of her couldn't help feeling sorry for Dolly, a large part of her was glad that Jassy had spoken out. It was about time that Dolly realised just what an effect she had on people.

A scrape of the chair, and Dolly was standing up. Vanessa and her daughters watched, waiting to see what she would do and say. But she didn't say anything and her face was a perfect blank.

They watched as she turned around and slowly walked out of the room. It was hard for Vanessa not to go and try to somehow comfort her after Jassy's tirade, but another part of her, the part that had been battered and bruised by Dolly over the years, kept her seated.

She looked across the table at Tilda and Jassy.

'Sorry,' Jassy said once her grandmother was out of the room. 'Was I wrong?'

'No,' Vanessa told her. 'A little unexpected, perhaps.'

'But she was picking on you. I hate it when she does that.'

'Me too,' Tilda said.

'You never say anything, Mum. You just take it,' Jassy cried.

Vanessa felt quite helpless under her daughter's scrutiny. 'I just try to keep the peace.'

'I would have said something a lot sooner if I were you,' Jassy insisted.

'Me too,' Tilda said.

Jassy looked at her sister. 'Well, you could have chipped in!'

Tilda looked stunned by this. 'I don't think I'd have dared go up against Grandma like that.'

'No, you were pretty impressive, Jassy!' Vanessa said.

'How come you've never stuck up for Mum, Tilly?' Jassy asked.

'What?'

'Why haven't you said anything to Grandma before?'

Tilda looked a little embarrassed by the question. 'I – well – I guess I've always been a little afraid of her.'

'Me too, darling,' Vanessa said.

'And you've always been closer to her,' Tilda added. 'You can get away with more than I can.'

'You think?' Jasmine said.

'Definitely!'

'Of course, you'll have to apologise to her,' Vanessa said.

'You're joking!'

Vanessa shook her head. 'I'm not. You'll have to make sure she's okay and that she's not brooding.'

Jassy didn't look pleased by this request.

'But maybe not just yet,' Vanessa added. 'I think we can let her brood for just a little while.'

It wasn't until after dark that Jassy ventured into Dolly's quarters. Jassy had just painted a brutal abstract and was now feeling miserable as she remembered her earlier outburst, which was funny because it had left her feeling exhilarated at the time. She'd never understood how feelings could swing from one extreme to the other so quickly. It was baffling. But she knew she had to apologise. Even if her mother hadn't asked her to, Jassy knew it was the right thing to do.

She knocked on the door and, when there was no reply, went inside.

'Grandma?' she called. She'd learned not to just charge into the room as her grandmother often dozed off in her chair. As a child, Jassy hadn't been able to understand why a grown-up needed to sleep during the day, but she was used to it now and took extra care.

Reynolds was by her feet in an instant and Jassy bent down to pick him up, her chin receiving a few enthusiastic licks.

'Jasmine? Is that you?'

'Yes, Grandma.' She walked forward, the dog still in her arms.

'I was asleep,' Dolly said, her face holding the softness of a gentle nap.

Jassy sat down on the chair opposite, Reynolds settling into her lap.

'You've been painting?'

'Of course.'

Dolly nodded. 'Good.'

'You should paint too,' Jassy told her.

'I'm too old to learn now.'

'No you're not. Nobody's ever too old to learn anything. I don't know why people say that. Anyway, it would do you good – get rid of your madness.'

Dolly frowned. 'I'm not mad!'

'Not as in crazy,' Jassy said. 'I didn't mean that. I meant madness as in anger. You know, how you're always cross. Painting would make you feel better.'

Dolly shook her head. 'I'm not going to learn to paint, Jasmine.'

Jassy sighed. 'Well, don't say I didn't try.' Her eyes glanced around the room as they usually did. There was always plenty to take note of, from the pretty pieces of silver and china to the large paintings that she loved to stare at, absorbing their colours and textures and wondering about the people from the past who had painted them. But then she remembered why she was there.

'Sorry,' she said.

'Pardon?'

'Mum said – I mean – I wanted to say I was sorry. For shouting at you. You know – before.'

'Yes, I remember,' Dolly said.

Neither of them said anything for a moment. Dolly stared out of her window at a garden she could no longer see in the darkness and Jassy continued to tickle Reynolds.

'Jasmine, I . . .' Dolly paused.

'What?'

'I don't mean to be mad – I mean cross.'

'Don't you?' Jassy was genuinely confused by this confession. Emotions, as far as she was concerned, should always be real and true and it baffled her that adults would sometimes muddle them all up, shouting at those whom they protested to love and laughing at things which weren't funny.

'It's just that I sometimes feel . . .' She gave a sigh and Jassy watched as her grandma twisted her large knotty fingers together. Jassy had sketched those hands on several occasions. They fascinated her, but they made her feel sad too because she'd look down at her own hands and wondered if they would look like her grandmother's one day and, if they ever did, would she still be able to hold a paintbrush?

'What do you feel, Grandma?'

There was a pause before she answered. 'Alone,' she said at last.

Jassy didn't understand. 'But you're not alone.'

'But I feel it. Sometimes. When I'm sitting here in this room, looking out of the window and remembering the past. My husband and my son.' She paused again. 'Both gone.'

'But we're still here – you have me and Mum and Tilda.'

'I know.'

Jassy saw that her grandmother's eyes seemed brighter than usual and realised that there were tears swimming in them.

'Oh, Grandma! Don't cry! I didn't mean to make you cry!' Jassy was up on her feet, Reynolds dropped unceremoniously to the floor.

'You didn't, darling. I'm just being silly.'

Jassy knelt on the floor by her chair, head in Dolly's lap.

'I hate it when people are sad. Marcus is sad about something and he won't tell me what it is. I've asked him and I think painting is helping him, but there's something he's not telling me.'

'Some people find it hard to talk. They're not all as open as you are,' Dolly said as she stroked Jassy's hair.

'I guess.' She looked up into her grandma's face.

'When your father died,' Dolly began, 'I felt as if a little piece of me had died with him.'

'I felt like that too.'

'I know you did, Jassy.'

'I couldn't stop crying.'

'I cried too.'

'Did you?'

Dolly nodded. 'Oh, yes!'

'But I never saw you cry.'

She took a deep breath. 'I didn't want you to. I didn't want anybody to. I thought things might change around here and that your mother – well – that she wouldn't want me living here anymore.'

Jassy gasped. 'You thought she'd throw you out?'

'Perhaps.'

'But she'd never do that.'

A resigned look settled on Dolly's face. 'Jasmine, your mother and I have never seen eye to eye.'

'I know, but that doesn't mean she'd make you homeless! I mean, where would you go if you didn't live here? This is your home!'

'Yes, I know that now. I was just going through a strange time. I wasn't thinking straight. I felt . . . vulnerable, alone.'

'But that's silly!'

Dolly gave a little laugh. 'Yes.'

'Because you have us. Your family.' Jassy got up and kissed her cheek. 'Oh, Grandma – you're crying again!'

'Tears of happiness, Jasmine. I'm happy. Really I am!'

Jassy shook her head. She would never ever understand grown-ups.

✦

The next morning was fine and bright. A languid summer mist filled the valley, promising yet another hot day.

Vanessa moved around the garden slowly, carefully, her eyes darting across the borders in search of the perfect blooms. She picked pink and red roses, snipping them cleanly with sharp secateurs; vivid-blue love-in-a-mist followed, and multicoloured sweet peas, lavender and sprigs of mint for a wondrous scent to lift the mood, all set off by the lovely acid-green of lady's mantle. She placed them all in a galvanised bucket filled with chilled water. It was a routine she'd gone through many times and one she never failed to find great joy in, but this bunch of flowers was different. This bunch was for a very special person.

Taking her flower-filled bucket into the house, Vanessa arranged the blooms and foliage with an eye she had trained herself from years of homemade displays. When she was happy with her creation, she tied it with jute string so that it was a manageable handheld bouquet which could be placed easily into a vase without giving the owner a panic attack.

She was just about to leave the house when Dolly entered the room.

'Are those for Jenna?' she asked.

'Yes,' Vanessa said without looking at her mother-in-law. A moment later, she heard Dolly shuffling back out of the room and she breathed a sigh of relief that the encounter had been blissfully brief. They hadn't spoken since the outburst in the morning room the day before, although Jassy had told her that she'd been in to apologise to her grandmother.

'She said she deserved it,' Jassy had reported back.

'Really?' Vanessa had said.

Jassy had nodded. 'She didn't say sorry in so many words, but I think she is sorry.'

Vanessa wasn't so sure about that. Dolly was probably sorry that she'd been humiliated, that was all.

Before she knew it, Dolly was back in the kitchen.

'Give this to Jenna for me, will you?' She held her hand out to Vanessa, unfolding it to reveal a gold necklace with a daisy pendant hanging from it.

'Isn't this the necklace you thought you'd lost?' Vanessa asked. 'Wasn't the jewellery box missing?'

'Oh, that was me forgetting where I'd put it,' Dolly said as if it was no big deal. She had no idea that it had caused Vanessa to doubt Jonathan's team and now Vanessa felt terrible that the thought had entered her mind.

'But Oliver gave you this,' Vanessa said, turning her mind back to the necklace and remembering the very day her husband had given Dolly the present.

'He gave me many things,' Dolly said. 'Many things I will treasure until I die.'

Vanessa stared hard at the old woman standing before her.

'But I thought you said Jenna was no good,' she said as she placed the necklace carefully in her jacket pocket. 'That she was trouble.'

'I've said a lot of things,' Dolly said. 'A lot of things I regret.' She looked directly into Vanessa's eyes. 'I only hope it's not too late.'

'Too late?'

'To b – be . . . to make . . .' Her voice petered out as she stumbled over her words. 'You know what I'm trying to say.'

'No, I don't,' Vanessa said, not wanting to let Dolly take the easy way out, not after all the years she'd suffered under her.

'I'm trying to say sorry,' Dolly blurted.

Vanessa had guessed that that was what her mother-in-law had been trying to say, or had hoped it was at least. She'd been waiting for an apology from Dolly for years now for the way she'd treated her but, now that the moment had actually come, she wasn't sure how to respond.

'What Jasmine said – it hurt me,' Dolly continued. 'It hurt me to realise that I'd hurt her by—'

'Hurting me?'

Dolly nodded.

'Well, you have,' Vanessa said. 'Over and over again. I've tried to be friends with you, Dolly. I really have.'

'I know,' she whispered.

'But you threw that friendship back in my face.'

'You took my son!' Dolly suddenly cried.

'No I didn't! I married him. He was still here, living under your roof. You saw him every single day. That's more than most mothers can hope for.' She paused. She didn't want to turn this into yet another fight. She wasn't even sure she had any more fight in her. So she took a deep breath. 'You did want him to marry, didn't you?' she asked gently. 'And to have a family of his own? You don't hate having granddaughters, do you?'

'Of course not.'

'Well, granddaughters need a mother, and I'm it! I'm the one your son chose and you're stuck with me because I'm not going anywhere.'

They stared at one another a moment longer before Vanessa turned her back on Dolly and moved across to the sink.

'I wouldn't want you to go anywhere,' Dolly said.

'Pardon?'

'I said I wouldn't want you to go anywhere.'

'Well, I'm not,' Vanessa said, turning around.

'Good!' Dolly said, and Vanessa caught the beginnings of a tiny smile on the old lady's face before she shuffled out of the kitchen.

'Oh, and tell Jenna she's not allowed to sell it!' Dolly said over her shoulder.

'Sell what?' Vanessa asked.

'The necklace!'

Vanessa smiled. What with Dolly's unexpected apology, she'd totally forgotten about the necklace.

Vanessa had left Orley a few minutes later. She'd spoken to Jonathan on the phone the night before and he'd given her an update on Jenna. She was doing well and, after several examinations, had been told she could go home if she had somebody to stay with her to keep an eye on her. They believed that this was an isolated experience brought on by emotional trauma and that, all being well, Jenna wouldn't attempt to overdose again.

Vanessa told Jonathan she'd call round and he'd given her the address.

'I'm sure she'd love to see you,' he'd said. Vanessa hoped so.

Jenna lived on a small housing estate on the outskirts of Hastings that was easy enough to find. Parking her car, Vanessa got out, lifting the bouquet – which had scented the car beautifully on its journey – from the backseat and approached the front door of number thirty-seven.

A young woman with scarlet hair opened the door.

'Oh, hello,' Vanessa said. 'I'm looking for Jenna.'

'I'm Sally, Jenna's friend. Come in.'

'How is she?'

'She's quiet. Really quiet. Which isn't like her. But she's eating.'

'Well, that's a good sign.'

'It is, isn't it?' Sally agreed. 'Come in. She's upstairs. I'll get her for you.'

Sally led Vanessa through to a small living room with a shabby sofa and a wonky table.

'Okay for a minute?'

Vanessa nodded.

'What lovely flowers,' Sally said as she left the room. 'Jenna will love them.'

Vanessa smiled, listening as Sally climbed the stairs. She then took a moment to look around the room, noting the peeling wallpaper, the threadbare carpet and the lack of things. There really wasn't very much in there. It looked as if Jenna had perhaps just moved in and her possessions hadn't yet arrived, or else she'd very recently had a huge garage sale in the pursuit of minimalism.

One thing Vanessa did notice was a strip of passport photos on a little shelf. She picked them up and saw Jenna with a handsome young man with dirty blond hair and an irrepressible smile. Was this the boyfriend who had caused so much trouble?

'Carl?' she whispered to the photo strip in an accusatory tone. 'Do you know how much damage that smile of yours has done?'

She put the photos down and caught sight of a pile of books on the wonky coffee table. With the instinct of a true bibliophile, she moved towards them and saw that they were all gardening books from the local library. She smiled as she noticed a small notepad and half-chewed pen beside them. Her intuition had been right with Jenna: she was keen to learn.

'Vanessa?'

Vanessa jumped and looked up to see Jenna coming into the room. The girl looked genuinely surprised to see her there.

'Hello, Jenna,' she said with a big smile, noticing how pale she looked, as if half of her blood had been drained from her. 'I wanted to bring you these.' She handed her the bunch of flowers.

'Wow – they're really beautiful.'

'I thought I'd bring Orley to you today.'

'Thanks. Nobody . . .'

'What?'

'Nobody's ever been this kind to me before.'

'It's nothing more than you deserve,' Vanessa told her. 'Shall I put them in a vase for you?'

Jenna frowned. 'We don't have a vase.'

Vanessa did her best to hide her surprise. She couldn't imagine a house without a vase.

'I'll look in the kitchen for something.' She walked through to the tiny kitchen, noting the stack of dishes that hadn't been washed and the old linoleum floor which felt sticky under her shoes.

That's when she saw the large tin barrel. It had once held biscuits – the sort people buy in bulk at Christmas – and she removed the lid to discover the end of a woebegone custard cream, which she promptly threw in the bin. She then washed out the crumbs and filled the tin with water, checking it was watertight.

'Have you any sugar, Jenna?'

'You want a cup of tea?'

'No. It's for the flowers.'

'Oh. Check the cupboard above the cooker.'

Vanessa did so and found a crusty packet of sugar that had partially solidified. She gave it a bash on the worktop and swirled a teaspoon's worth into the tin of water before placing the flowers into it. It looked less than satisfactory to Vanessa, who was used to fine china and cut crystal, but the flowers still looked glorious, if a little indignant.

She took them through to the living room and placed them on the table alongside the library books.

'I see you're reading about gardening.'

'Trying to,' Jenna said, 'but there's a lot of funny long words in them books.'

'Latin?'

Jenna frowned. 'What's that?'

'It's an ancient language that's used to classify plants. It can be very confusing, but you get used to it. Luckily plants have common names too. They're the ones we tend to use.'

'Thank goodness for that!'

Vanessa smiled. 'When I first moved to Orley, I didn't know anything about plants. I'd always had a garden growing up, but the garden at Orley only made me realise how very little I knew. It seems like such a daunting job, but you just have to break it down and learn the garden one plant at a time.'

Jenna sat down on the sofa and Vanessa joined her. 'You make it sound so easy.'

'It can be if you really enjoy it. I think if you have a passion for something, it doesn't seem like hard work.'

Jenna nodded as if understanding. 'I read in one of them books that there's an old country custom of testing to see if the soil's warm enough for planting.'

'And how do they do that?'

'By sitting on the soil with your bare bum.'

Vanessa laughed and Jenna joined in. It was good to hear her laugh again.

'Well, we don't do that at Orley,' Vanessa assured her.

'I'm glad to hear it, although I'm sure Oz would give it a go!'

They laughed again and Sally popped her head around the door.

'I'm just nipping to the shop. Do we need anything?'

'Chocolate,' Jenna said. 'Oh, and bread probably.'

'You got it.'

They listened to the door close and it was then that Vanessa remembered Dolly's necklace and reached into her jacket pocket.

'Dolly wanted me to give you something.'

'Oh?'

Vanessa handed her the daisy necklace on the gold chain and Jenna gasped.

'She gave this – to me?'

'Yes.'

'To keep?'

'Well, of course to keep!'

'But I don't deserve it.'

Vanessa placed a hand on Jenna's arm. 'Of course you do. There are a lot of people who really care about you, Jenna. You're special and we look forward to your days at Orley more than you can possibly know. In fact, I can't imagine the place without you now.'

Jenna gave a weak smile and tears shone in her eyes.

'Oh,' Vanessa added, 'Dolly told me to tell you not to sell it.'

Jenna looked genuinely shocked. 'I wouldn't! Not ever.'

'I know! I think she was just being cheeky.'

'I'll treasure it forever,' she said. 'Will you put it on for me, please?'

'Of course.'

Jenna handed the necklace to Vanessa and then lifted her hair from her neck.

'There you go,' Vanessa said once she'd fastened the necklace.

'I love it.'

'It looks beautiful on you.'

'Thank her for me, won't you?'

'You can thank her yourself when you next come to Orley.'

'You want me back?'

'Of course we want you back! Why would you even ask that?'

'Because I feel like I've let everyone down.'

'Oh, my dear girl! You haven't let anyone down. You've just gone through something really horrible – something nobody should ever have to go through. But we're all here for you. You know that, don't you? Tilda and Jassy send their love and I know Jonathan can't wait to get you out into the garden again.'

'I know. He said he needs my help in the greenhouse. The tomatoes are running riot.'

'Exactly! You're needed, Jenna. Never forget that.' Vanessa squeezed her arm. 'So, how are you feeling? I mean really feeling?'

Jenna sniffed. 'Everybody keeps asking that.'

'And what do you tell them?'

'What they want to hear. That I'm okay. That I won't do it again.'

'And is that the truth?'

Jenna looked up at her with bright, tear-filled eyes. 'I feel a bit lost.'

'Oh, Jenna!' Vanessa wrapped her arms around the girl and pulled her close as she cried. She wasn't sure how long they sat like that on the old sofa together, but Vanessa wasn't leaving until Jenna was all cried out.

'You know, when my husband died, I hit the very depths of despair. I didn't think I was ever going to get through that darkness. He was my soulmate, my one true love. I didn't think life was worth living without him.'

'Did you try to kill yourself?'

'No,' Vanessa said, releasing Jenna from her embrace as the girl began to calm down. 'But I was living a kind of death for a while. My daughters got me through it, reminding me that I had every reason to live. They used to take me into the garden, leading me by the hand like a child, and show me what was growing and the little things that needed doing. They'd leave my special trowel out in the hallway and line up my boots next to it.' She gave a little laugh as she remembered. 'I slowly found my way back into the world of the living and I'm so glad I did because look what was waiting for me.'

'What?'

'Jonathan. I never thought I'd find love again. I really didn't. I thought I'd ramble into old age on my own.'

'But that's you,' Jenna said.

'What do you mean?'

'People like you – you're lucky.'

'You call losing my husband to cancer lucky?'

'No, but you always fall on your feet. But people like me always fall on our faces.'

'That's not true and you mustn't think like that!'

'I can't help it.'

'Well, you should try. Starting today – right this minute in fact. You've got to be positive, Jenna. Positive things happen to positive people.' She smiled. 'You do believe that, don't you?'

Jenna gave a little pout. 'I guess I could try to believe it.'

Vanessa took a deep breath and then wondered if that was wise as she noted a huge mouldy patch of wallpaper in the corner of the room.

'There's something else I wanted to talk to you about,' Vanessa said. 'I've really loved having you at Orley. You work so hard in the garden and—'

'You're firing me, aren't you? You don't want me to come back.'

'No!' Vanessa cried. 'The very opposite in fact.'

'What do you mean?'

'I want to offer you a job. A part-time job in the garden.'

'But I don't know that much. You could find someone much better than me.'

'But I want *you*, Jenna!'

'Why?'

'You really have to ask?'

She nodded.

'Because you have spirit and determination. You have a wicked sense of humour and a willingness to learn. Because I like the way you ask me questions and really listen to the answers. Because I like you, Jenna.'

Tears had arisen in Jenna's eyes again. 'Really?'

'I want you as part of our permanent team at Orley. You know more than you think you do and you'd be working with Jonathan. An apprentice, if you like. He'd teach you everything you need to know. We want to open the gardens to the public and I can't manage it all on my own. Jonathan's team are doing a great job, but that's just two days a week and you've seen the size of the place. If Orley's going to do this professionally then that means hiring help.'

'But why me? Why not Andy or Oz or—'

'Because you've been doing a great job, and I've loved working with you. You've got a natural feel for the plants. Andy and Oz and the rest of the team – they're all great lads. They work hard, but they don't use their initiative like you do and they never give more than they have to. I don't think they care as much either. Just look at how you stayed behind to work the other day and how you're always making suggestions – really good ones too. And how hard you've been working with me in the south garden.'

'So this isn't just a pity thing?'

'Of course it isn't. I need your help. This is purely selfish on my part.' She paused, waiting for the girl's response. 'Of course, if you don't want the job, I could always ask Andy or—'

'No!' Jenna cried. 'That's my job. I'll take it!'

'You will?'

She nodded.

'Oh, I'm so pleased.' Vanessa hugged her tightly. 'I really didn't want to have to work with Andy!'

Jenna laughed and Vanessa was so relieved to hear her dear friend – and new employee – sound happy once again.

Chapter 21

A hot July slowly slipped into a sultry August. The roses were resting between flushes, the hollyhocks had reached skyscraper proportions and there were more tomatoes in the greenhouse than Jonathan's team could cope with.

'I've got tomatoes coming out of my ears!' Andy cried as Vanessa tried to get him to take a bag home with him.

'I've got them coming out somewhere further south,' Nat said. 'I swear my pee's turned red.'

'Please don't make me eat any more of them things,' Oz said, and Vanessa took pity on him.

'Fine,' she said. 'I'll make a sauce and bottle it for the fete.'

'What, sell it?' Oz asked.

'It's called adding value,' she told him. 'I'll cook it up with some onions, basil and herbs – all from the garden – and we can sell it for five pounds a bottle.'

'Cool!' he said with a broad grin.

Jonathan looked impressed. 'Want a hand with that?'

'I think I can cope.'

'He just wants a cut of your profits,' Andy said.

'You know all the money will go back into this project,' she told them. 'We're already planning what you guys will be growing next year.'

'Next year!' Oz shouted. 'We'll still be doing this in a year?'

Vanessa was a little taken aback by his apparent horror. 'Well, only if you want to be here,' she said.

Oz winked at her. 'Of course I want to be here. I was only messing with you!'

'Oh!' Vanessa said, mightily relieved.

'Oz has never had any sort of job for more than two months, have you?' Jonathan said.

'Two months?' Oz said. 'Are you kidding me? I've never lasted two months! Two weeks, more like!'

Jonathan shook his head in despair. 'Hey, Andy – are you keeping an eye on those cabbages of yours? Make sure the butterflies can't get through the nets or you'll end up with more hole than cabbage leaf and nobody will want to buy them.'

'Have you seen my beans, Jonathan?' Oz asked.

'I have, Oz. They're looking spectacular.'

'They're going to knock the socks off Andy's cabbages!' Oz said.

Jonathan grinned and Vanessa watched as he got back to work with a hoe. The rain of the week before had not only fed the flowers, fruit and vegetables, but the weeds too. She studied him for a moment. He looked so at home there working in the walled garden that it was now hard for Vanessa to imagine a time when he hadn't been a part of life at Orley.

She joined him.

'Hey,' she said.

'You okay?'

'I'm good,' she said. 'How's Jenna doing?'

Jonathan glanced over to where Jenna was pinching out side shoots on the tomatoes in the greenhouse.

'I think she's doing okay,' he said.

'Me too.'

'She loves her new job. This place is like a second home to her.'

'I'm so happy to hear that,' Vanessa said.

Jonathan and Jenna had started working in the south garden at Orley a couple of weeks ago and had made good progress, widening a border and dividing plants and cleaning out the large ornamental pond.

'Yeah. She talks about it incessantly on the ride home. It's driving me nuts!'

'No it isn't. You love it!'

'Yeah. I do.' He moved an inch towards her. 'I'll tell you something else. I love you.'

Vanessa blinked in surprise. Had she heard him right? Had he just told her he loved her as she was holding a garden fork in one hand and a rebellious thistle in the other?

'Jonathan . . .' she began, not quite knowing where the sentence was going.

'It's okay,' he said. 'You don't need to say anything. I said it because I wanted to, not because I expect you to say it too.'

'But I—'

'I hope you don't mind. I hope you don't think it's too soon and that I'm rushing things, because I don't want to put any pressure on you.'

'You're not. You're really not.' She took a step towards him and, even though she was aware that the whole team was watching their every move, cupped his face in her hands and kissed him fully on the mouth.

A huge cheer went up from the team and wolf whistles echoed around the walled garden.

'I love you too,' she said.

'There,' he said. 'I knew I could winkle it out of you!'

She gasped and slapped his arm, but she was laughing.

That evening, Vanessa thought it was about time that she told Dolly and her daughters about the fete she and Jonathan were planning. She'd

288

dropped a few hints about it over the last few weeks, but nobody had really been listening to her.

'So, what do you think?' she asked them now. They were sitting in the living room after dinner and, buoyed up with enthusiasm for absolutely everything since she and Jonathan had confessed their love for each other, she was ready for anything anyone might say. Sure enough, Dolly was the first to show her disapproval although she didn't express herself as callously as she might once have done.

'But we haven't had the fete since before Oliver became ill.'

'I know, Dolly.'

'So why now?'

'Because,' she began and then she took a deep breath, 'I'm ready. And Orley's ready.'

The three Jacobs women stared at her in silence. Tilda was the first to speak.

'When?'

'August Bank Holiday.'

'Oh, Mum! Everyone knows that the weather's always awful on bank holidays,' Tilda said.

'Yes, but the numbers of people visiting are always good then.'

'I'm not sure about this,' Dolly said.

'You don't have to be sure. You just have to support us. Well, you don't even have to do that,' Vanessa stated, 'but we'd like it very much if you did.'

Dolly scowled, but she was nodding too. 'Oliver would have wanted it, wouldn't he?'

'I believe he would have, yes,' Vanessa agreed.

'Then let's do it,' Dolly said.

Vanessa smiled. 'Great. Jonathan and the team will be so pleased that you're on board.'

'As long as I don't have to bake anything. My baking days are over,' Dolly informed her.

'Oh, that's a shame,' Vanessa said. 'Your coconut cookies were always bestsellers. Remember the year that Joan Keaton actually pushed Harriet Bradley out of the way so she could get the last few?'

Dolly gave a little smile and her cheeks flushed pink with pride. 'Well, maybe I could rustle up a batch or two,' she responded.

'That would be amazing,' Vanessa said, thinking how proud Jonathan would be of her for trying to win Dolly over with flattery. 'Jassy? How do you feel about having a fete again?'

Jassy shifted in her place on the sofa. She hadn't yet said anything. 'It won't be the same, will it?'

'No,' Vanessa said, guessing what was going through her daughter's mind. 'It will be the first fete without your father.'

Jassy nodded, seeming to take this in. 'I won't have to paint kids' faces, will I?'

'Not if you don't want to.'

'I definitely don't want to.'

'Okay, then.'

'But maybe I could set up a painting table. I could teach them. That would be acceptable.'

'That's a very nice idea, Jassy.'

'Marcus could help me.'

'Would he actually want to?' Vanessa asked.

'Oh, yes. Marcus does everything I tell him to.'

'You're so bossy,' Tilda told her sister.

'No I'm not,' Jassy said. 'I'm just full of good ideas.'

※ ❧

In his study in the north wing, Laurence gazed at his computer even though he wasn't really concentrating on it. Since Tilda had told him that she needed space, he'd kept his distance even though it'd been killing him. They exchanged only a few words when they passed each other in the hallway. Jassy had been keeping him updated on what was going on in her sister's life and it sounded like things were moving apace at Morton's studio in London. She was, apparently, spending a lot of time there and he couldn't help feeling a little jealous of the young music producer. How on earth could a boring financial adviser hope to compete with a dynamic music producer? he asked himself. He didn't have a hope, did he?

And so he'd decided not to think about competing. Tilda knew how he felt about her, and if that wasn't good enough then so be it. He wasn't going to make a fool of himself.

Anyway, he had his work, which was going surprisingly well. The wonder of word-of-mouth advertising was really beginning to kick in and he'd had a lot of new clients from the local area signing up for his services. Oh, yes, he had more than enough on his plate without any romantic complications. He was good and busy. He probably didn't have time for a relationship anyway, even if she changed her mind and came knocking on his door.

That's what he told himself anyway.

It was on one of those summer days when the air was so close that you started praying for rain that the incident occurred. It was as if the season had grown bored and tired of itself. Jassy was working with Marcus in the oast house, but neither of them was producing good work. It was too hot. Even with the door wide open, there was barely a breath of air to be found. Skinny had slunk off in disgust and Jassy was seriously wondering whether to take a dip in the pond. Grandma Dolly always disapproved of such behaviour. 'Unladylike,' she'd tell her, but, since Jassy's outburst, it was obvious that Dolly was making a real effort with everyone, and you could see her almost literally biting her tongue before speaking her mind.

Jassy shook her head, dismissing the thought of a quick dip as she saw Marcus struggling with his painting.

'You need some more blue,' she told him. 'Here – try this.' She passed him a tube of Prussian-blue paint.

'No,' he said. 'I don't want it.'

'The painting needs it,' she said. 'Never mess with what a painting needs.'

She watched him for a moment as he stood staring down at the tube of paint.

'Marcus? Are you okay?' His breathing seemed to be laboured. Was it the heat or was it something more sinister than that? 'Do you want to sit down?' Jassy reached an arm out, but he batted it away. Something inside him seemed to break and, before she knew what was happening, he'd kicked his easel over. It landed on the floor with a bang, the painting sliding off. Jassy screamed as Marcus's heavy boots stood on it, breaking right through the canvas.

'No!' she cried, but it was too late. There was no stopping him as he moved to the other side of the oast house where his paintings from the last few weeks were stacked. He picked one up and flung it across the room. Jassy screamed again.

'Marcus! Stop!' But he didn't seem to hear her.

Jassy ran out and on to the main house.

'Laurence?' she shouted as soon as she was in the hallway. 'LAURENCE!'

'What is it?' he said a moment later, appearing at the top of the stairs.

'It's your dad. He's gone mad.'

'What do you mean?' Laurence asked as he came down the stairs two at a time.

Jassy flapped her hands in front of her face as she tried to gather her thoughts. 'Be logical,' Tilda often advised her. 'In times of stress, you need to calm down and be logical.'

'Is there something I should know about Prussian blue?' Jassy asked, her face screwing up as she tried to navigate her way through the situation. That's when the trouble had started, wasn't it? With that innocuous tube of Prussian-blue paint.

'What are you talking about?'

'Oh, never mind!' Jassy said, slinging logic out of the window. 'Come on!' She grabbed Laurence by the arm and they ran through the north garden towards the oast house.

'Dad?' Laurence said as he entered. There were paintbrushes and broken jars all over the floor, but what was even more disturbing were the canvases that seemed to have been flung in what looked like an angry rage.

'Marcus?' Jassy asked, swallowing hard as she surveyed the scene. She'd been known to make a mess in her beloved studio, but she'd never achieved anything on this scale. All of his beautiful paintings destroyed. How could he have done that to himself after all his hard work?

And there was Marcus standing in the middle of the chaos. He was perfectly still now, his head slightly lowered like a beaten animal.

'Jassy?' Laurence said, turning to her. 'Would you mind if I took things from here?'

'You want to be alone?'

'Is that okay?'

She nodded, leaving the two Sturridge men together.

'Dad?' Laurence said tentatively. He wasn't sure how to begin, but he had to find out what was going on. 'Do you want to sit down?' He'd noticed a couple of stools had been knocked over and he went to pick them up. 'There,' he said a moment later. 'Come and sit down.'

Marcus did as he was told. He looked as if every ounce of energy had drained out of him.

'Can I get you anything? A drink?'

'No.'

Laurence sat in silence for a moment. A cool wind had arrived in the garden and the sky had darkened dramatically.

'I think it's going to rain,' he said, looking out of the oast house window before his eyes fixed again on the wreckage of the room. There were abstracts and landscapes and still lifes galore. Some had been punched through the centre and Laurence saw now that his father's right knuckles were covered in paint. Another – a painting of a row of blue bottles – looked as if it had been stamped on. But the thing that caught his eye was a portrait up against the opposite wall. Unharmed. He hadn't seen it when he'd first come in, but he studied it now. There was no mistaking who it was. Tara. His mother. With her dark wavy hair and the clear green eyes he'd inherited, she was just as he remembered her. Beautiful. What had been going through his father's mind as he'd painted her? he wondered.

'Dad – what's going on?' Laurence asked.

His father's face was ashen. 'I wanted to spare you this, son.'

'Spare me what? Dad?'

Marcus closed his eyes for a moment and exhaled slowly. 'Your mother. The day she died.'

Laurence swallowed hard. He had pushed and pushed his father to talk about that day but, now that he was going to, Laurence wasn't sure that he was ready.

'What about it?' he asked.

'She was leaving me.'

'What do you mean?'

'She was seeing somebody, Laurie.'

Laurence frowned. 'I don't understand.'

'She'd packed her bag. I removed it after the accident. I didn't want anybody to know,' Marcus continued. 'She was wearing that dress. That Prussian-blue dress that she loved so much. She'd bought it to wear for him.'

Laurence stared at his father as if he were speaking a different language and then shook his head.

'No, no. You've got it wrong.'

'She was leaving me.'

Laurence couldn't take in what he was being told. His mother had been leaving his father? No, that wasn't possible, was it? They'd been happy, hadn't they?

His mind was a maelstrom of jumbled memories. Had there been any clues? He tried to remember conversations he'd had with his mother, but there hadn't been any indication that she was unhappy, had there? Maybe there had. Maybe he just hadn't seen them because he'd been so wrapped up in his own world.

'Explain this to me,' he said at last. 'How did this happen? When did it happen?'

'I wish I could tell you,' Marcus said. 'I think we'd been slowly growing apart for some time. I sensed it for a while. Your mother wasn't happy with the hours I was working. It was one of the reasons I retired when I did. I thought that would make things better, but it didn't. It was way too late by then. She'd made herself a life with somebody else. I don't know when she met him. I don't think I want to know.'

'Did you try to stop her?'

'What would have been the point of that? She wanted to go, Laurie. There wasn't anything I could have done or said to make her stay. I could see she'd made her mind up.'

'But she never said anything to me.'

'What did you expect her to say on your brief visits? "Come and see the garden whilst the kettle's boiling. Oh, by the way, I'm leaving your father."'

'There's no need to be mean,' Laurence said. 'I'm trying to work things out here.' He rested his elbows on his knees and held his head in his hands as if needing the support. He'd had no idea what had been going on in his parents' lives. How could he not have known all this?

The answer was simple. He'd been too busy leading his own life and charging up the career ladder. And had that been wrong? he asked himself now. Surely it was only natural for children to grow up and move away from home and start making a life for themselves. But perhaps he should have spent more time with them both.

'Don't blame yourself,' Marcus said as if reading Laurence's thoughts. 'You couldn't have done anything even if you'd visited every single day. Your mother had made her choice.'

'But I had no idea things were so bad between you.'

His father shrugged. 'How could you? You had your life in London.'

Once again, Laurence felt a surge of regret that he hadn't spent more time with his parents.

'Why didn't you say something?' he asked his father.

'What could you do if I had?'

'I don't know – I could have tried talking to Mum.'

'You couldn't have said anything to change her mind, son.'

'I don't believe it. She wouldn't have just left you!'

'But she did. You don't understand. She was leaving me the day she died. She had a bag packed in the boot of the car. She'd gone. She'd gone for good.'

'Who was he?' Laurence asked with undisguised loathing in his voice.

'Someone she met through work. What does it matter?'

'I'm just trying to understand.'

Marcus took a deep breath. 'I was hoping to spare you all this,' he began. 'I really was.'

A strange peace descended between them as the sky continued to darken outside and the first drops of rain fell on the parched garden.

'Why didn't you just talk to me about all this?'

Marcus looked at him as if he'd just asked the most preposterous question ever.

'You never have time to talk.'

'What do you mean?'

'You're a workaholic,' Marcus said. 'I thought moving down here would change that but, if anything, it's made it worse.'

'But I've asked you over and over to talk to me about what happened.'

Marcus shook his head. 'You ask me what happened when you've got a spare ten minutes between making a cup of tea and taking a phone call. I can't open up to you in a ten-minute slot just because that's the time you've got available.'

Laurence frowned. Was his life really like that? He knew he'd been a workaholic in London, but was he still one now? When they'd first moved to Orley, he thought he'd made a conscious effort to make time for his father, but maybe it still hadn't been enough. Then, when Tilda had told him she needed space, he'd pretty much put his head down and worked as many hours as he could.

'But I've made an effort to spend time with you, haven't I?' Laurence said. 'I tried to involve you in things with me, like furnishing my rooms when we first moved here and the idea of us starting a garden together. Didn't I?'

His father gave a tiny nod. 'I know you did.'

Laurence took a deep breath, suddenly feeling exhausted.

'I'm sorry,' Marcus said. 'This is all my fault. I really didn't want you to know any of this and I'm sorry it's come out this way.'

Laurence once more became aware of the mess around them and hopped off his stool.

'Leave it,' Marcus said. 'I'll do it.' He stood up and Laurence watched as his dad picked up the couple of canvases nearest to him.

'I'm sorry,' Laurence said. 'I mean, if you ever thought you couldn't talk to me.'

Marcus turned to face him and there was a rawness in his eyes for a moment before he blinked and shook his head.

'I didn't exactly help things, did I?'

'What do you mean?'

'I mean by taking off to the other side of the world. It's just, well, I didn't have anything to keep me here.'

'I was here,' Laurence said.

'But you had your work. That's all you've ever needed.'

'Yeah? Well, maybe that was true in London, but it isn't anymore. I need you, Dad, and I wish – I really wish more than anything else in the world – that we could get this right. That we could start again.' Laurence could hear the emotion behind his words and was aware that if he spoke another word he'd probably choke up.

'Can you forgive me?' Marcus said.

'Forgive you?' Laurence was genuinely surprised by the question.

'For hiding all this from you.'

'I don't need to forgive you,' he said and then he laughed.

Marcus's forehead creased in confusion. 'What are you laughing at?'

'Us!'

'What about us?'

'You're incapable of talking and I'm incapable of listening. No wonder we're in a mess!'

Marcus gave a tiny smile. 'We have rather mucked things up, haven't we?'

The two men exchanged amused glances.

'But it's not too late, is it, Dad?'

'No, Laurie. It's not too late.'

Marcus crossed the brief space between them and then he did something he hadn't done since Laurence had left for his first day at school: he hugged him. And Laurence did something he hadn't done since he'd left for his first day at school: he hugged him right back.

Chapter 22

The clouds hung heavy over the Ridwell Valley on the morning of the fete. Tilda had been right to fear choosing the bank holiday weekend for their event, but Vanessa refused to be dismayed.

'It doesn't really matter what the weather's like, does it? This is England. People expect a few clouds!'

'We'll all have to wear coats and rain hats,' Tilda complained.

'And what about my painting table?' Jassy asked.

'Well, just don't use watercolours.'

Jassy pulled a face at her.

'Don't worry,' Vanessa said, 'we've got some canopies we can put over the stalls if the worst comes to the worst.'

But it didn't. Miraculously, just after lunchtime and with only half an hour until the fete opened to the public, the clouds cleared and the temperature began to soar. It was turning into one of those perfect days that people dream about when they think of summer. The sky was a peerless blue and the sun looked as if it had taken a solemn vow not to go anywhere for a good long while.

The yards of pretty bunting which had been taken down from the loft and hung around the stalls fluttered jollily in the warm breeze. The village had really pulled together to create the best fete ever. The WI had set up a table where they were selling cakes, biscuits, jams and chutney, and old Mr Taylor's plants were doing a roaring trade – as were Dolly's famous coconut cookies, with any crumbs being gobbled up by Reynolds, who was hiding under the tablecloth. Jassy had set up a long table near her grandmother where she and Marcus were giving demonstrations in painting, and Tilda was selling cut flowers fresh from the borders of Orley.

Jonathan's team had a table of their own where they were selling produce from the walled garden and Vanessa was helping them bag up the sales, which was pretty much a non-stop job. Both Andy's cabbages and Oz's beans were going down well with the crowd and there was a bit of friendly competition going on between them.

'I'm still way ahead of you,' Oz said.

'Rubbish!' Andy said. 'You can't count individual bean-pod sales against the sale of a large cabbage! Especially my cabbages. Just feel the weight of that!' he said, thrusting a cabbage at Oz.

'Put it down. I don't want to feel your bloody cabbages!'

'Language!' Jonathan said in warning. 'Remember what I said.'

The week before the fete had meant extra hours in the walled garden so that the team could make sure that everything was as perfect as possible for the big day. Jonathan had even done a dummy run with an old table, making each of the team take it in turns to practise selling to the public.

'Remember, no bad language and always say thank you when you take someone's money.'

There'd been a lot of laughter when Andy had pretended to be an awkward customer complaining about everything, but he was really pulling his weight now and seemed to be in his element too.

In a rare, quiet moment between customers, Jonathan leaned in close to Vanessa. 'I love your hat,' he whispered.

Vanessa's hands automatically flew up to the wide-brimmed straw hat with its large pink ribbon.

'In honour of your grandmother,' she said.

'She would have loved it. She'd probably have made you an offer for it.'

Vanessa laughed. 'And I would have declined because I'd have wanted to give it to her.'

He reached out and squeezed her hand. 'I wish she was here.'

'Me too. You know, I thought I might have to wear a rain hat with those clouds this morning.'

Jonathan shook his head. 'I had no doubt whatsoever that today would be just perfect.'

'Hey!' Jenna said, interrupting them. 'We've sold all your tomato sauce, Vanessa!'

'We're all out of strawberries too,' Andy announced.

'Remember that cold spring day when you were forking manure into the strawberry patch?' Jonathan said to Andy.

'How could I forget it? I was frozen and I stunk like a pig!'

'But all worth it now, eh?'

Andy grinned. 'I guess.'

Vanessa looked at the pride on Andy's face which he was doing his best to hide. But how could you not feel proud of having grown, nurtured, picked and sold something that wouldn't have existed without you?

'Hang on a minute,' Jenna said, bending down and retrieving something from under the table. 'There's an extra punnet of strawberries here.'

'How did they get there?' Jonathan asked.

A shifty look crossed Andy's face as he shrugged. 'No idea.'

Jenna took hold of them and was just about to place them on the table to sell when Vanessa whipped them away from her hand.

'No, no,' she said. 'Why don't we keep them for us? Stallholder privilege.'

Andy beamed her a smile and everyone began stuffing their faces with the ruby fruit.

'I'm just going to see how Dolly's getting on,' Vanessa told Jonathan once all the strawberries had been consumed.

'Want me to come with you as a buffer?' he asked, eyebrows raised.

'No need,' she told him. 'We're good.'

'Really?'

'Well, we're getting there,' she said and turned to leave, taking a deep breath and heading towards Dolly's stall. There was a small crowd around it and Vanessa recognised a few of the ladies from the village.

'I hope you've bought something from our team of hardworking gardeners,' she heard Dolly say to them as she nodded towards Jonathan's stall.

A couple of the ladies looked across to where Andy was attempting to juggle a couple of onions.

'Well, I think we've spent all our money here,' one of them said.

'That's rubbish and you know it,' Dolly snapped. 'You get yourself over there, Edna Greenaway, and show your support for our young ones! And tell all your friends in the WI to spend some of their money too. Go on now!'

Edna and her friend looked mightily affronted as they bustled away.

'And I'll be watching to make sure you actually buy something!' Dolly shouted after them, causing Vanessa to laugh.

'Good for you, Dolly,' she said.

Dolly shook her head and tutted. 'I heard them saying some dreadful things about our kids when they thought I wasn't listening,' Dolly said. 'Misconceived, prejudiced things.'

'Yes,' Vanessa said. 'I'm afraid we're still fighting that battle, aren't we?'

'And when I think of what Edna's Cyril was like as a young'un. She has no right to judge. No right at all!'

Vanessa looked across to where Edna and her friend were getting the hard sell from Jonathan as Oz bagged up some cabbages and tomatoes.

'Here,' Dolly said, passing a little tin to Vanessa.

'What's this?'

'Some of my cookies,' she said. 'I made an extra batch this morning for the team. Take them over, will you?'

'Don't you want to do that, Dolly?'

'No, no. I'll see them later once I've sold out here. You take them,' she said. 'And make sure Jenna gets a couple now, won't you?'

'I will. Thank you.'

Dolly nodded and Vanessa watched for a moment as her mother-in-law continued manning her stall, wrapping a couple of flapjacks for the village postman. How happy she looked, Vanessa thought. She was busy and needed, and she was absolutely thriving on it.

Laurence took in a deep breath of summer air as he walked across the lawn of the south garden towards the stalls. How beautiful it all looked. He still couldn't believe that this was his home now and that these people were his friends. Well, he hoped that Tilda was still his friend. He wasn't at all sure at the moment. They'd not swapped more than a handful of pleasantries recently and it was tearing Laurence in two, which was why he'd decided to do what he'd done.

Since the day his father confessed the truth about what had happened with Tara, there'd been a new closeness between the two men. They were learning to talk again, to share moments and thoughts, and his father had particularly encouraged him with Tilda.

'If you care about her, show her. Don't waste a single moment, son.'

His father's words echoed in Laurence's mind as he watched Tilda at her stall as she wrapped a big bunch of cut flowers in pretty paper for a customer. How at ease she looked, he thought, amongst her friends and neighbours. As if feeling his gaze, she looked up and smiled. He nodded and turned away, suddenly feeling anxious.

'Laurie?' she called a moment later and he turned to see her running towards him.

'Hi,' he said casually.

'Enjoying the fete?'

'Yes,' he said, aware of how very close she was to him. 'It's great.'

'Do try and get some of the bakery bits from the WI stall, although avoid Mrs Carlton's blackcurrant jam. It never sets properly and there are usually cat hairs in it.'

'Duly noted.'

They walked in silence for a moment, stopping by the edge of the pond.

'Laurie – I wanted to talk to you. To apologise.'

'Oh?'

'Yes, I – I don't know why I pushed you away like that. It was really—'

'You don't need to explain, Tilda. It's fine.'

'No, it isn't fine because I feel really mean and' – she paused – 'unhappy.'

He looked into her rosy face and the joy that had been there when she'd been selling flowers at her stall had disappeared. It was like seeing the sunshine vanishing from the summer sky.

'Why are you unhappy?'

'Because I hurt you.'

'No, you didn't.'

She looked puzzled. 'Didn't I?'

He swallowed hard. 'Well, I—'

'Because if I didn't hurt you then you couldn't have cared for me very much!' She looked affronted but there was amusement dancing in her eyes now and Laurence couldn't help but smile.

'I'm not going to puff up your ego by telling you that you broke my heart,' he said.

'But I don't want to have broken your heart. That's what I'm trying to say. I'm sorry if I hurt you. I never meant to. Really. I've been a mess and I was just trying to protect you from all that.'

'That's fine.'

'Is it?'

'I told you, you don't need to apologise.'

'So we're good?'

'We're good.'

They stared out over the pond, watching as an enormous green dragonfly settled on a lily pad, its iridescent body catching in the sunlight.

Laurence cleared his throat. 'So, how's the music?'

Tilda puffed out her cheeks. 'I'm kind of taking a break.'

'But I thought you and Morton were just getting going again.'

'So did I.'

'So what happened?'

She closed her eyes and groaned. 'He – he made a move on me.'

'Morton?'

She nodded. 'God, it was awful! He just sort of lunged at me one day in the studio. I was in the middle of singing a new song and it was going really well when he suddenly flew at me. He knocked the mic over and nearly knocked me over too!' She paused, hiding her face in her hands. 'I don't want to think about it.'

'I take it his move wasn't wanted by you?'

'No! It certainly wasn't. I thought we were business partners. I thought I could trust him. But he's just like everyone else – he wants something from me that I can't give him.'

'When did all this happen?'

'Oh, a few weeks ago.'

Laurence felt hurt by this admission. 'Why didn't you tell me?'

She shrugged. 'I couldn't bother you with something like that.'

'Yes you could.'

She looked at him and there was a tenderness in her eyes now. 'You're sweet. Thank you.'

He nodded. 'What will you do now?'

She sighed. 'Find another producer? One who doesn't want to change my image or force themselves upon me?'

'Well, they say third time lucky, don't they?'

'Yes, they do.'

'You'll find someone.'

'Will I?'

She was looking at him again with those blue eyes and it was all Laurence could do not to move forward and kiss her. But she wouldn't want that, would she? She'd just been complaining about how men were always trying to take something from her. If he made a move on her now, she'd probably push him into the pond, which might make for a memorable fete but probably wouldn't be the most comfortable of experiences.

'You'll find someone, Tilda,' he told her, and her hand reached out and took his and they looked at each other for an inordinate amount of time.

'I've been thinking,' she began.

'Oh?'

'Yes. I've been thinking that I've never gone out with an older man before. I've only dated men my own age.'

'And how's that worked out for you?'

'Terrible!'

He laughed and then he seemed to realise the significance of the moment with him standing there in the garden holding hands with her.

'Well,' he began slowly, 'I'm only about five years older than you.'

'Yes,' she said.

'That's not enough to get worried about, is it?'

Tilda frowned. 'Are you kidding? It's half a decade! That's a lot in music terms.'

'Hey, I can still enjoy the same music you do.'

'Well, as long as you like my music. That's all that matters, isn't it?'

'I love your music!' he told her.

'Good,' she said with a little laugh.

They stood holding hands a moment longer and then Laurence cleared his throat.

'Tilda?'

'Yes?'

He took a deep breath to steady himself, hearing his father's words once again: *Don't waste a single moment.*

The time had come to tell her – to show her.

'Come with me.'

'Where are we going?' she asked.

'Back to the house.'

'But the fete—'

'It won't take long, I promise.'

Still holding hands, they walked away from the crowds, sneaking into the house like naughty children. Laurence could feel his heart racing as they crossed the hallway, stopping at a door to a room he hadn't known existed until the day before. The blue drawing room.

If there was one thing he'd learned from his relationship with his father over the last few days, it was that time should never be wasted. Every minute counted and, if you didn't voice the feelings that you carried inside you, then you might well live to regret it just as his father did with his mother.

'What are we doing here?' Tilda asked. 'Laurie?'

'There's something I want to show you.'

'Okay,' she said, sounding the word slowly, anxiously.

Laurence opened the door into the blue drawing room, so called because of the beautiful old damask wallpaper, and Tilda gasped.

'Laurie!' she cried. 'It's a fountain of flowers!'

He nodded. 'There's no disputing that really, is there?'

She looked back at him. 'How did you know? I mean, how did you find out?'

'I was talking to your mum about the fete and she told me that, every year, your father would arrange a great fountain of flowers from the garden for her and that she wasn't allowed to see it until the very last person had gone home. It was his way of making the wonderful day last even longer.'

'Yes,' Tilda said. 'I remember every single display he made for her. Jassy and I would often help him choose the flowers from the garden. It was so much fun imagining Mum's face when she saw it.'

Together, they looked at the enormous display in front of them. It was placed on a small round table in the centre of the room and absolutely dominated it. Full of the best blooms of summer from roses and phlox to sunflowers and dahlias, the colours seemed to explode in the middle of that elegant room and the great spires of blue delphiniums shot into the air like jets of water. The fragrance was heavenly and Tilda automatically walked forward so she could inhale deeply.

'I can't believe you did this, Laurie,' she said, tears sparkling in her eyes.

'Well, I had a bit of help from your mum, Jonathan and Jenna. A lot of help actually.'

'But how did you keep it hidden?'

'Your mum assured me that you rarely come into this room and that you were so busy with your stall for the fete that you wouldn't realise that something was going on in here.'

'And what are you going to do with it?' she asked, reaching out a hand to caress the silky petals of a scarlet dahlia.

'What do you mean?' he asked, a little confused.

'I mean, are you going to raffle it at the fete?'

He frowned. 'No!' he said. 'This is for you, Tilda. Just for you! I made a donation to the fete to cover the cost of the flowers because I know your mum's been picking them from the garden to sell, but this is yours, Tilda. All yours.'

She looked genuinely surprised by this declaration and didn't speak for a moment.

'Nobody's ever done anything like this for me before,' she said at last. 'I mean, I've been sent flowers. Bouquets people have bought from florists, but nothing like this – not all picked by hand by the person giving the flowers.'

'Well, again, I had a bit of help,' he confessed with a sheepish smile.

'I love it!' she told him, sounding quite breathless. 'I really love it! Mum always said that Dad's fountain of flowers made her feel cherished and adored.'

'I know,' Laurence said. 'She told me that too. It's why I wanted to do this for you, Tilda. I wanted to show you how I felt.' He took a step towards her. He'd never felt more nervous in his life or more certain as he bent forward to kiss her.

'I cherish you, Tilda. I adore you. I love you.'

'And I love you too, Laurie.' She smiled up at him and there was something in that smile that spoke of the future.

As the sun slowly slipped westwards and the shadows began to lengthen on the lawn, Jonathan took Vanessa's hand and led her away from the stall.

'I'm so glad we did this,' she told him. 'The garden looks so alive again.'

'It likes being shared and looked at,' he said.

'It's a great big flirt.'

He laughed and they walked across the grass.

'What are we doing?' Vanessa asked.

'I want to abduct the good lady of the manor.'

'You mustn't keep calling me that!'

'Don't you like it?' he asked, stopping to look at her.

'You know I don't.'

He tilted his head to one side. 'That's a shame, because I find it very attractive!'

She shook her head in mock annoyance as they sneaked away from the crowds, making their way to the privacy of the walled garden and stopping in the cool shade of the fruit trees.

A blackbird ran down the red-brick path and disappeared behind the greenhouse and a song thrush was singing at the top of one of the apple trees.

Slowly, sweetly, Jonathan removed Vanessa's hat and bent down to kiss her. She closed her eyes, luxuriating in the warmth of his mouth and the feeling of being loved.

After losing Oliver, Vanessa had never thought she'd fall in love again, but here she was, standing in her beloved garden with the man she wanted to spend the rest of her life with, and she knew she couldn't be happier.

Acknowledgments

Thank you to Roy, Ruth, Gael and Judy. And to Emilie, Sammia and Sophie and the rest of the wonderful team at Amazon Publishing – I love working with you all!

Thank you to the National Trust staff at Bateman's in East Sussex. And a special thank you to Monty Don for his wonderful TV series and book *Growing Out of Trouble*, which inspired part of this story.

Author Biography

Victoria Connelly studied English Literature at Worcester University, got married in a medieval castle in the Yorkshire Dales and now lives in rural Suffolk with her artist husband, a young springer spaniel and a flock of ex-battery hens.

She is the author of two bestselling series, Austen Addicts and The Book Lovers, as well as many other novels and novellas. Her first published novel, *Flights of Angels*, was made into a film in 2008 by Ziegler Films in Germany. *The Runaway Actress* was shortlisted for the Romantic Novelists' Association's Romantic Comedy Novel award.

Ms Connelly loves books, films, walking, historic buildings and animals. If she isn't at her keyboard writing, she can usually be found in her garden, either with a trowel in her hand or a hen on her lap.

Her website is www.victoriaconnelly.com and readers can follow her on Twitter @VictoriaDarcy.